So Faithful a Heart

The Love Story of Nancy Storace and Wolfgang Mozart

Special Edition

Includes Book II

When Love Won't Die

The Continuing Story

K. Lynette Erwin

Alla Breve Books

MMXI

So Faithful A Heart
The Love Story of Nancy Storace and Wolfgang Mozart

When Love Won't Die
The Continuing Story

Copyright © 2011
K. Lynette Erwin
www.allabreve.org/storace

Special Two Book Combined Edition

Cover design by Alla Breve For the Arts
www.allabreve.org

Printed in the United States of America

ISBN-13: 978-1466326309

ISBN-10: 1466326301

Lovingly dedicated to Nancy Storace
whose story has waited too long to be told.

Foreword

To read an historical fiction, it is necessary to put aside our modern world. But that's the easy part. The real difficulty lies in being willing to take off our modern goggles and see life as it was lived centuries in the past without judgments that come from several hundred years of social evolution. This isn't easy, and there is so much we don't know. Even writers who have spent years in research can only imagine life before mass media, women's rights, the abolition of slavery, the overthrow of the monarchy, and the waning of theocratic governments.

This is a book that takes us to the eighteenth century to look at the life of a woman of the theater. At that time actresses were considered little better than prostitutes and few young women were encouraged to follow that path. Still, many did, not all of them women of loose moral character. Like women in our own time, many sought to be recognized and respected for their talents and hard work, stubbornly battling the stereotypes. However, also like modern women seeking acting or singing careers, some find themselves forced to acquiesce to the demands of the "casting couch" in order to find some small control over their lives. In the eighteenth century all women submitted to men, be they directors, fathers, brothers, or husbands. In this the wife was no different than the actress: she had a role to play, which was to see to the comfort and pleasure of a man. All women were held captive by this role, although the actress certainly appeared to have a more exciting life than the wife. While the wife may have looked at the actress with some envy for her supposed freedom, the actress probably looked at the wife, envying her security. Often, the pivot point between them was the husband, who required different things from the women in his life.

Which brings us to another problem when reading an historical fiction: that is the concept of marriage in an earlier time. In the eighteenth century a marriage was seldom made for love, especially between people of the noble, aristocratic, or educated working classes. The latter certainly had a little more access to romantic bonds, but the parents had the final say. After the ceremony it was back to life as usual; there was no honeymoon, and a steady parade of children usually followed, especially in those countries where the Catholic Church still held power.

With science teaching that a man needed regular sex to maintain his health, where was he to go when his wife was constantly pregnant, in post-partum confinement, or lactating? Men were expected to seek sexual release outside the marriage, something that few wives were threatened by. It was not his sexuality that made him loyal, but his sentiments. Falling into bed was not the sin, falling in love was, because that threatened the livelihood of the wife and her children. Therefore, men who could afford to do so kept mistresses and many wives were glad of it.

Likewise, the carrying, bearing, and raising of children were not the man's concern. A man was not part of the birth of his children, nor was he part of the washing, feeding, or diaper-changing. He was expected to support his family and to be a good provider. He was to see to their religious instruction and their social grooming, and that was all. The children of a mistress, especially, were not his concern; only the generous, financially solvent man supported his bastards. Most men did not even acknowledge their illegitimate offspring, leaving it to the mistress to seek abortions or send the children into servitude as soon as they were able to work. Ideally, the mistress took care of what birth control was available at the time.

These things seem harsh to us today, but to see the eighteenth century clearly, without our modern sensibilities intruding, we must force ourselves to remember that where these social issues are concerned, people were not like we are. The roles of men and women were clearly defined in an attempt to keep society civilized. In our century such roles are looked down upon as we evolve socially, each of us toward our own personal fulfillment, regardless of gender. Death was always around the corner, most people were grossly uneducated, and Europeans, although largely dominated by the Church, were not religious in the way that people are today. There was no fear of global self-annihilation, no Freudian analysis, and no modern American fundamentalism, which didn't take root until a hundred years later as a backlash to the liberal theology in both England and America. The world was a much larger place, and most people never traveled beyond their own city walls.

This is a book about two musicians who had seen most of Europe and had encountered other cultures, philosophies, and religious beliefs. They had been child prodigies, were worldly and educated, relatively tolerant, and unusually broad-minded. They were acquainted with many of the same people and had visited many of the same cities. When they met, they had to have recognized these similarities and they must have spent long hours in conversation about their mutual experiences. It is not difficult to imagine that they would have found these similarities comforting and even attractive.

As difficult as it is for us to slip beneath the skin of a person of the eighteenth century, it would be even harder for someone from that time to slip beneath ours. It is my hope that by reading this book you will truly get to know the characters and accept them for what they were, without modern bias.

SK Waller
Autumn 2009

Prologue

London, July 1817

*I*t was a warm and gentle summer afternoon at Herne Hill Cottage, a small, but fashionable country estate near Lambeth, just outside of London. A soft breeze blew, carrying upon it the delicious aroma of roses, lavender, and jasmine from the garden, through the open casements. She sat at her desk in the salon, feeling the sun as it streamed through the arched windows, enveloping her in its warmth as she fingered through a stack of old letters that were neatly tied into a bundle with a crimson cord. In front of her lay a guest list which she needed to read and approve for an upcoming charity event she was to host.

This can wait, she thought, pushing it aside, too distracted by the stack of letters before her to be bothered with something so mundane. She picked them up, fanning them beneath her nose to take in the aroma that she hoped might still linger on them. She remembered his scent well, a pleasing blend of citrus and spices from the West Indies mingled with the musky aroma of pipe tobacco. She untied the cord around the bundle and opened one of the letters dated June 1787. The parchment was stained with tears and ink runs from the many times she had read it. His voice was still fresh in her memory, and his broken, sometimes comical English that was riddled with double negatives and   was sometimes difficult to understand because of his thick German accent.

"Ma'am," the maidservant interrupted, giving a small curtsey. "There are two gentlemen at the door who insist they speak to you. I think they're German," she added.

"German?" Nancy replied, confused. "Are you sure they're German?"

"I suppose they are Ma'am. They're most insistent you receive them immediately."

"Did they say why they're here?" Nancy asked, perplexed.

"No, Ma'am, only that they must speak with you."

"Very well, then," she sighed. "Show them in and then prepare some tea."

Nancy rose from her seat as the men entered the room. Well-dressed and in their early to mid-thirties, they greeted her with polite bows as she extended her hand.

"Please sit down, gentlemen," she said as she gestured toward the settee.

"Thank you, Madame," one of them replied.

"My maidservant will be bringing some tea in at any moment. You must know we English never discuss anything unless it is over tea," she said chuckling. The men smiled and nodded.

"Forgive me if I seem impolite, but I detect by your accents you're German. I spent several years in Vienna and by the time I left, I spoke it well enough to carry on a respectable conversation. However, that was many years ago, and I have had little opportunity to use it since, so you will pardon me if I speak to you gentlemen in my native tongue," she said as she sat down.

"Yes, Madame," one of the men replied, "we are quite familiar with your reputation in Vienna. Signor Salieri and Herr Haydn still speak of you with great fondness as do others."

"Is that so?" Nancy replied, flattered she would still be remembered after so many years.

The maid entered with the tea tray and sat it on the table in front of Nancy and the men, who were seated across from her.

"So, gentlemen, what brings you here today?" she inquired curiously as she picked up the pot and began to pour.

"We were sent by an important gentleman who has employed us to inquire about the letters from Vienna…"

Her eyes narrowed. Who was this gentleman and how did he know about her letters?

Clearing his throat, the younger of the two men quickly added, "Our employer is writing a biography and would like to have these letters to add to his research."

"Who is your employer?"

"I apologize, Madame, but we are not at liberty to reveal his identity at this time."

"Well, gentlemen, I am not about to hand personal letters over to someone whose name I don't even know, if I indeed have what you think I have."

"I can assure you that he is willing to pay you generously for them," the older man said.

"And what if they're not for sale?"

"We are more than prepared to negotiate a sum with you, Madame."

Nancy sat silently looking into her cup.

"And I am prepared to tell you to convey to your employer that if I had these letters, they would not be for sale."

"We understand that no amount of money could replace the sentimental value that they must hold for you—"

"Nevertheless," she said as she gestured around the comfortable, well-appointed the room, "you can see I have no need to sell my personal belongings."

"In that case," the young man said as he noticed the stack of old letters lying on her desk, "we regret to inform you we have a warrant pending to confiscate them should you refuse our employer's generosity."

Seeing that he had spotted them, Nancy arose slowly, setting down her cup.

"Excuse me gentlemen, but I believe this conversation has reached its conclusion. Emma! Please show these gentlemen out."

The maid entered the room immediately and gestured toward the entry.

"Good day, sirs," Nancy stated firmly.

"You're making a grave mistake. We know you have the letters, and we will use whatever means necessary to obtain them. Take care, Madame Storace, you do not know with whom you are dealing."

"And you do not know with whom *you* are dealing, gentlemen," she said, her anger rising. She was a woman who didn't like to be controlled, not after all she had survived in her life. "You have been politely asked to leave. I don't believe I could have made my feelings on the matter more clear."

"This is not a stage play, Madame. I suggest you abandon the dramatics and discuss this with us in a civil manner."

"Dramatics?" she replied, fuming. "You've not begun to see the full range of my dramatic talent!" She slipped her hands through each man's arm and walked them to the front door.

"The nerve!" the older one responded. "You may live in a fine house and you put on some very fine airs, Madame, but we know that you were little more than his slut!"

Nancy opened the door, and shoving them onto the doorstep she shouted, "You take that bloody warrant and tell your employer to shove it up his sodding bum! And if you two bloody bastards ever set foot anywhere near my house again, I'll send for the constable!"

She slammed the door in their faces, falling back against it and catching her breath, her blood pulsing wildly in her temples. After a few moments, she made her way back to her desk and sat, picking up the letters again. Tears of anger and grief fell onto her cheeks.

"These are mine. They were for my eyes only!"

Chapter One

Venice, January 1783

*A*s Nancy entered the salon of her Venetian apartment, she could scarcely believe that in a few hours she would leave for Vienna, where she was summoned by Emperor Joseph II to be the prima buffa of his newly-formed Italian Opera Company. Strewn about the room, piled upon sofas and settees, and stacked on top of tables was a profusion of trunks and bandboxes, some of which were still in the process of being packed.

Anna Selina Storace, (who was known as Nancy to her closest friends and family), was barely seventeen years old when an emissary of the Emperor came to Venice to scout out some singers for His Imperial Majesty's new theater company. Nancy was among those in whom he was most interested, and once he saw her on the stage of the Teatro San Samuele, he wrote that Vienna could greatly profit from her talents. The Emperor's reply was swift and certain: "Hire her at once!"

Almost from the moment she arrived in Italy from London in 1778–barely twelve years old–with her Italian father, Stefano, and her English mother, Elizabeth, Nancy was a sensation, a celebrity in the world of comic opera. Her flamboyant, expressive stage presence and impeccable singing, combined with the fact she was educated, unlike most singers of her day, made her one of the most sought-after performers in all of Italy. Indeed, the Emperor offered her a salary far above any performer of her type anywhere.

"Ann!" her mother called from one of the bedchambers. "Are you certain you have everything? Did you pack that lovely fox fur muff your brother sent to you from England?"

"Yes, Mother," Nancy called back, rolling her eyes, a sharp note of irritation in her voice.

Elizabeth could be fussy and overbearing at times, and her need to manipulate and control the people around her had worsened since her husband's death just two years before. She wasn't overly enthusiastic about leaving her comfortable life in London in the first place, but Stefano insisted, believing an Italian tour was the only way to launch their daughter's singing career successfully.

Elizabeth Trusler, the youngest daughter of the proprietor of the Marylebone Pleasure Gardens in London, met Storace when he came to London from Italy to play the bass violin in Marylebone's theater orchestra. Stefano fell in love with the pretty, graceful Elizabeth and they were married in the summer of 1761. The following April, Nancy's older brother, Stephen, was born and Nancy came along later, in October of 1765.

Both children exhibited extraordinary musical abilities from an early age and Stefano, who greatly admired Leopold Mozart and the manner in which he'd educated his two "wonder children", had determined his own children would receive the same kind of education and exposure. Both Stephen and Nancy were taught to play the harpsichord as well as sight singing, harmony, counterpoint, and composition. Stephen learned to play the violin and Nancy studied the harp as well as the guitar. Nancy began singing publicly at the age of eight; Stephen was sent to study composition at his father's alma mater, the San Onofrio Conservatory in Naples.

Knowing that taking Nancy to Italy to begin her career would be lucrative, Storace began planning the family's journey abroad. It was a less than enthusiastic Elizabeth who reluctantly agreed to her husband's wishes. After Stefano's unexpected death in Naples, Stephen decided to return to England to take care of his father's estate, as well as to start a career of his own as a composer for the London stage, leaving Elizabeth and Nancy alone in Italy to fend for themselves.

Elizabeth entered and saw Nancy sitting atop of one the many trunks lying about the room, kicking her feet in rhythm against the side and gazing out the window into the Venetian dawn, lost in a daydream.

"Anna Selina!" she called out sharply, startling Nancy out of her reverie and onto her feet. "There's still much to do and little time left before our coaches leave. Michael will be here soon. Now get up from there and help me!"

Nancy looked around, frustrated by her mother's demands. She gestured wildly and exclaimed, "Good God, Mother! What is there to pack? We have enough luggage for five coaches! And how will we ever accommodate Mick's trunks?"

"Don't be so dramatic, child!" Elizabeth snapped, hurriedly turning to go finish her packing. "You exhaust me with your exaggerations."

Nancy hoped Michael would arrive soon, because he had a calming effect on her mother which always helped ease the tension that existed between them. Nancy and Stephen met Michael Kelly a few years earlier while in Liverno. They'd seen him come off a ferry onto the dock, a handsome, young man with wavy blonde hair that flowed freely to his shoulders.

"Look at that girl wearing boy's clothes," Nancy exclaimed rather loudly to her brother.

Michael, a bold, outspoken Irishman, turned and replied, to Nancy's astonishment, "You are mistaken Miss, for I am a very proper he animal, and quite at your service!"

They instantly embarked upon a friendship that lasted their entire lives. In Bath, before traveling to Italy to begin a stage career, Michael had studied with Nancy's former voice teacher, the castrato, Venanzio Rauzzini. Kelly had a velvety tenor voice, which had a softer quality and color than the brighter, more strident Italian tenor. He also possessed the marvelous gift of blarney, which Nancy found wonderfully charming and which endeared Michael to her even more. Michael was also hired by the Emperor, along with the Italian baritone, Francesco Benucci.

No sooner had Elizabeth left the room than there was a knock at the door. The maid opened it to find Michael dressed in his traveling clothes and greatcoat, ready to help the Storace women gather their luggage and line it up near the door for the driver to begin loading onto the wagon.

"Nancy, me darlin' dove," he said enthusiastically as he kissed her on the cheek. He was like a brother and with Stephen away, it was most certainly a comfort to have him there. "Are you ready to be leavin' soon?"

"I suppose so. I'm certain Mother packed the entire city in here, along with a few gondoliers!" she giggled. "She's always been a pack rat, but this is ridiculous. The sight makes me dizzy!"

She laughed as she crossed her eyes and stuck her tongue out unbecomingly, twirling about, trying to disorient herself. Michael broke into a fit of laughter. Always energetic and effusive, Nancy never seemed to be off stage. It was this energy that charmed him and everyone else who encountered her.

Although not considered a beauty by the standards of the age, Nancy was pert and sassy, with a sweet little heart-shaped face, large dark, expressive eyes, and a tiny turned-up nose. Having inherited her father's Italianate features, she had a dark, olive complexion and a head of thick dark chocolate brown hair that she wore piled in ringlets that cascaded down her back. She was of small stature, with a petite, but round and pleasingly ample figure that appealed to the men who saw her on stage.

She was dressed in a green wool travel suit adorned with brass military style buttons on the waistcoat, jacket, and cuffs. Her mother bought her a lovely black felt tricorn hat with gold bullion trim along the edges and a cockade of bright green and iridescent blue peacock feathers mixed among the more subdued but elegant brown pheasant feathers. The outfit was finished off with a pair of black kid leather gloves.

Michael noted that she looked rather grown-up in her travel clothes, a sight which seemed rather incongruous with her childish antics. Elizabeth, who heard all the commotion, made her way into the salon to find Michael enjoying Nancy's pranks.

"I'm glad you're here, Michael, but for goodness sake, stop paying her so much attention!" she fussed as Nancy continued to bounce and twirl about the room, her eyes still crossed. "You're only making her worse!"

Michael feigned a somber expression as he tried to stifle his laughter. Nancy, who paid little attention to her mother's fuming, went on trying to divert his attention.

Finally, Elizabeth grew impatient with Nancy's clowning and stomped her foot as she called out, "Ann! Stop this instant!" Nancy froze in place as the room spun around her head. Woozy from the twirling, she weaved and darted for a few moments, and then she tripped over one of the boxes, nearly toppling to the floor.

"God knows that child is going to be the death of me, yet," Elizabeth sighed. "It's her father's fault for indulging her. He never controlled her when she acted like this," she complained.

"Ah, but Madam," Michael said, defensively, "she's delightful. Thank God for bestowin' that energy upon her, for 'tis those exasperatin' antics of hers that keeps a roof over your head and food on your table," he said, reminding Elizabeth that without Nancy, who was the primary breadwinner of the family since Stefano's death, that she would most certainly be destitute.

Feeling vindicated, Nancy wore a haughty smirk. Michael knew how to put Elizabeth in her place in such a clever way that Elizabeth didn't realize what was happening.

"Well, now," he exclaimed as he gazed around at the massive task before him. "We should get to the business of moving all of this out onto the landing so we can get goin' on time. Can't keep His Majesty waiting ye know!"

"Wolfgang, you must sit still. Bitte," Joseph barked at the fidgety Mozart, who impatiently submitted to his brother-in-law's attempt to paint a portrait of him at his fortepiano.

Gathered in the salon of Mozart's apartment was his wife, Constanze, who was a few months pregnant with their first child, and her sister Aloysia and Aloysia's husband, the noted Viennese Shakespearean actor, Joseph Lange, who enjoyed painting as a hobby. As the sisters sat near the stove and sewed, they chattered over the latest Viennese gossip.

"The new singers will be arriving any day now," Aloysia said, waiting to see if she would get a rise out of him. She knew he was frustrated with the Emperor for closing down the German theater in order to launch the new Italian company. As the Emperor's elite opera troupe, they would perform Italian comic opera exclusively. This move would inevitably put many of the German singers and actors out of work and would force composers of German Singspieler and serious opera to adjust to the new style.

"You know what I think about that," he muttered.

Mozart, who had just experienced a huge success with *Die Entführung aus dem Serail*, had hoped to write another Singspieler for the German theater when it was announced that it was to be closed.

"We have a German Emperor whose national theater is Italian! Tell me what kind of shit sense that makes!"

Thrilled that her brother-in-law had swallowed the bait, Aloysia rejoined with a reply intended to provoke him even further: "Well, I suppose if we're going to be fashionable, then we must adjust, even if it means that some of us will have to change our stodgy, old-fashioned ways and compose opera that appeals to modern audiences."

Aloysia, Constanze's older, prettier, and more talented sister, was Mozart's sweetheart before she threw him over for a count who'd kept her as his mistress, promising her a brilliant Viennese singing career. After she broke Mozart's heart, he turned to Constanze for comfort and companionship, and ended up marrying her a year later, in part because of a trap that Frau Weber used to ensnare him.

Aloysia never let Mozart forget it was because she threw him over for another man that he was her brother-in-law instead of her husband. She enjoyed spitting at him like a cat and watching him dodge, and she took every opportunity to engage in this heartless sport.

"Aloysia, don't be cruel!" Constanze snapped.

Aloysia waited patiently for Mozart's reply.

"My husband is well aware of the adjustments he has to make to meet the demands of the Emperor's new theater," Constanze continued in his defense. "He's more than capable of meeting the challenges better than any composer in Vienna!"

Mozart paid no attention, and changed the subject.

"I hear that new soprano—what's her name? Anna Storace…yes, that's it." He glanced at Aloysia to see if he was having any effect on her. "I hear she's marvelous—the best that Europe has ever heard! His Majesty had to offer her quite a large salary in order to acquire her," he continued, still checking for Aloysia's response. "She's the highest paid singer in all of Europe, and she's only seventeen years old," he said, watching her fidget. "I've also been told she can sing as well as act, a combination I've yet to find in any singer, so far."

Aloysia quickly retreated into her sewing, insulted by his insinuation that her acting skills were less than adequate. Storace could easily outshine her, usurping her long-held and comfortable position as the most popular singer in Vienna. Constanze glanced up over her sewing and gave him a triumphant grin. A long, uncomfortable silence ensued before Lange finally put down his paintbrush and attempted to change the subject.

"The theater management is holding a reception at the Hofburg. They've invited all of the city's composers, actors, singers, and theater patrons to meet the new company."

"Benucci and Storace are supposed to give a concert as well," Mozart added. "I'm looking forward to hearing them. We'll see how these Italians measure up to our German singers. Let's see just how ready they are for the Viennese!"

☙Cs

The journey to Vienna was short compared to the one Nancy traveled from London to Italy, but even two days in the same coach with her mother was almost more than either of them could bear. Fortunately, Michael kept the tension at bay with his chatter. Still, his incessant talking and maudlin stories of his "sainted Mither" back in Ireland grew quickly tiresome.

Francesco Benucci, a quiet, odd-looking Florentine who traveled with them, was a brilliant singer and actor. Just a little younger than Elizabeth, he reminded Nancy of her brother—soft spoken, a little shy, and delighted by her. He was married, but he never spoke of his wife and children. He spoke no French and of course, no English, but since Nancy spoke Italian, she had no difficulty conversing with him, and she enjoyed his company tremendously.

During the second day of the journey, the conversation turned to the subject of Mozart, whom everyone knew by reputation. They knew he enjoyed worldwide fame as a gifted musical prodigy from a remote town in Austria and he was known to be virtuosic on the fortepiano as well as the violin, but that as an adult, he was emerging as a gifted composer.

Nancy had heard of his opera, *Idomeneo, Re die Creta* and of his German opera, its title she couldn't pronounce. However, he hadn't composed any Italian comedies that she knew of. Perhaps he was working on one for them!

She felt as if they were kindred spirits, owing to the many things she believed they had in common, and she was anxious to meet him. Those commonalities were a great source of pride for Nancy, setting her apart from other actresses who were regarded as just a step above common whores. She would never allow herself to be lowered to that position. She was much better than that, she knew, for she was educated in the same manner as the great Mozart!

Elizabeth wasn't sure she could trust Mozart around her daughter, for she had heard gossip about him and his reputation with young women. Although it was said he was married, that fact had little effect upon her, knowing marriage rarely kept any man from indulging in flirtations and assignations with whatever pretty girl happened to be available to them— especially if she was as attractive, gifted, and flirtatious as her daughter.

The group arrived in Vienna, tired and a little sore from the long, bumpy ride, but otherwise happy and anxious to get to work. They were met at the customs house by Count Orsini-Rosenberg, who came to personally welcome them. He showed them to their apartments, not far from the Hofburg, which was the main Imperial complex. The Burgtheater was located just across the way in the Michaelerplatz. Their accommodations were fashionably appointed, with white baroque marble fireplaces, ornate chandeliers and sconces, and enough space to accommodate several people, including a cook and a full maid staff.

Nancy had never lived in such luxury; she was impressed that she commanded such lavish accommodations.

When their trunks and boxes were delivered to their apartments, Rosenberg informed them that they had three days to rest from their journey before they were to report to the Burgtheater to begin rehearsals for their first production. Before that, however, they needed to prepare a short concert for their formal reception.

Nancy aghast, marveled at the opulence of her apartment and she stood in the center of the main salon, twirling in a slow circle as she gazed up at the beautiful, sparkling chandelier of Bohemian crystal suspended over her head, watching as it threw rainbow prisms around the room.

Emperor Joseph II of Austria

Chapter Two

On the day of the grand reception, Nancy was up early to be dressed in her most elegant court gown. Wigs, which for the most part were out of fashion on an everyday basis, were an absolute requirement when at court, so her hair had to be pinned and capped in order to ensure that the heavy wig would stay in place without slipping around, or worse, falling off. This was a laborious routine which could easily take up the better part of a day.

Nancy hated the confinement that court attire brought with it—the tight and uncomfortable stays, the hot, heavy fabrics, layers of skirts, and narrow shoes that pinched her toes. The construction of the gown's bodice and sleeves forced her upper body to stay in an upright, almost sway-backed position, limiting and restricting the movement of her arms and hands to within only a few inches. Whenever she had to sing while wearing such attire, she instructed her maid to lace her stays loosely so she would have room to expand her rib cage, and breathe properly.

When she finally emerged from what she was convinced was a torture chamber of the lowest order, she transformed from a pert and sassy little actress into a lovely and elegant young woman of the court. Her gown was of raw polished butter yellow silk which hinted of subtle peach tones when the light caught it just right. The underskirt was made of heavy ivory satin and was ornamented with rows of lace and satin ribbons, with little seed pearls sewn in the shapes of flowers. The stomacher was decorated with graduating bows and ivory lace and the narrow upper sleeves stopped at her elbows, where they erupted into rows of cascading lace and ribbons that enveloped her delicate forearms. Her blond wig sported a corsage of ivory silk roses and ribbons and a spray of seed pearls fastened to little gold wires, with two white ostrich plumes erupting from the top. Her face was powdered pale, her lips and cheeks rouged, and one little black velvet beauty patch was fastened to her right cheek.

"La Storace!" Michael exclaimed in sheer delight when she appeared, still wrestling with her stays and wiggling around in an attempt to loosen them even further. He had been waiting for her in the salon, eager to escort her to the reception. He bowed with a flourish when he saw her.

"Nancy, you're the picture of loveliness! Me darlin' dove's a lady!" He could hardly believe the transformation. She looked like a duchess.

"I'll be glad when this whole affair is done and over with and I can get out of these wretched clothes! Good God, Mick, I can't bloody breathe!" she cursed as she picked up her fan, turning so he could drape her cloak upon her shoulders.

"Ah, but 'tis worth it, Nancy. To a man's eye, anyway."

"Bugger you men! I'll never understand why you can't appreciate the female sex in our natural state. God knows you're impatient enough when it comes time to disrobe us."

Laughing, he ignored her complaint. "Local gossip has it Mozart will be there," he said, changing the subject as Nancy gazed into a large gilded mirror, giving herself one last look.

She could always count on Michael to bring her the local gossip. He seemed to have a nose for it, and he kept up with it far better than she cared to. Nancy, who was easily engrossed in her work and other more important affairs, found local gossip tedious and a waste of precious time. She had better and more interesting things with which to occupy her time and mind, so she paid little attention. One rarely saw her standing in a corner with other actresses chit-chatting over who was seen with whom, or who had taken whom as whose mistress, and 'Oh I can't believe she's with him! He's such a scarecrow!' It simply wasn't in her nature. However, on this particular occasion she was extremely interested, for his gossip pertained to Mozart, a man in whom she had a vested interest.

"Truly, he will be there?" she asked as she turned around. Michael extended his arm.

"Indeed, love, he will be there," he teased. "At least that's what gossip promises. They tell me he'll be with his brother-in-law the actor, Joseph Lange and his wife, Aloysia, who considers you potentially her greatest rival," he continued as they strolled out the door of her apartments.

"Oh, does she now? Only potentially? I see my reputation has preceded me." Nancy tossed her head back and laughed. Good, she thought. Perhaps that means Mozart is just as interested in me as I am in him.

She knew she was going to give the Viennese singers a run for their money, but she hadn't realized that they were already starting to run. She hadn't even appeared yet, and already the rivalries were forming. It didn't bother her in the least, for she was highly competitive, and she always won. No one would top her at her game, not even Aloysia Lange. The stakes were always high for Nancy, in all things. It was either all or nothing at all where she was concerned. That philosophy had already served her well against all her competition and it would continue to serve her in Vienna.

They arrived at the reception to find all of the city's musicians and musical patrons were there. Anyone with any reputation in the world of music and theater was there—composers, singers, actors, court musicians, nobility, patrons, and the wealthy and influential. It was a gala event held in the Festsaal, a large Baroque hall with a soaring ceiling and golden chandeliers. The buffet tables were laden with rich food and drink, ladies were dressed in their finest, and gentlemen were in their silk brocade coats and satin breeches, donning their finest perukes. A small orchestra made up of strings, a harpsichord, and a few winds, played as the guests mingled and enjoyed the food, bragging and gossiping, and congratulating themselves and others for being titled, wealthy, clever, and important.

Nancy met many people, including the new court poet and librettist, the Venetian Abbé, Lorenzo Da Ponte. Da Ponte was an odd and colorful character, with a reputation for being quite a ladies' man. He'd come to Vienna upon his own reference, and through his devilish charm and gift of persuasion, he had managed to talk the Emperor into hiring him. He'd never held a position in any court, nor had he ever written a libretto, as far as anyone knew, yet he was hired without vitae or references. He and Nancy quickly established a rapport as he promised he would create many spectacular roles for her.

Antonio Salieri, the Imperial Court Composer whom she had already had the pleasure to meet, and with whom she had worked with over the past weeks, was also there. It was in one of his operas that she would make her debut, and already he was greatly impressed with her skill and ability not only as an actress, but also as a gifted musician. He was pleased with her work ethic, for she was one of the hardest-working, most dedicated actresses he had ever known, always punctual, always knowing her parts, and always contributing to the well-being of the entire production.

Salieri brought with him his favorite singer, and mistress, Catarina Cavalieri, who had most recently sung the role of Konstanze in Mozart's *Entführung aus dem Serail*. Despite the Italian name, which she had adopted to ensure employment in Joseph II's new Italianate capital, Cavalieri was in fact Viennese. A short and round, but attractive blonde, she and Nancy had met and were already establishing an amiable friendship.

15

"You must point him out to me, Catarina," Nancy whispered as she sipped a glass of punch

"Point out whom?"

"Mozart, silly goose!" Nancy giggled as she continued to look, wondering if she could guess which one Mozart might be.

"Well," Catarina paused in thought, "he's quite diminutive, I'm afraid, but he has an interesting face. I can't describe it really. Very large eyes and a prominent nose. He's not what one might expect, not at all imposing in appearance, but beware his eyes, Nancy! That man can cast a spell on any woman with those big, sad eyes. Personally, he brings out my maternal instincts, scarce as they may be. He's always well turned out, but there's always a loose thread, a wrinkle in his coat, or that one loose curl that slips out over his left eye when he's performing, or dancing, or who knows what else..."

The two women giggled together. Suddenly, Catarina poked Nancy in the side with her elbow. "Look," she exclaimed, pointing her sight in the direction of a small man wearing a lavender silk suit with a bright green and gold satin embroidered waistcoat. He stood drinking champagne with another man and a slender, willowy woman. He laughed and carried on with them as if they were very familiar with one another. "That's Mozart!" Catarina whispered.

"Which one?"

"The one in the lavender suit. The other one is the actor, Joseph Lange, his brother-in-law, and the woman is Aloysia, Lange's wife and older sister of Mozart's wife. Aloysia is one of the biggest gossips in town! I would watch out for her. Word has it she's already out for blood where you're concerned."

"I've heard," Nancy replied, uninterested in Aloysia. She was only interested in Mozart and what he had to offer her as the new prima buffa.

"Come!" Nancy ordered, setting her glass on a tray and slipping her arm through Catarina's, pushing her in the direction of Mozart and his party.

"Where are we going," Catarina asked, startled by Nancy's audacious move.

"You're going to introduce me. You don't think I'm simply going to stand around and wait, now that you've pointed him out to me, do you? Now get going!" They approached Mozart and his party and, as they drew nearer, Mozart glanced over, recognizing Catarina.

"Madame Cavalieri," he exclaimed enthusiastically, with a bow.

"Herr Mozart." She returned a polite curtsey.

"It is a distinct pleasure meeting you here," he replied. "And tell me," he said as he glanced at Nancy. "Who is this tasty little morsel with you?" Instantly scanning Nancy from the top of her head to her shoes, taking her in all in one long glance, he continued, "I don't believe I have seen her before. Please, you must introduce me at once," he said, taking Nancy's hand and gently bringing it to his lips to kiss.

"May I present to you Mademoiselle Anna Storace."

Mozart's eyes grew round and his smile, which already took up a great deal of his face, expanded to take it over entirely. He had a magnificent smile! Handing his champagne glass to Lange, he exclaimed, "Ah, La Storace!" He gestured with a deep bow and a decorative flourish. "May I present myself to you, Mademoiselle? I am Wolfgang Amadé Mozart and entirely at your service!"

"Herr Mozart, it is an honor," Nancy said, her fan in full flutter over the lower half of her face. She gave him a deep curtsey.

"This is the esteemed actor, Joseph Lange," he offered, politely gesturing toward Lange, who took Nancy's hand and offered a low bow, not as flamboyant as Mozart's, but polite all the same.

"I'm honored, Mademoiselle. May I say that I am rather intrigued by the fact that you're English. Are you well versed in Shakespeare?"

"Oh, indeed!" she replied enthusiastically. "I'm very familiar with his works. I am of a habit to memorize a sonnet a day, for it helps me hone my memorization skills," she said proudly.

"Mademoiselle, this is my wife, the celebrated soprano, Aloysia Lange."

Aloysia stepped forward and offered a shallow curtsey. "A pleasure, Mademoiselle," was all she said, her jealous rivalry already in full bloom.

Nancy ignored the chill and replied with a deep curtsey, deferring to Aloysia's reputation in Vienna. "I know of your fine standing among the Viennese, Madame, and I look forward to working with you in the future."

"I hear you are to entertain us with a taste of your talent, Mademoiselle," Mozart interjected in an attempt to break the ice, which had frozen what was an otherwise warm introduction. "I can't tell you how I look forward to hearing you sing. Pray, tell us what you will offer us this afternoon," he went on enthusiastically, already charmed by her appearance and obvious intelligence.

"I've chosen some arias by Paisiello and a favorite of mine by Handel, *Let the bright Seraphim* from *Sampson*, as well as one of the Countess' arias from the Salieri piece which opens in two weeks," she said, nervously. She suddenly realized this would be her first time to sing for Mozart, who could be rather critical. "If I may, I need to excuse myself because I believe it is almost time for me to take my place for the concert." She glanced over and saw Benucci and the orchestra starting to take their seats. Michael shook Benucci's hand, then took his seat as well.

"Of course. I look forward to speaking with you afterward," Mozart said, bowing to her as she left to make her way toward the orchestra.

Such a warm and demonstrative man, she thought as she took her seat next to Benucci for the start of the concert. Not at all what I expected. Somehow she had been under the impression that Mozart would be serious and austere, more like the descriptions her father had given her of Leopold Mozart, who was reported to be rather stern, and at times overbearing.

Benucci was the first on the program and as he stood for his part he was greeted by enthusiastic applause. He sang brilliantly, his full, round, baritone voice filling the hall. Everyone was impressed, including Nancy. There was no question that His Majesty did well in hiring him. Next, it was Michael's turn to sing, his performance so brilliant that the entire hall broke into enthusiastic applause at its conclusion.

These two left Nancy feeling a little intimidated, but when her time came, she slipped into character and rose from her seat with confidence, taking center stage.

Mozart, who had made his way close to the front so that he could better watch her technique, was already impressed. He was never attracted to ethereal beauty—the wispy, willowy, shallow, muddle-headed type that was all charm and no substance and was considered fashionable. He desired intelligence and a little spit and sassiness, and he already perceived that Nancy met up to his criteria.

Nancy sang beautifully, her favorite Handel piece bringing thunderous applause from the entire audience, including Mozart.

"Ah, she sings like an angel. And what technique!" he said aloud, relieved that everything that was said of her was true.

Nancy's voice was unusual. There was a deeper, darker quality to it than most of the sopranos Mozart knew. She wasn't exactly a lyric, but neither was the voice weighty. It lacked some of the flexibility of a coloratura such as Aloysia, or even Cavalieri, but there was a richness, warmth, and sensuality about it that he found intriguing. He had to compose an opera for this singer. He could take Vienna by storm with this girl!

After the concert he waited as others approached Nancy to offer their congratulations and wishes for her success. He wanted to get her to himself so he could find out more about her, and he was willing to wait a long time in order that he might capture her undivided attention. After the crowds dispersed and everyone seemed interested in returning to their champagne and gossip, he approached and offered his accolades.

"Brava!" he said with a bow. "Yours is a lovely instrument—such warmth, such emotion and expression, especially in one so young. You're an absolute song bird!" He chuckled, remembering a bit of English from his stay in England during his youth. "A little yellow budgie!" he said in his thick German accent. Nancy glanced at her gown, instantly understanding his joke, and broke into laughter.

Because of Mozart's extended travels in England when he was a small child, he learned to speak English well enough to communicate effectively, however, it had been a while since he spoke it and his vocabulary was rather rusty. Nancy, who knew very little German—only what she studied when she learned she would be coming to Vienna—felt most comfortable speaking Italian, a common language among the city's educated classes.

"You're amusing as well as gracious, Herr Mozart. And your English is quite good!" she said, still laughing.

"Grazie, you are most kind Signorina, but please, don't call me Herr Mozart. It sounds like you're talking to my father."

Nancy was a bit taken aback at this familiar suggestion, and her laughter trailed off into an uncomfortable silence. He hesitated a moment as he observed her reaction. Realizing they had not known one another long enough for him to extend her such a courtesy, he quickly apologized. "Perdono, Signorina, I don't mean to be impertinent, it's just that…" He hesitated once again. "Well, it's just you seem so familiar to me, as if we've met before. Of course, that's quite impossible. I haven't been to England since I was a boy and I seriously doubt you were yet born."

"Please, don't apologize. I do understand, for I have felt it as well. I admit I've been very anxious over meeting you, but your humor and generosity have served to quell my anxiety. I hope we will have many more opportunities to become better acquainted."

"As do I, Signorina," he replied as he kissed her hand. "I will be at your premiere. I pray you will see fit to join my party and me at Café Milano afterward; it is where we always go to celebrate after an opening. Your charming and lovely presence will add grace to our otherwise oafish company."

"Thank you. I shall consider it. Until then?"

"Until then," he echoed.

∞CR

Nancy debuted at the Burgtheater to an enthusiastic audience. The Emperor was duly pleased with his entire company, including Nancy, with whom he was especially charmed and delighted.

Afterward, Michael escorted Nancy and her mother to Café Milano. When she came through the door, the entire café burst into applause, along with shouts of "Brava!" from all around. She curtseyed, bowing her head in acknowledgment as she secretly scanned the room for Mozart from over the top of her fan. Spotting him at a table near one of the windows, she transferred the fan to her left hand and gently opened it, glancing in his direction, making it clear that she desired to sit with him. Mozart, who was anxiously awaiting her arrival, understood her signal perfectly and approached her and her party, inviting them to sit with him.

"Mademoiselle, we meet again," he said as he bowed, taking her hand to kiss it. "Once again, I am honored by your company."

Nancy smiled and returned with a curtsey. "This is my mother, Elizabeth Storace."

Mozart turned to Elizabeth, and in a more subdued manner than was usual, he bowed and said, "It's an honor to meet you, Madame."

Elizabeth curtseyed to Mozart and replied rather coolly, "The honor is returned, sir."

Nancy then gestured toward Michael. "I would also like for you to meet my dearest friend and colleague, Michael Kelly."

"Ah, the great O'Chelli! It is a pleasure, sir," Mozart said enthusiastically.

"'Tis an honor to finally meet the great Mozart I've been hearin' about," Michael said.

"So, Mister O'Chelli, I have only recently learned that you're Irish and not Italian, as was first believed by most. There has been some confusion over the pronunciation of your last name."

Michael was relieved that Mozart brought the subject up.

"Indeed, sir, I am Irish and proud to say so, and me surname is pronounced simply 'Kelly' without an 'O' at the beginin'," he explained. "I'm afraid His Majesty is under the mistaken impression that all Irish names have an 'O' in front of them."

"Well, then, Michael Kelly it will be from now on!" Mozart said as he and Michael seated the ladies. After he sat down, he turned to Elizabeth. "I get the distinct impression, Madame, that we have met before, although I'm not quite sure where."

"We have indeed, Herr Mozart," she said with a glimmer of warmth in her voice. "You were just a child. It was when you came to Vauxhall to play while you and your family were in England. You met my husband, who instructed you in the finer points of the bass violin." She smiled warmly, and Mozart's grin widened as her words sparked his memory.

"I remember! That was your husband? Please forgive me, but I didn't make the connection."

She smiled again as Nancy watched in sheer amazement at how easily he seemed to win her mother over. Elizabeth usually wasn't easily won. She had a very keen sense about her, enabling her to sniff out a person's true character almost instantly. If one made an enemy of Elizabeth from the beginning, there was no redeeming himself, but if, however, one made a friend of her, he was always a friend, no matter what.

"And where is your husband now, if I may ask? I take it he did not travel with you to Vienna. Is he in England?"

Elizabeth's eyes lowered as she explained to him that Signor Storace had passed away three years earlier during Nancy's employment in Naples.

"That is why it was necessary for me to accompany my daughter," she explained. "She is not yet of age. My son, Stephen, who is a violinist and composer, returned to England shortly after my husband's death."

"My deepest condolences, Madame," Mozart said with heart-felt concern in his voice. "Your husband was a fine man and a gifted musician. Take comfort in knowing that all who knew him share your loss."

"Thank you, sir. You are very kind."

The four engaged in an evening of pleasant conversation, and recollections of times past. They shared a little gossip here and there, which Mozart seemed to enjoy almost as much as Michael, and discussions of the transition in which Vienna's musicians found themselves with the Emperor's decision to discard the German theater for the Italian opera.

Finally, Elizabeth, who was not used to keeping such late hours, announced that she was getting tired and needed to return home. Nancy was still energized from all the excitement and wasn't ready to leave, so Michael offered to escort Elizabeth home and then return to enjoy the rest of the evening with his new friend. Mozart was happy to volunteer to watch over Nancy until Michael's return. After they left, he turned to her.

"A good woman, your mother. I thoroughly enjoyed meeting her."

"You were very kind to her, Mozart. She never wanted to leave England, and then, after Papa died, it seemed worse for her. She was devoted to him, but I don't think she ever forgave him for taking her away from her home and her family and friends. She misses them tremendously, most especially the Linleys."

"The Linleys?" Mozart acted as if he had just seen a ghost. "You know the Linleys?"

"Well, of course we do! They're one of the most prominent musical families in England. Our families have known each other for years. Of course, the sisters are much older than I, so I never knew them well, but there was some talk between our parents of the possibility of a betrothal between Thomas and myself. But then, of course, he had that terrible boating accident several years ago and, well…"

At the mere mention of Thomas, Mozart's eyes misted over. He pulled a handkerchief from his pocket and dabbed them as Nancy watched in confusion over what she might have said that elicited such a reaction from him.

"Forgive me," he said after he composed himself, "but I've not heard anyone speak his name in years. We were the dearest of friends. We met in Italy when we were boys. He was so very gifted and we were almost exactly the same age. Like brothers, we were. When we parted, our fathers had to physically tear us away from each other." He choked back another wave of tears and then continued. "The news of his death hit me very hard, and when you mentioned his name and that you might have been engaged, well, it took me by surprise," he explained, looking down as he folded and unfolded his handkerchief.

"I'm so very sorry, Mozart. I had no idea," Nancy replied, not knowing what else to say.

"How could you have known?" he said, as he broke from his trance. He noted an expression of empathy in Nancy's face that he thought was remarkable for one so young.

"Your friends are very dear to you, Mozart. It's quite evident," she said, smiling warmly.

"Yes, they are. We don't choose our family, but we do choose our friends."

In the weeks following, Mozart announced to Nancy that after the birth of his first child, which was expected sometime around mid-June, he had plans to travel to Salzburg with his wife to spend some time with his father and sister. He also planned to meet with the librettist, Giovanni Varesco, to discuss the possibility of an Italian comedy from a libretto entitled, *L'oca del Cairo*, which would have a part in it that he thought, would be suited to her.

"Damned arrogant, these librettists!" Mozart said as Nancy and Michael sat with him at the tavern discussing it over beer. "Do you know that shithead Varesco actually had the gall to tell me that his text shouldn't require any alterations and should I desire any, he would require more money?" He laughed sarcastically as he took another sip from his beer. "I wrote back to him and explained that I liked the plot, but I considered his proposal preposterous. I can assure him his text will not be pleasing unless the music is good, and the music will be compromised if the text isn't right. Therefore, if the opera is to be a success and he hopes to be rewarded accordingly, he must alter and recast the libretto as much—and as frequently—as I wish! The ass hasn't the slightest knowledge or experience of the theater and yet he makes such demands!" He took another large draught from his stein.

"Well," Kelly replied, "have you considered askin' the new court poet, Da Ponte, to write a libretto for you?"

Mozart leaned back, crossed one leg over the other and pondered the idea a moment before answering. "I haven't given the notion any thought," he replied, cocking his head a bit and then rubbing his chin. "But that might not be a bad idea at all." He paused again, shaking his head. "I'll wait until after I meet with Varesco to decide. There are too many things going on right now with the baby nearly due and travel plans to make. Plus my wife has the notion in her head that before we leave, we should move out of our apartment and put all of our belongings in storage to save on rent while we're gone."

He rolled his eyes and rubbed his brow. "I'm no good with domestic details. I leave that all to her. 'Whatever pleases you, little mouse,' I say to

her. Then, I come to the tavern to drink with my friends!" He laughed as
he held up his stein.

Little Raimund Leopold arrived on time and Mozart couldn't have
been more proud, or pleased. The trip to Salzburg was scheduled for the
end of July, after Constanze's confinement was over and they were
assured the baby was healthy. After some thought and consideration, it
was decided it would be best for them to leave the baby in Vienna with a
wet nurse. He would be in good hands as Mozart had interviewed several
nurses, choosing the very best one he could afford. Constanze's mother
and sisters were there as well so there would be a number of women to
look after him. It was common enough for a couple to refrain from taking
an infant on a long journey. Fear of the dusty roads, changes in climate
and water, and other conditions made traveling with an infant both unsafe
and inconvenient, but they suffered anxiety over the decision nevertheless,
especially considering he was barely six weeks old.

"Are you sure we've made the right decision, Stanzerl? He's still so
tiny," Mozart questioned as he hovered over the cradle.

"We can't take him, Wolferl. He's too young. The roads are dusty and
I don't trust the mountain air in his lungs. He's not used to it, not to
mention how laxative the water is in the mountains," she replied, not
entirely confident of their decision, but trusting God to protect their son.
She was, in fact, trying to talk herself into it.

"Papa will be extremely disappointed, not getting to see his first
grandchild."

"I know," she sighed, "but he will just have to understand." She
looked around the room to make certain the things they were taking with
them were being kept separate from the things that were going to be put
into storage. When they returned, they would move their little family into
a newer, bigger, more fashionable apartment in the Trattnerhof.

"If I hadn't promised Nancy that I'd be speaking to Varesco about
that damned libretto, I'd postpone the trip until the baby was bigger and
stronger, and then we could take him with us," he bemoaned as he lifted
the infant out of the cradle and held him in his arms. Fatherhood agreed
with Mozart. He always loved children, and now he had one of his own,
he wondered how anyone could be cruel or neglectful to a child. "But
you're right, Mauschen, he's too young, and we're leaving him in the best

of care, so I suppose it's best we let it go at that." He sighed as he held the baby close to him for as long as he could.

Constanze felt a pang of jealousy at the mere mention of Nancy's name. In a cold and catty attempt to hurt her sister, Aloysia shared with her the local gossip that was already flying around Vienna about Mozart and the new English actress. However unfounded it was, it disturbed Constanze because word had already gotten around Vienna that Nancy wasn't like the other actresses, that she was educated like a man and that she commanded a higher salary than even Benucci, which was completely unheard of. She knew her husband had his little love affairs, which was entirely acceptable socially, as long as he was discreet. The sin was when a man fell in love with another woman, thus threatening the financial security of his wife and offspring. And what man, especially a man like Mozart, who was highly attracted to intelligent, educated women, could resist a girl like Nancy?

"So it's true then," she said as she packed the last of the baby's things into a basket.

"What's true," Mozart asked as he held the baby, rocking and cooing.

"About you and that Storace girl," she said as she swallowed hard.

"What about it? We're friends," he said, looking up in confusion over her sudden line of questioning.

"Is that all," she asked, her back still toward him.

Mozart laid the baby down carefully and covered him with a blanket.

"What do you mean, 'is that all'? Of course, that's all. She's a singer and I'm a composer. We're colleagues and friends. What is all this about, Stanzerl?"

"Aloysia tells me the gossip around town is that you're smitten with her. She's seen you together, and everyone says that it's true."

"Of course, Aloysia! Stanze, you know Aloysia shares this horseshit with you because she's jealous. You know she'd say anything to get to you. I can't believe you would believe such nonsense! I love you, Stanze," he whispered as he folded her in his arms. He began to playfully nibble on her ears and down her neck. "To tell you the truth, I've missed you since the baby arrived. We haven't... well, it's been a long time," he whined. "I'm almost glad that we're leaving the baby here so that we can have some time alone, like we used to," he whispered as he continued to nibble.

Constanze giggled, and as he pulled her closer to him, she smacked him hard on the backside.

"Ooh!" he screamed out with glee. "She wants to be a naugh-ty girl! Stanzi-Marini is a naugh-ty, naugh-ty girl!"

Placing both of her hands squarely on his chest, she pushed out of his embrace and laughed, "You're a silly man! One could die from putting up with such a silly man! Now hurry. They'll be here soon to get our things and we're not nearly done with all the packing."

He would have to say something to Aloysia about this. He couldn't have her passing gossip to Constanze when it was so hurtful and caused her to doubt his love for her. How dare she do such a thing? Thankfully, they would be in Salzburg for a few weeks. Perhaps that would give enough time for the local gossip mongers to move on to something else, something with more substance to it.

ಬುಗ

August came, and with it a performance of the company's first completely new opera, a piece by Paisiello based on the French playwright Beaumarchais' *Il barbiere di Siviglia*. It was a smash hit, the Viennese going absolutely wild over it, and at the center of its success was their new darling, Anna Storace. All the local gossip sheets were hot with news of its success.

"Listen to this, Nancy, me darlin'," Michael said as he looked up from a piece he was reading in a theatrical review. "'Storace sang like an angel. Her lovely eyes, her snow-white neck, her fine bosom, her fresh mouth made a charming effect.' I think this one's in love with you, me dove."

"Humph!" was her reply. "Who is that anyway," she asked, leaning to read over Michael's shoulder.

"It's Zinzendorf again." Michael laughed.

"Zinzendorf! He's a fat old fool. All he ever writes is about my 'fine bosom and fresh mouth'! Good God, what a bloody bore. The man needs a blow," she fumed. "I wonder how it's going with Mozart and Varesco in Salzburg?" she wondered out loud, changing the subject. "I miss him. He's become a good friend."

Michael sighed, his jovial mood and expression suddenly serious as he looked up from his paper. "I heard that their wee one died several days ago. Madame Lange broke the news the day after.

"Oh, no, Michael, it can't be! He was so fond of that child, and so proud."

"People lose children. It's the way of things. You know that."

"But Mozart's not just any person. He won't take this news well. I know it will break his heart."

It was several months before they saw Mozart again, for it wasn't until early the following December that he and Constanze returned. He arrived home after having had no success in obtaining a libretto that suited him, so he set his sights on another project. He decided to embark upon a series of subscription concerts, which he felt would bring a good amount of money, and buy him more time to find the right libretto. And although he covered his grief well, those whom he counted as his friends saw beneath his polished pretenses.

Much had happened in Vienna over the months, most notably the arrival of a new English violinist by the name of John Fisher. As soon as he returned, Mozart heard the gossip from his sister-in-law of how Fisher came and almost immediately garnered the reputation of a drunkard and a brute. He was reported to be an old family friend of the Storaces, arriving in Vienna on sabbatical from Oxford shortly after the death of his wife. This news concerned Mozart, but since neither Nancy nor Michael ever mentioned Fisher, he supposed that there was little substance to the rumors, and he let it go without further thought.

It was a joyous reunion when Mozart saw Nancy and Kelly again and rekindled the friendship that had been suspended by several months of separation. They shared with him the success of the past season and of how Nancy and the entire company, who had almost cancelled their contracts due to salary disputes with the Emperor, won a three-year contract, as well as a dramatic salary raise. Mozart was pleased to learn that they would be staying for at least three years, giving him more time to find a libretto with the right part in it for Nancy.

Michael Kelly

Chapter Three

At the premiere of Mozart's newest piano concerto, Nancy was introduced to Baron Gottfried van Swieten, a good friend and great admirer of the composer and his music. The Baron, a diplomat and civil servant, was an amateur musician of the highest order. He was infatuated with Baroque fugues, an appreciation that was evident in his love for the music of Bach and Handel, having collected many of their scores for his personal library. Every Sunday afternoon the Baron held an in-home musicale to which he invited Vienna's finest amateur and professional musicians, some of them nobles, to sing through the cantatas and oratorios. Mozart was a regular attendee at these musicales, often serving as the paid accompanist.

"Perdono, Signorina Storace," he said with a bow and a flourish. "I wish to take this opportunity to offer my most sincere accolades to your immense talent."

Nancy, who was still not accustomed to the formality of the Viennese court, or to the protocol of an employee of the court, giggled with delight and thrust her hand awkwardly toward the Baron so he might kiss it. She replied a little too enthusiastically, which only served to amuse and delight the already enamored gentleman.

"I'm so pleased to make your acquaintance, Your Excellency. I've heard of you from Mozart. He speaks ever so fondly of you. I know of your admiration for the music of Bach and Handel, the latter of which I am very familiar."

"But, of course. Tell me, are you familiar with *Messiah*?"

"Oh, quite!" she replied, clapping her hands with glee. "I've sung the soprano solos on several occasions. May I present Mister Michael Kelly, who is also familiar with Handel's works. His rendition of *Every valley* is one of the finest I've heard!"

"Excellency, it is a pleasure," said Kelly, bowing. "I should inform you that my friend may be a bit overly enthusiastic regarding my talent, but nevertheless, I am quite the admirer of Handel's music."

"Ah, but this is quite fortuitous because I am hosting a reading of *Messiah* this very Sunday in my home. I would be honored if both of you could attend and entertain us with your renditions of some of the solos. Please say you will. I shall not take no for an answer."

At noon the following Sunday, they arrived at van Swieten's home and were escorted into a large library, where the walls were lined with shelves of books and maps, and the many scores for which he was famous. They were pleased to see Mozart, who was busy tuning an elegantly painted and carved fortepiano.

"What a pleasure to see you. I was wondering when van Swieten was going to invite you," he exclaimed cheerfully. "This will be entertaining. I was getting a little bored with all the old farts and bluestockings. God knows we could liven things up a bit around here," he teased with a twinkle in his eye.

Nancy and Kelly had at last developed a warm friendship with Mozart, often meeting him at soirees, musicales and other gatherings around the city. There were also occasions when Mozart and Nancy saw each other at the Trattnerhof casino, where, when she could steal some time from her hectic rehearsal and performance schedule, she would go with Michael to gamble and enjoy a bit of diversion.

She and Mozart enjoyed playing games of chess, which she always won and then teased him mercilessly. Mozart, who was competitive in all things—not just music—didn't generally like losing, but he found losing to Nancy at chess was a stimulating experience. There was something overwhelmingly charming about the way her brown eyes sparkled and danced when she called "Checkmate!", bouncing up and down in her chair, her young bosom bouncing right along with the rest of her. It was so charming, in fact, that he found ways to let her win without letting on that he was doing so on purpose.

Mozart took Nancy's arm and led her to her chair. "You're looking quite lovely today, Mademoiselle," he said flirtatiously, admiring the peach silk frock that so perfectly complemented her skin color. "I'm certain your singing will be every bit as lovely. Your seat is positioned right here next to mine, and at just the perfect angle for me to watch your technique," he said with a roguish grin.

Nancy gave him a smack on the backside with her fan and replied to him through gritted teeth, "Mind your manners, you rascal. This isn't the casino."

Once the music began, Mozart's playful and flirtatious demeanor changed. Suddenly nothing else existed but the music. Nancy admired his ability to lose himself so completely that he became oblivious and indifferent to all else, including her. This aspect of him captivated and intrigued her and, ah! there was that curl Catarina had warned her about, as well as his soulful, yet intense eyes. She wanted to know him better. She felt a connection to him and to his relationship with the music that she couldn't define, but she knew she would have to have more of this part of him.

At the conclusion of the overture, Michael stood and sang the first recitative and the accompanying air, *Every Valley*, which was followed by the chorus, *And the Glory of the Lord*. Nancy and Michael were amused as the group, made up primarily of Viennese men and women, with the occasional Italian, struggled with the English pronunciations. On several occasions they would stop the music and defer to their English guests on how to correctly pronounce some of the more difficult words. Then after Nancy stood and gave her rendition of the air *But Who May Abide*, she was greeted with thunderous applause by the gathering, who were most notably impressed by her skillful manipulation of the difficult melismatic passages in the prestissimo section.

After the session was concluded, Mozart approached her. "Excellent," he exclaimed. "You sing Handel well. Tell me, do you know the aria from *Rinaldo*... what is it called?"

"*Lascia ch'io pianga*. It's one of my favorites," she replied, delighted he was so familiar with Handel's operatic pieces.

"Of course, that's it," he said softly as he gazed at her. "I'd like to hear you sing it one day soon. Your performance today so inspired me that I know that should I hear your rendition, I would be moved to tears."

Afterward, Mozart invited Nancy and Michael to ride with him in his carriage to the Milano, where several of the musicians planned to meet. The mood at the café was festive and light and Nancy felt like she was finally finding a niche within the tight circle of Viennese musicians, who up until this point seemed rather unfriendly and standoffish. They were suspicious of the Italians and resentful of outsiders who took their jobs at court. But today she had impressed all, including Mozart, who was the most difficult to please.

He insisted Nancy take a seat beside him so they could talk, while Michael could do little else but listen and drink. No longer was she simply a charming actress with a pretty voice with whom he liked to flirt, she had intellect too, and Mozart's sudden recognition of that pleased her.

"So tell me, with whom did you study?"

"My father was my first teacher," she answered proudly. "My brother and I were educated in the same manner as you and your sister. When I was eleven I was given to the castrato, Rauzzini, for vocal instruction. I studied with him for two years before I began my tour of Italy. We both studied with him," she said, trying to be polite and include Kelly in the conversation.

"I composed my *Exsultate, jubilate* for him when I was seventeen," he said, not without a touch of pride in both his voice and his bearing. "What a dear man, and such talent. Little wonder you have excellent technique, especially with your breath management through long melismatic passages."

As the three spoke of music, travel, and their diverse performance experiences, Mozart hung on to every word Nancy offered. For the first time he realized how intelligent she was, and how completely fascinating, not like any of the other actresses he'd met, who were vapid and shallow, like Aloysia. No longer was he simply content to be charmed by her. He wanted to know her inside and out.

ᔥᔣ

It was a blustery February afternoon and Mozart had just returned home from the music shop, where he purchased some paper. The moment he walked through the door, he heard an unpleasantly familiar sound echoing from the bedroom. He went in to find Constanze hanging over a porcelain basin, retching. She was pale and drawn, her eyes sunken and her dark locks askew across her forehead.

"Stanze!" he cried out, terrified she was seriously ill. He couldn't stand it when his wife was sick because it made him feel insecure and afraid. It reminded him of years before when he was alone with his mother in Paris and she took ill. He didn't know how to care for her and when she died, he blamed himself. Consequently, whenever Constanze became ill, he felt responsible.

"Don't worry, Wolfgang, it's nothing. It'll pass as it always does," she replied, unaffected by her husband's startled reaction. She made her way back toward the bed and crawled in, complaining that if she didn't lay back down she would faint.

"What do you mean, it will pass as it always does?"

She placed the pillow over her head and snapped, "For God's sake, Wolfgang, I'm going to have another baby! Now go back into the other room and do whatever it was you were doing, and leave me alone!"

"Another baby? When?"

She sat up, looking at him as he stood helplessly, his eyes glazed over and mouth hanging wide open. Sometimes, he really could be a bother. "Not for a while," she said impatiently. "I'm only a couple of months along, so it's going to be a long summer. Now go back to your work and let me sleep. You know when I'm like this, sleep is the only thing that makes me feel better."

He tiptoed toward the bed and sat down beside his grumpy wife, tenderly stroking her tousled curls to one side and kissing her right in the middle of her forehead.

"Another baby. Mauschen, I'm so pleased!" It had only been a few months since their little Raimund passed away and the thought of another child excited him, filling him with hope that perhaps this time things would go better.

"Good. I'm glad you're pleased. Now go back to your work, you silly man, and let me sleep before I puke on you." She managed a weak smile and patted him affectionately, then turned back over and buried her head in the pillows as he pulled the covers over her. He checked the stove, making certain she would stay warm, and then he tiptoed out of the room, closing the door behind him.

Married life agreed with him for the most part, but he found the drudgery of day-to-day living and simply trying to survive a bigger struggle than he'd anticipated. Sometimes he allowed himself to wonder if his father hadn't been correct when he'd advised him to remain single until he'd made his fortune. If he'd followed that advice, he could have kept himself free for his music, and free from the worries and cares that domestic struggles brought into a man's life. Still, he loved Constanze and he worked hard to be a tender, attentive, and loving husband.

He was glad he lived in Vienna where there were so many places to escape to when things got a little overwhelming at home. He enjoyed meeting his friends at the casino or at the Milano after concerts or theater performances. He learned, however, that if he was out with friends and Nancy had been among them, it was best for him not to mention it to his wife. There was still gossip around Vienna, and it was still getting back to Constanze through Aloysia.

One evening as he and Nancy played chess in the casino, Mozart inquired about John Fisher. He was curious about the rumors that Fisher was living in the Storace's apartment.

"So is it true that Fisher is living with you and your mother," he asked as she contemplated his next move.

She remained silent, sipping her cider.

"Yes, it's true," she finally answered. "He moved in with us a couple of weeks ago."

"Nancy, why? Haven't you heard what's said about him? He has one of the worst reputations in the city. There are already numerous establishments in which he's no longer allowed, due to fist fights and drunken brawls."

Nancy felt a lump rise in her throat and she swallowed several times to relieve it before she was able to offer an explanation. "He's an old friend of the family. When he came to Vienna, Mother was so starved for old friends and English company that she invited him to spend several evenings with us. Things just seemed to develop from there, and before we knew it, she invited him to live with us." She hoped this answer would be enough to satisfy his curiosity, but he continued to press her for more information.

"But that doesn't make sense. Is he courting your Mother?"

"No," she replied, hesitating. "He's engaged to me. We're to be married in a few weeks."

His face grew ashen. "You've got to be joking! Please tell me you're not in love with him. For God's sake, he's got to be nearly three times your age. Nancy, please explain this to me in a way that will make some kind of sense!" He hoped there was some way he could persuade her to reconsider.

"It's a purely professional arrangement orchestrated by my mother to help further my career. As to how it will do that, I'm at a loss. It's her way of insuring we will return to London when my contract with the Emperor is up, I suspect. She hates Vienna and she'll stop at nothing to see we don't stay. I've told her she can go back to London if she wishes. I'm of age now and I can take care of myself, but she won't hear of it. Stephen is in London, but that isn't enough. She wants me there too. This marriage is her way of being in control."

Elizabeth Storace—just like Papa, Mozart thought bitterly.

"Promise me one thing, Wolfgango," Nancy continued after a long moment of uncomfortable silence. "Promise me you will remain my friend, that you won't let this come between us. I couldn't bear it if I thought I would lose you. Your friendship means more to me than anything."

"Of course, Nancy. Friendship is the strongest bond on earth and there is no friend dearer to me than you…but I'm frightened for your safety."

"Please don't worry. Fisher has never hurt either of us, despite the rumors. He has been a gentleman. In fact, he's rather charming, and he is very witty. He can be a bit pompous and self-important, but he's a handsome and intelligent man, so I suppose he's entitled to a little self-importance," she replied, trying to offer Mozart some reassurance.

"Just promise me that if you ever need me for anything, you will come to me. I quite demand it."

"I promise. Thank you. You're the kindest of friends."

Nancy suddenly remembered that she left a score in her dressing room which she needed to study before the next afternoon's rehearsal, so Mozart offered to walk her to the theater so she could retrieve it, and then walk her safely home. When they left the casino they changed the topic to something more pleasant. However, Mozart's thoughts still drifted to their earlier conversation.

It was only a short walk from the Trattnerhof to the Burgtheater, just a few yards to the square, and across to the Hofburg. They arrived at the stage door, where the guard recognized them and allowed them passage within.

The backstage area was dimly lit by some sputtering candles in sconces on the walls. Nancy's dressing room was only a short distance down a narrow corridor, so she asked Mozart to wait for her while she went to retrieve the score. She took a candle from out of a small wooden box lying by the backstage entrance and lit it off of one of the wall sconces.

Mozart loved the look and smells of the theater backstage. The aroma of dusty velvet mixed with sawdust, human sweat and stage make-up captivated his innate sensuality, and the thick, red velvet curtains reminded him of the draperies that hung in the bordellos he'd visited once or twice. Perhaps it was also because of the many clandestine encounters he had witnessed between so many actors and actresses, backed up against the walls or hiding behind heavy, velvet curtains, unashamedly indulging their heated passions between acts. Whatever the reason, being backstage always aroused him, especially when he was in the company of a beautiful woman.

In only a few minutes Nancy made her way back up to the corridor to where Mozart stood waiting. Her hair was piled loosely on the top of her head with curls cascading partially down her back and little wisps softly framing her heart-shaped face. Her golden skin reflected the dim candlelight, giving her a soft, almost iridescent glow.

She looks good enough to eat, Mozart thought. He still couldn't separate his thoughts from their earlier conversation, and despite his claims that he was concerned mostly for her safety, he couldn't escape the vivid pictures in his imagination of the wedding night, and what would take place between Fisher and Nancy in the sanctity and privacy of the bedchamber. The thought of Fisher touching her was almost more than he could bear.

"Is there nothing you can do to prevent this marriage?" He hesitated a moment and looked around nervously before he spoke again. "I can't stand the idea of Fisher's hands on you!"

Nancy was taken aback by his sudden outburst. She stepped back slightly and peered into his eyes. They pierced into her, and she was mesmerized.

He slowly reached out for her and placed his hand around her waist, his fingers resting in the small of her back, where he could feel the taut firmness of her stays, which caused her to arch backwards ever so slightly, her cloak and music score dropping to the floor. As he fixed his gaze on her, his eyes darted back and forth as if he were taking in her entire face and expression, reading her every thought and emotion, and conveying to her the depth of his own feelings.

"He can hypnotize any woman with his eyes," Catarina's voice popped into her mind, but she didn't care. She had never been peered into before, nor touched in such a manner, and she felt a surge of warmth rising from her breasts all the way to her head. It was dizzying and exciting, and she wanted more. She arched back further, inviting him closer. She let a small gasp escape as he drew her to him and with his right hand, lifted her dimpled chin towards his face and kissed it softly. His lips began to search for hers as she parted them slightly, allowing his tongue to slip between her teeth and softly touch hers.

Slowly, he backed her against the wall, his mouth making its way along her jaw line, down her supple throat to the tops of her firm but tender breasts, which were slightly exposed and accentuated by her stays and the low, open neckline of her gown. His hands searched up and down her waist, pulling her in even closer until she could feel the firmness of his thighs through her thick skirts. He paused momentarily to gaze into her eyes, which were filled with longing and anticipation, and he lifted her into his arms to carry her to a nearby divan, a set piece, which sat in a corner of one of the stage wings. He softly lowered her upon the divan and quickly removed his greatcoat, tossing it onto the dusty floor, and returning to her.

Reaching up, she touched his hair, and then his face, which was surprisingly smooth and soft. Timid, she could think of nothing to say, so she let her body and hands speak for her, and as he lay upon her, kissing her mouth, she whispered, "Yes."

Taking the lead, he carefully lifted her skirts and positioned himself over her and gently parted her legs. She reached out to him and pulled him to her, resting him between her thighs, and with her hands she groped for the buttons on the front of his breeches as he covered her face, mouth, and throat with his kisses. They kissed and groped, and fondled until he could bear it no longer and he gently thrust himself inside of her, meeting her maidenly resistance.

Stopping short, he whispered, "Nancy, you're a virgin. I'm sorry. I didn't realize... I'll stop if you don't—"

She laid a finger to his lips, silencing him. "Shh…" she whispered. "It's all right. I want it to be you," she replied softly as she took his face in her hands and drew his mouth to hers. "Love me, Wolfgango."

He wasted no time in obliging her, and with a single hard thrust he broke through, sending a sharp jolt of pain, mixed with an odd sensation of pleasure and warmth, surging through her. Her body shuddered slightly as she let out an audible gasp.

"Ai!" she cried softly. "O Dio," she exclaimed as he thrust into her again, the pain dissolving into warm sensations of fullness and pleasure, the like of which she had never felt before. The pace of his movements increased as she instinctively met them with her own, their excitement and pleasure mounting.

Soft cries arose from her throat and she threw her head back as their mutual passion reached its fervent culmination. Her sweet little noises thrilled him even further and he pressed into her as if he were trying to crawl inside and hide forever.

"Mein Gott!" he whispered as he kissed her tiny ears ever so tenderly and allowed her little body to go limp in his embrace. Then, he lifted her face toward his and fingered a stray curl that fell to the middle of her forehead.

He never knew passion to overtake him so quickly, nor so completely. This was a different love than he'd ever known, profound and sensual, the touching of two souls. He lay with her, only the sound of their breathing permeating the silence of the vacant theater, basking in the warm afterglow, holding her close to him and wishing that the moment would never end.

The next morning, Nancy awakened to the sound of her mother's voice beckoning her to get up and dressed. She allowed a gentle sigh to escape as she lazily stretched her arms toward the ceiling, recalling the previous evening's encounter. Her head lay cradled upon her soft pillow, as she remembered his soft and supple hands, his tender but firm, confident touch, and the warmth of his lips gently caressing her body. Suddenly her tender memories were invaded by the dark realization that this was the day that she and John Fisher were to go to register for their marriage license.

Wolfgang A. Mozart

Chapter Four

*A*ugust arrived hot and unforgiving. It had been a busy summer for Mozart with subscription concerts, pupils, and various performances and concerts in the homes of his wealthy patrons. He was grateful for the busy schedule for it meant work, and work meant money, something he needed more of now that Constanze had entered her confinement. The doctor's bills were piling up. This pregnancy had been more difficult than the first, and she needed more care. Constanze, whose moods could be erratic under normal conditions, was particularly moody and grumpy, and the stress was beginning to show on Mozart, who had been making more frequent outings to the casino and the taverns. But as much as he enjoyed the relief that his various diversions provided, it simply wasn't the same without Nancy.

Nancy married John Fisher in late March and the local gossip reported that he'd started beating her almost from the moment they exchanged their vows. It seemed she was off stage more than on, due to unexplained injuries and illnesses. The Viennese audience was starting to become impatient with the situation, and Mozart wondered how long the Emperor would allow this to go on before he replaced her permanently with her understudy. Mozart hadn't seen or spoken to her since the night at the theater, and he tried not to think of it. However, in moments of weakness, or when domestic life was particularly difficult, he couldn't help himself. He still didn't understand how it had happened, or what it was that caused his affections toward Nancy to deepen the way they had. It confused and disturbed him.

"I love my wife," he repeated to himself. Constanze was a good wife and she provided him with all the domestic comforts and conveniences that a wife should. She was a good friend and companion when she wasn't in one of her moods, which lately seemed more frequent than not. When it came to their marriage bed, she was a sweet, generous, and playful lover, allowing him to indulge himself whenever he wished. In turn, he was thoughtful and kind, never demanding his husbandly rights when she wasn't feeling well, or when it was her time of the month.

Things had been different with Nancy. Making love to her had been intense and emotional. It was as if their souls had been locked in the act of passion along with their bodies. Both of them had been moved to tears and when he walked her back to her apartment that night, he could barely tear himself from her. This was a passion that left him craving more, an addiction that could never be satisfied by the playful slap-and-giggle he found with his wife. He told himself that he had to put it out of his thoughts; it was something that could not be. He couldn't allow himself to dwell on it.

John Fisher was a tall, slender, handsome man with cool, slate blue eyes, a head full of dark, thick hair with slight graying at the temples, and an austere, almost noble bearing. He was forty-one years old when he came to Vienna, nearly three times Nancy's age. An old friend of the Storaces from their theater days at Vauxhall, Fisher had served as the principal violinist when Stefano was the director of the orchestra there. When he came to Vienna on sabbatical from Oxford, he immediately found Nancy and her mother with the intent to re-establish ties with his old friends. Nancy's fame, especially her good standing with the Emperor, could prove lucrative for him.

Nancy didn't remember him, for she was far too young at the time that he and her parents were friends, but she'd heard her mother speak of him on several occasions, and always very fondly. She mentioned that he had a tendency toward self-importance and pontification, believing everyone was entitled to his expert opinion whether or not they asked for it, but most generally people shrugged it off. What she didn't know was that after he was widowed only shortly before he came to Vienna, he had taken to strong drink as well as to whoring and had earned a reputation in Oxford as a drunkard and a man of violent outbursts. What no one knew was that this sabbatical was forced by the university heads. Perhaps some time away would cool his temper and save his tenure.

It was a cruel stroke of fate that Nancy's first passionate encounter, the one that would usher her into womanhood and leave her feeling beautiful, respected, and loved, would be followed by the most brutal and humiliating experiences of her life. The man whom Nancy promised wasn't as bad as the gossipmongers claimed turned out to be her worst nightmare.

The abuse began immediately. In fact, Fisher turned into a different person the instant they took their vows. As soon as they arrived home he began barking out orders to the maids to have his things moved into Nancy's bedroom.

"Schnell!" he shouted as the young maids went running, hauling his heavy belongings through the apartment. "Things are going to change around here! No more of your indolence, or your backtalk, you German swine!"

When one of the maids dared to raise an objection, he replied with a box on the ears, and it wasn't unusual for him to pick up a nearby chair, a vase, or anything within his reach and hurl it at the offending girl. Elizabeth took to hiding in her room, never daring to raise an objection however much she regretted the match she had orchestrated. Of course he never laid a finger on her, but Nancy and her poor maids didn't fare as well.

The first beating took place only two days after their wedding, when Nancy and Michael came back to the apartment after going to the Milano with other members of the company following a performance. They were laughing over his inebriated state and Michael, in a fit of drunken gaiety, buried his face in Nancy's bosom. Nancy pushed him off of her, taking his arm and walking with him up to his own apartment, where she helped him get settled in for the night so he could sleep it off. When she returned to her own apartment, Fisher met her at the door with a leather strap in his hand and hit her with it, calling her a whore.

By the middle of April, word of the beatings had gotten out to the Viennese gossipmongers, for Nancy was taken out of several performances due to her injuries. They knew it was only a matter of time before Rosenberg grew impatient with Nancy's frequent absences. She did the best she could to keep up with the grueling rehearsal and performance schedules, which were especially busy that spring and summer. She wasn't going to allow herself to be replaced if she could help it. If nothing else, Nancy was determined.

Fortunately there were some weeks spent at Laxenburg, the Emperor's summer palace and hunting grounds, where Fisher, being a spouse, wasn't invited. Nancy enjoyed a little respite then and was grateful for the time away from both work and her husband. Upon her return to Vienna, however, she found the situation at home was as bad, or worse, than before.

She hadn't seen Mozart the entire spring or summer, for after the night when she returned late with Michael, she was afraid to go out to the casino or to the Milano. It didn't matter how early or late she returned, though, because Fisher always found a reason to be angry with her, so she was subject to his foul moods on a daily basis.

When he dragged her into their bed and forced her to submit to her conjugal duties—and unspeakably vile debaucheries—she closed her eyes and escaped to a place where she was loved and adored, and treated with respect and tenderness. She imagined being with Mozart in a lush, expansive garden with trees and a softly flowing river, lying in the grass. There, he made tender love to her on the daisy-strewn lawn, the birds and the breeze their only music, and the sky their only witness.

There were also times when she felt a sense of overwhelming guilt over her thoughts of him. What if she really was like other actresses and nothing but a common whore? Sometimes she believed that Fisher's treatment of her was penance for her sin of loving a married man. Fisher always called her a whore; what if he was correct? And although she was neither a Catholic nor religious, she sometimes walked to St. Michael's to sit in one of the back pews where no one would see her, and pray to God to forgive her for loving a man who belonged to someone else.

Giovanni Paisiello was composing a new opera, *Il re Teodoro*, to premiere at the Burgtheater in late August, with Nancy singing the lead female role. It was to be a grand and prestigious occasion, attended by the entire court. Also in attendance would be the heir of King George III of England, the Prince of Wales. Nancy was especially excited about the Prince's attendance, and was determined she would do everything in her power to gain his approval.

It was only a few days before the day of the royal command performance, and Nancy had managed to keep Fisher off of her for a couple of weeks. Fisher, who was a vain man, took particular pride in the fact that it was his wife who would sing the female lead in the premiere, and was particularly careful about not striking her. He still yelled and carried on, but his vanity kept him from hitting her for the time being. He had much to gain if the Prince found favor with his wife and became a patron when they returned to London.

Forced to stay at the theater after the dress rehearsal for some last minute costume fittings, and late by only half an hour, Nancy found her husband sitting in the salon at the fortepiano when she walked in the door. He had been drinking and the entire salon reeked of rum.

"You're late, madam. Where have you been?"

"I had to stay a little while," she replied cautiously. "There were some last minute wardrobe changes and I had to be re-fitted for two of my costumes."

"I heard voices outside. You weren't with Mozart again were you? I've heard the rumors about you two."

"It's just gossip, John" she said, turning away from him to hide her face, afraid that her expression would betray her true feelings. "I haven't seen him in months. I was with Kelly. He walked me home from the theater before he went to the casino. He was meeting some of our friends there, I think."

"That Irish pig! What do you see in him anyway? He has no talent, he can't sing, and he can't act. And I've heard from some very reliable sources, my dear, that he's not even a good fuck," he grunted, growing more and more agitated.

"He's a dear friend, John, one of the dearest I've ever had, and I wouldn't know about his sexual prowess because I've never slept with him."

"The hell you haven't! You're an actress! You've slept with every useless musician in this whole bloody city!" he said, cursing and staggering as he got up and made his way toward her.

"I'm very tired, John. I need to go to bed now. I have a long day tomorrow. The rehearsals are getting intense. Our Crown Prince is arriving tomorrow. Perhaps you might want to take my carriage out to the Stubentor to see him arrive with his entourage. I hear it's going to be quite the spectacle!"

Her attempt to pacify him was to no avail. He grabbed her by the waist and pulled her toward him with such a strong force that it caused her head to snap back, sending a surge of pain up the back of her neck all the way into the top of her head. He pushed into her, rubbing his pelvis in a circular motion and putting one hand on her buttocks he bent her back and began to unbutton the front of his breeches with the other.

"No, John, not tonight!" she protested as she pushed him away.

"Shut up!" he snapped as he smacked her across the face with the back of his hand, a large ring cutting into the soft flesh of her cheek.

"John, please, stop!"

"I told you to shut up, you bloody whore!"

Nancy struggled out of his grasp and fell to the floor, but as she tried to get back up, he grabbed her again and dragged her into the bedchamber where he tossed her onto the bed. Despite her weeping and crying out, trying to convince him to stop, he was too agitated and enraged, and he positioned himself over her and began slapping her face and head, boxing her ears, and then beating and punching her with his fists. Finally, he gave her one last blow to the head, knocking her out. After she stopped struggling he had his way with her.

Nancy wasn't sure how long it was before she came to, but when she awoke, Fisher was still lying on top of her, passed out, drunk. Weak and dizzy, she somehow managed to push him off of her. Afraid that moving him might have wakened him, she lay still for a moment, listening to his breathing. Both of her eyes were swollen from the blows to them, but she managed to sit up on the bed, a massive, overwhelming surge of pain gripping her entire body, and she grew dizzy and nauseated. As she climbed down from the bed, she saw the bloody linens and realized that she needed attention. She tried to stand, but the room moved in circles, and she fell to the floor and vomited. After several moments she was able to get to her feet, maintaining enough balance to leave the room.

As she closed the doors behind her she leaned against the wall and made her way to the salon. She was cold and shivering from shock, so she found her cloak and managed to put it around her shoulders. As she made her way to the front entrance she heard a door opening in the corridor. She froze, terrified that Fisher had awakened and would find her trying to escape. She knew if he found her he would kill her. She was relieved, however, when she heard her mother's voice. She had been hiding, as usual, in her bedroom.

"Are you all right," Elizabeth asked in the dark.

"I'm fine. Go back to bed. I'm going out to get some fresh air. Don't worry."

As quickly as she could, she slipped out the front entrance of her apartment and onto the stair landing. She leaned up against the wall so she could have a moment to think about what to do and where she should go. She wasn't sure how late it was because she didn't know how long she had been unconscious, so she didn't know if Michael would be home or not. Besides that, his apartment was on the floor above hers and she knew that she couldn't manage the climb. She decided the best thing would be to get to the theater where there might still be someone who could help, and where the guards would refuse Fisher entrance, if he showed up.

It took all the strength she could muster to make it down the stairs to the ground floor, and to the building's entrance. When she got there, she managed to push the door open by leaning into it with all her might, sending excruciating pain surging through her entire body.

The street was still illuminated by the lamplights, which meant it wasn't yet dawn. Hopefully someone was still at the theater. She made her way down the narrow street to the Michaelerplatz where she noticed the theater lights were still lit.

"Good," she thought aloud. "Now, if I can just manage to cross the square." She leaned against another building, catching her breath and regaining her strength. It took several moments for her head to clear. Her legs felt as if they weighed a thousand pounds each and her entire body was wracked with excruciating pain. Just as she was about to make her way across, she heard the loud clip-clop of horses' hooves and the rattle of a carriage driving over the cobbled stone street. The carriage stopped and out stepped a small man in a pale green suit.

"Nancy! Is that you?"

She recognized that voice! Her vision was blurred and her head felt like it was about to explode with the throbbing pain as she strained to see the person who approached her. As he drew nearer, he exclaimed, "Mein Gott! Nancy!"

Mozart. It was Mozart! He kneeled down to examine her more closely under the lamp light, horrified by the gruesome sight before him.

"Help me, Wolfgango," she whispered, her voice so pitifully weak that he could barely hear her. "He's going to kill me."

Mozart cradled her in his arms and stood. The pain surged through her entire body, and she moaned.

"I'm so sorry, little bug," he whispered in her ear. "I've got to get you into the cab so I can take you to get help. Do you understand?"

She nodded as he carried her to the cab. He called the driver to come down to open the door and help him get her in. Mozart then got inside and turned and poked his head back out the door and called out once more. "Klosterneuburg! The Waldstätten estate, at once!" He leaned over her as the cab lurched away from the curb, heading toward the Schottentor gate leading out of the city to the small village, which lay about five miles to the north of Vienna. "Nancy, can you still hear me?"

"Yes," she answered weakly.

"I'm taking you to the Baroness Waldtstätten's. She's a friend of mine. She'll take excellent care of you and you'll be far enough away that Fisher won't be able to find you." He looked up towards the cab's ceiling and prayed silently, crossing himself. "Dear God, let her be all right! Please!"

Struggling to remove his jacket, he rolled it up into a ball and gently placed it under her head as a pillow. He arranged her cloak so that she was completely covered and then he sat back for the remainder of the drive.

The Michaelerplatz, Vienna

Chapter Five

The cab pulled into the circular drive of the Waldstätten estate just outside of Vienna. As he stepped down, Mozart motioned for the driver to help him with Nancy, who was unconscious. He carried her up the steps to the entrance of the manor, calling out for someone to let him in. Finally, after what seemed far too long to the anxious Mozart, a porter opened the door, instantly recognizing him. Startled to see the tiny woman lying unconscious in the composer's arms, he beckoned Mozart to enter quickly.

In the sitting room, he found a soft, over-stuffed settee and carefully laid Nancy there. As he looked about the room for something to use to cover her, he barked out an order to the porter. "Get the Baroness! Schnell!"

After a few moments, the Baroness, startled and perplexed by the commotion, entered the room and saw Nancy drawn and pale, but coming to, Mozart kneeling by her side speaking her name softly in an attempt to rouse her.

The Baroness was an elegant woman in her late thirties, quite wealthy, a little coarse and outspoken and influential in the Viennese court. Estranged from her husband, she kept an elegant home in Vienna in the Leopoldstadt, but whenever the Baron was on one of his long excursions abroad, she usually made her way back to the country to enjoy the peaceful living the large family estate afforded her.

She and Mozart met when he first came to Vienna in 1781, and she was quite taken with him. They developed a warm and amiable friendship and Mozart never hesitated to call upon her for assistance of any kind. He went to her in similar fashion when he was engaged to Constanze and she and her mother quarreled. The Baroness took Constanze in without question. Anything for her favorite genius.

When she saw Nancy, she recognized her immediately, for as one of the patrons of the Emperor's theater, she was in regular attendance at the opera. Appalled by Nancy's broken and battered condition she inquired, "Who did this to her?"

"It was that dog of a husband of hers, John Fisher! You know, that English violinist," Mozart replied, his voice full of venom and outrage.

"Mein Gott," she exclaimed, moving closer to Nancy and kneeling down to see her face more closely. "Friedrich!" she called the porter, who stood just outside the entrance to the room. "Wake three of the maids to help us get her cleaned up! Mozart, help me get her up the stairs to a room. There's one very near the top that is quite comfortable."

Mozart bent over Nancy and gently lifted her, placing one of her arms around his neck. He followed the Baroness into the corridor and up the stairs to a large bedchamber, and placed her softly upon the bed, as two maids lit candles and started a fire in the furnace. Soon the third maid came in carrying a large pitcher and basin of water, several rags, bandages, and a jar of green salve. The Baroness led Mozart back into the corridor so that the girls could undress Nancy and begin to care for her.

"It's late, Wolfgang. You needn't stay. We will take good care of her until she's able to return to her own apartment."

"Oh, no, Elisabeth, please. I would much rather stay. I'm too sick with worry to leave now," he said, trying not to betray his tender feelings.

The Baroness quickly perceived that there was something deeper in Mozart's regard for Nancy than he was willing to divulge, and as she cocked her head, her eyes narrowed into two tiny slits as she allowed a knowing grin to curl her lips.

"Very well. Go back down and wait for me in the salon. We'll get her cleaned up and changed, and then you can sit with her." She lifted the hem of her negligee and turned to go back into the room, and then hesitated, looking over her shoulder at Mozart, who was making his way to the stairs. "Don't worry, Wolfgang. She'll be fine." She went back into the room, closing the door behind her.

The maids were in the process of cleaning and dressing the cuts and bruises on Nancy's face, and gently placing cool compresses on the bumps all over her body. The Baroness leaned over, spoke quietly to one of them, and asked if there were any broken bones.

"No, Madame," the girl replied, "I don't believe so."

"Good, then. At least that's a blessing. Go into my bedchamber and find one of my chemises to put on her. And take her dress with you and have it washed and made into rags. It's torn and stained beyond repair. I'll send for some of her things in the morning. She'll stay with us for a while, until she's well enough to return home."

"Yes, Madame," the maid said as she curtsied, and then turned to gather up Nancy's things.

Soon Nancy was sitting up in the bed, a soft, linen sheet draped over her shoulders to cover her, and fully conscious and aware of where she was. Still very weak, she tried to object to staying, but the Baroness was adamant.

"I won't hear of it, Liebling. You'll stay until you're well enough to be moved. And don't worry about Rosenberg. I'll tell that stingy old fart that he'd better find a way to get this stopped, or I'll remove my patronage from the theater. And if I remove my patronage, my friends will do the same. I'll have some tea sent up. The maid will be in very soon with something for you to put on and in a few minutes I'll go get Mozart. He's waiting, rather impatiently, in the salon."

As she walked to the set of wing doors, she motioned for a maid to come closer. "Get some laudanum from my dressing table. She's going to need it for the pain."

Although in excruciating pain, Nancy began to feel the results of the care that was so generously lavished upon her by the Baroness and her servants, and she thanked her for her kindness. More, she felt tremendous relief to be far from her husband.

One of the maids brought in a clean, silk chemise, along with one of the Baroness' pretty dressing gowns. She was helped to a large, comfortable chair in the corner of the room and a soft knitted blanket covered her lap. A small, round, mahogany table was unfolded in front of her and a tea tray was set upon it. A maid poured her a cup of warm medicinal tea, made from tree bark to help ease her pain. Moments later, she heard someone at the door.

"Nancy, it's Wolfgang. May I come in?"

"Yes," she called out, weakly.

He was greatly relieved to see she was conscious and sitting up, although still rather weak and pale. He knelt by her so he could get a better look at her face, and was nearly overcome by the sight. There was a large gash on her left cheek and both of her eyes were swollen and black. Her lower lip was cut and swollen and, although he couldn't see them, he knew there had to be cuts and bruises all over her body. Tears welled in his eyes.

"What kind of a man could do this to your sweet face, little bug?" He took her hands and lifted them up to his lips to kiss her fingers. Then, as he turned them over in order that he might kiss her palms, he saw the bruises around her wrists, evidence that she was held down by force against her will and violated. The horrified look in his eyes betrayed his shock. He couldn't bring himself to ask the indelicate question that sprang to his mind. Besides, he already knew the answer.

Humiliated and ashamed, Nancy pulled her hands away and buried them in her lap, hiding them in the folds of the blanket. Turning away from his gaze, she began to weep.

In a fit of blind rage, he leapt to his feet and declared, "I'll kill him! I swear by God, I'll kill that dog and leave him lay in a pool of his own stinking blood!"

"Don't be a fool, Wolfgang. Fisher is twice your size and strength. I don't need for you to champion me. I will work this out myself." She paused a moment. "Besides, the Baroness has already promised to pull her patronage from the theater if Rosenberg doesn't find a way to stop him."

She paused again and sighed, her tone softening. "Please, Wolfgango, this is women's business. Let women take care of it."

Confused, he stood in silence for a moment, then, after he battled down his rage, he pulled the chair over from a desk. "I didn't mean to offend. I only want to help."

"But you have helped, Wolfgango. I don't know what I would have done had you not found me and brought me here. You've done all you can—all that is appropriate for you to do," she said as she turned away again. "I'm not yours to champion. I'm not your wife, and I refuse to be your mistress."

"What are you saying?"

She began to weep again. "I don't know what I'm saying," she sobbed. "I feel so ashamed! Fisher says I'm a whore. On our wedding night he knew…"

"What did he know," Mozart asked cautiously.

"He knew he wasn't the first," she said as she hid her face in her hands.

Mozart said nothing as he rose from his chair and walked to the other side of the room. He felt an overwhelming since of guilt. "I don't know what to say, Nancy. I'm so sorry," he said as he hung his head.

"It's not your fault, please don't blame yourself. It wouldn't have mattered one way or the other with him. He would have done this, anyway."

"You're not a whore," he said as he turned to her. "I didn't think you as such when we…"

"We have to forget that night. I care too much for you, Wolfgango, and I could too easily fall in love," she confessed.

"But Nancy, I…"

"Just go now, please," she said as she turned her face away. "I can't talk about this now. I appreciate your concern, and all you've done, but it's time for you to leave."

"Very well, then," he conceded. "I'll check in on you in a few days." He then turned quietly and left.

Nancy awoke the next day to see the late afternoon sun streaming in through the arched bedroom window, patches of orange light casting an amber glow over the entire room. Startled at first, not remembering where she was, or why she was there, it took her several moments to recall the terrible event of the previous night.

"Baroness Waldstätten," she whispered as the fog began to lift, "I'm at her estate. Wolfgang found me. I ran away… Fisher… he tried to kill me!"

She flew into a panic as the terrifying images of the night before began to dart through her memory, like flashes of white hot lightening—Fisher's crazed expression, the brutal beating, his large fists hurling toward her face, the excruciating pain, the blood, her escape from her apartment, and Mozart.

"Wolfgango!" She said his name aloud as her panic began to subside. "He brought me here," she recalled with a sigh of relief. "I'm safe now."

I wasn't very kind to him, she thought, recalling their conversation. There were so many jumbled thoughts and images trying to invade her all at once that it was too much to grasp. She couldn't think of him yet. It was too painful, too confusing.

She tried to raise her head but an intense, sharp, pain shot through her entire body, from the top of her head to her feet and she sank back onto the soft, eider down pillow. Across the room stood an oval looking glass. Her vision was so blurry the night before that she could barely see at all. Her vision greatly improved, she could make out her reflection in the mirror. Horrified at the swollen black-and-blue creature starring back at her, she turned her face away, buried it in her pillow, and wept. The salt tears stung as they trickled from her eyes onto her cheeks, invading the open cuts left by Fisher's ring.

How could he do this? What did I do to deserve such cruel treatment? After a few moments, she heard the doors creak open and in walked an elegantly dressed woman with light brown hair which was fashionably coiffed.

"Good afternoon, my dear," she said cheerfully, her voice as elegant as her appearance and her dark blue eyes expressive and kind.

She leaned over Nancy and examined her face. "The swelling is down considerably. I can see your pretty eyes. And don't worry about scars. We put some salve on your cuts, an old family recipe…works like a miracle! I've called my private physician to give you a thorough examination. He'll be here later this evening. I've also arranged for some of your things to be brought here," she added. You'll be staying for a while. You won't be well enough to move for several weeks."

"But the premiere! The Prince!"

"I went into the city today and spoke with Rosenberg. I'm afraid you've been replaced by your understudy." She spoke softly, trying to break the news to her as easily as she could.

Nancy broke into heart-wrenching sobs, this new disappointment being the final blow. Elisabeth sat beside her on the bed and stroked her hair as a mother would an upset child. "There, there, now, I know it's distressing, but not to worry. Your position with the company is secure," she assured her. "I threatened Rosenberg to pull my patronage if he didn't do something about that animal. He promised that he would speak to the Emperor immediately. You won't have to worry ever again."

"But what can they do to insure that?"

"I have no idea what they're planning," she said as she shook her head, "but rest assured it will be taken care of. You will have no more worries where he's concerned."

"I can't begin to thank you enough for what you've done on my behalf, Madame," Nancy said, extending her hand in gratitude.

Elisabeth took her hand in hers and smiled warmly. "Think nothing of it. I'm only glad that Mozart thought of me when he found you. And speaking of Mozart," she added, "I ran into him today and he was most anxious to receive word of you." She searched Nancy's expressions for any signs of affection.

Nancy began to fiddle nervously with the lace on the edge of the bed sheet. "It was a miracle he found me, Madame. I'll always be grateful to him. He's the dearest of friends."

Elisabeth listened, wishing Nancy would speak of their conversation the night before, but she hesitated to pry. Time and trust would reveal more. She had a way with young women. Once she gained their trust, they had a way of readily betraying their deepest secrets.

"He must regard your friendship as dearly as you do for he seemed quite relieved when I told him you were going to be all right—that all you needed was time and rest."

She went to the doors. "I'm having some food sent up. After you've eaten and have rested a little, the physician will come take a look at you. If there is anything else I can do, please, do let me know," she added, graciously.

"Is my mother all right? Does she know where I am," Nancy asked, suddenly remembering that she'd left Elizabeth alone with Fisher.

"She's fine. Rosenberg sent a messenger with word of your safety. She doesn't know where you are yet. We have to keep that secret until Fisher is dealt with. After that, we'll send word to her of your whereabouts so she may come to visit you."

❧⊗❧

The weeks spent with the Baroness Waldstätten were healing for Nancy, who spent a great deal of her time lounging in the estate's many gardens and quiet spots, reading, writing letters, and doing needlework.

Rosenberg sent word that the Emperor had evicted Fisher from the Imperial apartments, and in addition, he was given two months to leave Vienna altogether. He assured Nancy that she wouldn't have to deal with Fisher again and encouraged her to take all the time she needed to recover and regain her strength. Her position with the company was secure, just as the Baroness had promised.

Michael brought Mrs. Storace for regular visits, during which she brought news from Stephen, who was nearly frantic with worry. Nancy wrote to him several times and assured him she was doing well and that the Emperor had insured her safety. Stephen was unsatisfied with Nancy's word alone and decided at the end of the year he would make a trip to Vienna to check the situation out for himself.

There was also distressing news concerning Mozart. On the evening of the premiere of the Paisiello opera he collapsed and had to be removed from the theater and driven home. Word was he'd suffered from an attack of his kidneys, a chronic condition from which he'd suffered since childhood.

It was a warm September afternoon and Nancy sat in the garden doing her needlework when the Baroness came and asked if she could join her. Since coming to stay at the Waldstätten estate, Nancy enjoyed many hours of leisure with Elisabeth, which they spent in conversation over numerous subjects, including music, art, the theater, and England. Elisabeth observed Nancy kept many things hidden, that her innermost thoughts and emotions were shrouded behind a wall of secrecy that was nearly impenetrable. She believed although Nancy was nearly healed of her physical wounds, the emotional scars remained.

"What glorious day," she exclaimed as she looked out over the garden.

"Indeed it is, Madame," Nancy said as she looked up from her work to view the sky. "We've had a stretch of beautiful weather for several days now. I've enjoyed the opportunity it has afforded me to indulge my more indolent nature by sitting in this beautiful garden nearly every day for the last week."

"The fresh country air must agree with you, dear. Your strength seems to be returning."

Nancy smiled as she watched the cat chase a butterfly as it flitted across the lawn, around a large trellis laden with pink roses. "I simply adore this garden. One day I shall own a cottage in the country and have a garden filled with fragrant tea roses."

Elisabeth closed her eyes and drew in a long breath of fresh air. "I think it's time for a picnic," she said. "I haven't entertained friends in a while. With the weather cooperating as it is it's about time I do!"

"That sounds delightful, Madame. When," Nancy asked as she continued her stitching.

"I've already set the date for this Saturday. Your friend Michael Kelly tells me Mozart is feeling much better and is in need of an outing. He spent three weeks cooped up during his illness and needs some fresh air and company." She paused to see if there was any response from Nancy. "I've invited both of those charming rascals to be our guests for the entire weekend." She giggled and hesitated a moment more. "And I *know* you're in love with him," she added, humorously.

"I don't know what you mean. Who am I in love with?" Nancy chuckled nervously, startled by Elisabeth's bluntness.

"I knew the night he brought you here."

"I'm afraid, dear Baroness, that I don't know what you're talking about," Nancy said trying to put her off.

"Oh please, Nancy, you can't hide such things from me. You know me too well by now. It's useless. I can see it in your eyes every time someone even mentions his name."

Nancy had never spoken of her feelings for Mozart to anyone, and there were times she felt as if her heart were going to burst. Perhaps if she shared them with the Baroness, she could help her sort them out. She sat silently for several moments and ran her finger over the stitches in her needlework before she finally replied.

"Yes, I'm in love with him," she confessed. "I didn't mean for it to happen. We were simply good friends." She paused, struggling to gather her thoughts. "We found many things in common, and we loved spending time together playing chess and discussing music. Then, one night, after we'd been at the casino, he walked me to the theater. I had just told him I was engaged to Fisher. He was terribly upset over it."

Elisabeth sat, listening intently.

"It happened there." Tears welled in her eyes. "It happened so fast. He put his arms around me and kissed me, and then…"

"He made love to you," Elisabeth added as delicately as possible. She was thrilled to have made this much headway.

Nancy nodded.

"Was it your first time," she asked, gently coaxing her to reveal more.

She nodded again. "It was so… I don't know…so beautiful. I never felt like that before, and no man had ever touched me in that way… He was gentle, and so tender," she said, blushing.

"And then you married Fisher."

"Yes," she whispered and burst into tears.

Elisabeth put her arms around Nancy and held her close. "Everything will work out," she spoke softly. She reached into her pocket and pulled out an embroidered handkerchief and wiped Nancy's eyes.

"I believed Fisher's cruelty was my penance for loving a man who isn't my husband."

"Nonsense! Do you really believe loving can ever be a sin?"

"Well, loving him is, isn't it? He's married. All I could ever be is his mistress."

"And what's wrong with that? As long as one is discreet, the arrangement is perfectly acceptable."

"But we have so much more. We're friends. I refuse to cheapen the relationship by stooping to that position," Nancy exclaimed indignantly.

"You feel the friendship would be compromised?"

"Yes."

"Do you still love him," Elisabeth asked, trying to press her point.

"Yes, I do, but he can't love me. He loves his wife," Nancy shouted, as she began to lose patience with the conversation.

"What is it with you English and your staunch insistence on marital fidelity? Do you not understand that marriage is purely a social arrangement to ensure that a man's line remain pure? It has nothing to do with love. Men don't marry for love. They marry a woman who will take care of them, make good homes and give them children."

She looked at Nancy, who remained with her back turned.

After a few moments she sighed, and said, "Yes, you're right. He loves her. She makes a good home for him and gives him children as heirs. She's a good companion. She sees to his meals, his laundry, and his health, and she keeps his bed warm at night. What man wouldn't want a woman to do those things for him? But you're different," she continued. "He doesn't merely love you, Nancy; he's *in* love with you. You excite him. You stimulate his intellect and stir his emotions. You're his best friend, his muse. As his wife, Constanze owns his loyalty and his name, but you, my dear, are his lover, for you're like him."

She paused as Nancy thought on what she had said, and then she asked, "Why would you ever want to be his wife when he's chosen you to be his lover?"

Chapter Six

*I*t was a sultry afternoon as Sophie went through the apartment opening every window in an attempt to catch any breeze that might bring some comfort to the household. Her sister Constanze reclined on a settee in the salon, which seemed to be the coolest room for the moment. Her swollen feet were propped up on two pillows, and as she fanned herself, she thought that God chose the cruelest of seasons for her to endure the last phase of her pregnancy.

"I'll be gone for a couple of days, Stanze," Mozart called from the bedchamber, where he gave himself one last look in the mirror. He was looking forward to a few days away. Being stuck indoors without the society of his friends had made him agitated and restless.

"But what if the baby should come while you're away?"

"Sophie knows to send word to me should that happen. I won't be far away and I can be home within an hour. You've already said that it shouldn't be time for another week or so." He told her he was engaged to play for a soiree the Baroness was holding for a group of her aristocratic friends from several neighboring villas.

She wanted to go with him. Certainly she needed the diversion as much as he. She petulantly threw her fan down on the settee. "Sophie, open the windows wider!"

"They're open as far as I can manage, Constanze," Sophie replied, tired of her sister's foul mood.

"I wouldn't leave you like this, Stanze, if we didn't need the money," Mozart said, striding into the room to kiss the top of her head and pat her belly.

"Don't paw me!" she snapped. "It's too hot, and I feel like I'm about to burst!"

"My poor little wife," he sighed. "Why don't you send out for an Italian ice? It might help."

"That does sound good." She looked at him and smiled sheepishly. "Forgive me for being such a shrew. It's almost over," she sighed as she turned onto her side, trying to find a comfortable position. "You've been cooped up in this apartment with me for too long. Go and enjoy yourself. Sophie will take good care of me."

He felt guilty for leaving Constanze in such a miserable state, but not guilty enough to turn down the Baroness's invitation. Besides, he thought, it will be good for me to get out of her hair. I always seem to say and do the wrong things when she's like this.

He pulled his watch from his waistcoat. "It's time for me to go. Kelly will be here soon. I'll see you on Monday." He kissed her and left.

Upon their arrival at the Waldstätten estate, Mozart and Kelly were escorted into the grand salon, where the Baroness gave them a warm reception.

"Gentlemen, what a pleasure to see you! It's good to see you looking well, Mozart."

"I can't thank you enough for your gracious invitation, Madame. I was about to go mad, sequestered in that apartment for so long!"

"It's my pleasure. And there's someone else who's been rather anxious to see you. She's in the garden," she said with a grin. She turned to Kelly and took his arm. "Come Mr. Kelly; let us proceed to the music salon. I have several new scores that have only just arrived from England. I think you might enjoy looking at them."

Mozart hurried out to the garden, where he found Nancy lounging on a wicker settee, engrossed in a novel. She wore the latest English fashion—a crisp summer frock made of cream-colored cotton with organza ruffs encircling the sleeves and neckline and cinched at the waist with a puce ribbon. Her hat was a straw one, embellished with ribbons that matched the one at her waist. Her feet peeked daintily out from under her skirts to reveal a pair of cream-colored satin mules, decorated with fine embroidery in light brown and puce. Her face appeared to be miraculously healed of the ghastly wounds inflicted upon it only a few weeks before.

But ah! she looks like a portrait, he thought as he stood for a moment to take in the charming scene.

"Nancy!" he called out at last, in a loud whisper. She looked up cheerfully and saw his broad smile.

"Wolfgango, my God, it's you!" she said as she sprang to her feet and ran to him. He scooped her into his arms and held her in a warm embrace.

"You're absolutely beautiful! I can't tell you how good it is to see you looking so well!" He took her by the hands and held her out so that he could get a better view.

"And what of you? I heard you were ill."

"Oh that," he said waving it off. "I was, but I'm much better now and the sight of you doing well has certainly revived my spirits!" He gathered her up in his arms once again.

"I can't thank you enough for bringing me here," she said softly as she took his hand and began to walk with him. "The Baroness has been extremely kind, and we've grown rather fond of one another. I will miss her company when I return to the city next week."

"Next week? That's good news, for you've been sorely missed."

There was a long pause before Nancy stopped and turned to look into his eyes.

"Wolfgango, I've been thinking a great deal about our last conversation, that night… I seemed ungrateful and I'm aware that it appeared that I was casting blame on you for the situation in which I'd found myself."

"You don't know how I've tortured myself. I couldn't bear the thought that I may have unwittingly invited Fisher's wrath upon you because I allowed my passions to burn out of control."

"Please forgive me for placing that burden on you. It wasn't your fault, Wolfgango. You didn't force yourself upon me. I wanted you to be the first. I invited you... and I'm still inviting you," she offered, as she gazed longingly into his face.

He hesitated for a moment as he pondered. He wasn't sure if he could trust her affections, yet it was evident she had given this careful thought, and they appeared genuine. Perhaps it was safe for him to open his heart to her again.

What do I have to lose, he thought. It's only an innocent love affair. Kelly's been nagging me to take a mistress for a long time, so what would it hurt?

At last he took her face in his hands and gently brought her lips to his when Michael and the Baroness suddenly entered the garden, arm-in-arm. A liveried servant followed them, laden with an enormous wicker basket filled with food and wine for their picnic.

Holding an already half-consumed glass of wine, Michael lifted it. "Nancy! Good to see you lookin' so well, me dove! Come, you two, we're headin' out to the lawn to enjoy this fine picnic which the Baroness has so graciously provided for us!"

Frustrated that his tender advance was thwarted by their sudden intrusion, Mozart shook it off as cheerfully as he could. "Mick, you inconsiderate ass! Did it never cross your mind to pour a glass for me?"

Michael laughed. "Well me friend, I shall make it up to you as soon as we reach our destination. Come now, our carriage awaits us!"

After getting into the open carriage, they drove to a lovely spot in the middle of the estate where a small grove of pear trees stood, their boughs filled to capacity with ripe fruit. The servants had already set several lounge chairs beneath the trees along with some tables for the wine and glasses. As the women laid out the ground cover and opened the picnic baskets, Kelly and Mozart strolled over to the wine tables where Michael opened a bottle and poured a glass for Mozart.

"So I see she's taken kindly to you again, Wolfgang." Kelly smiled as he handed him the glass.

"I don't know what you mean, Mick," Mozart replied cautiously.

"What a bloody damned liar you are!" Kelly sipped his wine and watched the two women unpack the food and serve it onto the plates. "It's written all over your face what you're feelin' for the girl! Ya wear your heart on your sleeve, lad."

"She's not a girl anymore, Mick. She's a woman," Mozart said indignantly.

"That she is—a very charming woman. There's nothin' more attractive to a man than a beautiful woman who's in love with 'im. Problem is, you're in love with her as well."

Mozart shot Kelly a fiery glare as if to say, "How dare you?"

"Don't deny it, Wolfgango. You know it's true. I know I've been encouragin' ya to take a mistress, but I didn't mean her. Nancy's not mistress material—she's not like other women. She's the type ya fall in love with and stay in love forever. And don't think I don't fight with me own tender feelins' for her—I always have, but I know better than ta let meself stray down that path."

Mozart sipped his wine and stared blankly into the distance.

Kelly paused for a moment and allowed what he said to sink in before he added, "You're a married man, and now you're about to become a divided man," he said, concerned that his two dearest friends were about to venture down a dangerous path that would lead to nowhere but pain for them both.

"I understand ya have deep feelins. God knows it's easy to fall in love with her, but I'm tellin' ya it's goin' to bring both of ya nothin' but heartache. Mark me words. Have a lovely time and enjoy her tender company for the time bein', but don't fall in love."

He patted Mozart on the back and walked to where the women were seated.

Mozart remained at the table for a moment, sipping his wine and mulling over Michael's unsolicited advice. Mick means well, he thought, giving his friend the benefit of the doubt. He's protecting her. That's commendable, but Nancy's a woman now and she's made her decision, as I've made mine. He'll have to respect that.

He poured another glass and then walked to where his friends sat under the cool shade of a large pear tree. Finding a spot near Nancy, he removed his coat and lowered himself comfortably in a reclining position next to her. "What do we have?" he asked as a plate of roast chicken, various cheeses, bread, grapes, and strawberries was passed to him. "Madame, this is fare fit for a king," he exclaimed cheerfully as he looked across to the Baroness, who sat with Michael's head resting comfortably in her lap.

The dog, Mozart thought enviously. He certainly didn't waste any time!

He snickered as Michael shot him a mischievous glance and winked, causing the two of them to burst into fits of boyish laughter. Then he rolled onto his back and laid his head in Nancy's soft, inviting lap. Nancy watched as the other two unashamedly flirted back and forth, and she took her cue, feeding Mozart from his plate, popping grapes, bits of roast chicken, and ripe strawberries into his mouth. He gazed at her wistfully as she fed him, and they giggled when she sometimes missed his mouth and the morsel dropped into her lap.

Their conversation was light, consisting of gossip and of the latest fashion trends, the Baroness complementing Nancy on the lovely new frock she wore which had arrived from England the day before—a gift from her brother.

"Look at all the lovely pears!" Nancy said later as she looked up into the tree. "They look ripe, and so delicious!"

"Would you like one," Mozart asked.

"Oh, thank you," she exclaimed, as he stood and looked up. "Pears are my favorite!" She watched him eagerly as he reached into the lowest branches to retrieve several of the ripest pears, enough for everyone in the group.

He tossed some of them in Michael's direction, and as he caught them he laid them beside himself and the Baroness. Then Mozart handed one to Nancy and sat down beside her.

They were very ripe, indeed, and as they ate, the sweet juice ran down their chins onto their fingers. Mozart gazed with delight as Nancy took bite after lingering bite, and held the juicy fruit in her mouth for a moment, rolling it around on her tongue, before chewing and then swallowing. As the sticky juice ran onto her fingers, she licked them, placing each finger, one-by-one, into her pink mouth and drawing each one out slowly in order to get every sweet drop. The sight was almost more than he could bear and he had to lay his coat discreetly upon his lap in order to conceal his excitement.

Très charmant! What a darling little mouth she has, Mozart thought. What I wouldn't give to have it all over me! His impure thoughts raced as he tried to keep his arousal concealed, his eager eyes fixed upon Nancy's charming mouth as she relished the last delicious bite of her pear.

When they finished eating, the women decided to take a stroll in the shaded orchard as the men napped.

"My dear," the Baroness said as they drew far enough away that the men couldn't hear. "You were utterly enchanting! You had our Wolfgang eating out of your hand!" she said, impressed with Nancy's stellar performance.

"I did do rather well, didn't I?" she announced proudly.

"He couldn't take his eyes off of you." Her blue eyes sparkled as they burst into giggles.

"That might be just a little excessive, I'm afraid, but I did rather enjoy watching the expression on his face," Nancy confessed.

"His expression? He fairly rose to the occasion," Elisabeth exclaimed as they broke into girlish laughter once again.

As the yellow afternoon sun faded into orange, they decided that it was time to go and freshen up before the evening's activities, so they packed the food back into the baskets and boarded the carriage to return to the house. Entering the manor in happy conversation, they said their adieus and retreated to their respective rooms, and then later emerged, dressed in appropriate evening attire, the women in silks and taffetas and the men in silk suits.

After a lovely supper, they decided that a friendly game of faro was in order, so they strolled leisurely into to the music salon as they continued to chatter and gossip, and sat at the card table in a far corner of the room. Michael, who was notoriously bad at the game, lost every hand to Nancy, who promised to hold him to his debts, insisting that he couldn't charm his way out of paying them. Throughout the entire game, Mozart, who sat next to Nancy, kept inching his foot closer and closer to hers, only to learn that when he touched her, he would receive a playful kick, causing him to pull it back. This under-the-table footsy game went on between them the entire time, and at one point, she kicked him so hard that she nearly upset the whole table, causing everyone to burst into laughter.

After the game, the Baroness moved to an armchair. "Let's have some music!" she announced, gesturing broadly. "I have three of the most gifted musicians in all of Europe right here in my salon and I demand you share your talents! You first, Mozart!" She gestured to the fortepiano which sat beside an ornately painted harpsichord. "Play something new for us!"

Mozart, who never shied from the opportunity to perform, went to the fortepiano and placed his hands upon the keyboard. He thought a moment before he spoke. "I have just the one," he said confidently as he sat, "a new sonata that I completed only recently."

All listened intently, in amazement and delight as Mozart played. Once again, Nancy was taken in by his intensity and his ability to lose himself in the music—that loose curl again, in the middle of his forehead, and the tiny beads of perspiration that trickled down his brow that he didn't even seem to notice. Several times as she listened and watched, her heart raced as the blood rushed into her cheeks, forcing her to wave her fan across her face to cool them. She felt her longing for him return, an emotion that she had been forced by her difficult circumstances to keep at bay, but now she felt safe in rekindling.

Next was Kelly who sang some Irish airs as Nancy accompanied him on the fortepiano. Most were songs that neither Mozart nor the Baroness had ever heard, but found delightful. At one point they danced as he sang sweetly on, enchanting the entire company with his lilting Irish brogue. When he finished, Nancy stood and smiled broadly as Mozart and Elisabeth applauded enthusiastically.

"It's your turn, Nancy, dear. We've not heard from you yet," Elisabeth said as she slipped her arm through Nancy's and led her to the harpsichord.

Mozart turned and walked to the wine table to pour himself another glass as Kelly moved from the fortepiano to take a seat to listen.

"Why don't you sing that ravishing little aria that you performed for me the other day?" she suggested as she gracefully positioned herself at the keyboard. "I'll accompany you."

"What is it, Nancy? We'd love to hear you," Michael said cheerfully as he made his way to a comfortable, overstuffed settee.

Mozart stood with his back turned, pouring himself another glass of wine. "It's probably a bawdy little pub song that she learned back in England!" he said, but almost before he could finish his sentence, the Baroness began to play. He stood motionless as Elisabeth played the first several measures of the music, instantly recognizing the continuo. His emotions overtook him as he remembered the day at the Baron van Swieten's home when he suggested to Nancy that one day she should sing this aria for him. It was on that very day that he realized he had begun to fall in love with her.

"*Lascia ch'io pianga, mia cruda sorte…*"

He turned, his gaze intense and fixed upon her.

"*…e che so spiri, la libertà!*" Her voice was plaintive and full of longing. She understood perfectly well the suffering of which she sang.

"*Let me weep over my cruel fate, for I long for freedom. I pray for mercy for my sufferings!*"

Mozart stood transfixed, overcome with tenderness for this young woman who stole his heart in that very moment.

"*Il duolo ingfranga, queste ritorte, de miei martiri, sol per pietà!*"

Their gaze met across the divide as she sang to him.

"*Have pity! Shatter my chains out of mercy for my suffering!*"

When she finished there was only silence. She had ripped her heart from herself and held it out for everyone in the room to see.

God knows it's easy to fall in love with her, but I'm tellin' ya it's goin' to bring both of ya nothin' but heartache.

Kelly's earlier warning echoed through his thoughts, but it was too late. She had captured him completely.

Finally Kelly broke the silence by quietly suggesting to the Baroness that they take a turn around the rose garden, leaving Mozart and Nancy alone in the salon.

Nancy, who remained stationed by the harpsichord, watched intently as Mozart sat his wine glass on the table and silently crossed the room toward her. As he drew nearer, she saw the tears that pooled in his eyes and her heart began to race once again as she felt the blush return. He stood close to her, barely breathing, and gently enveloped her in his arms, pulling her to him. She wrapped her arms softly around his neck and closed her eyes as he kissed her tenderly on the forehead. They stood together in silence for several moments holding one another in their arms. Then, without a word, he took her by the hand and led her out of the salon, into the great hall and up the stairs to her bedchamber, quietly closing the door behind them.

The moonlight streamed in through the window, providing the only light as the lovers took one another in their arms. She stood in its sliver beam as he slowly unlaced the back of her bodice, leaning occasionally to kiss the tender nape of her neck and run his fingers softly across her shoulders. As the bodice fell, revealing her stays, he turned her to face him and kissed her neck and throat, making his way down to her bosom.

He drew her in closer, his arms wrapped completely about her waist. As he tenderly kissed her breasts, lingering in the soft cleavage, she ran her fingers through his thick, chestnut hair, and finding the end of his queue ribbon, she gave it a gentle tug and released his clubbed queue, his shoulder-length hair falling in one long wave down the middle of his back.

He gazed intently into her eyes, smiling as he removed his coat and laid it across the settee at the end of the bed. As she gently untied the lace stock at his throat she kissed him on each cheek and softly brushed her lips along his jaw line. He could feel her moist breath against his cheeks as her mouth moved closer to his. When their lips finally met, they locked together in one, lingering, breathless kiss.

He slowly went to his knees, kissing her body, which was still held tightly in place by her stays. He reached around her waist and untied the laces that held up her skirts as well as her panniers, and they fell to the floor and collapsed around her feet. Little by little they unwrapped each another as if they were elegantly wrapped gifts, each layer giving way to another layer as their excited anticipation mounted.

She unbuttoned his waistcoat and slid it off of his arms. Setting it aside, she un-tucked his shirt, allowing it to hang loosely from his shoulders. She slowly slid her hands up under his shirt where they stopped at his chest and rested in the soft tuft of hair. This sent waves of excitement surging through him and he felt the urge to finish unwrapping the lovely gift that stood before him, waiting to be ravished. He turned her around once again and, as quickly as he could, he unlaced her stays, not as slowly as he did when he unlaced her bodice in similar fashion.

Finally he scooped her up into his arms and, placing her on the bed, he playfully kicked off his shoes. Then he climbed on the bed and positioned himself over her, gazing down into her two huge dark eyes. At last she wore only a silk chemise which was so sheer that he could see through it to make out the dark outline of her nipples. He laid himself on top of her and began to kiss them through the thin fabric, sending waves of intense pleasure throughout her entire body. She began to arch her back and cry out softly.

"Dio, Wolfgango!"

He rose to his knees and unbuttoned his breeches, sliding them off of his legs along with his stockings leaving only his shirt hanging loosely from his shoulders. Then he reached up the hem of her chemise and untied the satin ribbons that held her stockings in place and slid them off of her legs. As he positioned himself above her, the moonlight shone through the iridescent fabric of her chemise revealing the soft, curvaceous outline of her body. He could see the dark triangle of hair that lay between her thighs and he exclaimed, "My God, Nancy, you're so incredibly beautiful!" He fell upon her, covering her face, her lips, her chin, her neck, and her ears with his kisses.

He ran his hands along her entire body stopping at her breasts where he lingered, cupping them in his palms. Her nipples were firm and erect. He closed his eyes and desperately searched for her mouth with his, and when he found it, he kissed her passionately and hard, pushing his tongue through her teeth and running it along the bridge of her mouth. She parted her legs, allowing his hips to rest between her thighs. She felt his excitement as he rubbed against her pushing and giving way, allowing himself to just touch the soft, wet entrance to her body and then pulling away, teasing her, making her cry out for him even more.

"Take me, Wolfgango. For God's sake, take me now!" she cried out once more, wrapping her legs around him. In an instant he was inside of her and she met his thrusts with hers, cries of sheer ecstasy escaping from her with every push. He hardly breathed, his passion mounting with her every cry. Then, suddenly, a shudder ran through him and he cried out before he collapsed between her breasts. He buried his face in her hair which fell in loose waves about her shoulders, and he took in its fragrance. It smelled of lavender and rosewater, and in that tender moment, he thought she was the sweetest, most magnificent creature that God had ever put on the earth.

The morning sun streamed in through the window, replacing the moonlight which had been the only witness to their congress the night before. They lay sleeping, still wrapped in their tender embrace. Being the first to awaken, she turned to her lover and stroked his face, gently tracing the outline of his eyes, his nose, and mouth, and then leaning into him, she tenderly kissed him. Her kiss awakened him, and he opened his eyes to find her smiling down, her dark eyes misty and aglow with tender affection.

"Good morning, Wanze," he said as he took her hands and kissed the knuckles.

"What does that mean," she asked as she giggled playfully. "How did you pronounce it?"

"I said, 'VON-sah', he repeated slowly. "It means 'little bug', my little bed bug," he replied with a yawn.

"Wanze, Wanze, Wanze, Wanze," he repeated over, as he pulled her to him and gently tickled her sides. She burst into giggles as he tickled and rolled her all over the bed, taking a nibble at one of her ears once in a while for good measure.

Nancy sat up and as she cradled his body between her legs, she took his face in her hands and drew it toward her moist lips, kissing his mouth.

"Mmm... Must have more of that," he said as his lips searched for hers again, locking in a long, wet kiss. He rolled her over again and began to kiss her all over her body through her chemise, laughing and giggling as she slapped at his hands when he slipped them up under to pinch her on the bottom. It didn't take long before all the playful indulgences gave way to more intense pleasures, and once again they found themselves wrapped around one another's bodies, engaged in yet another passionate interlude.

Throughout the rest of the following day and into the night they remained sequestered in Nancy's bedchamber, only emerging to retrieve the trays of food that were left by the door, complements of their gracious hostess. Then once they had eaten their fill, they resumed their lovemaking, and in the between times they talked of music and dreamed together of the opera that Mozart would compose especially for her, and how together they would bring Vienna to her knees.

Monday morning arrived too soon, and as Mozart packed his bags to return with Michael to the city, Nancy's eyes filled with tears. "When will I see you again, Wolfgango?" she asked, as he pulled her close and gave her a tight squeeze.

"I don't know, Wanze. You have a busy rehearsal schedule when you return, and I have work to catch up after being ill," he said softly as he laid her head upon his shoulder and gently stroked her hair.

"Perhaps we can at least meet at the casino once in a while."

"Of course we can. Nothing will change. We simply have to be more discreet, that's all. And we can meet in your dressing room as well." He grinned and winked playfully as he kissed her lower lip which was stuck out in a pretty pout. "I see that pouty lip, Little Bug. Pouty, pouty lip, a perch for birds to take a shit," he teased.

She began to cry.

"Oh Wanze, please don't cry. I can't bear your tears," he said as he enveloped her in his arms. "It's going to be all right, I promise. We'll have plenty of time together. You'll see." He gave her one last tight squeeze and a lingering kiss before he picked up his bags and carried them down the stairs to the entry, where Kelly stood waiting for him.

The Baroness came to bid them a fond farewell and to thank them for making the weekend so lovely. "We must do this again very soon. It was delightful," she said as she turned her gaze toward Kelly. Then turning to Mozart, she continued, "And I *know* you enjoyed yourself, you rascal!"

He shot her a devilish grin as he took her hand and kissed it. "Indeed, Madame. I thank you. It was just what the doctor ordered." He took one last look at Nancy who stood at the top of the stairs, and blew her a kiss. Then he followed Kelly out the doors and down the broad steps to the waiting carriage.

Another week passed and as late summer turned into autumn, Nancy returned to work at the theater. She was greeted warmly by all of her colleagues, as well as her audience, who were genuinely happy to see her return to the stage. Those terrible months were all behind her and she re-emerged a stronger, more confident young woman as well as performer. Rosenberg remarked to her on several occasions that her performance, which was always outstanding before, was even more so since her break. Her time with the Baroness as well as the separation from her wretched husband did her good. Nancy was eternally grateful to the Baroness, who remained her friend and confidante long after she returned to Vienna.

It was only a short time after Mozart's return from the Baroness's estate that his son, Karl Thomas, was born. Extremely pleased and proud, he once again took to fatherhood quickly, as he had done after the birth of his first son, who had lived for so short a time. Nancy was happy for him, knowing what his children meant to him and understanding how the loss of his first child had devastated him. She prayed that this child would survive.

They continued to meet when they could at the casino and sometimes with Kelly at the café, but it was a much rarer occasion when they were able to sneak away for a quick encounter. The night of her return to the stage, Mozart sneaked into her dressing room and waited for her to come back so that they could indulge in some post-performance delights. But, however wonderful it was to be with each another in whatever manner or place they could manage, they both longed for another opportunity to meet at the Baroness Waldstädten's and relive that delightful weekend which had served as the carefree beginning of their new love affair.

Constanze Weber Mozart

Chapter Seven

Nancy awakened on a cool late October morning feeling dizzy along with a sour stomach. If I move, I just know I'll be sick, she thought as she lay motionless. Perhaps if I lay still a moment it will pass.

She hoped that she hadn't come down with the fever that was going through the rest of the city. She didn't have time to be ill, and she feared that Rosenberg's patience would wear thin if she asked for more time off.

She laid as still as possible, waiting for the churning in her stomach to settle before she attempted to get up. Suddenly, overwhelmed with the urge to vomit, she leapt out of bed as quickly as she could and ran behind the large screen in the corner and bent over the chamber pot, heaving until she'd emptied her stomach. Returning weakly to her bed, she curled up into a ball, lying perfectly still as not to invite another wave. Despite her best efforts, it came again, this one even worse than the first.

I can't get sick, she exclaimed to herself. I don't have time for this. Suddenly she remembered; she was late. She counted the weeks since her last time on her fingers.

It was just two weeks before the weekend that Mozart and Kelly came to visit, she calculated, frantically. She held out her fingers and counted them again, this time aloud. "Oh, my God! No, it can't be!"

Suddenly, another wave hit her, this time exacerbated by her panic, but she failed to make it to the chamber pot and the rancid, smelly contents spilled out onto the floor. As she looked for something to clean up the mess, she heard a knock.

"Ann, are you all right?" her mother called to her.

"Please, Mother. Not now."

How was she going to explain this? She knew that it couldn't be Fisher's. She hadn't been with him since that night, and she got her time just shortly after that. In fact, quite miraculously in all the times that she had been with him it never happened.

Wolfgango, she thought. "Bloody hell…it's his," she whispered as she placed both of her hands gently upon her belly, looking down at the soft, fertile spot where his child was growing inside of her.

"Ann, may I please come in?" Her mother's voice sounded anxious. When Nancy didn't answer, she opened the door and cautiously peeked in. She found Nancy bent over the floor, cleaning up a puddle of vomit and gasped. "What in heaven's name, child! Are you all right?"

"I'll be fine. I'm not feeling well this morning," she replied, trying to appear calm.

"You can't afford to be ill. What will Count Rosenberg say," she asked, knowing as well as her daughter that she was still in a precarious position with her employer. "Get back in bed. I'll get Antonia to come and clean this up," she ordered, as she left the room.

As she climbed back into bed, Nancy's thoughts began to race back to the night at the Baroness's when Mozart led her by the hand into her chamber and made love to her. She knew it had to have happened then.

What am I going to tell Mother, she asked herself, frantically. She's not stupid. She'll know it isn't Fisher's. Oh, never mind her! What am I going to tell Wolfgango? What if he never speaks to me again?

The anxiety over Mozart's possible reactions sent another wave of nausea, and as she cupped her hand over her mouth, she ran again for the chamber pot, barely making it in time. She bent and heaved over the pot, but this time nothing came out. She sank to the floor in the corner and pulled her knees to her chest, fear and panic driving her frantic emotions.

There are remedies. I'll write to the Baroness and tell her. She'll know how to help me, she thought resolutely. She looked down at her belly as tears of repentance and remorse poured from her eyes. I can't do that to his child! How could I have thought such a terrible thing?

When Elizabeth returned with the maid and found Nancy huddled in the corner behind the screen, crying, she instantly knew the nature of her illness. "Dear God, Ann, you're not…"

Nancy stared up blankly and said nothing.

Elizabeth, who didn't want Antonia to hear what was about to transpire between them, hurried her along with the cleaning and instructed her to close the door on her way out. "Ann, get up," she said coldly.

Nancy did as she was told, pulling herself up off the floor. She made her way back to the bed where she sank in and pulled the covers over her head, as she did when she was a child and knew she was in trouble.

"This child isn't Fisher's, is it?"

"Why do you ask, Mother? You already seem to know everything," Nancy snapped back, still hiding under the sheets.

"I'm not going to accept this behavior from you. Now I want to know who this baby's father is!" she snapped.

Nancy sat up and shot back in resentment at her mother's condescension. "It's Mozart's! The baby is his! There, are you satisfied now? I'm not a child, so stop treating me as one!" she shouted angrily. She lay back down and turned her back, sobbing.

Shocked and dismayed by the news, Elizabeth sat on the bed beside her daughter and stared absently at the wall, gathering her thoughts.

"How did this happen," she asked calmly, looking down at her hands as she buffed her nails with her fingertips.

"In the way these things usually happen, Mother. Do you want me to give you the full bloody account?"

"He didn't take advantage of you, did he?"

This intrusive line of questioning offended Nancy, but she realized that her anger wasn't going to solve anything. Besides, she knew Elizabeth would keep on as long as she kept giving her sarcastic replies. She forced herself to stop crying and wiped her tears with the back of her hand.

"No," she hiccupped, "he didn't take advantage of me."

"Are you in love with him?"

"No, I'm not in love with him," she replied, a little too adamantly. "It was just one of those things. He came with Kelly to visit me one weekend while I was with the Baroness. We had a little too much wine and one thing led to another and, well, now I'm up the duff."

"Don't be vulgar, Ann."

"Mother, just go away, please, and leave me alone," she said flatly, curling into a tight ball and covering her head with her pillow.

Elizabeth rose and went to the door, pausing a moment. "You'll have to let the management at the theater know of this. Be prepared for the possibility that you will have your contract revoked."

"You'd like that wouldn't you? I'll get the sack and have to return to England with you. You always get your way," Nancy replied hatefully.

Elizabeth allowed Nancy's cutting accusations to wash over her unnoticed. "We'll allow people to assume that the child is your husband's.

No one will know the difference. At least then you won't be saddled with the reputation of being Mozart's whore," she shot back coldly as she left the room.

Nancy lay alone in her bed wondering how things had gotten so complicated. Just when life was beginning to turn around in her favor—Fisher was gone, her career was going well, and she was with the man she loved—now this had to happen. She didn't understand. Life is cruel, she thought.

"Mother doesn't help," she whispered. "I wish Papa was here." She started to cry again. "Why did he have to be the one to die?"

Her thoughts drifted back to the day he died, nearly four years before. On his deathbed he made Elizabeth promise that she would stay in Italy and continue to support Nancy in the furthering of her stage career. Elizabeth agreed to it, but Nancy knew it was with great reluctance and only out of a sense of obligation to her dying husband that she honored his last request. Nancy was lying in his arms when he took his final breath, her head lying upon his chest as she strained to hear his heartbeat. She knew when he was gone because his heart, which had already slowed considerably, stopped beating altogether.

She imagined him sitting beside her on the bed, gently stroking her tousled curls and calling her "Bella" and telling her how special she was. She would tell him all her troubles and he would hold her in his strong arms and comfort her.

"What is troubling you, Bella Anna?"

"Oh, Papa, things are such a mess. I loved a man, and now I'm having his child. What do I tell him, Papa? What if he stops loving me?"

"Then you will go on, Bella. You are strong."

"I don't feel strong, Papa. I feel tired. I'm so bloody tired."

"I know you, Anna. I've never known you to give up, no matter how weary you become. Don't you remember when you were a bambina, and you'd be so sleepy that you could hardly hold your eyes open? You'd fuss and fight, and run in circles around the room to keep from falling asleep. I would have to hold you tight against my chest so that you could hear my heart."

"I remember."

"I would say to you, 'You hear that heart beating, little Anna? It's beating just for you.' Then you'd wiggle up close to me and yawn, and you'd fall fast asleep."

"I remember, Papa."

"Listen to my heart, little Anna. It's still beating just for you."

"I'm listening, Papa," Nancy whispered as she fell into a deep, restful sleep. "I'm listening."

∞∞

The following day, Nancy went to Rosenberg to inform him of her condition.

"Signora Storace, please be seated," he said as he smiled and motioned her to a chair across from his desk. Nancy curtseyed politely and thanked him as she sat. "What brings you here today?" he asked cheerfully.

She hesitated a moment to gather her courage. "Excellency, I came to inform you," she paused. The words were difficult to get out. "Sir, I am with child." There, she'd said it. "That wasn't too difficult," she thought. She looked across the desk, nervously watching for a reaction.

As he leaned back in his chair, he laid a finger to his lips, his eyes fixed intently on her. Then, after several moments, he stood and replied. "Indeed," he said matter-of-factly, as he walked around to the front of the desk and leaned against the corner, crossing his arms in front of him.

"Well, this isn't the first time one of my actresses has come to me with such an announcement, but in light of the fact that you have only recently returned from a month's leave, this news comes at a rather inconvenient time."

"I know, Excellency," she replied nervously as she swallowed hard. She began to feel queasy.

"I have no choice but to retain you for the next several weeks, until I can inform His Majesty," he continued. "He is away in Hungary at present and he, of course, has the final say in such matters. However, in light of this news, we will be forced to retain Signorina Laschi. She had plans to return to Italy this week, but since circumstances have changed, she will have to remain."

Nancy instantly recognized this as a threat to replace her with her understudy. "I can still work," she said firmly, looking him square in the eyes.

"And you will be expected to work, Signora, or I guarantee you that you will lose your position with this company," he replied sharply. "As much as I would regret having to take such action, we simply cannot retain an employee at such a salary as you are paid, who is continually absent, no matter how legitimate the reason. Do I make myself perfectly clear?"

"Yes, Excellency. I understand."

"Your next call is in an hour. I expect you to be there on time." His voice softened as he continued. "I'll have a chair placed in one of the wings for you so you won't have to be on your feet when you're not on stage, and should you become ill," he tried to put it as delicately as possible, "there will be a receptacle nearby."

"Thank you, Excellency. I appreciate your consideration," she replied gratefully as she rose from her seat, curtseyed, and started for the door.

"Signora!" he called to her in a softer tone, fearing he had been too harsh.

"Yes, Excellency?" She turned and looked at him.

"Please rest assured that I will do my very best to influence His Majesty in your favor. You have my word on it. We don't want to lose you. You're the finest actress that has ever graced this stage," he added with a warm smile.

"Thank you, Excellency. You are most kind." She curtseyed once again and left.

Although she knew Rosenberg would keep his word and fight for her to retain her position with the court, she knew she was still at considerable risk of being fired. Rosenberg was in her corner. He liked her. He knew how hard she worked when she was there. The question was never her work ethic or her talent, but rather the fates that conspired against her and forced her frequent absences. She knew she had to do something on her own behalf to reinforce his defense of her position, but what?

"Think, Nancy, think!" she said aloud. "There must be something I can do." Then, she remembered her brother. Stephen's coming next month from England for a visit," her thoughts raced ahead. "A commission! What if I can get the Emperor to commission Stephen to compose a comic opera for the Burgtheater, with me cast as the heroine?

Stephen, who had been back in England for nearly two years, had never composed a complete opera on his own. He had, however, composed a couple of insert arias for her in productions at the Burg, to which the Viennese audiences responded enthusiastically.

If I can get a commission for Stephen, he'll have to stay for several months, perhaps even close to a year.

This was good.

But how do I gain an audience with His Majesty, she wondered. I'll have to do it through someone who already has his ear, she thought. But whom? She paused for several moments, and then she remembered. "Zinzendorf!" she said aloud.

Count Karl von Zinzendorf was the privy finance minister to Joseph II, and wrote as a theater critic for various Viennese publications. He was quite enamored with Nancy, and had written an early article, remarking on her "fine bosom" and "fresh mouth". The wheels continued to turn in her head.

He has the Emperor's ear. I'll make him an offer. He thinks he's in love with me, and he probably will do anything I ask, if I return… certain favors.

Oh God, what was she thinking? Was she so desperate that she was willing to stoop to act like that which she swore she would never become?

How could I bear to do such a thing? She cringed. But if I don't do something I'll lose my job and Mother will have me back in England so fast my head will spin. Then I'll never see Wolfgango again, and I absolutely could not bear that, she argued with herself.

She took a deep breath. She knew what she had to do. Then it's decided. I'll arrange an appointment with the Count tomorrow afternoon.

Count Karl von Zinzendorf

Chapter Eight

*I*t was nearly time for the rehearsal to start. As the cast gathered backstage, they stood in little groups of two and three, conversing and sharing the latest gossip. They were all surprised when Luisa Laschi walked in, for they thought she was supposed to return to Italy.

"I don't know why I am here! I am a-supposed to go back tomorrow," she exclaimed, shrugging. "Den I receive da message from Rosenberg dis morning, and he say for me to report to rehearsal dis afternoon."

She strutted around the stage, gesturing as if she were acting in a scene. "The little principessa probably has-a da sniffles or someding," she said dramatically, mocking Nancy as she pressed her hand to her forehead and pretended to faint.

Luisa was a pretty, young Italian actress with a fine, clear voice, a nice figure, and a great deal of stage presence. She had been hired in early September when it was clear that Nancy would not return to work any time soon.

"That's enough, Signorina," Benucci chided. He was in charge of the afternoon's rehearsal and he had little patience with this catty little diva, especially when she mocked his friend. All of the regular cast members were loyal to Nancy as well, knowing what she went through with Fisher, and they were ready and willing to defend her against any little upstart who might try to move in and take her place.

As he had promised, Rosenberg sent word earlier to have a chair placed in the wings with a lidded chamber pot on a side table, and when Benucci walked in and found the set-up, he became concerned. When Nancy entered through the backstage door, she made her way down the corridor to her dressing room.

"I'll be just a moment!" she called out to the cast who were waiting for her onstage.

She entered to find a note lying on her vanity table, and she instantly recognized the handwriting. Wrapped inside the note was a thin rectangular box covered in black velvet. She hurriedly opened it and read:

Just a little something for my Wanze. Before I'm finished with you, you'll be dripping in garnets!

W.

She opened the box to find a stunning tooled silver bracelet, encrusted with little oval and square-cut garnets, and accented with tiny marcasite stones.

Oh, Wolfgango, she sighed. What's going to happen to us now? She didn't have time to think about it then. It was time for rehearsal to start and Rosenberg had made it abundantly clear that tardiness would not be tolerated. She quickly removed the bracelet from its box and fastened it around her wrist as she made her way to the stage.

When she walked in, Laschi remarked, "Dio in cielo! The principessa has-a decided to grace us with her presence!" She bowed to Nancy as if she were royalty.

"Let's get to work," Nancy replied coolly, paying no attention to Laschi's taunts.

"Den what in-a heaven's name, am I doing here," Luisa asked haughtily, gesturing in the air.

"You're here because Rosenberg said you're to be here and His Majesty is paying you!" Benucci snapped. "Now sit your fat ass down and shut the fuck up!" he ordered sharply as he snapped his arm and pointed to the row of seats designated for understudies. He turned to Nancy, who looked pale, and asked gently, "Are you all right, Anna?"

"I'm fine, Francesco," she replied with a smile. "Grazie."

The first part of the rehearsal was difficult. Several times, she felt herself getting ill and had to rush offstage and avail herself of the chamber pot, but as concentrated on her work and set aside personal circumstances, she found it much easier to take care of the job at hand. After about the third time that she had to rush off, Benucci, understood and gave her leeway. He was extremely kind and gentle, and even gave the cast a few more breaks than usual so she could rest.

I can do this, she thought as she felt her confidence return. Papa was right, I *am* strong!

After the rehearsal she returned to her dressing room and sat at her vanity. As she peered into the mirror she observed how pale and tired she looked. When she raised her hand to touch her face, the bracelet that was still fastened around her wrist caught her eye. She hadn't had time earlier to take a good look at it so she held it up closer to the light. It shimmered and sparkled, the deep red stones turning almost purple when certain facets caught the light. It was stunning, and obviously quite expensive.

Garnet, she thought, the stone of profound love. She opened the note that she'd left sitting on the vanity top along with the bracelet box, and read his words again.

Before I'm finished with you, you'll be dripping in garnets.

Suddenly there was a knock and a man's voice quietly calling for her. "Wanze, it's me. May I come in?"

She looked into the mirror in panic. Reaching up with both hands and pinching her cheeks several times, she pressed her lips together to bring some color back into them. If she had known he was coming, she would have used some rouge.

"Come in, Wolfgango."

He entered and saw her sitting in front of the mirror wearing his bracelet.

"Ah! You've opened it!" he said as he placed his hands on her shoulders. He leaned over and kissed her cheek, giving her ear a playful nibble.

"Do you like it?" He gazed at her through the mirror, beaming with pride. "Garnets are fiery and passionate. Just like you."

"I adore it, Wolfgango. Thank you. I'll treasure it always," she said as she looked anxiously at his proud reflection in the mirror. Should she tell him now? And if she did, how would he respond?

He wrapped his arms gently around her shoulders, placing his hands on the exposed tops of her breasts, and then he began to kiss her neck. She rested her hands on his, relishing the tender moment which she thought might be their last. He took her by the hands and began to pull her into his arms, but when he looked into her eyes, he stopped suddenly.

"Wanze, you don't look well. You're so pale," he observed, as he softly brushed her cheek with the back of his hand.

"I'm simply tired." She lowered her eyes so that he could read nothing more. "I think I'm still a little weak, and today's rehearsal was a bit of a strain," she offered, hoping he wouldn't press her any further. She knew he wanted her and she didn't wish to put him off. She needed him to make love to her.

"We don't have to. I can be such a dog!" he said, chuckling softly.

"Oh no! We have so little time together as it is, and I, well, I'm feeling especially tender right now and I want you to. I need to feel your touch."

Tears welled in her eyes and he smiled as they sparkled in the candlelight, making her eyes look especially misty and soft. He was both touched and disturbed by her melancholy mood, and he held her close, resting her head upon his chest. "I hear your heart beating," she said.

"It's beating for you, my love." He held her chin and raised her lips to his and kissed her. Then, he led her to the settee where he sat her down and held her in his arms for several moments before he tenderly made love to her.

🙙🙛

"He's such a good baby!" Constanze crowed to her sisters as she rocked little Karl. "And he has such a healthy appetite—just like his father!"

Shortly after Karl was born, the Mozarts moved to a larger and more fashionable apartment on the Schulerstrasse near St. Stephan's Cathedral. Mozart, who had been very successful with his subscription concerts earlier in the year, was in a much stronger financial position than in the years before and he and his little family were beginning to enjoy the fruits of that success. The only thing that eluded him was a choice Italian libretto with a good part in it for Nancy that would make a name for him in the world of Viennese theater.

"Speaking of babies," said Aloysia, who was busily knitting a jacket for her nephew, "word is on the streets that La Storace is expecting."

"No," Constanze exclaimed, wide-eyed. "Really?"

"I feel sorry for her," Sophie replied sympathetically. "No woman deserves the kind of treatment she got from that awful husband of hers. Now she has to have his child. It doesn't seem fair."

"I've heard that Rosenberg still hasn't decided her fate. Word is that she may lose her contract over it," Aloysia continued, smugly.

"Oh you're just jealous because Rosenberg won't hire you anymore because you're so insufferably haughty and ill-tempered that no one can get along with you!" Constanze replied.

Sophie snickered, trying to stifle her laugher. You tell her, Stanze, she thought. The Weber sisters had all grown weary of Aloysia and her conceited pretenses.

"Where do you get all this gossip, anyway," Constanze asked Aloysia, wondering why she always seemed to be among the first to hear things.

"I'm an actress," she replied, looking down her nose, ignoring Constanze's chastisement. "When there's news, we're always the first to get the dirt and the first to report it," she continued as she held up the jacket to examine the sleeves. "Anyway, I think it serves her right. She thinks she's so much better than the rest of us because she's English and she's educated. Basta! Someone needs to educate her on how to choose a husband!"

"Like you did so well..." Sophie muttered under her breath.

Although Constanze felt a certain amount of jealousy over Nancy, due mostly to the rumors that Aloysia continually brought back to her regarding her husband's affairs, she didn't believe that the English singer deserved to be punished simply because she had been married off to a brute. Despite her occasional tinges of envy over Nancy's education and obvious appeal to men like her husband, Constanze felt very secure regarding Mozart's affections and was grateful that she wasn't married to a man who beat her. Mozart was good to her, providing her with a secure home and a good name, and that was all she needed. Besides, actresses never made good wives. Aloysia was proof of that. They were too vain and self-centered, and they didn't know the first thing about taking care of a man, so Constanze felt no insecurity regarding her place in her husband's heart.

It wasn't until a couple of days later that Constanze thought to mention the news of Nancy's pregnancy to her husband. He was in another room playing billiards and simultaneously composing another new piano concerto. She had just put the baby down for a nap when she passed the room where he worked, pausing in the doorway.

"I suppose you've heard the news about Nancy, haven't you?"

"What's that?" he said as he focused on the shot he was lining up on the table.

"She's going to have a baby."

He stood suddenly erect, allowing the cue stick to slip from its position.

"Who told you that?" His palms began to sweat.

"Aloysia did, just the other day. I got so busy with the baby that I forgot to mention it to you. She says that the Emperor might revoke Nancy's contract. I really don't understand why, I mean she's married, after all. I think it has more to do with the fact that she's been out of commission too much over the last year, and the theater management is nervous about more absences."

Mozart went back to his game and tried to re-align the shot he'd lost.

"So I suppose this means you may be composing your opera for a new buffa," she added nonchalantly as she walked away.

Mozart attempted for several moments to battle down his shock, but to no avail, so he decided to abandon the game and the concerto and go to the tavern. Grabbing his greatcoat and hat, he called out to Constanze that he was leaving.

When he arrived at the Hungarian Crown, he found his regular table and sat. As he waited for his beer, his mind raced. He was aware of the very real possibility that the child was his, and it placed him in a delicate position between his duties and affections to his wife, and to the woman whom he had taken as his mistress. He'd done what Kelly had warned him against, and fallen in love with Nancy. There was no sin in the taking a mistress, but to allow oneself to fall in love and divide one's affections— that was the sin.

He was torn. Society and the Church demanded that he be true to his duties to his wife and family. He'd pledged to Constanze all his loyalty and worldly goods, but what about the woman to whom he'd pledged his heart? What would it do to her if he disassociated himself from her as he knew he should?

Constanze doesn't seem to suspect anything, he thought as he took a gulp from his stein. And I know Nancy. Even if it is mine, she'd never say so.

He remembered the last time that they were together in her dressing room. She hadn't felt well and she was pale and extremely emotional. "Ach du Scheisse!" he cursed aloud as he stared blankly out the window.

She wanted to tell me then, but she was afraid. He leaned his forehead against his hands and ran his fingers through his hair. I don't know what to do, he agonized.

His honor and reputation in Vienna were at stake. He wasn't a member of the noble class who could callously put a woman away or pay her off, denying his bastard child. If it were known that he was the father, he could lose his livelihood, his possessions, and everything he worked so hard for his entire life. If he didn't cut himself off from her, he could be ruined.

But I love her, he thought, as he allowed himself some empathy for her situation. How can I abandon her after all she's been through?

He took several draughts from his beer and continued to think things through. There's nothing else to be done, he concluded with regret. The choice was made when I married. As much as it breaks my heart to do so, I have to end the affair now.

ᔥᔥ

It was several days before Nancy was able to get an appointment with Count Zinzendorf, but when he learned that his favorite soprano was coming to him with a request for a favor, he was giddy with delight. Her appointment was scheduled for three in the afternoon, so he thought that he would impress her by serving English tea and scones with clotted cream.

When she arrived, she was escorted to a large, fashionably appointed salon in which hung several Baroque paintings of plump, rosy, nude women, along with several gilded carvings in the shape of fat cherubs.

"Signora Storace!" he said gleefully as he took her hand and placed a wet kiss right in the middle of it. "How delightful to see you looking so well!"

Zinzendorf was a round little man with a face that was as round as his belly, his gouty over-stuffed physique a testament to his years of privileged living. His small upturned nose, as well as his cheeks, glowed shiny pink, and when he smiled, the corners of his mouth reached from ear to ear.

"Excellency." She curtseyed.

"Please, Signora, take a seat." He motioned to an elegantly upholstered wingback. "I have ordered tea from England to be served to you, as well as these lovely scones. I pray they are to your liking," he said smiling, eagerly awaiting Nancy's approval at his thoughtful gesture.

Before her lay a silver tray upon which sat a lovely china teapot adorned with hand-painted English roses, as well as shepherds and barefoot shepherdesses, with matching cups and saucers. Nancy hadn't tasted scones since she'd left England nearly seven years before, and the clotted cream looked as sweet and fresh as the cream her Aunt Mary served in her pastry shop in London.

"Oh this is quite lovely, thank you." She gazed eagerly at the scones, relishing the taste of her home.

"Will you do me the honor of pouring, Signora?"

"Why, of course. My pleasure," she answered prettily as she picked up a cup and placed it delicately upon the saucer. She laid a gold strainer across the cup and poured the tea through.

"Sugar?"

"Indeed, dear, two lumps," he answered enthusiastically as his eyes traveled to her bosom.

"Lemon or cream?"

"Lemon, a generous squeeze, please." He rubbed his chubby fingers together in anticipation. "But please, allow me to pour your cup."

"Thank you, Excellency."

"Sugar, my dear?"

"None for me thank you, but I would adore some cream." She reached for a plate on which to place a scone, leaning forward enough that her bosom fell fully within his sight. With a knife, she placed a generous slather of cream on the scone, spreading it over the top and allowing some of it to get on the ends of two of her fingers, and as she handed him the plate, she licked them with the tip of her pink tongue.

His eyes narrowed as he watched her tongue gently flick the thick cream off the end of each tiny finger, and he shifted uncomfortably in his chair.

"So, Signora," he began, "I have been informed that you have a request to make of me."

"Yes, sir," she replied sweetly, as she took a sip of her tea. The tea was warm and soothing and served to settle her queasy stomach, which was growing queasier by the moment as she dwelt upon the price she would most likely have to pay for her request.

"My brother, Stephen, who works with Lord Richard Brinsley Sheridan as an assistant in his theater in London, is coming to visit me in January."

She paused a moment to draw in a long breath and take another sip of tea. "Stephen was trained in musical composition at the conservatory in Naples, and has shown tremendous promise as a composer of comic opera," she continued as she picked up a scone. After she took a small bite and chewed it delicately, she continued.

"My proposal is this: Since you serve as His Majesty's minister of finance, as well as in an artistic capacity as a theater critic, and because you have His Majesty's ear, I should like to humbly ask if you might make a request of the Emperor on Stephen's behalf. I am requesting a commission for my brother to compose a comic opera, in Italian, for His Majesty's theater, with me cast in the leading role."

She drew in another long breath and took another sip of her tea, peering up at him from behind the cup in coquettish fashion.

"Well, Signora," he said as he leaned back in his chair, crossing his legs to conceal his aroused state, "this is a rather complicated and large request. His Majesty, with his excellent taste, is naturally very selective when it comes to his theater. Why even Mozart had to work for several years to finally obtain a commission for his first Viennese production."

His eyes traveled over her body, taking in her entire, voluptuous form. "This would be your brother's first opera?"

"Yes Excellency, it would be, but I can assure you that he is up to the task, and I would be eternally grateful and indebted to you," she softly pleaded as she lifted her skirts just enough to reveal a shapely calf.

"I shall require some time to think on it, Signora," he answered back, pressing her to reveal more.

"Oh, but sir, we have little time, for he is already preparing to leave on his journey, which will take up to three weeks. It is of the utmost urgency that this request be fulfilled immediately, or I am afraid that it will be too late. Because of the urgency of my request, and because I fully appreciate the great trouble it would require of you, I am most willing to reciprocate with my utmost gratitude in the most immediate fashion."

She stood in front of him and removed her fichu, unlacing the ribbons that closed the front of her bodice.

His eyes traveled eagerly up her form along with her fingers as she pulled the ribbons through each grommet, finally laying her bodice open and allowing it to slip from her shoulders to the floor. Then she reached across and up, sliding her chemise to one side, revealing the smooth, bare, honey skin of her right shoulder. As she advanced toward him she slid the other side of her chemise off of her left shoulder, allowing it to fall, completely baring her breasts. She stood directly in front of him, and he reached out and took one breast in each of his hands, closing his eyes as he kneaded and fondled them, his arousal growing.

When he opened his beady eyes, he placed his hands upon her shoulders, pressing down gently, forcing her to her knees. He then took one hand and unbuttoned the front of his breeches and placed his other hand on her back, between her shoulder blades, pushing her closer so that he could slide his member between her breasts. He lingered there a while, moving his hips up and down. Then, placing his hand on the back of her head, he pushed her face down, forcing her mouth onto him.

"You're nothing but a whore! All actresses are sluts!" She heard Fisher's voice in her head and nearly stood up to run out of the office, but with firm resolve, Nancy refused to run from the accusation, or act out the revulsion she felt. She was a woman in a man's world, after all, and she had to do whatever was required to make her way through it and get what she wanted.

You men are so simple, anyway, she thought. Nothing but big babies. Give you a tit and tell you how big you are, and you're butter in the hand. If we're sluts and whores, she silently argued, it is only because you men have made it impossible for us to be otherwise! You and your over-estimated self-importance and your pathetic little cocks!

When she emerged from the front entrance of Zinzendorf's house Nancy cupped her hand over her mouth and ran toward a group of shrubs and leaned over them, vomiting.

Two weeks later a message arrived from the Emperor informing Nancy that he would offer Stephen a generous commission to compose an Italian comic opera for the following theater season.

Chapter Nine

*W*eeks passed and Nancy received no word from Mozart—no notes left on her vanity table, no knocks on her dressing room door, no invitations to meet at the Milano—only silence. Her worst fears were realized and she resigned herself to the cruel idea that he had silently abandoned her. She put the garnet bracelet back into its box and instructed Michael to return it to him with no explanations. He would understand. The pain of what felt to Nancy as abandonment on the part of her lover was only lessened by the happy anticipation of seeing her brother again after three long years of separation.

Stephen arrived in early January to the joyful and enthusiastic greetings of his mother and sister, as well as his dear friend, Michael Kelly. Nancy was especially glad to see her brother, as he was a great source of friendship, support, and encouragement. As children, they were close and until he left to study in Italy when he was twelve, they were rarely, if ever, separated.

Because his commission from the Emperor was his first major work, Stephen was understandably nervous and he decided that he should seek some guidance from a more experienced composer, preferably one who was up on what was most fashionable and one who was familiar with the Viennese audience and its likes and dislikes.

"Kitten," Stephen asked, calling her affectionately by the pet name he'd given her when they were children, "what do you think of Mozart?"

"What do you mean," she asked, a little taken aback. Stephen knew that she and Mozart were friends, but surely their mother hadn't shared the truth about him being the father of her baby. "I think of him fondly. We're dear friends."

"No," he said, shaking his head, "I need someone to help me with my opera. You know how anxious I am about this." He nervously thumbed through the libretto he'd chosen for the piece. When the commission arrived, Stephen was stunned. He couldn't believe that he had been chosen over so many more qualified local candidates, including Mozart, to compose an opera for the Viennese national theater, and he wasn't at all confident that he was up to the task.

"I think Mozart would be an excellent choice," she answered truthfully. She had no desire to exercise vindictiveness against her ex-lover, nor did she wish to seek any financial support or recompense for the child. Still she was deeply hurt that there was no word from him since last she saw him. She understood why the affair ended, but he'd expressed no emotion, no anger, no remorse, no sorrow, nothing since that day, and she wondered if he really ever loved her, if the whole affair had just been a casual fling on his part.

"Good! Then I think I shall pay the maestro a call tomorrow," he said as he opened the libretto and began to study.

∞∞∞

As Mozart passed through the main salon on the way to his music room, a pretty sight caught his eye. Constanze was leaning over the secretary entering some figures into the household accounts, her left elbow planted firmly on the desktop, propping her chin up with her hand. Her sweet, round backside, which was hidden under her skirts, was stuck up in the air, an inviting temptation for her playful husband, who always seemed to be in the mood for a romp whenever the opportunity presented itself.

Instantly his thoughts reverted from the manuscript that lay on his fortepiano in the music salon to the delightful interlude that could take place between them if he would but take full advantage of the charming situation. He went down on all fours and tried to sneak up on her, but the creaking of the floor boards gave him away.

"I can hear you." She giggled.

He snickered.

"I know what you're doing," she said as she giggled again and continued to write.

He snickered again.

In the next instant, she could feel him crawling under her skirts, and as she laid down her quill, she felt his warm, wet kisses all over her bottom.

She smacked the back of his head through her skirts, yelling and giggling at the same time. "Oh, stop! Stop it, silly Mandl!"

He brought his head out from underneath her skirts and stood and grabbed her by the waist, turning her to face him. Then he pulled up the back of her skirts and cupped his hands around her bare buttocks, playfully drawing her close to him.

"Stanzerl-Manzerl puddin' pie, I kissed her arse and made her cry!" he teased as he nibbled her neck.

She giggled again and grabbed his buttocks in return, giving them a firm squeeze. He squealed like a piglet and then they both laughed. Then just as they were locked in a lingering kiss, they heard someone knock.

"Ach du Scheisse!"

"Let it go," she pleaded as she continued to fondle his backside, moving her hand to the front.

"I can't, Stanzerl. It might be something important." He pushed her hand away, the mood completely ruined.

"But don't worry, little mouse-wouse," he said as he pulled away from her embrace with a playful wink, "I'll be back for you later." There was another knock and he quickly ran into another room to put on a waistcoat to conceal the results of his recent antics and then made his way back to the door. "I'm coming!" he shouted impatiently, as there was yet another knock.

He got to the door and opened it to reveal a young, olive-skinned man with dark brown hair and large, dark brown eyes standing before him, wearing a heavy English greatcoat and a fashionable English round hat, and carrying a rather large leather valise. Mozart thought he recognized the young man, but he couldn't seem to place him.

"Herr Mozart?"

"Yes," he replied, still perturbed over the interruption. "What do you want?"

"I'm Stephen Storace, Anna Storace's brother," he answered, as he waited for Mozart to acknowledge the connection.

"Of course," Mozart said nervously as he motioned for Stephen to enter. "Please, come in."

"Thank you, sir."

"What brings you here?" He was afraid of what Stephen's answer might be. He led him through the foyer and into the salon.

"I have business with you, sir."

"Constanze, come and take this man's coat," Mozart called out as he motioned for Stephen to sit on a nearby settee. There was only one matter of business that he could imagine Nancy's brother having with him, and he felt a large knot begin to form in his stomach. As Constanze entered the room, Mozart gestured to her. "This is my wife, Constanze."

Stephen bowed politely. "It's a pleasure, Madame."

"Constanze, this is Signora Storace's brother, Stephen. He's here all the way from London."

"It's a pleasure to meet you, sir," Constanze said as she curtseyed, a sparkle of curiosity in her eyes as she looked Stephen over. "Please, let me take your coat." As she took it from him, Mozart motioned with his eyes toward the door, indicating that he wanted her to leave them alone. As soon as she was gone, he shut the doors, leaving them to talk privately.

"Please, sit down," Mozart said, gesturing again toward the settee.

Stephen removed his hat, and took a seat as Mozart sat in a large chair directly across from him.

"What is the nature of your business, Mister Storace?" He leaned back into the chair, nervously rubbing his fingers together.

"Well, sir," Stephen began.

Mozart drew in a long breath, preparing for the worst.

"You may know that I received a commission from His Majesty, the Emperor, to compose a comic opera for your national theater."

Mozart let out a silent sigh of relief. However, when he had a moment to think on it, he was a bit confused, as well as a little dismayed. How had this young, English unknown received such a commission?

"No, I had not heard."

"I don't know what my sister has told you of me, but I am a capable composer, if I say so myself, but I'm inexperienced. To receive such a commission without my ever having composed a work of this scale has me rather overwhelmed."

Mozart sat listening intently, interested in what this obviously intelligent young man had to say. He reminded Mozart very much of Nancy, who had the same proud bearing and spirit about her. He liked him already.

"I have come to you, Maestro, in recognition of your great talent and your reputation as one of the finest composers in the Vienna, to ask if I might humbly sit under your tutelage as I compose this opera. I'm willing to pay well and would consider it a great honor if you would take me on," he concluded, anxiously awaiting Mozart's reply.

"Show me what you brought," Mozart said as he leaned forward extending his hand.

Stephen opened his valise and pulled out four different works: a chamber piece for strings and winds, a full-scale orchestral piece, and two insert arias, which he had composed for Nancy and which she had already sung in a few productions at the Burg. His hands shaking, he handed the manuscripts to Mozart.

Mozart took them, stood, and walked toward a table in the corner of the room, laying them flat so that he could better look at them. Stephen got up from his seat and moved near Mozart so that he might be able to answer any questions the maestro might ask. As he read through them, Mozart stroked his chin, sometimes uttering little guttural sounds, indicating the things he liked or about which he was curious.

"Good voice-leading here," he said, pointing to a phrase in the chamber piece. "Excellent use of the suspension."

Stephen smiled proudly.

"There are some problems with the phrasing here. A bit too... how would one say it? Too disjointed." When he began to look at the arias, he smiled. "You know your sister's voice well." He chuckled warmly.

"Yes, Maestro, she has a unique quality. I've not heard another voice quite like it."

"Indeed." Mozart smiled, nodding in agreement. "It's a very warm and expressive voice. Not quite as flexible as it should be, but it has a seductive quality nonetheless that I've not heard in any other soprano." He turned, looking Stephen in the eye. "Tell me, Storace. Just what is it that you want me to teach you?"

"I want you to teach me how to compose opera, Maestro," Stephen replied confidently. "I know how to compose for the human voice, but connecting the different components together with the adjoining recitative to create a continuous line and musical theme, is the challenge. As I said to you earlier, this will be my first major work."

Mozart rubbed his forehead and thought for a moment. "Well then, it will be a pleasure. We start tomorrow, for we've no time to waste."

The next day, Stephen arrived to begin work. The libretto he'd chosen was by Brunati, entitled, *Gli sposi malcontenti*, and Nancy's role would be a dramatic rather than a comic one.

Mozart found Stephen to be an astute, musically intelligent, and sensitive composer. A quick study, Stephen was eager to learn and was receptive to all of Mozart's instruction, and Mozart soon regarded him as one of his favorite students as well as a friend.

A couple of weeks after Stephen began his instruction he was invited, along with Nancy and Michael, to be guests in Mozart's home for a special evening. Mozart honored his friend, mentor, and fellow composer, Joseph Haydn by composing a series of string quartets for him, and he decided to present them at a private musicale. Mozart worked long and hard on these quartets, spending many arduous hours literally sweating over them, and he was extremely pleased and proud with the results. Stephen was excited and honored to have been asked by Mozart to play the violin parts at the premiere of these important works.

As they arrived at the Mozart apartment, Nancy held tightly to Stephen's arm, finding security in staying near him. When Mozart opened the door to find Stephen, Nancy, and Kelly standing in the entry, he greeted them warmly, giving Nancy a polite kiss on the hand and commenting on how well she looked and how good it was to see her. She responded in kind, offering a warm greeting, for she was genuinely happy to see him after so many months, even if it was under such strained circumstances. Nancy's pregnancy was quite obvious by this time, but Mozart tried not to notice, preferring to remain in denial over the child's parentage.

"And who is this charming lady?" Haydn remarked as they entered the room. "Why have I not yet met her?"

Mozart smiled and replied, "Papa, this is Signora Anna Storace. Signora, this is Joseph Haydn, whom we all refer to affectionately as 'Papa'."

Haydn was a warm, informal, earthy man, with no affectations whatsoever. To speak with him one would never know that he was one of the most intelligent, respected, and loved of all composers in Vienna.

"At last," Haydn said with a warm smile as he took Nancy's hand and kissed it. His gray-blue eyes danced and sparkled. "You are as charming off the stage as on, my dear."

"Thank you, Herr Haydn," Nancy replied.

"No, it's 'Papa'! I insist. None of this waiting for a polite period before we can use familiar terms with one another! You're an honored and respected member of the musical community here in our fair city; that already makes us friends."

"Then 'Papa' it shall be from now on," Nancy said with a warm smile.

When Nancy was introduced to Constanze, she had expected the wife of Mozart to be more educated and a little more worldly, but to her great surprise, Constanze was a bit on the plain side and she had no experience in hosting a soirée, especially one that was attended by so many of Vienna's musical elite. It was evident that Mozart was worried that his wife might say or do something that would embarrass him in front of his more educated and sophisticated friends and guests. Still, Nancy found Constanze to be likeable and polite, and despite her desire to dislike her lover's wife, she found herself warming to her.

After the quartets were played, the men gathered to discuss them over the punch bowl, Stephen joining in with Mozart and Haydn as if they were long-time friends. Nancy was extremely pleased to see Stephen getting on so well with Mozart, but she longed to be included in their discussion of the quartets, being more interested in what was deemed men's business than she was in the women's idle chatter about weddings and births, and the latest fashions that had arrived from Paris. She sat alone in a nearby chair and strained to listen to their discussion as she, too, was interested in hearing what Mozart had to say about how these quartets came about.

Thinking that Nancy was lonely, Constanze took her by the arm and led her to a settee so that they could become better acquainted. Looking for something that they had in common, Constanze brought up the subject of Nancy's pregnancy.

"When is your baby due?"

"Oh not until June," Nancy replied, a little uncomfortable with the subject.

"I'm sure you'll make a wonderful mother," Constanze said, searching for a way to compliment her. "Babies bring such joy into a home. Why you wouldn't believe what joy our little Karl has given us. Wolfgang is so proud of his son," she said, smiling proudly. "Karl makes our family complete."

Nancy didn't know how to respond. Thus far the only things her baby brought to her were pain and separation from the one she loved. Constanze's comments, although not intended to be unkind, seemed a bit insensitive to Nancy in light of the fact that there was no home or husband for her to bring her child into. She began to search for a way to politely change the topic when she noticed the garnet necklace that was around Constanze's graceful neck.

"What a beautiful necklace," Nancy remarked as she leaned in closer to get a better look.

Constanze put her hand up to her throat and touched the necklace. "Oh, yes, it was a birthday gift from my husband. It was only a few days ago, and the garnet is my birthstone. I didn't have the heart to tell him that I don't like it though. It's much too gaudy for my tastes, and it's so heavy. It doesn't even look like something I would wear. But you know how men can be; they don't understand such things. And what makes it worse is he probably paid a small fortune for it!"

Upon closer examination, Nancy noticed that it was an exact match to the bracelet that Mozart gave to her several months earlier. Hot tears stung her eyes as she remembered his promise in the accompanying note to have her "dripping in garnets". She realized that he must have bought the bracelet and the necklace together as a set, and gave her the bracelet that night before her rehearsal, intending to give her the necklace at a later time. It was obvious to her that after the affair ended he decided to give it to his wife as a birthday present instead.

"Please excuse me, Frau Mozart," Nancy said suddenly, standing, "I must go and find my brother. All at once I'm not feeling well."

"Oh I understand completely. It's all a part of your condition. I can't tell you how many times I had the same thing happen. I do hope you feel better soon."

"Thank you. It was lovely meeting you," Nancy said as she tried to conceal the tear that made its way down her cheek.

Nancy quickly found Stephen, who stood in another part of the room, still conversing with Mozart and Kelly. When she slipped her arm through his, he noticed that she was upset, so he walked with her to another part of the room where they could speak in private.

"What's the matter, Kitten?"

"May we go now, Stephen? I'm not feeling well and I want to go home and lie down."

She turned her gaze toward Mozart, who was still talking and laughing. Mozart glanced suddenly toward the corner where Nancy stood with Stephen and became visibly distracted. He could tell that Nancy was crying, and he wondered if Constanze had said something unkind to upset her.

"Of course we can," Stephen said as he wiped a stray tear from her cheek. "Let me go and say goodnight to our host, and we'll be off."

Stephen walked back to the group of men and excused his sister and himself. He thanked Mozart for the lovely evening and congratulated him for the fine quartets, and then he retrieved Nancy and they left.

Later that night, as they were getting ready for bed, Mozart asked Constanze if she knew why Nancy was so suddenly upset.

"I couldn't tell you. It was the strangest thing. She noticed the necklace you gave to me for my birthday, and as I was telling her about how I thought it was such a lovely and thoughtful gift, she got up and left."

"Hm," he grunted. "Divas!" he said, pretending to be indifferent to the situation. He knew what had upset her. "You never know what the hell's going to set them off."

⁎⎇⎈

Over the following weeks it became clear that this was not going to be an easy pregnancy for Nancy, who was frequently ill and suffered with extreme fatigue and fainting spells. At one point during a performance of *Il re Teodoro*, Benucci had her sit for her big aria, hoping that it would stave off the frequent fainting spells which seemed to plague her on stage. By this time, Benucci had grown quite fond of Nancy and had it not been for the fact that she was with child, he would have already pursued a love affair with her. However, being of a quiet and sensitive nature, he didn't wish to heap any more scandal or stress upon the girl, who was already plagued with such to the point that she was near her breaking point.

It was an unseasonably warm and balmy March afternoon as Nancy stood in the music salon in Mozart's apartment, rehearsing for a concert she was to give the next day at the Mehlgrube. Mozart was hired by the Burgtheater management to be her accompanist and she was to sing several arias from her repertoire.

Constanze was out taking a stroll with Leopold, Mozart's father (who had arrived in February from Salzburg for a lengthy visit), so they were alone except for the servants. Things were stressful in the Mozart home because of Leopold's visit, so Wolfgang was relieved to have everyone out of the house and to have some time to engage in what he considered a relaxing activity.

Nancy felt unusually well that day, and as she stood in the rectangular, closet-like room with its faux marble walls and ornately carved ceiling, going over with Mozart what she was to sing the next day, she suddenly felt very close to him again. They were a remarkable team and she felt confident whenever he accompanied her. As they rehearsed, they joked, laughed, and carried on as they had before, as if none of the unfortunate events that plagued their relationship had ever happened. It felt like the friendship of the old days.

Suddenly, the breeze blew through the open casements sending the music flying across the room, scattering it on the floor. Nancy was unable to bend over to retrieve it, so Mozart politely offered to do it for her. It was a fairly tight squeeze in the small room and as Mozart stood to place the manuscript back on top of the fortepiano, he stumbled and fell into Nancy. As he did, he thrust his hands out in front of him in order to shield her from the full impact of his weight. He was able to soften the impact by dropping to his knees as he fell, which landed him directly in front of Nancy's protruding tummy. Despite the voice inside of him warning him not to place himself in a compromising position, he couldn't help but place his hands on the mound that was the child growing inside of her.

The impact of the fall, although greatly softened by Mozart's careful maneuvers, caused Nancy to fall back against the wall, and she felt the baby startle. Mozart felt it too, and despite the awkward position in which he found himself, he lingered there for several moments, his hands still resting upon her belly.

Knowing the child was his, he desired to feel it once more. Suddenly the baby moved again and this time Mozart gazed up at Nancy who looked down at him, relishing the moment.

"It's all right," she said softly. "Go ahead. If you'll apply just a little pressure you can feel it better." She laid her hand on the top of his head and felt his soft chestnut locks between her fingers. She looked at the ceiling and smiled.

He waited silently for the baby to move again, and when it did, he laughed a little and said, "It's a strong one like you, Nancy."

After lingering there for several moments, he suddenly stood and cleared his throat and they proceeded together to sort out the mess of manuscript that lay askew on top of the fortepiano.

ჳႥႬჳ

With Mozart's help and instruction, Stephen was able to complete his opera in just a little less than two months, and rehearsals began immediately following. It was clear to Stephen that getting Nancy through this to the premiere was not going to be an easy task. Between her grueling performance schedule and her difficult pregnancy, she was also rehearsing another new piece by Salieri entitled *La grotta di Trofonio*, in which she was to sing the role of Ophelia. In addition to stage rehearsals, there were separate musical rehearsals that took place, sometimes in Mozart's apartments, and other times in the Storace apartments. Stephen's opera was scheduled to premiere on June first, and Salieri's, a couple of months after, shortly after Nancy's postpartum confinement would be completed. Despite the fact that the premiere fell within a few weeks of the time when Nancy was due to give birth, the Emperor felt that he had already given her too much time off and his demands were imperative; she would sing at the premiere even if it meant she would give birth to her child on the stage.

Nancy began to show signs of distress. She had trouble sleeping at night due to physical strain and nightmares about Fisher. She would awaken screaming in terror after seeing Fisher's fist coming toward her face, and she would look down an abyss into a pool of blood. Stephen would hear her terrified screams and come rushing into her bedchamber, taking her into his arms and rocking her until she settled to sleep. This went on for weeks, and combined with the other stresses that were mounting upon her, things were beginning to look dismal for Stephen's premiere.

It was mid May, only two weeks before the premiere and Mozart was going over some last minute changes in some of Nancy's arias with her and Stephen in their apartment. He had been through a whirlwind of a spring between his father's extended visit, which inflicted terrible conflict in his household. As a result, Constanze was moody and grumpy, and that with his unusually hectic and grueling performance schedule were almost more than he could take. Tensions ran high as Nancy, who was in an agitated state, clashed with Mozart over a change that he proposed in her big act one aria.

"This has to be changed," he said, pointing to a series of melismatic passages that, under normal circumstances, would offer no challenge for her. Under the current conditions, however, they presented problems that she couldn't seem to correct. "You simply don't have the stamina to carry these off right now, Nancy," he continued, trying to convince her that the changes had to be made.

"If you would take this tempo just a little faster here, as I've asked you to do over and over again, I would be able to make it through."

"We can't, Kitten," Stephen replied, frustrated by his sister's unwillingness to cooperate with their suggestions. "The tempo has to remain slower there to reflect the melancholy mood."

"I'm only asking for a slight change of tempo, gentlemen. I'm not asking that you rewrite the whole bloody opera! Humor me!"

This type of discourse continued throughout the entire session with every change that they proposed in every piece until finally, Mozart reached his breaking point and flew off the handle with her.

"God damn it, Nancy!" he shouted, standing and knocking the manuscript in front of him across the room. "Basta! I've had it with your whining and your tantrums! We're trying to help you and you're treating us like shit!"

Nancy turned and faced him with fire in her eyes. "And just who has treated whom like shit for the last eight months?" she shouted.

Stephen, who didn't want to be a part of the argument decided that this was a good time for him to excuse himself, so he slipped out of the room and go for a walk to the nearest tavern.

"What do you mean? I've barely spoken to you. I've barely even seen you. I haven't had time to wipe my own arse this whole goddamned spring much less think about you!"

"Of course, forgive me. I forgot my place for a moment. I had been under the mistaken notion that we were lovers and that you were supposed to care!"

"What would you have me do? I'm a married man. I have duties to my wife and family. I thought you understood that!"

At that, she turned on him and through clenched teeth shot back, "Your duties didn't seem all that important to you when you left your pregnant wife at home to go off to the Baroness's to spend the weekend fucking me, did they Wolfgango?"

His head swam as a knot formed in his stomach, his tongue sticking to the roof of his dry mouth.

"And what of your promises to me and to the child you created during your weekend of wanton pleasure?" She waited, seething, for his reply.

He stood silently for several moments before he spoke again. "Then you're saying the child is mine?"

"Yes, Wolfgango," she snapped. "Of course it's yours. You can't tell me you believed for one second that it could be Fisher's, or anyone else's for that matter."

She began to cry. "And what is it that concerns you? Whether or not I'm going to hold you financially responsible for the child? Well you can relieve yourself of that, because I don't need your money or your support. 'Oh, Wanze,' she scoffed, 'my heart is beating for you! Before I'm finished with you, you'll be dripping in garnets!'."

Then she turned back to face him. "The necklace your wife wore that night matched the bracelet you gave to me! How could you, Wolfgango?"

She fell sobbing, into a heap on the settee.

Mozart stood in the middle of the room reeling, his head swimming with the hateful venom to which he had been subjected. Something inside told him that he should take her in his arms and comfort her, but then her seething words rang through his ears again, and his heart hardened. The anger welled inside, so instead, he turned and grabbed his hat and headed for the entrance.

"I don't have to take this shit! I already have a wife!" he shouted as he slammed the door on his way out.

"Who does she think she is, speaking to me like that?" he grumbled as he kept walking, passersby looking at him as if he were mad. "I've done my best to help her, damn it! I even took her brother in as a student as a personal favor. I didn't have time to help him with that damned opera, with all the other things I had going! And where's my goddamned commission from the Emperor? Fuck them all!"

When he reached the Graben, he ducked into a tavern. He could always think better with a few beers in him.

It had been a long and arduous spring full of activity, concerts, and a long visit from his father. The busy schedule was difficult enough to manage, but with Leopold added into the mix, it had become hellacious. Leopold arrived in February and he had only gone back to Salzburg three weeks before. Wolfgang's head was still spinning from that alone, with all the tension from his father, who hated Constanze. He had to keep his father entertained, along with that boy, Heinrich, who his father brought with him, not to mention all of Leopold's concerts, which he had to attend. Then, when his father wasn't home, he had to listen to Constanze's constant nagging and complaining. Now Nancy hit him with this news, throwing it at him with all the venom and vitriol she could muster. He was almost nauseous by the time his first drink arrived, but the cool, foamy brew eased the knot in his stomach and soothed his frazzled nerves almost as soon as he took the first swallow.

I can't think about this right now. Besides, Nancy said I didn't have to worry about her asking for support, so there's nothing for me to do about it anyway.

He remembered the conversation that he'd had with Kelly that day at the Baroness's estate. He'd warned him not to fall in love with her, that it would only cause pain for both of them.

I fell in love, he thought as he took another drink. But I never said I loved her. Not in so many words, anyway, he argued with himself.

Nancy's stinging accusations hit him like poisonous arrows. *And what of your promises to me and to the child you created during your weekend of wanton pleasure?*

What promises did I ever make? he replied in his mind. Besides, I didn't notice that you weren't having a pleasant time with me. All those pretty little noises and cries... That was acting, I suppose. Hah!

He had to ponder it a while longer. Suddenly the picture of her standing beside the harpsichord at the Baroness's invaded his thoughts. It happened then. In that single moment, she captured him completely. He was lost forever.

Be honest, Wolfgang; you did exactly what Kelly warned you not to. You fell for her and you allowed her to fall for you.

Suddenly he understood what Kelly meant about becoming a divided man, for now he found himself divided between his loyalty and obligation to Constanze and the woman he truly loved.

Chapter Ten

Mozart wasn't sure how he was going to handle the delicate situation with Nancy. Her last words to him were cutting and cruel, and they hurt him deeply. As much as he understood the cause of her anger, he wasn't ready to make himself vulnerable to another attack, so he thought it best to put off talking to her until after the opera's premiere when her nerves might be less on edge. Besides, he didn't see how things would ever change between them where her child was concerned. He could never acknowledge it as his and he was afraid that might be every bit as hurtful to her as his sudden and silent abandonment of their affair.

He looked forward to a restful summer after the whirlwind spring that had sapped him of his energy. First there was the premiere of Stephen's opera and then there would be little or no demand on him until August or September. Perhaps he would do a little reading and spend some time lazing with his wife and son in the Prater.

Constanze backed out of going to the premiere at the last minute, claiming that she had a headache. It didn't concern him, for he much preferred to attend these events alone, or with his friends, so that he could go to the Milano afterward and stay as late as he wished. Only then did he have the freedom to flirt with any pretty girl who caught his fancy, without Constanze's watchful eye on him.

When he arrived at the theater he was escorted to his box, which was about three quarters distance away from stage right. He looked around at those who had already been seated.

There's Zinzendorf. He never misses one of Nancy's premieres. Ah, Baroness Waldstätten, he thought as he caught her eye, giving her a nod. And there's Salieri with Cavalieri, Rosenberg, and Pezzel...

Nancy heard a knock on her dressing room door.

"Kitten, it's me. Are you nearly dressed? It's almost time," he called.

"I'm ready," she replied, patting her bosom with a bit more powder. She stood, giving herself one last look in the mirror and grabbed her fan. As she made her way down the corridor she saw Stephen standing at the end.

"Break a leg," he said as he kissed her cheek. He left, then to take his place with the orchestra.

Nancy had trouble focusing. Everything was blurry and a little dim. She was tired.

"Positions!" the stage manager whispered loudly as the overture began. Nancy couldn't find her entry point. Where was it?

"Madame," the stage manager whispered, "Your position please!"

Where was it? She couldn't remember. Ah, there it is, she thought as she saw Benucci moving into place. She made her entrance next to him.

As the curtain rose, she walked out onto the stage along with Benucci, and began to sing the first notes. Things went along fairly well, although a couple of times she had difficulty remembering her blocking, but when it came time for the first trio, she could barely get through it. As she exited, the stage manager met her and asked, "Madame, are you all right?"

"I'm fine," she replied as the curtains and the walls around her began to spin. "I'm feeling a little dizzy. Please, I need to sit before my next entrance."

She was led to a chair.

"May I have some water?" She listened as the next scene played out, and when it was almost time for her cue, she stood and made her way back to her next position. It was nearly time for her first big aria, the one in which her character grieved the loss of her husband's affections.

"Positions!"

She positioned herself for her entrance, and she walked on stage, the first measures of her aria began to play.

As I cry out, oh God,
I cry for freedom;
I cry out for restoration,
but they give none.

After only a few bars she stopped singing and gazed out over the audience.

Everyone is looking at me, she thought in sudden terror. They know about Mozart. They know what I've done. They know how Stephen got his commission.

"What's she doing?" the stage manager whispered.

"Oh my God, what's wrong with her?" Kelly exclaimed in horror as he watched from the wings.

Stephen looked up from where he sat at the harpsichord and tried to get her attention. Thinking that she had lost her place, he mouthed the words to her.

In his box, Mozart leaned over the rail.

"What's she doing? She has no rests here," he thought aloud. "What's wrong with her?" He arose and exited his box, making his way out of the house to the backstage entrance, fearing that something was terribly wrong.

They all know I'm a whore. My mother knows. Look, there he is. He knows I'm a whore. He doesn't love me anymore. No... no... he never loved me... he never loved me at all. He's laughing at me! They're all laughing at me, Zinzendorf, all of them are laughing...

Standing in the middle of the stage, she began to weep. She wandered around crying and muttering to herself. Suddenly she fell into a heap on the floor, sobbing.

Stephen silenced the orchestra and jumped on the stage as Benucci joined him from the wings. The audience began to buzz in confusion and speculation.

"Kitten," Stephen whispered as he knelt next to her. "What's the matter? Please, what's wrong?"

She gave no response. Stephen motioned to Benucci to help. The men picked her up and helped her to her feet so that they could get her off the stage and back to her dressing room. By this time Mozart was standing in the wings with Kelly.

"My God, Mick, what happened?"

"She collapsed. The poor girl couldn't take the strain any more," he said as tears poured down his cheeks.

Mozart stood in shocked silence as he watched Stephen and Benucci lead Nancy by the arms into her dressing room. Stephen led her to the settee and held her as she continued to weep. Benucci watched helplessly. When Mozart and Kelly appeared in the open doorway, her hysteria only increased.

"I'm sorry, but I'm going to have to ask you to wait outside," Stephen said quietly as he motioned to Benucci to close the door. Mozart saw the tears in Stephen's eyes. They moved to wait on a bench in the corridor.

Stephen held his sister in his arms, rocking her and trying to soothe her by softly cooing and brushing the loose hair from her eyes. It was a long while before she finally stopped crying and fell into an exhausted slumber with her head in Stephen's lap.

"Francesco, go ask Mozart if he would lend us his carriage to take her home."

When they arrived at the apartment building, Mozart got out of the carriage first and opened the door as Stephen took Nancy in his arms and carried her up the stairs to their apartment. Elizabeth, who had already gone home so that she could be there when they arrived, heard the carriage drive up and met them at the door to let them in, but when Mozart tried to enter, she blocked his way.

"I think it would be best for you to wait outside," she said coolly.

Dismayed by her cold treatment, he did as she requested, remaining in the landing until Kelly came up the stairs. "Madame Storace won't let me in," he said, visibly upset.

"She's blamin' you for what's happened to her daughter."

"Me? What did I do?" he sputtered indignantly. "It's that animal she married Nancy off to that did this. Mrs. Storace has no one to blame but herself!"

"That may well be, but…" Michael shrugged.

After what seemed an interminably long time, Stephen came to the door and motioned them to enter.

"We've got her settled now, I think. At least she's sleeping. Thank you for your help."

"I'm so sorry about your premiere, Stephen," Mozart said, observing the disappointment in Stephen's face. "I don't know what to say. I've never seen anything like this before."

"It's my fault. I saw it coming several days ago. I should have replaced her with Coltellini then, but Ann begged me to let her go on. I agreed, against my better judgment, and this is the result," he said with a sigh.

"She's a hard-headed spitfire, she is," Michael remarked. "She'll keep goin' till the bitter end."

"And that's exactly what it came to. I'm afraid it'll be the end for my opera as well."

"No, no," Mozart said shaking his head. "It'll go on as scheduled. You'll have to put Coltellini in for a while, but after…" he paused. "Well, after the child is born, she'll be ready to get back to work, I'm sure. Just give her some time."

They spoke for several more minutes until Stephen thanked them again and wished them a good evening. As Mozart turned, Stephen stopped him.

"Maestro, thank you for everything," he said as he managed a weary smile. "I couldn't have done this without you."

Mozart patted him on the shoulder. "You're a good man, Storace, and a fine composer. It is my pleasure."

Not long after, Mozart walked into his own apartment to find Constanze rocking baby Karl. "What are you doing home so early," she asked as she looked up, surprised to see him.

"There was an incident at the theater. The show had to be stopped," he replied quietly as he walked past her to their bedchamber to change out of his suit.

"What do you mean?" She laid the baby in his cradle and followed after him.

"Nancy collapsed on stage."

"Is she all right? What about the baby?"

"I don't know. She was asleep when I left their apartment. No one said anything about the baby. No one really knows what happened. She just stopped in the middle of her aria and started to cry, then she collapsed. She'd open her mouth and nothing would come out."

"Poor thing," Constanze remarked, shaking her head. "It's probably all about that husband of hers. Having to carry his child… it must have been too much for her to take," she said as she laid her head on his shoulder. "I'm so fortunate to have a good husband," she sighed.

He put his arms around his wife and said nothing. After she left to check the baby one last time, he finished undressing, blew out the lights, and went to bed.

The next morning Aloysia arrived loaded with gossip about the night before—gossip that had already spread like a wildfire through the city. But to her dismay, Constanze already knew everything in full detail.

Finally, for once I know more than her, Constanze thought smugly.

Mozart didn't sleep well. All night he lay awake tossing and turning as the scene repeated itself over and over in his mind. He couldn't seem to erase Nancy from his thoughts. It was nearly dawn before he finally fell asleep, so Constanze shut the door to afford him some quiet. When he awakened, it was nearly one o'clock in the afternoon, so he got up, dressed and headed over to the Storace apartment to check on Nancy. He was met by Antonia, the maid, who barely opened the door, peeking out to speak to him.

"Good afternoon," he greeted her politely. "I came to inquire about Signora Storace. How is she today?"

She stepped outside onto the landing, holding the door to the apartment slightly ajar, but not offering him entrance.

"I'm sorry, sir, but I can't let you in. I have strict orders."

"But how is she?"

"There's little change, sir," she said with emotion. "She slept fitfully during the night. She has nightmares and when she is awake, she doesn't speak. Mostly, she sits in her bed and cries, but no sound comes out."

"And her brother, how is he?"

"He's barely left her side all night, or all day," she replied. "I've never seen a brother who is so devoted. I worry for his health as well. If he keeps up this kind of vigil he'll collapse too, I'm afraid."

Mozart wanted to ask about the child's welfare, but he feared approaching the indelicate subject with her. "Please tell her that I stopped by," he said as he hung his head. "Tell her that I'm very concerned...I mean, my wife and I are very concerned and we send our best wishes."

"I will, sir."

&OCB

A week passed and still there was no change in Nancy's condition. She rarely if ever uttered a word, and when she did, it was only in direct response to questions to which the answer could be a simple yes, or no. She mostly slept, as the nightmares seemed to have subsided. When she was awake she sat in her bed, silently staring at the wall. Her mother and brother took turns keeping vigil, making sure she was as comfortable as possible and trying to get her to eat.

There was a steady stream of notes, messages, flowers and gifts from friends, theater patrons, the theater management, and people from all over, wishing her a speedy recovery and return to the stage. Stephen read every note to her as it arrived, and when flowers were delivered, Elizabeth put them in a vase and brought them to Nancy's bedchamber. None of these things, however, seemed to bring about any change.

It was the middle of the night when Stephen was suddenly awakened from a deep, restful, sleep by a blood-curdling scream coming from Nancy's chamber.

Another nightmare, he thought as he got up and searched in the dark for his dressing gown. He lit a candle and shuffled towards her room, preparing himself to console her for the next half hour. When he entered, however, he found her standing on the floor in a puddle of water mixed with blood, shivering. "Please," he shouted, "someone help! She's bleeding!"

Elizabeth rushed into the room, dressed only in her nightdress and cap, and saw Nancy standing in the puddle with Stephen behind her, his arms wrapped around her shoulders looking helpless.

"Mother, something's terribly wrong!"

"No, nothing's wrong, Stephen," she said calmly as she took Nancy by the hand and moved her out of the puddle of her baby's water. "She's in labor. Go wake Antonia and tell her to get the midwife. I'll take care of her until you get back."

Stephen looked bewildered, but relieved. He nodded. "All right," he said. "I'll get dressed."

"Hurry now, there won't be much time." Elizabeth turned her attentions to Nancy. "Let's get you out of this wet gown and into something dry."

She pulled the sopping nightgown over her daughter's head and then helped her into a dry one. Then she laid Nancy down on the bed and removed the duvet, preparing the bed for the birthing process. In a few minutes Nancy began to cry out.

"It's all right, Ann," Elizabeth said gently. "Look at me. Take a deep breath and look at me."

Nancy did as her mother instructed.

"Now, let the breath out slowly… very slowly."

Nancy blew out, her eyes fixed upon her mother's face. In a few moments, the pain began to subside.

"That was good," Elizabeth said as she smiled, stroking Nancy's hair. "Another one will come soon and you'll do the same thing. Do you understand?"

Nancy nodded and Elizabeth smiled.

"Good. You're doing very well. I'm proud of you."

In less than an hour, Stephen and Antonia came in with the midwife to find Nancy lying on her side, gazing intently into her mother's eyes. Elizabeth was holding her hand, talking her through another pain. The midwife instructed Stephen to go into the salon to wait.

"It looks like it's going well in here," she said cheerfully. "I'm not sure you need me at all."

Elizabeth smiled, but kept her gaze fixed on her daughter. "I've done this twice myself. It comes naturally, I suppose."

As the pains grew more and more intense, they knew it was getting very close to time for Nancy to push. They positioned her sitting upright on the end of the bed, placing a large basin on the floor beneath her to catch the remaining water, and the blood that would pour out when the infant was expelled. Antonia had already brought a basin of warm water, some twine, and a pair of scissors, along with several rags. A swaddling blanket was laid on the end of the bed so that after they cleaned the baby off, they could wrap it up before handing it to the mother. When another pain came, the midwife instructed Nancy to bear down.

"Push! That's good, you're doing fine, dear."

Another one came and she cried out.

"No, don't scream, dear. It only tires you. Just push. Push as hard as you can," she instructed. Nancy followed the midwife's instruction and bore down, straining and pushing as hard as she could, using every bit of strength she could muster. After a few more pushes, the top of the baby's head was visible to the midwife as she bent underneath to observe and to manipulate the baby's head and shoulders into place. "All right, girl, just one more and it's out."

She didn't have to push very hard this time and the baby slipped right out into the midwife's hands. As she turned the infant over and looked between its legs, she called out, "It's a girl." She handed the baby over to

Elizabeth, who cleared the mucus from her nose and gave her a good spank on the bottom so that she would cry and suck the air into her lungs.

Instinctively, at the sound of her baby's cry, Nancy held out her arms, but instead of handing it to her, Elizabeth took the infant to the basin, where she gave her a thorough examination. There was no question that Mozart was the father. She looked almost exactly like him. Elizabeth bathed the baby gently and rubbed some oil into her skin to prevent chafing, and then she swaddled her tightly in a blanket. She turned to take the baby to Nancy, who had been cleaned up and lay comfortably against her pillows. Nancy held her arms out once again, and as Elizabeth laid the infant in her daughter's arms, she turned to the midwife and thanked her for her help.

"My son will pay you. Thank you."

Outside the room, the midwife found Stephen, who was waiting rather impatiently, and gave him the good news regarding his sister and his new niece. He paid her, and she saw herself to the door.

"May I come in now," Stephen asked as he knocked quietly on Nancy's door.

"You may," he heard Elizabeth's voice call from the other side.

As he entered, he found Nancy sitting in bed, holding her baby in her arms. She was smiling and there was a glow in her eyes that he hadn't seen since the whole ordeal began. He was greatly encouraged.

"Oh, Kitten," he exclaimed as he moved toward the bed. "She's beautiful! Just like you!"

Nancy held her baby up so that he could get a closer look at her, her eyes beaming with pride.

Elizabeth pulled Stephen aside and said to him, "She can't keep it, Stephen, it's a bastard."

"No, it's not. She's married," Stephen replied, shocked.

"It's not Fisher's, Stephen. She told me it wasn't. I don't know whose it is," she lied, "but we can't keep it and risk Fisher thinking it's his, and laying claim on Nancy and the child later. Besides that, I won't raise a bastard."

"I don't think that's your decision to make, Mother. Besides, you're not the one who will have to raise the child. She will, and until she can speak for herself, the child should remain with her."

"Stephen, look at her," she exclaimed, pointing at Nancy. "She went mad on that stage a week ago and she isn't recovering. She may never recover, and I'll be left to raise her bastard child! I won't have it, I tell you. I won't!"

With that, Elizabeth walked to the bed and took the baby from Nancy's arms. Nancy panicked, holding her arms out, wordlessly pleading for her mother to give it back, but Elizabeth ignored her and turned, dashing out of the room with the baby in her arms.

Stephen followed after her, calling out, "Mother, what are you doing?"

"I've decided, I'm taking it to the foundling home. It's best to do it now before Ann has a chance to get too attached to it."

"Mother, you can't!" Stephen pleaded. "You'll break Ann's heart! Mother, please don't do this!"

Ignoring his pleas, she ran out the front door, leaving him to console his sister who was in her bedchamber, sobbing hysterically. Stephen paced in front of the doorway trying to decide what to do. Should he follow after his mother and insist that she return with the child or leave her to do as she wanted and he deal with his sister? He paced into the salon and leaned against the hearth.

I'm a bloody coward, he thought.

"Stephen, be a man! Speak for your sister!" He heard his father's accusing voice ringing in his ears.

Elizabeth had always been difficult and overbearing, and had it not been for the fact that their father knew how to handle her, she would have overrun him as well. After Stefano died, young Stephen endured two miserable years alone with Elizabeth and his sister in Italy. When he could endure it no more, he decided to return to England, telling them that as the man of the household, he needed to settle his father's affairs. In truth it was because he simply couldn't tolerate his overbearing mother. He felt guilty for abandoning Nancy, but he felt that if he stayed, Elizabeth would have surely driven him to madness. He wasn't as strong as Nancy, who could stand up to Elizabeth most of the time. When she couldn't stand up to her, then she was almost always able to outwit her. He couldn't help but believe that had he been with them when Fisher came to Vienna, that Elizabeth would never have orchestrated the ill-fated union and things wouldn't have ended up this way.

"Goddamn you, Mother!" he screamed. "How dare you run off and leave me to console her?" He slipped to the floor and began to sob. "I'm not strong like you, Kitten. Please forgive me."

When he finally returned to Nancy's chamber, Stephen noticed a dramatic change in his sister's mood as she slipped back into the silence that had overtaken her before. The crying ceased and as she wiped the tears from her face with her sleeves, she lay back down, turning away from him to stare out the window at the sun that was just beginning to rise.

Elizabeth's carriage arrived at the entrance of the new state hospital, which included a home for orphaned children. She could make out the infant's features better in the early morning light than in the dim candlelight of Nancy's bedchamber. It looked even more like Mozart than she'd noticed before. She had fair skin—not olive like her daughter's—and the nose and mouth were unmistakably his.

The baby began to cry with hunger and Elizabeth knew that she had better hurry and get her in so that the nuns could begin to care for her properly. She entered into a great marble hall with a large, imposing desk set to one side, where a nun was seated. Elizabeth approached her, hoping that since she couldn't speak German, and the nun probably didn't know any English, she would be able to converse with her in Italian.

"Perdona me Sorella. Parlate italiano?"

"Si," the sister nodded.

"I've brought you an orphan newborn that I cannot keep," she continued in Italian. She thought about what she had said and decided to tell the nun the truth. "No, that's not the truth, Sorella. Forgive me. It is my daughter's baby," she confessed. "She does not wish to keep it and has requested that I bring it to you."

The Sister looked at the baby and asked, "How old is this child?"

"An hour, perhaps two," Elizabeth replied. "She's hungry and needs proper care and nourishment as soon as possible."

"And why has your daughter chosen to relinquish this child?"

Elizabeth thought for a moment before she answered.

"Again, truthfully, Sorella, my daughter did not make the request directly," she confessed as she bowed her head in shame. "She has gone mad and is unable to care for it. It is a bastard, and therefore, I am not in the position to care for it, either."

She looked up at the Sister and spoke directly to her. "The child would fare better if she were placed in a loving home where she could flourish."

The Sister smiled and as she took the infant from Elizabeth's arms, she handed Elizabeth a release form. As she read it over, she saw a place where she could give them permission to contact her should the child be placed, or should she die. She thought for a moment before releasing such information, but she was afraid that should Nancy ever recover and remember what she had done with her baby, she could at least be consoled by the fact that it was given to a good home.

God, forgive me, she thought as she put quill to paper and began to sign. He must forgive me for my daughter never will.

ᏸᎧᏣ

Soon it was July and there still was no change in Nancy's condition. Since the birth of her daughter the month before, she remained in complete silence, her face and eyes affixed on some far off distant place outside of her window; no amount of coaxing or consoling could bring her back. Stephen was beginning to believe that his mother was correct when she'd said that Nancy might never recover, although he wondered how much the loss of the baby contributed to her condition.

On a sultry morning, a letter arrived from the founding hospital. It read, starkly, *Female child, Storace, deceased.* There was no word of her having been christened or if she was given a Christian burial. Elizabeth prayed that if Nancy ever recovered, she would remember nothing about the birth; she could then tell her daughter that it had been stillborn.

Friends and family continued to gather around to comfort and console Nancy in an effort to bring her back. Twice since the birth, Mozart came, but was always turned away by the maid. Michael came every day and sat reading to her out of her favorite book of Shakespeare's Sonnets, and twice she was visited by Antonio Salieri. Nearly every day she was visited by Benucci, who often wept as he left.

ᏸᎧᏣ

The hot July sun bore down on the lawn as Mozart and his little family lazed under a large Linden tree near a pond at the Prater. The park was abuzz with activity: children playing games on the lawn, mothers pushing their infants in prams, couples sitting on rugs eating Italian ices, roast chicken, fresh strawberries, and fresh mozzarella cheese with basil on sliced tomatoes, drizzled with olive oil.

Constanze watched as baby Karl, who was a little over ten months old and who was already beginning to toddle, pulled himself up on the lawn and tried to chase the butterflies that flitted by, only to fall onto his backside when his chubby little legs couldn't carry him fast enough. This was the indolent summer Mozart had promised himself and his family and he was enjoying it to its fullest with no guilt or remorse. As he lay upon the blanket in his stocking feet, he read; another luxury that he'd promised he'd indulge in over the summer.

He loved to read all sorts of subjects ranging from science and philosophy, politics and religion, to the gossip columns in the newspapers. He also enjoyed reading plays, especially the works of Shakespeare and some contemporaries such as Schiller, Goethe, Voltaire, and Rousseau. However, on this day he read a rather new work. In fact, it was so new that it had premiered in Paris the year before in 1784, and from what he'd heard, it had caused a riot. It was by the French playwright, Pierre Beaumarchais and was entitled, *La Folle Journée, ou Le Marriage de Figaro.*

He lay on the blanket and sipped his beer, laughing out loud at the antics of Figaro, who was the Count's barber and valet, Figaro's fiancée Susanna, who was the Countess's saucy little chamber maid, and Cherubino, the fourteen year-old boy who was in love with love. It was a frothy, delightful play, based on the Commedia dell' Arte tradition, with a bit of late eighteenth-century politics thrown in for good measure.

As he continued to read, the wheels in his head began to turn, for the composer in him never rested, and he started to think that this play might make an innovative comic opera. As he mulled over the characters in his mind, he thought of the different singers in the Italian opera company.

Benucci is of course the bumbling Figaro, and we could use one of the women dressed in boy's clothes for Cherubino, and Nancy! She has just the spit and fire needed for Susanna. She *is* Susanna! Then he remembered that Nancy was still secluded in her room, not speaking, and he put the book down, allowing his mind to rest on her.

She's been through such a terrible year, he thought. It all started with that husband of hers! The righteous indignation welled inside of him. "f only I'd had the chance I would have killed that ass.

As he thought on it further, however, he couldn't help but wonder if he hadn't hurt her almost as much as Fisher, except that the bruises he inflicted were to her heart. He remembered the night at the Baroness's when she'd sung the Handel piece and how his heart went out to her as she sang of suffering and longing for freedom from pain. He'd fallen completely in love with her then.

No, I will not accept the blame, he argued with himself. I never intended any harm. That's the difference. Ah, Nancy, he sighed. What am I to do?

He turned to watch Constanze as she sat on the lawn playing with their son, holding him in her lap and kissing his fat little fingers. She was a good wife and a good mother, and he cared for her a great deal, but she'd never ignited his soul. She was pretty enough with her large dark brown eyes and thick, straight, dark hair that hung like a drape. She was charming and sweet, with a playful sense of humor, very like his. But after he met Nancy, he found it difficult not to compare them and find his wife lacking.

He thought back to the days when he'd rented a room from Constanze's mother not long after he'd arrived in Vienna and split from Archbishop Colloredo's service. Frau Weber saw opportunity to still bring Mozart into the family after the break-up with Aloysia and she manipulated things in such a way that he and Constanze often found themselves in tempting and compromising situations. Then when they finally succumbed and went too far with their petting, she forced him into a contract of marriage with her daughter, threatening to ruin him if he refused. He married Constanze in August of 1782 and Nancy arrived in Vienna the following January.

I shouldn't have married, he thought with regret. If only I had waited six months.

He had never known a woman like Nancy. She was independent, intelligent, educated, and outspoken. She possessed a wicked sense of humor, which played itself out beautifully both on the stage and off, with an air of confidence and strength that he had never observed in any woman he'd ever known. To him, she was a woman who thought like a man and that fascinated him. Then when they became friends he discovered the many things that they had in common, not the least being their mutual love and dedication to music. She was his musical peer in many respects and that was her greatest appeal.

How could I have resisted her? I'm only a man, he thought as he picked up the book, opening it to where he'd left off.

Act I, *Le Nozze di Figaro*

Chapter Eleven

*I*t was yet another hot mid September afternoon and Elizabeth was out shopping, enjoying a day away from caring for Nancy. Stephen wandered through the apartment opening every window he could in order to catch what breeze there was, if any. He was barefoot, wearing only a pair of cool linen breeches and his thinnest cotton shirt with the tails left hanging out, the sleeves rolled up to his elbows. On his way down the hallway toward the salon, he suddenly met with a sound that he hadn't heard in over three months.

Could it be? he wondered as his heart skipped a beat. "It's Ann! My God, she's singing!"

Plaisir d'amour ne dure qu'un moment
Chagrin d'amour dure toute la vie.

The last three months had been harrowing at best. After the loss of her child, Nancy only seemed to slip further and further away from them. They tried everything to bring her back, reading to her from her favorite book of Shakespeare sonnets, sitting her at the table to watch as they played her favorite card games, even sitting with her at the fortepiano and playing her favorite music, but nothing could coax her from her world of isolation and silence. Stephen once suggested that they invite Mozart to come visit with her, knowing their dear friendship, he thought it might help, but he met with a near violent response from his mother at the suggestion. They had tried all that they knew and were nearly ready to give up hope that she would ever recover.

Elizabeth insisted that Stephen and everyone close to Nancy who knew, keep silent about her condition. Word was on the streets that she suffered from a strange case of chronic laryngitis brought on by hysterical trauma, but all who were close to the family knew she suffered a deeper madness that was more than Elizabeth was willing to divulge.

He paused a moment to make sure he wasn't hearing things and then he tiptoed into the salon so as to neither startle nor disturb her. As he approached the scene, he could barely contain his emotions. There she sat upon a small gilded chair, singing and playing her guitar. Her voice was clear and strong, and he swore they were the most beautiful sounds he had ever heard. He stopped in the doorway, listening as she continued to sing, totally lost in the music and completely unaware of his presence.

The pleasure of love lasts only a moment
The pain of love lasts your whole life through.

When she finished, she sat quietly and laid her face upon the body of the guitar, strumming and picking it, taking in the sound and feeling the vibrations through her cheeks. She allowed the sounds to fill her entire being, remembering how music used to fill her heart with complete, indescribable joy. When she looked up and saw her brother standing in the doorway, she smiled and said softly, "Hello."

"You're back. We've missed you." His voice quivered.

"I've missed you too. But don't worry, I don't think I'll be going there ever again."

"Oh Kitten," he cried, "We thought you were lost forever." He ran to her and scooped her up in an embrace.

As her arms enveloped him, she whispered in his ear, "I love you, Stephen. Thank you."

&⊃⊂&

"Pardon me, Wolfgango, if I'm interruptin' your work," Kelly said as he entered the Mozarts' salon. "But I've got some news that I think would be best comin' from a friend than by way of local gossip."

"No, not at all Kelly, please, have a seat." He gestured to a chair across from the settee.

"I've just come from the Storace's where I've been to see Nancy."

"And what news," Mozart asked anxiously. "Is there any improvement?"

"Well that's what I came ta tell ya, boyo," he said with a grin. "I thought it best ya heard this from me so you could have the chance for an honest reaction."

"What, Kelly? Is it good news?"

"Indeed, quite. It seems Stephen was makin' his way down the hall from one of the other rooms in the house earlier this mornin' when he heard singin' comin' from out of the salon."

Mozart's eyes grew large. "Yes?"

"Well it was Nancy singin', of course. She was sittin' there bright as day strummin' her guitar and singin' as beautifully as if she hadn't missed a day. Stephen says he was quite overcome with the sight of it."

"Ah! Excellent news, Kelly," Mozart exclaimed. "Very good. I knew she'd come back to us—to her work. She needs her work. It's what she lives for. I'm so glad she's getting better."

Kelly was a little surprised by Mozart's seemingly cool response. This wasn't quite what he expected.

"I think after things settle down a little over at the Storace's, I'll get with Stephen and see if we can't come up with an idea for a little comic piece to welcome her back—perhaps even to perform on the night of her return to the stage. Yes," Mozart exclaimed. "That's it—a little welcome back cantata!"

Finally, Kelly spoke up. "Are ya hearin' yerself, Wolfgango? This is the woman ya fell for—who stole yer heart and who we thought we'd lost ta complete madness. She's made a miraculous recovery and all ya kin say is that yer happy that she can return to her work?"

Mozart's expression grew somber. "I can't think of that now, Kelly…I can't. You were right. I can't divide myself like that. I love my wife and I refuse to destroy what I have for something that could never be." He took a deep breath. "Don't take me wrong. She's a dear friend, and I care for her deeply. I'm overjoyed that she's recovering. It is truly miraculous, but please understand that I simply can't."

"Very well," Kelly said, as he stood. "I just thought you'd like to know. I'll be seein' meself out then."

"Thank you again, Kelly. I appreciate you bringing the news."

ක

When she returned to rehearsals, Nancy's colleagues clapped and cheered. Benucci presented her with a bouquet of roses, kissing her tenderly on the cheek, barely containing his emotion. Salieri, whose newest opera, in which she would premiere in only a few weeks, gave her a medallion of St. Cecilia, the patron saint and protector of musicians.

After her four long months away from her duties, Nancy made a triumphant return to the stage as her audience cheered, and threw flowers. It seemed all of Vienna was there to greet her and as the bouquets and blossoms piled around her feet, she bowed and waved for several moments before she was allowed to sing. At the conclusion of the final act, Stephen, Mozart, and Salieri performed a little piece that they composed together, for which Da Ponte wrote the text, entitled *Per la Ricuperata Salute di Ophelia* (Upon the recuperation of Ophelia), a silly little cantata celebrating Nancy's return, which made her and the entire audience roar with laughter.

She returned to her dressing room afterward to change from her costume, and remove her stage make-up so she could later join her friends at the Milano.

"Are you nearly ready? I'll wait for you here so that we can walk together," Nancy's friend Celeste, called out as she peeked through the open dressing room door.

"That's all right. Go on ahead, carina, I won't be long. Francesco has already offered to escort me."

After she changed back into her own clothing, she sat at her vanity and began to remove the heavy stage make-up, which after her long absence felt good to have on again. It was good to be back. It was right, and for the first time in over a year, Nancy felt the joy and vitality of her life returning to her.

Later they arrived at the Milano to find Mozart, Salieri, Stephen, Kelly, and Mozart's newest student, another young Englishman, Thomas Attwood, waiting for them.

"Brilliant performance tonight, Anna!" Salieri raised his glass to her.

"Brava, indeed," seconded Kelly. "A triumphant night!"

Everyone joined in raising their glasses in celebration. "Brava, Ophelia! Brava!"

"So, Storace," Lange said, turning to Stephen, "I hear you're to return to England soon."

"Indeed, sir. I have employment there, and I was only given twelve months sabbatical from my present position in order to fulfill this particular commission. However, I do wish to see my sister return to the role I composed for her before I take my leave," he said smiling as he turned to her.

"It's back on the docket for December, I believe," Salieri said, "so you'll be cutting it close, but perhaps you'll get to see her in at least one performance before your departure."

"It's a good piece," Mozart interjected, "especially fine for a first work. It should receive a fair amount of play," he said as he patted Stephen on the back.

"Well, Mozart," Salieri said jovially, "It looks as if you'll be losing one fine English pupil only to gain another." He gestured to Thomas Attwood, who sat next to Michael. "Tell us, Attwood, what brings you to Vienna?"

"Why, Mozart, of course. Stephen wrote to me several months ago and informed me of his work with him. He highly recommended that I consider coming to Vienna to study with him as well. I took his recommendation into consideration, and here I am," he said as he placed his hand on his heart and tipped his head to Mozart.

"It seems you've developed yourself quite a glowing reputation among the English," Salieri said as they all laughed good naturedly. Mozart smiled and shrugged.

"Much of that reputation is due to the Linley and Storace connection," Attwood added. "They're two of the most prominent theater families in all of England. We're looking to introduce Italian comedy there, and Mozart has been most willing and available with his assistance."

"None of this would have come about without my sister," Stephen announced proudly. "She's the one who obtained the commission for me in the first place, although she has never disclosed to me exactly how she accomplished it," he added as he peered in her direction in hope that she would divulge her secret.

"Please, Nancy," Mozart chimed in. "How did you manage such a feat?"

Nancy put her glass of champagne to her lips and replied coyly, refusing to divulge any of the details concerning her encounter with Zinzendorf. "I have my connections, gentlemen."

"Ah, she's keeping secrets. How like a woman! They quietly manipulate our lives, and then they refuse to let us in on it," Mozart said as he took a large swallow from his drink.

As the evening progressed, and the conversation flowed along with the champagne, Mozart noticed flirtations taking place between Nancy and Benucci, who were sitting directly across from him at the table. It started when Nancy whispered into Benucci's ear and then broke into coquettish giggles, followed by Benucci slipping his arm around her waist and squeezing her tightly. He suspected that things were going on under the table that caused Benucci's expressions to freeze as sweat ran in little droplets down his temples. Mozart could imagine only too well what she was doing with her hand under there, and the scene in his mind caused him no small amount of discomfort as he shifted and squirmed about in his seat.

It can't be, he thought, pricked with a tinge of jealousy. What the hell is she doing with him, of all people?

As the crowd dwindled and people began to disperse, Benucci, Nancy, Da Ponte and Celeste left together, walking down the street toward the Imperial apartments where they all lived. Michael hung back to bid good night to Mozart and as they exited the café, Mozart watched from a distance as Benucci slipped his arm about Nancy's shoulders and pulled her close.

"What's with them?" Mozart asked as they paused together in the doorway.

"It looks like he's taken quite a fancy to her."

"Humph!" Mozart grunted indignantly.

Michael patted Mozart's shoulder. "What did ya expect?" They turned to walk up the Kohlmarkt in the late night quiet. "She deserves some happiness, especially after all she's been through. Ya wouldn't deny her that now, would ya?"

"No, but Benucci?"

"And why not, lad? He was kind and attentive to her all the months she was ill."

"He's married too, if you recall." They walked on further in silence before Mozart spoke again. "Mick, I'm torn," he admitted. "I don't know what to do with this... with her..."

"I thought you said you couldn't care anymore, Wolfgango. Is that not what ya told me when I came to ya and gave ya the news that she was recoverin'?"

Mozart sighed. "Yes, I know, I know…"

I warned you, boyo," Kelly replied sympathetically. "She's an easy one to love, that Nancy, and she's hard to forget, but forget her you must."

They hung their heads in silence and walked until it came time for them to go their separate ways, then they bid one another good night and headed for their homes.

ဆၢ

Everything started out badly. As soon as he awakened, Mozart knew it wasn't going to be a good day. He was glad that he had appointments that would take him away from the apartment. Constanze had spent the entire night up and down with Karl, who was teething and who spent the most of the night screaming in pain. She'd tried everything—rubbing his gums with brandy, giving him chicken bones to gnaw on, and rocking him, but nothing seemed to soothe or settle him. She finally brought him into bed and laid him on her breast, where at last they both fell into an exhausted slumber, moments before dawn. Only an hour later, as Mozart attempted to get out of bed without waking them, he caught his knee in his nightshirt and slipped, falling upon the mattress and startling both Constanze and the baby, who began to cry all over again.

"You clumsy man!" she barked. "Why can't you be more careful? I just got him to sleep," she moaned as she sat wearily up in the bed, holding the screaming child to her shoulder and rocking.

"I'm sorry. I tried to be careful, I really did," he pleaded.

She turned to her husband and snapped, "Just get dressed and find a place for yourself out of my sight!"

Grumbling, he threw on his banyan to await the arrival of his valet, who always shaved and dressed him, and styled his hair. He made his way into the music salon where he prepared his morning coffee, and by the time he was ready to sit down with his first cup, Primus arrived to begin Mozart's toilette.

It was mid October and he was in the throes of composing one of the most challenging, and exciting works he had ever attempted. He had finally settled on *Figaro* the month before and he and Da Ponte had an appointment to meet at the Hungarian Crown to discuss the first act and to work out some of the complicated staging that needed to be written in the libretto to support the action, keeping the actors moving smoothly through their entrances and exits, on and off the stage. It was the first time ever that a composer worked so closely with his librettist in the process of the actual writing, so that the action and the music would fit together seamlessly and flawlessly with the text.

Mozart was full of impatient, kinetic energy, and Primus had to chase him all over the apartment to finish dressing him. As he flitted from room to room, he searched for notes—ideas that he'd written on little bits of parchment and left lying in the place where the particular inspiration came to him. At one point, he accidentally stepped on one of the baby's wooden pull toys that lay on the floor. He cried out in agony as he grabbed his foot with one hand, hopping about on one leg.

"Scheisse!" he cursed as he turned his foot over to examine the bottom, where a little bruise was already beginning to form. "Why doesn't she pick these Gott verdammt things up?" he yelled as he hopped over to the divan so that he could get a better look at the damage, Primus following closely behind, holding a curling iron and queue ribbon in his hands as he tried to finish dressing the maestro's hair.

When at last he was finished with grooming and dressing, he tiptoed again through the bedroom, where Constanze and the baby were fast asleep. Silently he went into his music salon to retrieve the musical sketches and outlines that he had already completed for act one. As he tiptoed back through, he stopped and softly kissed the baby on the top of his curly head, and left, quietly closing the door behind him.

When Mozart arrived at the café, he found Da Ponte waiting in the back room, which they'd reserved for the entire day so that they could work without any interruptions. Da Ponte noticed as Mozart approached the table, that he walked with a slight limp.

"So what's up with you, Mozart? Did your horse step on your foot while you were squatting to take a shit or something?"

"Domestic life," Mozart exclaimed. "Let me give you some advice about marriage, Lorenzo," he said as he sat down at the table, "Don't get married! You'll only regret it."

"The only marriage I'm concerning myself with at the moment is Figaro's," he replied as he reached to open his leather portfolio.

Mozart ordered a breakfast of cold meats, cheeses, fruit, a soft-boiled egg and coffee, and then set to work.

126

"The challenge we've got here," Da Ponte began as he pointed to a line in the text, "is the fact that we've got to keep Cherubino hidden from the Count, but visible to the audience at the same time. My thought is to hide him under the bed."

"It won't work," Mozart objected, shaking his head. "The audience has to be able to hear him as well as see him. We'll lose him under there. Besides, Susanna has to be able to interact with him during this whole discourse between the Count and Bartolo. It has to be a more convenient hiding place."

They both sat silently for several moments mulling it over when Da Ponte had an idea. "What about a chair? A large wingback."

"How would that hide him? He'd still be in plain sight."

"Not if Susanna covered him with a furniture drape," Da Ponte said, smiling.

Mozart held his chin in his hand and thought for a moment before answering. "It's a good idea," he conceded. "He's hidden, yet still in plain view, and he can poke his head out from underneath the drape and interact with Susanna all at the same time. It would be amusing."

The hours passed quickly as the two men worked and discussed, argued and sweated over every detail, of every action, of every gesture, of every scene in the first act. By the end of the day they were completely exhausted and ready to go home, most certainly after Mozart received the tab that they ran up for the copious amounts of food, deserts, and beer that the two of them consumed in the process.

As they packed the manuscripts back into their portfolios, Da Ponte looked up. "Damn, this is good, Mozart. I've never seen or heard anything like it!"

"I think you're right, Mozart replied confidently. "We're going to take Vienna by storm with this one!"

Day after day, as the work continued, the two realized that they were creating something completely new and different. Mozart told him that he wanted the scenes to be so real that the spotlighted prop in most scenes was a large, rumpled bed, so Da Ponte set about to give him all that he asked.

From the very beginning it had been Mozart's intention to write the role of Susanna around Nancy and to make the character to fit her like a glove. Susanna *was* Nancy, and during the process of characterization, he couldn't help but fall in love with her all over again, for Susanna possessed all the intelligence, personality, wit, and fire that had attracted him to

Nancy in the first place. He instructed Da Ponte to place Susanna in every act and every scene, expanding the role from the secondary place it held in the original play to the most prominent, pivotal, and important role in the story. It became obvious to Da Ponte that Mozart had developed an emotional attachment to Susanna and he wondered if it wasn't rooted in something deeper.

"But you know, Wolfgango, it's Rosenberg's intention to cast Nancy in the role of the Contessa and Laschi as Susanna, don't you?"

"No, no, no! Laschi is all wrong for the part. She can't act! And there's no comparison between the two regarding musical ability. Nancy's skills and training are far superior. We must have Nancy as Susanna!"

Da Ponte paused for a moment and leafed through the pile of manuscript on Mozart's fortepiano--the musical sketches and outlines which Mozart had already begun for the opera--and thought for a moment before he spoke.

"I'm not sure that the Viennese audience will accept Nancy in a secondary role," he replied cautiously. "They've already seen her as the Contessa in *The Barber of Seville*. And as you know, in that piece, La Contessa is the primary female role."

"What do you mean 'secondary role'? We've already written Susanna as the primary role in the libretto! What the hell are you talking about, Lorenzo?"

"I mean we can't bill Susanna as the prima in this opera. Susanna is a servant. This isn't one of your Singspielers, Mozart. This is a piece for His Majesty's National Theater. The Emperor and his noble audiences will not take kindly to the billing of a servant over a countess. You know that."

"Then don't bill Susanna at the top for God's sake! What difference does it make?" Mozart blustered.

"But Nancy is the prima buffa. She's the highest-paid performer on that stage. She always gets top billing. If she is cast as Susanna, she cannot be billed at the top. I don't know if I can convince Rosenberg..."

Mozart chuckled sarcastically. "Da Ponte, my friend, you were the one who presented yourself to the Emperor without any references, having never written a libretto, and convinced him to hire you as his court librettist. Indeed, sir, I do believe you have the ability to convince Rosenberg to cast Nancy as Susanna." He glared at him and continued calmly. "Now do it."

As Mozart insisted, Da Ponte went to Rosenberg and appealed to him as the theater's director to allow them the artistic license of casting Nancy in the role of the maidservant, understanding full well that it would mean that she wouldn't receive top billing, but explaining to him the reason why they felt it was necessary. Rosenberg, who wasn't fond of Mozart to begin with, took some hard convincing before he finally conceded to the idea, most certainly because he liked Da Ponte as much as he disliked Mozart and would agree to most anything Da Ponte asked.

All the acts at last completed, Mozart and Da Ponte went over the last scenes of act four when he pointed to the text that was to be used for Susanna's aria—the one in which she would switch clothing with the Countess and sing as if to the Count, but in reality, she would sing to Figaro.

"No, no, no," he objected, "this is all wrong."

"What do you mean, it's all wrong?" Da Ponte asked, confused.

"I mean, it's all *wrong*, Lorenzo," he replied impatiently. "It's not the right mood. It's too sultry, too coquettish."

"Good God, Wolfgango, she's trying to seduce him," he argued. "She's supposed to be sultry!"

"No, she's really singing to Figaro, who is by this point, her groom," Mozart continued to argue. "I want it suggestive, but innocent, and very tender. She's not seducing him so much as she's inviting him to have his way with her. She's giving herself to him," he insisted. "Submission. This is love she's singing about, not a mere romp in the garden. She's a bride, after all."

"I'll be happy to write it over for you," Da Ponte replied, suspecting that something deeper lay beneath the surface of Mozart's objections. "I just need to know what it is you want."

"I want something private, in a garden with night birds, a silver moon, and flowers and babbling brooks—something romantic, suggestive, but not overtly seductive."

"You're the composer. I give the composer what he wants, and if he wants birds and flowers then he gets birds and flowers!" He had never worked with such a demanding composer. Mozart challenged him, and Da Ponte enjoyed meeting up to it.

"Good. When can you have it ready for me?"

"I can have it for you tomorrow."

"Excellent," Mozart said, with a note of satisfaction. "We'll go over it then."

The next day, when Da Ponte returned with the revised text, Mozart took it from his hand and read silently.

At last comes the moment
When without reserve, I can rejoice
In my lover's arms: timid scruples,
Flee from my heart,
And do not come to trouble my delight.
Oh how the spirit of this place,
The earth and the sky, seem
To echo the fire of love!
How the night furthers my stealth!

Come, do not delay, oh bliss,
Come where love calls thee to joy,
While night's torch does not shine in the sky,
While the sky is still dark and the world quiet.
Here murmurs the stream, here plays the breeze,
Which refreshes the heart with its sweet whispers.
Here flowers smile and the grass is cool;
Here everything invites to the pleasures of love.
Come, my dearest, and amid these sheltered trees
I will crown your brow with roses.

"Perfetto! Lorenzo, you're amazing! This is exactly what I wanted! I can already hear her singing this," he said as he closed his eyes and pictured Nancy standing in the middle of a moonlit garden, the breeze blowing softly through her hair.

"It was nothing. I get a picture in my head and then I paint it with words. Our Susanna will sound rather lovely singing this, I think."

"I agree." He headed to the fortepiano to begin laying out a melody to the text. "She'll be irresistible."

"Indeed," Da Ponte replied softly. "I think she already is." He watched Mozart slip into another world where only he and his music existed. "I'll let you get to your work now," he said as he turned to leave. "I'll show myself out."

৩০০৪

As Stephen sat at the desk mapping out his return route to England, Elizabeth paced and fidgeted nervously. "Mother," he said as he looked up from his maps. "You can still come with me. There's nothing says you have to stay here. Ann is of age now and Mick will watch after her."

"I will not leave her here alone, Stephen, and that is my final word on the subject! She's had too difficult a year and I still fear for her health. I refuse to leave her in this godforsaken place by herself," she said, determined to find a way to get back to England with her daughter in tow.

"But she still has another year left on her contract and she's already confided in me that she will complete it. She's determined to redeem her reputation with the Emperor and seek yet another four-year contract with him. She's quite set on the idea."

Elizabeth continued to pace. "I will not stay here another four years. I simply cannot bear the thought of it. I miss my family and friends. I miss England," she said as she broke down and wept.

Stephen was familiar with this manipulative ploy. He'd seen his mother use it countless times against his father, who, as a man, was more apt to give in to a woman's tears than to her anger. As a consequence it had hardened him to his mother's emotions and whenever she cried, for whatever reason, legitimate or not, his walls went up.

Just then, Nancy came through the door, returning from the theater where she had been rehearsing for her reappearance in Stephen's opera. As she entered, she found her mother standing in the middle of the salon crying.

"Whatever is the matter," Nancy asked gazing at Stephen fearfully, afraid that they'd received a piece of distressing news.

"It's all your fault!" Elizabeth lashed out. "After all I've endured these past three years in this place, and now your brother tells me that when you finish this contract you want another four years! I can't do it Ann. I tell you, I won't! I want to go back to England with your brother when he leaves next month," she said as she tried to compose herself.

"What do you mean it's my fault?" Nancy replied enraged. "What about your part in all of this? Most of what I've been through has come about through your scheming and manipulations to get me back to England in the first place!" she shouted angrily. "Vienna is the highest success that any actress can attain in Europe, and thus far I have been a grave disappointment. I have to stay so I may redeem myself, and nothing you can say or do is going to stop me!"

"And what of me? I'm alone here. I have no friends. Vienna is a strange place full of people with strange customs and an odd-sounding language that I cannot understand or speak. As always, Ann, you and your selfish need to further your career, along with your pursuit of fame and glory, take precedence over the needs of your family!"

Nancy turned away in disgust. She had heard all of this before and could almost predict what her mother would say next. She turned to Stephen, glaring at him as if to say, "How can you sit there and let her say these things to me?" He sat in silence allowing their mother to go on with her accusations, feeling powerless, once more, to intervene on his sister's behalf.

"I blame your father for a great deal of this," Elizabeth continued. "He always indulged you and put these ideas of celebrity into your head with all his talk of the Mozart children and the fame that they attained through their travels. He wanted the same for you," she said dramatically.

Nancy was always amused whenever Elizabeth accused her of being over-dramatic, claiming it was a trait she got from her father.

"He wanted it so badly that he was willing to sacrifice his own career, my happiness, and even the security of our family to attain it. And of course, before he died, he made me promise that I would remain in Italy with you so you could make your reputation there. Well, I've fulfilled that promise, and then some." She paused and thought a moment. "I only promised Italy. I never promised Vienna, and I'm tired now and I want to go home."

What could Nancy say? She could never argue with Elizabeth when she played the martyr and win, so she did as she always did and placated her long enough to keep her at bay, allowing herself enough time to think up a solution.

"You win, Mother," Nancy conceded, the wheels in her head already turning as she thought of a way to thwart her mother's plans. "I'll sit down this minute and write a letter of resignation, and then I'll submit it by hand to Rosenberg this afternoon."

She walked to the secretary, where Stephan rose to give her his seat. She pulled out a piece of parchment. Elizabeth was silenced. She followed Nancy, watching over her shoulder as she penned the letter to the Burgtheater management. "I'll make it effective the end of this year, that way we'll be free to return with Stephen when he goes."

She watched as Nancy folded the letter and then lit the burner under the little pot of sealing wax. When the wax was completely melted, Nancy spooned a little onto the letter and then pressed her seal into it.

"There, it's done. Are you happy now, Mother?"

Elizabeth said nothing as she turned to leave the room, brushing Stephen with her hand as she passed. After their mother closed her bedroom door, Stephen rushed to Nancy and exclaimed, "Kitten, you don't mean it! Don't let her manipulate you into this!"

"Well, I didn't notice my noble brother rushing to my defense!" she snapped at him sarcastically. "You always appear to take her side, Stephen, so she thinks she has you. It was two-to-one; I was out-numbered. So what choice did I have?"

Stephen didn't offer any word on his own behalf, but simply hung his head in shame, pictures of that awful night when he allowed Elizabeth to snatch his sister's child out of her arms and take it to the orphanage still vivid in his memory. He held tremendous remorse for his cowardice in the face of his mother that night, and he proved timid again by failing to confront her regarding this.

"Don't worry," she said as she tucked the resignation in her leather folio and walked to the hall to gather her cloak and hat, "I have a plan. She hasn't won yet," she said, as she flashed him a fiendish grin and opened the door. "I'll be back later."

When Nancy arrived at the theater, she found Rosenberg in his office, so she approached his secretary with a request for an immediate audience. She entered his office to find him sitting at his desk going over the performance schedule for the next year.

"Ah, Signora Storace, I'm glad you're here. I've wanted to go over this schedule for the new season with you for some time. We have several new pieces next year, including a brand new one by Mozart that has quite a large part in it for you," he said as he glanced up at Nancy over his spectacles.

"Indeed, Excellency," she replied cautiously as she took a seat in front of his desk.

"But first, we need to discuss the business that brings you to me this afternoon," he said cheerfully. "I might add before we move on to the subject at hand, that we've all been quite pleased with your performance since your return. His Majesty is extremely pleased and has instructed me to inform you that if this coming year goes as well as the last two months, he is prepared to extend your contract for another four years."

"Well, sir," she said as she took a deep breath. "That's partly why I am here..." She pulled the letter of resignation out of her folio. "Before you read this, Count Rosenberg, I wish to inform you that this was not my idea, but my mother's, and that I wrote this under great duress beneath her watchful eye. However, I am here to submit this to you in order to placate her, in hopes that you will understand that I had no choice but to do so, despite my own misgivings."

She handed the letter to Rosenberg, who looked at her in confusion. As he broke the seal and began to read, his confused expression dissolved into laughter as he peered back at her.

"She is serious about this? She thinks that simply because you submit this letter that we are bound to let you out of the last year of your contract?" he asked, amused.

"Yes, Excellency," she replied as she looked down into her lap, "I'm afraid you don't know my mother very well. She can be a silly, arrogant woman sometimes," she sighed, relieved that Rosenberg didn't seem concerned by the request.

"Well, Signora," he replied as he arose from his chair and reached for a quill. "I will make this decision right now," he said firmly, as he proceeded to dip his desk pen into the inkwell, and then write across the bottom of the letter.

After he signed his name, and sprinkled it with some drying sand, he turned it so that Nancy could read what he'd written. She leaned over the desk and looked. Written in bold letters above his signature was the single word, DENIED. As she looked up at him, a satisfied grin crept over his face. "There now, Signora. I expect that should do well enough, don't you?"

"Yes sir. It will do quite nicely," she said cheerfully, as she returned his smile. "Thank you, Excellency. You are very kind and I am most grateful."

ഇൗൽ

Nancy's reappearance in her brother's opera was a huge triumph. Aware of the significance of the occasion, the audience called her back for several encores and at one point called for Stephen to come up out of his place at the keyboard to join his sister in one of the duets. The Emperor finally had to stand and silence the crowd, which would not be satisfied until Nancy agreed to finish the scene with an extra aria.

It was upon this triumphant note that two weeks later Stephen set off for England with a commission for yet another opera from Emperor Joseph in his pocket, this time won by his own merits.

"I shall miss you, dearest," Nancy spoke tearfully as she stood in the entrance of the customs house to see him off.

Stephen grabbed her up and held her in a long embrace. "I shall miss you, too, Kitten," he replied tenderly. "But I'll be back next autumn with another new opera for you. In the meantime, you keep Mick in line and don't let Mother wear you down," he said as he kissed her on the cheek.

"Write to me every week."

He took out his handkerchief and gave it to Nancy to blow her nose, and replied, "Of course I will, and I'll send presents, too. And if I can, I'll send some of those peppermint ribbons you love so much."

They gave one another one last embrace and Stephen boarded the coach.

Elizabeth was too angry and distraught to go with them to the customs house, so she said her good-byes at the apartment, and afterward threw herself, sobbing, upon her bed as Stephen closed the door behind him. Her plans to return to England thwarted once again, by Nancy's skillful outwitting.

Elizabeth Storace

Chapter Twelve

*T*he winter season had already opened with a brand new opera from the newest composer in town, Vicente Martín y Soler. Everyone was abuzz about the opera's success, as well as its dashing and handsome Spanish composer. All of the Viennese actresses vied for his romantic attentions. Then there was the annual February fête at the Emperor's palace at Schönbrunn, where Nancy had the audience in tears of laughter with her comic impression of the notoriously arrogant and well-known castrato, Luigi Marchesi. In addition, rehearsals had already begun for Mozart's *Idomeneo*, which was to be presented in a concert performance at the Palais Auersperg during Lent, and in which Nancy was to sing the role of Ilia.

It was a frigged January afternoon as Mozart sat in his music room at the fortepiano, rehearsing Ilia's act three aria in which she asks the breezes to carry her confession of love to Idamante, who has gone to battle the sea serpent. The warmth of Nancy's voice seemed to soften the chill in the air which had invaded the room from outside, and he didn't seem to notice the white puffs of steam that poured from her mouth as she exhaled.

> *Zeffiretti lusinghieri, Deh volate al mio tesoro:*
> *E gli dite, ch'io l'adoro, Che mi serbi il cor fedel.*

"That's it, Nancy! Smooooothly…yes…yes," he coached as he raised his hand in the air. "Lovely…hold that now…crescendo…now let it trail off…yes!" He stopped playing and sighed, "Oh how I wish you could have been my original Ilia! How Munich would have adored you, Nancy!"

"I'm afraid I'm far too Italian for the Bavarians," she replied, knowing the Munich audience's less refined reputation. "I fear at times I'm too Italian, even for Vienna!" She laughed.

It's good to hear her laugh, again, Mozart thought as he leafed through the manuscript, searching for another place in the score to go over with her.

"Basta! The Viennese," he replied with a sneer. "They only feign refinement. They'd love to be Italian, but they can't bear to separate themselves from their Weisswurst und Bier! Put a busty tavern wench on stage singing a bawdy tune and all the snobs at court will sing along, waving their sausages in the air!"

Together they burst into a chorus of laughter that echoed through the marble walls of the small music chamber, the joy of the friendship that they both feared had been lost, at last returned.

છબ્ડઉ

Rumors flew around Vienna for several weeks that Mozart and Da Ponte were working on an adaptation of the French play, *The Marriage of Figaro* and everyone speculated over when it would appear on the theater docket. Nancy was especially curious, for Rosenberg mentioned something in their last private meeting about a new Mozart opera that had a large part in it for her, that was to premiere during that season. She remembered how Mozart promised her many times, often in the heat of passion, that one day he would compose a part for her that would make her remembered for all time.

On a cold afternoon, the cast gathered on stage to hear the announcements for the new lineup and to receive their part assignments for the season's opening show. Secretly, Nancy hoped the announcement would come through that Mozart's new piece would be the one to open the spring lineup.

She noticed some new faces, most of them Italian, as well as a young Viennese girl, who couldn't have been more than eleven or twelve years old whose name also was Anna. Benucci arrived shortly after Nancy, and when he saw her standing mid-stage, he slipped out from the wings behind her and gave her a playful pinch on the bum. This startled her, causing her to jump forward. She let out a scream, followed by a fit of giggles. "You're naughty, Cecco," she said, still giggling as she reached around to slap his backside with her closed fan.

"So have you heard what they're giving us today? I keep hearing rumors about Mozart and Da Ponte. I don't know if they're true, but it's the hottest gossip in town. Men are even placing wagers in the casinos and taverns."

Nancy turned to him and with a playful little pout replied, "I thought we were the hottest gossip in town."

"Ah, tesora, we are," he said as he pinched her again.

Suddenly, Rosenberg and Da Ponte walked on stage from the wings and Rosenberg called for order.

"All right, everyone settle down now," he called out loudly. "We've got a lot of work to do today and little time to do it."

When Nancy saw Da Ponte enter with Rosenberg, she knew it had to be true; they were handing out the parts for Mozart's new opera! Her heart began to flutter and she grew excited for she could only imagine how wonderful it would be.

"All right, folks," Rosenberg continued. "I know most of you know this gentleman standing next to me, but for the newcomers, this is Signor Lorenzo Da Ponte and he is His Majesty's court poet. Signore Da Ponte is the librettist for this piece, so if there are any questions concerning your parts they should be addressed to him. The composer for this particular opera is Mozart, with whom I'm sure you are all familiar."

At the mention of Mozart the entire cast began to whisper.

"Settle down people," Rosenberg called out again. "I'm going to call out your name and the part you will play and Signor Da Ponte here will hand you your libretto. Benucci! You're playing Figaro."

"Then it *is* Figaro! The rumors were correct!" Nancy whispered to herself as she jumped up and down with excitement.

"Signora Storace! You're Susanna, the Contessa's maid, who is engaged to Figaro."

As she advanced forward to receive her libretto, Rosenberg pulled her aside. "You need to take this home immediately and get started on it. It's a huge part. You're in every scene."

Nancy's eyes grew large as Da Ponte handed her the libretto and she began to thumb through it, stunned by the number of times Susanna's name was printed on the sides of the page along with the coordinating lines. She hugged the libretto to her breast as she made her way back to her place next to Benucci, who was already thumbing through to find all of his parts.

"Your part is enormous, Anna. I've never seen anything like it. You're going to be exhausted!"

After all the librettos were passed out, Rosenberg called to them again. "Now, the music for the third and fourth acts is not yet completed, so we don't have full scores to pass out. But we do have music for acts one and two, so you may pick those up on the tables as you leave."

Four acts? Nancy thought, reeling at the idea of the amount of music she would have to learn. The average comic opera only had two acts—three at the most—but this one had four, and she was in every scene.

"Read-throughs for act one begin tomorrow, which means Benucci and Storace will be first. Make sure you check the schedule before you leave. There are a lot of characters in this piece, and some of you are playing double and triple roles, so I don't want anyone missing a read-through because you didn't check the schedule!"

Nancy made her way backstage to the slate that hung on the wall next to the door. As she read down the line, she realized that she was the only one in the entire cast whose presence would be required the whole day.

"Would you like to join us at the Milano, Nancy?" Michael called out to her from across the stage, where he stood with several others.

"I don't think I'd better tonight, Kelly. I've got too much studying to do," she replied as she waved to them. "Perhaps another night," she said as she turned to leave.

When she arrived home, she went immediately to her chamber and began to read the entire piece so that she could understand the plot. It was a complicated story with many characters, a great deal of bait-and-switch and mistaken identities. She was a little shocked to read how suggestive and, at times, overtly seductive it was. The part of the fourteen year-old page, Cherubino, was to be played by a woman, Dorotea Bussani, who was one of the newcomers with the cast.

A woman dressed in a man's clothing on stage? How naughty! I know that had to be Wolfgango's idea, she thought as she smiled, remembering a time he asked her put on his shirt, waistcoat, and breeches and prance about the room in them. She recalled that it had in fact led to one of their most heated lovemaking sessions ever. When she got to the fourth act and read the text to her aria she was moved by its sweetness. It was charming and playfully seductive. She knew that he meant it to be their love song.

As she blew out the lights and slipped under the covers into her soft bed, she continued to muse over what she had just read. It had been nearly a year since she'd allowed any tender feelings for Mozart into her heart. By necessity she'd allowed it to harden where he was concerned, for it was simply too painful. But now what was she to do with this? She decided that she would have to wait and see what would transpire between them over the coming weeks.

ೋസ

January in Vienna was most often cold, wet, and blustery, and the January of 1786 was no exception. Already there had been so much rain, snow, and sleet that the Danube was overflowing her banks and flooding was all too common in the low-lying areas. Fortunately the Viennese were far too engaged in the festivities of the Carnival season to pay much attention to Mother Nature's wrathful winter vengeance unless it affected them directly.

To stave off the gloom of the harsh winters, the Viennese celebrated Carnival with an entire season—six weeks, to be exact—of parties, masquerade balls, fêtes, musicales, revelry and merry-making of every kind. Mozart was especially fond of parties, especially balls, for next to music, dancing was his favorite activity, and he was known as one of the best dancers in all of Vienna.

Nancy, too, was an excellent dancer and one of the things she enjoyed most about life in the Holy Roman Catholic Empire was the Carnival season. England, being protestant, didn't engage in such festivities so this was something rather new and exciting, as Carnival was unique to the Catholic nations of Europe.

Every Carnival season a grand masquerade ball was held at the Redoutensaal, a magnificent room in the Hofburg with a high, imposing ceiling decorated in the neo-classical style with gilded crown molding and scenes painted in pastel hues on the ivory wall insets. It was lit by six imposing chandeliers made of heavy Bohemian leaded crystal. Everyone who was anyone was there, including the Emperor, all of the gentry, members and employees of the court, and all the court musicians.

The costumes were as magnificent as the setting, ranging from the demure and whimsical, or characters out of Greek mythology, to local legends and villains. All wore colorful and intricate masks in order to disguise their identities, enabling them to exercise their more lustful, excessive, and sinful natures without threat of disclosure. Mozart's favorite disguise was that of Harlequin, from the Italian Commedia dell 'Arte tradition.

As he walked into the imposing hall, no one recognized him, but neither did he recognize anyone else for all were masked. He was met with a palate of colors, textures, and sounds that were almost overwhelming; bright greens and blues, yellow, puce, crimson and black. There were wigs of all sizes, colors and styles, feathers, pearls, gold chains, and sparkling jewels of every size, cut, and color. There were laces, satins, brocades, velvets, and taffetas that made swishing noises as the wearer passed by. The hall was alive and kinetic with music and laughter and the champagne flowed while the guests drank, ate, and danced, whizzing and twirling by him, the ladies with their heads tipped back in wild laughter and the gentlemen with their arms around their waists, touching one another in places on their bodies where they wouldn't normally dare touch in public.

He stood and panned the room, looking to see if there might possibly be someone he would recognize, when a young woman dressed as Columbine whirled by him and smiled prettily as their gazes fixed upon one another. She wore a black-and-white striped satin bodice with a petite black lace collar that encircled her delicate throat and a colorful calf-length diamond print skirt held out by several layers of petticoats. Her tiny feet were attached to two shapely calves adorned with little black slippers that sported laces which criss-crossed up her calves and tied at the top. Her dark hair was fashioned in rows of pert little sausage curls that bounced as she danced and she wore a tiny little round white hat that sported a large red silk rose blossom and was tied neatly under her chin with black satin ribbons. Her mask was white and covered only the top half of her face, and had one painted red tear that fell from the right eye-hole.

How charming, he thought as he watched her dance away. As she circled by again, Mozart held out his hand and she took it, leaving the one with whom she was dancing to find a new partner.

In 1786 the waltz was brand new, and all the young people were dancing it. Deemed "the dance of the devil", it was regarded as immoral by the older sect, for as the couple danced they touched one another, the lady placing her hand upon the man's shoulders and the man placing his around the lady's waist. In addition to the touching, was also the fact that as they danced they twirled and spun around the room making themselves dizzy. This dizzying effect was made even stronger after a few glasses of champagne were consumed. It was the most popular dance in Vienna and Mozart loved it.

As Harlequin and his pretty little Columbine waltzed several turns around the room, they gazed curiously into one another's eyes and smiled, but neither uttered a word. Neither recognized the other, but as they danced they both got the overwhelming sense that the other was someone they knew. Finally, Harlequin could stand it no longer and he led Columbine to a window on which hung two thick, heavy red velvet draperies adorned with gold fringe, pulled back with large, ornate gold tassels. He tucked her behind one of the drapery panels and wrapped his arms around her waist and pulling her close to him, he kissed her long and passionately. She let escape an all too familiar gasp and then she whispered his name. "Wolfgango!"

"My god, Nancy, it's you," he exclaimed as he released her and stepped back. "I apologize…I, I, didn't realize…" he stammered as he bowed and backed away from her.

Startled, confused, and still dizzy from the champagne and dancing, they paused for several moments as they gazed through one another's masks, each recognizing the pair of eyes gazing back at them. "Please forgive me," he said finally, as he bowed again. He turned then and disappeared onto the crowded dance floor, leaving Nancy standing breathless and alone at the window.

ഇരുൽ

"Come, ladies and gentlemen, let's get started!" Mozart called out as he clapped his hands. The cast gathered around the fortepiano that sat in the middle of a large hall that served as the rehearsal room in the theater. "I need Susanna and Figaro up front please. We're starting from the top of the first act." He sat at the keyboard and played the intro leading into the first scene of act one where Figaro counts out the measurements on the bed.

"Cinque… dieci… venti… trenta … "

"Now, at this point, Figaro, you're to turn and start measuring Susanna," Mozart said as he stopped playing and took the measuring stick from Benucci, so he could demonstrate. "You're not actually measuring the bed so much as you're measuring to see if she will fit into the bed. Do you understand?" He laid the stick against Nancy lengthwise and pretended to measure her.

"Trentasei… quarantatré… "

He started from the bottom of her hemline and began to move up, measuring her until he reached her bosom, and when he got to Nancy's eye level his gaze caught hers, and they both blushed. The other members of the cast snickered when they saw the two blushing, except for Benucci, who stood with his arms folded, his expression somber.

He went to Mozart and snatched the measuring stick from him. "I get it, Maestro," he said indignantly.

Michael, whose entrance wasn't until the next scene, watched with marked interest during the whole first half of the rehearsal as the two peacocks fanned their plumage for one another in an effort to win the peahen, each vying for Nancy's attentions and each one growing more and more agitated at the other as they went. Finally, when it was time for a break, Michael pulled Mozart aside. "What were you doin' back there, Wolfgango?"

"What do you mean, Kelly" Mozart asked, perturbed. "We were rehearsing!"

"No, I'm talkin' about what you were doin' back there with Nancy. I was watchin' and Benucci was just about to tear into ya."

As Michael spoke, Mozart glared across the room at Benucci, who stood with Nancy in his embrace. Several times he leaned over her and stole kisses, nibbling on her neck as she giggled and ran her hands up and down his chest. The sight of the two of them shamelessly pawing one another was almost more than he could take.

"They're disgusting. I can't stand it."

"Then what are you goin' to do about it? You're goin' ta have ta make up yer mind, Wolfgango."

Mozart stood silently for a moment and turned again and glared at the two lovebirds across the room. Then he turned back and stared at the floor. Finally he looked Michael in the eye. "Nothing, I'm going to do nothing. I'm going to get over it and continue with this rehearsal. This is my play and nothing—nothing is more important," he replied proudly as he turned to go back to the fortepiano to begin the second half.

As the first several weeks of rehearsals passed, Mozart controlled his jealousy by staying focused on the task at hand. He couldn't be distracted by the little love affair going on in front of him, for he knew it would be detrimental to the success of his opera.

When *Idomeneo* played during the Lenten season at the Palais Auersperg, Mozart was so moved by Nancy's sensitive and tender portrayal of Ilia that he decided to pay her a visit in her dressing room afterward to tell her so.

As he knocked on the door he called out to her, "Nancy, it's Wolfgang. May I come in?"

"Of course."

As he entered, the familiar sight of her sitting at her dressing room vanity, the aroma of perfumes, powder and stage make-up mingled with her own unique scent, and the soft amber glow of her skin in the candlelight nearly overwhelmed him. He had to stop and draw in a long breath in order to compose himself before he could speak. Her back was to him as she sat facing the mirror, and she smiled warmly as she saw his reflection.

"So how did I do, Maestro?" she asked, cheerfully.

"You were perfect. That's what I came to tell you. I was touched by your performance today. Thank you." He gazed at her in the mirror as he had done so many times before. He remembered the tender and often passionate interludes that began with just such moments as this.

"I know how much you love your *Idomeneo*," she replied warmly. "I wanted this performance to be perfect for you." She hesitated as she looked away from him.

"Nancy, I…" he moved toward her as he spoke. In that very instant he wanted to take her up in his arms and tell her how he loved her and how his heart yearned for her. He wanted to lay her softly upon the divan and make love to her as he had done so many times before.

"Anna, it's Francesco," Benucci suddenly called to her from just outside her door.

"In a moment, Cecco," she replied, startled by the interruption. "I'm almost ready," she called to him as she wiped tears from her eyes.

"I should go now," Mozart said, looking nervously around the room. "It sounds as if you have plans and I don't want to keep you. I…well, I just wanted to tell you how wonderful you were." He smiled as he placed his hat on his head and made his way for the door.

"Wolfgango," she said softly as she turned from the mirror to face him. "Thank you. It was thoughtful of you to come and tell me."

He nodded and left.

෨෦ൠ

"What do you mean you want to change my act four aria?" Nancy exclaimed. "Is there something wrong? Do I not sing it well?"

"No, Nancy, that's not it at all," Mozart replied, trying to soothe her diva's temper. "It's simply not appropriate for the scene. We can't use a big bravura aria there. It doesn't fit."

"So you're saying I have to give up my big aria—that the prima buffa, the star of the entire piece doesn't get to sing her showcase aria? That's absolutely absurd! You're such an ass, Wolfgango!"

"But I promise I'll make it up to you at another time, Nancy—really I will. And in the meantime I'll compose a new aria that's so tender and so sweet that people for all time will know that this was composed especially for you. You'll be immortalized."

At the next rehearsal when Nancy entered the stage in act four, Mozart and Da Ponte settled back to listen to the new aria and for the effect it would make on the scene.

As the strings gently plucked out the soft pizzicato intro, Nancy strolled into place under the painted night sky, surrounded by a set depicting a peaceful, magnificent garden where in the center stood a lovely, romantic pavilion.

Gently, ever so tenderly she sang, *Deh vieni non tardar, O gioia bella…*

As Mozart had hoped, the new piece that was demoted from the big showcase bravura aria to a simple cavatina fit the scene perfectly. It was amazing how just the rewriting of the music—not even a change of text— could make such a difference. It was everything he promised it would be—tender, moving, simple, and gentle, and most of all, Nancy sang it beautifully. After it was all said and done, even she had to admit that Mozart was right, and deep in her heart, she knew that he meant it to be their love song. She was immortalized, indeed. From that point on, history would remember her as Mozart's first and most beloved Susanna.

As opening night swiftly approached, the rehearsals grew more and more intense. Between the difficulty of the music, the complex staging, and the fact that Mozart was beginning to experience some problems with some of his singers, tensions ran high and quite often spats and quarrels would break out among the singers over little, insignificant issues.

On stage, Nancy couldn't have been more pleasing to Mozart. She was absolutely perfect as Susanna and he rarely, if ever, had a quarrel with her. Offstage, however, was an entirely different matter. It seemed to him that every time he passed her in the wings or in the corridor, or perchance met up with her at the café or the casino, during a rare opportunity for diversion, she was with Benucci, which only irritated him. He did his best to avoid her in private situations whenever possible.

One evening after a particularly stressful rehearsal, Kelly invited Mozart and Da Ponte to walk with him over to a nearby tavern to have a few drinks to unwind. When they arrived, they found that several of the cast were there as well, including Nancy and Benucci. The three of them chose a table in the corner and ordered, as Mozart sat and stared across the room, where the two sat and drank with friends. Nancy sat on Benucci's lap and laughed, carrying on with him unashamedly, not even noticing that Mozart had entered the tavern. Da Ponte observed his fixed gaze and turned to see at whom he was staring.

"That's certainly the oddest couple I've ever seen," Da Ponte said, gesturing across the room. "He doesn't seem her type."

"Yes, but they're bloody good together on stage, you have to admit," Michael replied as he took a drink from his beer.

"That they are," Mozart agreed. "They're perfect, and I'm at least grateful for that," he sighed as he drew a long draught from his beaker.

"Well they're about the only principals who are at this point," Da Ponte moaned. "I'm starting to get really nervous about that Bussani woman. Cherubino's too important a role and she's just not putting out like she should. I wrote that character to steal the whole goddamned show and thus far she's not doing it!"

"And I pray that Laschi gets those last measures in the act two finale right or the whole thing is going to come crashing in on top of us all," Mozart said as he wiped his brow with his handkerchief.

"It's a tough piece," Michael said. "Everyone's workin' extra hard on it. I don't know of a tougher one out there. It's a good cast. We'll get it down before it opens, gentlemen. Just you wait and see."

Opening night arrived with all of its usual difficulties; costumes that still weren't quite right, sets that didn't move on and off smoothly or quickly enough, and all the anxious butterflies that flutter in the stomachs of the actors and actresses performing a piece for the first time.

Mozart flitted, paced, and hovered around backstage, barking out orders and calling out to various cast members, reminding them to correct trouble spots, keep the tempo steady in that measure, or to sing out at various points so that the orchestra won't drown them out.

When Nancy arrived at the theater, she found a small gift with a card attached from Mozart, lying on her vanity. When she opened the card, it read:

My dearest Susanna,

On the day we met I vowed that I would compose an opera for you. I pray that it is all that you hoped it would be, and more. You are the fairest of songbirds.

Your devoted
WM

She opened the box to find a lovely cloisonné brooch in the shape of a yellow parakeet, studded with sapphires, commemorating the day that they met at the grand palace reception, three years before.

Oh Wolfgango, she thought. What a sentimental creature you are. Why must we be distanced like this? Say the word, and all will be forgiven.

With the exception of the first act, which went badly because of the antics played by some disgruntled singers, as well as some of Martin y Soler's hired cabals from the audience, the opening was a huge success.

After the first act was completed, Mozart, who was quite distressed over the mishaps and interruptions, came up from his place in the orchestra to the Emperor's box to assure him that the rogue singers (primarily the Bussanis and the Mandinis), were properly rehearsed and knew their parts. They were only acting out, he assumed, due to their disgruntlement over some issues backstage that most likely had to do with Soler's opera having not been chosen as the season's premiere. He pleaded for the Emperor to inflict discipline upon them, a request that His Majesty was only too happy to oblige, also threatening Rosenberg with his job. Thus the rest of the performance went without incident.

Nancy and Benucci were brilliant and all of their arias were encored, as well as all the large ensemble pieces. The whole opera, which was already three hours in length, lasted six hours because the audience demanded that every number be encored, some even twice, causing the Emperor to have to decree that in the next performances that solo numbers would be the only ones to be repeated. By the end of the six-hour performance everyone was exhausted, and there was still the opening night cast party to attend at the Milano, where everyone would wait for the Emperor's review to come in, as well as word from the various private soirees held throughout the city by local theater patrons.

After Nancy changed out of her costume, she went to the Milano accompanied by her usual entourage. When she and Benucci made their entrance there was a loud cheer from the crowd that had already begun to gather. Mozart, who sat near the front entrance, motioned for them to come and sit with him. He was extremely pleased to notice that Nancy wore the brooch that he'd given to her, and he swelled with pride at his ability to give his leading lady such a lovely, meaningful, and costly present.

"Your performance tonight was impeccable," he complimented her. "Susanna stole their hearts."

"She most certainly did," Benucci interrupted. "You completely charmed them, mia principessa," he cooed.

Mozart bristled at Benucci's attempt to trump his congratulations and he sat puffed up like a toad as Benucci continued to sweet-talk and nuzzle her, completely dominating the conversation as well as Nancy's attention. Finally, when he'd had all of it he could take, he got up from his seat and noisily shoved his chair underneath the table in an attempt to startle them out of their trance and make Nancy aware of his disgust. "Excuse me, Signora, but I think I'll join Signore Da Ponte and his party," he said to her coldly as he bowed and then walked to the other side of the room, where Da Ponte sat with Rosenberg and other members of production team.

Moments later, he felt a hand touch him softly upon his shoulder, and he looked up to see Nancy standing behind him. "I would like to speak to you privately, please, Maestro," she spoke formally, as not to arouse the suspicions of those within hearing distance.

Mozart excused himself and they moved together to the back of the room, away from the crowd.

"What was the meaning of that display over there?"

"What display? The only display I was witness to was the disgusting one across the table between you and your horse-faced cavalier!"

"How dare you!" she exclaimed, outraged by his arrogance. "Just who do you think you are? You... you... bastardo!"

Suddenly she grabbed him by his coat sleeve and dragged him into one of the empty back rooms, shutting the door behind them. "I don't understand you, Wolfgango!" she exclaimed furiously. "What is this all about?"

"Well I certainly don't understand you lately, Madam," he replied indignantly. "You're behaving like a whore and I always thought you were better than that!"

"So I'm a whore now? Simply because I'm trying to get over you and find some happiness after the mess my life has become?"

She paced in front of him, angry tears spilling from her eyes. "I know that I wasn't supposed to, but I fell in love with you and my heart broke in two when our affair ended when I," she hesitated, "when I learned I was with child."

"I had no choice," he barked. "I didn't want to hurt you, but I had to end it. I could have lost everything—my family, my career, my future prospects!"

"I understood that, really I did, but you acted so coldly. One day you were speaking words of affection and tenderness, giving me intimate, costly gifts and making love to me, and then the next, nothing. You expressed no remorse, no sorrow or even anger. Your silence spoke more loudly than any of your words of affection. I could have borne your contempt more easily than your cold indifference!"

"I was afraid. I didn't know what to do," he tried to explain. "I wasn't even sure that the child was mine."

He took her in his arms and as he did so, she fell into him and buried her face in his chest. Then, suddenly, she began to beat him with her fists, her anger resurging. "How could you not have known, Wolfgango? Did you think that I would have slept with anyone else after I confessed my love for you?"

She pulled away and began to pace again. "Mother took her from me. Did you know that? The only thing I had left of you, and she ripped her from my arms and left her to die in an orphanage! My family thinks I don't remember, but I have full recollection. I wasn't as mad as everyone believed me to be."

This news took him completely by surprise, for rumor had it that Nancy and her mother claimed that the child was Fisher's and that they didn't care if it lived or died. He was disturbed by the cruel implications of such rumors, believing them to be completely uncharacteristic of Nancy. Now his suspicions were confirmed and it injured him to learn of the additional pain that she was forced to endure, as if the terrible burden she had already borne wasn't enough.

"I don't know what to say. My poor Wanze, you don't know how I've agonized..." he said as he tried to take her in his arms again.

"I don't need your pity! I'm sick to death of everyone's sympathy. 'Oh poor Anna, she's such a delicate little lunatic!' I'm not so fragile that I break that easily," she exclaimed hostilely as she pulled away. "We were such good friends, Wolfgango. Now I wish we were never lovers!" She threw herself dramatically onto a nearby divan.

He knelt beside her. At last, he understood. She'd believed all the time that he never loved her, that he had abandoned her out of callous indifference. What else could she have believed?

"But meine Wanze, don't you know that I love you?" he whispered softly. "I've always loved you. From the moment I first saw you at that reception three years ago, you stole my heart." He leaned over her gently and kissed her hair, laying his cheek upon her soft curls. "I tried three times to visit you during the months you were in seclusion, but each time, I was turned away at the door. I was sick with worry, Wanze, but I didn't know what to do. I couldn't reveal my affections for you, or how concerned I was for fear of suspicion," he continued as he stroked her cheek. "I've been so jealous seeing you with Benucci that I could hardly stand it."

"But I don't love, Benucci," she sobbed, her face still buried in the divan. "I only went to him when I thought you didn't love me."

"But why him?" he asked, with sudden, characteristic indignance.

Nancy arose slowly. "Because he was kind to me," she said as she wiped the tears from her cheeks. "After all I had been through with Fisher, I needed a man's kindness. He was there every day and was so gentle and attentive. But I still loved you, Wolfgango. I wanted him to be you."

"I've missed you so much, Nancy. Please forgive me, sweet angel," he whispered as he kissed her. "I thought I was going to go mad!"

She held him and stroked his hair. "I thought I'd never hold you again, Wolfgango," she whispered. "But what do we do now? We can't let anyone know. It's still too dangerous."

"Then we'll keep it very secret," he said as he held her face in his hands, covering her eyes, nose and lips with soft kisses.

"You know when I go back out there, I'll have to pretend that nothing has changed," she warned him. "Francesco can't know—no one can."

He nodded. "I know. I understand," he assured her.

"When can I see you again?"

"I'll leave you a note in your dressing room. It could be a while before I can work something out, but I'll let you know as soon as I do," he promised, smiling.

Nancy stood, smoothing her skirts and started toward the door when he stopped her once more.

"Wanze," he said as she turned to him, "You were truly magnificent tonight."

She smiled warmly. "Thank you, Wolfgango. It's a divine opera," she replied as she slipped out the door.

Francesco Benucci

Chapter Thirteen

"So how long are you to be gone, this time?" Constanze sighed as she watched her husband choose the clothing his valet was to pack for his trip to Laxenburg.

"Several days," he replied flatly, his concentration focused on what he would need during his stay. "There's the performance of *Figaro* the first night and then I'm giving two concerts within the same week, and I'm accompanying for several others," he continued as he held up his bright green satin suit and examined it, contemplating the occasion for which it might be worn.

Schloss Laxenburg was a generous palatial estate in the countryside, several miles outside of Vienna. Of all of Emperor Joseph's estates, this was his favorite because contained within it were his finest hunting grounds, several lush gardens dotted with pavilions, small forests, wooded paths, a large, picturesque, pond with row boats, picnic grounds, spas, and green lawns which were ideal for all sorts of outdoor entertainment. In addition to the grounds was the palace, which housed a small theater, ballrooms, a large banquet hall, casinos, and several estate rooms. It sat just on the edge of a tiny village that boasted many fine shops, cafés, wineries and taverns, all designed to accommodate His Majesty, his retinue, and his noble guests. Whenever the Emperor took his summer recess, he generally brought his opera company along with several other musicians and performers who were housed in a row of luxurious apartments not far from the theater, and while there, were given free reign of the grounds and use of all the estate had to offer. It was a place of beauty, relaxation, indulgence, sensual pleasures and delights for the enjoyment of the Emperor and his honored guests.

"I wish I could go," she whined as she reclined on the bed and propped up her swollen feet.

Constanze, who was nearly six months along with their third child, had already spent the majority of the difficult pregnancy laid up with various complaints and was particularly grumpy and ill-tempered, and it was beginning to wear on her husband's generally good nature and affability.

"You know you can't, Stanzerl, so there's no point in whining about it," Mozart replied impatiently. "Even I wouldn't be able go if I wasn't one of the hired musicians," he reminded her.

"I'll bet it's lovely there." She sighed as she propped her feet up on a pillow and laid her head back. "All lush and green, with all the finely dressed ladies and polite gentlemen."

"Yes, it's quite lovely." He was still engrossed in the task of choosing his clothes. "But we have access to many of the same luxuries and entertainments at the Prater," he said, trying to appease her. "Why don't you ask your mother or one of your sisters to take you and Karl there for a picnic one day while I'm away? That would be a nice diversion for everyone."

"I don't want to go to the Prater. I'm bored with it. Besides, my feet are entirely too swollen for me to leave the house and my back aches too much for all that walking. She paused and looked around the room, trying to think of a way to steer the conversation in the direction she wanted it to go. "Who all will be there?" she asked coyly, changing the subject.

"The usual people, I suppose. All the gentry, of course, and the retinue and court musicians."

"Will Nancy be there," she asked curiously, looking for a heightened response from him.

"Well I imagine she'd have to be there, now wouldn't she?" He couldn't understand why she would ask such a ridiculous question. She was starting to wear on his nerves.

Constanze bristled at his impatience and as he turned to examine a pair of shoes, she shoved her tongue out at him. Several moments of silence passed before she spoke again. "Is she still seen with Benucci?"

"As far as I know," he replied, trying to appear indifferent. "They were together at the casino after the last performance a couple of weeks ago." He laid several pairs of silk stockings on the bureau, not offering her any more information on the subject than what she asked.

"They seem the odd couple to me," she continued. "They were wonderful together in your opera, but off stage I should imagine that they're strange."

"It's nothing unusual, Stanzerl." He turned to face her. "Leading ladies often take to their leading men off stage. It happens all the time." He was afraid of where the conversation was headed.

"And what of leading ladies and their composers," she asked, venturing down the path which he had already predicted she would go.

"I suppose that happens, too, but I'm not sure I like where you're going with this. If you're suggesting that some impropriety exists between Signora Storace and me, I can assure you that even if the temptation were there, we've not the time, for she is as busy with her performance schedule as I have been with mine," he replied defensively. "And between that and her involvement on the side with Signor Scarecrow, I seriously doubt she has time for, or interest in, any illicit affairs with me," he said as he laughed, trying to erase any doubts from her mind.

Secretly he wondered if what he had just said to Constanze wasn't true. It had been nearly six weeks since the opening night of *Figaro* after which Nancy and he had their encounter at the Milano. However, in the weeks since, there seemed to be little change in their relationship save for an easing of the tensions between them and an only slight easing of his jealousies over Benucci. There had not been time for any consummation of their declarations of love and Mozart had begun to wonder if her affections for him were cooling. Nancy's involvement with Benucci seemed to him as impassioned as ever, as he frequently saw the baritone entering and exiting her dressing room before and after performances, as well as hugging and kissing her backstage. He was beginning to wonder if what she perceived as indifference on his part for over a year hadn't hurt her more deeply than any short but impassioned renewal of their affections could heal.

Constanze noticed as he seemed to slip into his own world at that moment—something that was not at all uncharacteristic of him, especially lately, and since she wasn't getting the response she wanted, she simply shrugged and proceeded to get up and leave.

"See to it that Primus packs an extra shirt or two," she said breaking into his reverie. "It's likely to get warm and you'll need some extras if you want to freshen up in the middle of the day. Oh, and look in the top drawer." She pointed toward the bureau. "Mama tatted some new laces that you might want to take with you," she said as she left the room.

&⁊⊂⊗

Nancy always enjoyed the summer recesses at Laxenburg, for even though she did keep up a rather busy schedule while there, her mornings were most generally free, with an occasional day between performances as well as a more relaxed atmosphere than in the city. Even the Emperor's mood was more casual and it wasn't above him to stop and converse with the members of his theater troupe if he encountered them on the grounds while out and about riding his horse. It was on just such an occasion two summers before, when she and Michael had been riding through the grounds in a carriage, that they encountered the Emperor on his horse. He stopped and asked them how they were enjoying their stay and if there was anything that they needed. In characteristic fashion, Nancy replied rather impetuously, "It is rather hot. Would you be so kind as to fetch us a glass of water?" The Emperor, who was always delighted and charmed by Nancy's often crude candor, replied that he would be most obliged to have one of his servants meet her request, and rode on to see to it that it was done.

This summer's performance schedule was unusually busy but Nancy would still have her off days when she would enjoy picnicking on the grounds, taking long walks in the pleasure gardens, sitting under one of the pavilions and reading, and spending the evenings at one of the many balls, concerts and parties, or gambling with the gentry in the casinos.

On the night of the opening performance, Nancy arrived in her dressing room to find a small, red velvet box tied with what appeared to be a black satin queue ribbon, with a note attached. Upon further examination, she realized that it was from Mozart. She sat down and quickly opened the note and read it.

Meine Wanze,

Please accept this gift as a token of my most profound affections. I fear that I have failed once again in communicating the depth of my emotion for you. I await your word, and should my proffered love be rejected, please know that I could not endure not seeing you again as my adorable little Susanna.

Il Bastardo

She opened the box to reveal a pair of exquisite drop earrings in gold, with a large oval garnet in the center of each, encircled by a ring of tiny diamonds. She pulled some parchment out of a drawer and quickly wrote out a reply, then put her head out the door and called for a page.

"I want you to give this to Herr Mozart, who will be in the audience tonight, but not until the fourth act when my aria begins," she said as she handed him the note and a gulden for his services. Then just as she shut her door, she spied Benucci making his way toward her dressing room.

Damn it all! she thought. Will he never leave me alone?

In the weeks since her conversation at the Milano with Mozart, Benucci had become suspicious, and as a result, rather possessive, which unnerved her to no end. It was difficult for her to find any time away from him to spend with Mozart. She began to fear that Mozart was put off by it and, knowing his tremendous jealousy for Benucci, she thought that his affections for her had waned as a result. She was finally relieved to learn that he was as ardent as ever and she didn't want Benucci to interfere with the passionate interlude she hoped would take place between them after the performance that night.

Benucci called to her, so she quickly tucked the box containing the earrings, along with the note, inside of a drawer in her vanity and replied, "Yes, Francesco, I'm here. You may come in."

He entered to find Nancy lying prostrate on the settee grasping her belly and moaning as if she were in tremendous pain.

"Whatever is the matter, Bella?" he asked as he knelt beside the settee.

"Caro, I am so very embarrassed," she muttered.

"Embarrassed, Carina? Whatever for?"

"I don't know how to tell you, for it is quite indelicate…but…" she hesitated. "Oh what an inopportune time for me to get my monthly! And we were so looking forward to the time alone in this lovely place. Now it looks as if I'll be spending the entire week confined to my room, except for performances, of course and then there's the ball tomorrow night. Of course I have to make the obligatory appearance with Mozart, but I'll probably leave after the first dance or two," she said, hoping she could pull off the deception.

Benucci, who was rather upset by the news that his week-long tryst with Nancy was to be halted by Mother Nature's vengeance, gazed at her, crest-fallen, and tried to conceal his disappointment with concern.

"Will it last the entire week?"

"Oh yes, most assuredly."

"Well, is there anything you can do to ease the pain?"

"The pain will eventually ease up, but, well, I won't be able to…"

"Oh, I understand, Carina," he assured her. "I would never demand that of you while you're..." he said as he lowered his eyes.

"I think that after the performance tonight, I'll go back to my apartments and have a glass of wine and lie down. I'm sorry, Cecco."

"No, no, it's fine," he said shaking his head. "I understand. I should leave now and let you get into your costume. I need to be getting into mine as well," he said as he leaned over and kissed her on her forehead.

"All right, I'll see you in a little while and I'll be just fine," she added to reassure him.

"Good, then. I'll see you on stage."

She felt a tinge of guilt over the way she put him off, especially after he had treated her so kindly over the last months, but she was determined that nothing was going to keep her from her long-awaited tryst with the man she loved. She had done far worse than lie in order to get what she wanted, recalling her encounter over a year before with Zinzendorf. This was nothing.

Mozart entered the theater and took a place near the back, for he wanted to be nearer the doors where a page could more easily spot him, should he receive word from Nancy. As he found his seat, he nervously pulled out his watch and checked the time. It wasn't long before the theater was full—some of the gentry who lived in the area and hadn't made it into the city to see the premiere performances were there, but it was mostly the local peasantry who enjoyed the opportunity to see a quality performance, at no cost to them, a gift from their sovereign.

As the overture began, he fidgeted and squirmed as he waited nervously for word from Nancy. He was disappointed when none came and when she entered the stage for the first scene his heart sank as he realized that he may have waited too long to declare his affections for her, and in so doing, allowed hers to cool for him.

As the first act dissolved into the second and the second into the third, his heart began to sink further. A lump rose in his throat as he realized that his opportunity with her had been lost, most likely forever. When the fourth act began with Barbarina's plaintive aria about the loss of a pin, he almost got up to leave, but decided to stay at least until he could hear Nancy sing the aria he had always considered theirs, but now most likely she sang for Benucci. She entered, looking as darling as ever, and began to sing, causing his heart to sink deeper with every note. Suddenly, as she turned, she lifted her skirt just enough to reveal his black satin

158

queue ribbon tied just above her left knee, and he let escape an audible gasp.

Could it be? he asked himself nervously. She must have received my gift! But what word from her?

Suddenly, a page leaned over him from the back and handed him a note, which he quickly opened to read.

Caro Wolfgango,

Beloved, do not delay, the night is falling. Hasten where love's delight is sweetly calling, until the stars grow pale, and night is waning, while the world is still and calm is reigning. Hurry, my beloved, and meet me at Diana's Temple.

Tua Susanna

He was overtaken with elation at this development, and he struggled with himself to sit through the rest of the opera. As soon as the curtain fell, he ran outside to the garden, knowing that Diana's Temple was a large pavilion in a most wooded, lush, and private spot. It was a little distance from the theater, but once he arrived, he stood within the latticed Baroque pavilion and waited there under the cover of a vast blanket of stars for Nancy's arrival.

After about three quarters of an hour had passed he could see her petite silhouette appear in the distance, approaching the clearing where the pavilion stood. He ran to meet her and they swept one another up in an embrace.

"Oh my love, my very heart," he whispered as he covered her face with kisses. "I thought I'd lost you. I feared I'd taken too long—that you'd grown weary of waiting."

"I would've waited forever, Wolfgango, for there's no one I love as you," she exclaimed as she held him closely.

"I've fallen in love with you, Nancy. I'll say aloud that I adore you," he defiantly declared. "I've been afraid of allowing myself the joy of this emotion, fearing the consequences of such affections, but it only tore me apart and made my longing for you even deeper. Right or wrong, I can't put aside what I feel any longer, Wanze. Right and wrong be damned; I've made my choice."

He held her face in his hands and gazed into her dark eyes that were filled with adoration for him, and he kissed her passionately, covering her mouth, cheeks, and eyelids with warm kisses. Within a few moments he was taking her by the hand and leading her back down the moonlit path toward her apartments. At one point she let go of his hand and ran playfully ahead of him, darting behind trees and giggling as he chased after her. When he found her at last, tucked behind the trunk of a large chestnut tree, he wrapped his arms around her and kissed her until she broke away again. Running down the path, he caught up with her, and took her hand in his once more, raising it to his lips, kissing each delicate finger.

Once they were secretly ensconced within her candlelit bedchamber, they removed each another's clothing, and he swept her into his arms and laid her softly upon the canopy bed. The warm breeze blew in gently through the open casements, carrying the sensual fragrance of night blooming jasmine and roses. And as the moonlight streamed through the windows, it created shadows of their silhouettes upon the wall next to them, mimicking their every move as they rolled about on the bed, fondling and caressing one another's bodies and removing the ribbons and combs that held the other's hair in place. As she rolled her over on top of him, her hair fell gently down over her shoulders, creating a soft, dark, velvet-like frame around her face. He sighed as he took in the lovely sight. Finally, he positioned himself above her and gazed directly into her eyes and declared, "Tonight I will make you mine."

He kissed her mouth, parting her lips with his tongue, allowing the tip to gently glide along the edge of her teeth. His kisses became more impassioned and as he laid himself on top of her, he placed his hands on her thighs and gently parted her legs revealing the soft, pink, moist opening to her temple, the sacred place that was filled with a wealth of treasures and delights, which she declared belonged to him alone. As he entered her she let a soft cry escape and she took him deep inside. She cried out once more and arched her back, raising her breasts high, her nipples firm and erect with arousal. He put his mouth over one of her nipples and began to kiss and lick it with the tip of his tongue, his thrusts reaching deeper and deeper inside of her and growing more rapid and desperate with each heated moment. Suddenly she threw her head back and began to moan and cry. "Ti amo, Wolfgango!" she cried out as the tears streamed down her cheeks.

"Meine liebes Anna!" He suddenly buried his face between her breasts and thrust hard and deep into her, causing her to wrap her legs around him completely and dig the tips of her fingers into his back.

In an instant they were completely entwined in one another and, with one great outcry, they reached the peak of their ecstasy, melting into each another's bodies and covering each another's faces with impassioned kisses. Then as their passion slowly dissolved into a warm glow, he laid his cheek between her breasts and listened to her heart as it beat rapidly, only slowing as she became more relaxed.

Soon they were lying in a tender embrace in complete silence, and in awe of the overwhelming and dangerous love that they defiantly declared on that starry night. Just as the glow overtook them and began to lull them into a contented slumber, he pulled her in close to himself and kissed her once more, declaring, "You will always be mine, Wanze."

After about an hour passed, Nancy awakened still wrapped gently within her lover's embrace. As she gazed lovingly upon him while he slept, she ran her hand softly across his cheeks and traced the outline of his face with her fingers. She arose and found a sheer dressing gown and put it on. She went to the table to pour a glass of wine. As she took a sip and allowed it to linger upon her tongue, her eyes drifted back to her lover, who was still asleep, so she crawled gently back upon the bed, holding the glass, and positioned herself next to him, sitting just above his head. She dipped the tip of her finger into the glass and touched his lips with a single drop of the wine. As the drop ran into his mouth, he awakened and took the glass from her. He took a sip and kissed her, allowing the wine to pass from his mouth into hers.

"Mmmm…" she moaned with pleasure as he continued to kiss her, almost spilling the wine, "I want some more."

He held the glass to her lips and she took another sip, then leaned forward to kiss his mouth, parting her lips slightly as she touched his, passing her sip of wine over his lips and onto his tongue.

"Are you hungry?" she asked him as he kissed her on her cheeks and along her jaw line.

"I have a voracious appetite," he replied fervently, "especially when the food is so delicious," he said as he continued to kiss down her throat and to her breasts.

"I'm being serious," she giggled as she playfully pushed his face away and then lifted it to kiss him. "I can have the maid bring us something. I'm always starving after a performance, so the cook has food prepared for when I return."

"Absolutely." He gazed into her eyes and gently stroked her cheek.

Nancy summoned the maid and, in a matter of only a few moments, she brought a tray laden with roast capon, cheeses, olives, artichoke hearts drizzled with garlic and olive oil, sweet blood orange segments and ripe strawberries.

As Nancy filled their plates, Mozart found his shirt among the pile of clothing which they left lying on the floor in their moment of passionate haste, and slid it on, and plopped himself back upon the bed, pulled the sheet up over his legs and waited for her to return. He fixed his gaze upon Nancy, who stood with her back to him as she filled the plates. Her dressing gown was made of a sheer, embroidered, peach silk organza, which revealed the soft curves of her form—her tiny waist, the firm, soft, roundness of her buttocks and the fullness and suppleness of her thighs.

It was the first time he ever had an opportunity to take in a woman's entire nude form at one time, for when one engaged in marital relations, the couple always remained partially clothed. Even when he made love to Nancy at the Baroness's he was too shy and polite to undress her completely. He had never even witnessed his own wife fully unclothed. However, this night was different, for the lovers made an unspoken decision as they undressed one another that there was to be nothing left between them. All was revealed in a level of intimacy that eluded even the marriage bed, for this was not about duty to the Church, to one's spouse, to family, or to society. Theirs were the purest and most profound expressions of love, passion, and sensual pleasures that could be experienced between two human beings.

When the plates were filled, she found him reclining against the headboard, propped up on some pillows, gazing at her intently, a smile playing upon his lips. "Why are you smiling?" she giggled shyly as she handed him his plate and climbed upon the bed.

"Ah, Madame, I have been enchanted by the most stunning, most beautiful creature in the world!" he exclaimed as he took the plate from her.

"Indeed?" she said as she picked up a piece of capon from her plate and plopped it into his mouth.

"Mmm…indeed."

"Pray tell me about this enchanting creature," she whispered, playing along with his fantasy as he fed her an olive from his plate. "Could it be a Nymph?" she asked.

"Ah, no, not a Nymph, for although this creature possesses the ability to woo with her hauntingly lovely voice, and she is exceedingly intelligent and beautiful, she is not bent on the cruel destruction of the object of her wooing," he said as he gazed into her eyes.

Nancy laid her plate aside and pulled back the sheet, lifting his shirt up around his waist. "Perhaps, then, she is not a creature at all," she said as she bent over to kiss his thighs. "Perhaps she is a goddess," she suggested as she covered them with soft, wet, kisses.

"Oh, indeed," he sighed as he laid his plate aside and closed his eyes, allowing the sensation of her moist lips to overtake him as they softly brushed his most private parts. "She must be a goddess!"

Before long, she sat upright and straddled herself upon him. As she began to rock slowly and gently back and forth, he opened his eyes and whispered, "Oh yes...most definitely a goddess!"

As she continued to rock gently, she picked up the plate and began to feed him from it once more in an effort to distract him so that his excitement could mount slowly. "So tell me more of this goddess, for she sounds quite intriguing."

"Oh she's very exotic," he replied, going along with her efforts. "She's from a strange, far off island kingdom to the west, where they speak an incredibly odd-sounding language and eat puddings made up of things about which one doesn't want to know," he teased.

"And what does she look like?" she continued as she gestured toward the glass of wine that was sitting on the small commode at the head of the bed. He smiled, then picked up the glass and took a sip from it, and handed it to her. As she sipped, she continued to rock gently, waiting for him to continue with his description.

"Oh, but she is the fairest of the goddesses!" he said as she handed the glass to him to sit back on the commode. "Her skin is like amber honey and her eyes are black and deep," he said as he grasped her hands and intertwined her fingers between his, holding them palm-to-palm against his. "Her mouth is warm and moist and her lips are red and sweet like berries. Her throat is soft and supple and her shoulders are delicate," he continued as their mutual excitement grew. "Her hair is the color of coffee and is scented with lavender and jasmine, and her breasts, oh, her breasts," he sighed as his eyes rolled back into his head, "are firm and tender, like twin rosebuds."

They grew silent as the pleasurable sensations began to grow in strength and intensity. He opened his eyes so that he could witness her passion as it mounted, her breasts growing firm and erect as little droplets of perspiration ran down between them, and the delicious scene only served to increase the intensity of his pleasure.

Finally, in one sweeping moment, she let out a cry, her breasts reaching toward the canopy overhead. His body stiffened and he began to moan. He closed his eyes and his head turned from side to side as the intensity mounted. Then suddenly as he turned his head to his left, he opened his eyes and witnessed the shadow upon the wall that mirrored their congress. The sight of her arched silhouette mounted in pleasure on top of him was more than he could take and it pushed him completely over the edge.

"Ach du lieber!" he cried out as it overtook him. "Mein Gott!"

Their bodies shuddered in ecstasy as he spilled himself into her. He took her face in his hands, pulling her toward his mouth, engaging her lips in a long and passionate kiss. At last, she collapsed upon his chest, her hair covering his face and her body, warm and relaxed. He wrapped her in his arms and held her close for several moments before rolling her over and covering her face with kisses. He had never felt such emotion for another human being and as he gazed down upon her gentle expression, his eyes brimmed with tears that fell like raindrops upon her face. As he wiped his tears from her cheeks, she spoke to him in a whispered sigh.

"I adore you, Wolfgango."

The morning sunlight found them still entwined in each other's embrace. Being the first to awaken, he kissed her softly on the forehead as he pushed aside the stray curls that drifted onto her face during the night.

You're so lovely, Wanze, he thought as she lay slumbering in his arms. I am completely smitten.

He continued to hold her, not wanting to leave the secluded and intimate place where all night they'd engaged in the tender consummation of their vows of love. Knowing that he was to be engaged later that day in two separate concerts, he realized that he needed to get up and make his way back to his apartments where he could dress and ready himself for the business of the day. A tinge of sadness stung his heart at the thought of leaving her there alone, for in a very real sense he felt as if he were being forced to leave his bride alone in their marriage bed, so he lingered a moment longer and allowed her to sleep undisturbed within his embrace.

At last, when he knew that he couldn't tarry any longer, he gently unfolded himself from her sleeping form and pushed some pillows against her in hopes that they would serve to take his place, if only long enough for him to dress and make his way out without disturbing her slumber. He found his clothing in the place where it was left lying the night before, and dressed himself quietly.

Suddenly she stirred and awakened enough to realize that he no longer lay beside her. "Why are you going, Wolfgango," she asked, a little disheartened to find him dressing to leave.

"I'm sorry, Wanze. You were sleeping so peacefully that I couldn't bear to awaken you," he replied, softly. "I'm engaged in two concerts this afternoon and I have to leave so I can prepare for them."

"I suspected as much, but I was hoping that we might have a little more time before we had to be off on our separate ways." She sighed.

"But there'll be much time for us to be together. I won't be engaged again until tomorrow night when I accompany you in your concert. And then there's the ball tonight, at the palace," he reminded her. "I'll be your escort, of course."

Suddenly Nancy remembered the excuse that she made up to put Benucci off, and she was seized with a moment of panic. "But what do I do about Benucci?"

"What about him," he asked indignantly.

"I'm sure he assumed that after our obligatory dances, I'd be spending the rest of the evening with him. Of course I don't want to, but I don't know how I'm going to get out of it."

"Well how did you get out of being with him last night?"

Nancy cast her eyes down and began to finger the ribbon that tied her dressing gown. "I'm too embarrassed to tell you," she said, blushing. She sat for a few moments and thought about it before she confessed. "I told him a lie."

"What kind of a lie?" he asked with a mischievous grin.

"I told him that I was having my time and that I would have it all week."

Mozart burst into a fit of laughter and threw himself across the bed.

"I don't see what you find so humorous about it," she replied indignantly, smacking him on the backside and sticking her lip out in a pretty pout.

"Now that's my little Susanna," he said as he rolled over and took her in his arms. "Sometimes you are just too darling for words!" He kissed her pouty lip.

"I really must be off now, meine Liebe," he said reluctantly. "I wish I didn't have to leave you, but I'll be here early this evening to walk with you to the dance. Then afterward, perhaps we can go walking in the gardens and then enjoy a late supper."

"That sounds wonderful," she replied as she laid her head upon his shoulder. "I love you, Wolfgango."

"And I love you, Wanze," he said as he gave her one last kiss and headed for the door. "I'll see you tonight."

The dance that opened the Laxenburg recess was a gala occasion at which the Emperor was always in attendance, along with his noble guests and various court officials and employees. This meant that formal court attire, including wigs, were in order. For the occasion, Nancy chose a lovely gown made from two contrasting colors and fabrics—the bodice of a deep teal moiré trimmed with white organza lace around the neck and sleeve openings. The skirt was made of a soft pink taffeta, dotted with embroidered roses in burgundy silk thread throughout the fabric. She wore a blonde wig which sported a single queue that fell down the middle of her back and in which she wore a corsage of burgundy silk roses. To add the perfect accent, she wore the garnet earrings that Mozart gave to her the night before as a token of his affection.

When Mozart arrived, he was directed to the salon to wait. He looked handsome in his nankeen yellow suit in raw silk, with a lightly embroidered coral waistcoat—a picture of elegance and refinement as he waited rather anxiously for her to greet him.

He didn't see her when she first entered the room, for he stood at the window, his hands clasped behind his back, peering out into the night sky, recalling the events of the night before at Diana's Temple, when under the very same sky, he declared his undying affection for her.

"Wolfgango," she spoke his name sweetly.

As he turned, he was met with what he believed to be one of the loveliest, most exquisite sights he ever beheld. There she stood all dressed in blue and pink, with flowers in her hair, her charming dark eyes peering into him from over her fan.

He took her hand and twirled her slowly so that he could look at her from all sides. "My darling, you are enchanting!" He was unable to take his eyes off of her. "I shall be the proudest peacock at the ball!"

"I'm wearing your earrings," she said as she tipped her head to one side, making them sparkle as they caught the light.

"Indeed you are, and they look exquisite against your skin." He took her by the waist and pulled her in close. "I have half a mind to skip the dance and take you to bed this instant and ravish you, except that it would be an utter shame for me not to take you out and show you off."

It was a balmy evening and as they walked to the palace, they passed several other couples, all dressed in their finery, leisurely strolling the walkways which were lit with colorful Japanese lanterns, placed in rows along the edges of each path. As they strolled with her arm tucked into his, they could hear the pleasant din of cheerful voices engaged in conversation, the sounds of laughter rising in the distance, and the playful giggles of young lovers as they ducked behind the occasional tree or into a nearby archway to engage in a little petting along the way.

At one point Mozart, who was easily stimulated and aroused by the sights and sounds around him, took his irresistible lady by the hand and tucked her behind a large topiary. There he proceeded to kiss and fondle her up and down, lifting her skirts so that he could raise one of her legs and run his fingers up her delicate silk stocking past the pretty pink satin ribbon which held it in place, to the soft, smooth skin of her thigh and around to her buttocks.

"Mmmm…" he moaned as he nibbled her lip, "perhaps I should have ravished you back in your apartments. I don't know if I can wait all night," he whined playfully.

When they arrived at the palace, they were announced as they entered the ballroom, and greeted by the Emperor and his guests of honor. Mozart puffed up with pride as His Majesty complemented both of them, once again, on the successful opening of *Figaro*, and then he escorted his lovely Susanna to the middle of the floor to begin the allemande.

The ballroom at Laxenburg was decorated in typical ornate Baroque fashion, the walls lined with white Corinthian columns sporting gold sconces with heavy lead crystals hanging from each globe. The wall panels were ornately gilded on the edges and painted with lush, pastoral scenes in soft pastels, of lovely young men and women dancing and playing flutes and guitars. The ceilings were frescoed with pastel pink and blue skies and puffy white clouds with fat cherubs perched upon them, peering down to gaze upon the dancers on the floor below. Two enormous and ornate crystal chandeliers hung from the ceilings, illuminating the entire room with the bright but soft glow of the hundreds of candles contained in each of them.

All eyes were on Mozart and his pretty partner as they bowed and curtseyed to each another, and began to dance. As they fell into two lines, the ladies on one side and the gentlemen on the other, they turned shoulder to shoulder and stepped forward in sync several steps, before facing one another as the gentlemen took their partners by the hand and twirled them gracefully until they ended up on the opposite side. Then they all stepped to one side, the gentlemen to the right and the ladies to the left and, extending their hands across the divide, they took the hand of the lady or gentleman in front of them and made a skip-hop step to the right. Then the left-over lady and gentleman on the opposite ends skipped into the divide and took one another's hands and faced forward to promenade down the middle of the two lines, each couple following suit until they were back in their original places with their original partners. Each time Nancy returned to Mozart, she beamed with delight.

In one corner of the room, standing near the refreshment tables, was Benucci, who saw as Mozart entered with Nancy on his arm and unashamedly escorted her to the middle of the dance floor. As he sipped from his glass of champagne, he seethed with hurt and humiliation as he recalled the night before when Nancy called off their engagements.

It wasn't at all unusual for an actress to set her cap for the composer of a new opera and carry on a passionate but short-lived affair with him, especially when the composer featured her as prominently as Mozart featured Nancy in *Figaro*, but Benucci didn't care. He was insulted by her throwing him off in the fashion in which she did, so he stood in the corner and watched as the two of them danced, allowing his hot Italian temper to seethe.

When the dance ended, they bowed and curtseyed, and Mozart took Nancy's arm and led her gracefully off the floor. "I'm dying for some champagne," he said as he set his thirsty gaze upon the refreshment table. "But look who's there." He tipped his head toward Benucci, who was throwing back glass after glass of champagne, glaring at them from across the room.

"I saw." She snapped open her fan and glared back. "He doesn't look very pleased," she said nervously.

"No, he doesn't. I think I'll wait until he decides to move," Mozart said, wondering how many glasses Benucci would consume before his temper would flare and cause a scene.

Just at that moment, Nancy felt a gentle touch on her shoulder and when she turned, she was greeted by a warm and familiar smile.

"My dear, what a pleasure to see you again." the Baroness exclaimed.

"Madame!"

"And Mozart, what a double pleasure to see the two of you together," she said as she extended her hand to him.

"The pleasure is all mine, Madame." He bowed, kissing the Baroness's hand.

"I must tell you that I was simply enchanted by your *Figaro*, Mozart," she said as she took Nancy's arm. "And this little lady, oh my…My dear, you were simply stunning. I returned for the second performance the next day and would have returned for the third, but I was called away."

"I'm overjoyed, Madame. I was rather concerned over how it would be received, but I have heard so many gracious compliments that my concerns have been arrested," he said as he glanced again toward the refreshment table to see if Benucci was still there. When he saw that he was gone, Mozart turned to the two ladies and offered them some champagne.

As he headed for the table, the Baroness took Nancy by the arm and pulled her out away from the fray and opened her fan to hide her face so she could speak candidly. "I'm thrilled to find you here with Mozart. I thought that after your rather unfortunate incident, it was over between you."

"As did I, Madame. In fact, we've only just been reconciled in the last two days."

"Well he looks rather, dazed, Nancy dear. What have you done to win him back," the Baroness asked curiously, gazing at Mozart who was detained at the table by several gentlemen who wished to congratulate him over *Figaro*.

"It seems that I never lost his affections. There were simply…well, there were complications…"

"You know that there are ways to prevent such complications," the Baroness replied discreetly.

"Yes, I know that now. I've taken measures to prevent it from happening again."

"Good then. Lovers can't enjoy one another with total abandon when they're concerned with such matters. He'll love you more for it, be assured."

Just then, Mozart returned with the champagne, smiling broadly and notably more relaxed than he was when he had left them moments earlier.

"I watched as you two lovely ladies gossiped and I simply won't be satisfied until I know what passed between you," he said as he handed each one of them a glass.

"Signora Storace and I were simply discussing the virtues of peace of mind and complete abandonment, and how it is conducive to love," she replied as she held up her glass. "Rest assured your secret is safe with me. Indeed, I'm very happy for you both. Now, if I may excuse myself, I believe that I see the Countess Thun over in that corner, and I desire to speak with her."

"Of course, Madame. It was a pleasure beyond compare," Mozart replied as he bowed to her.

"Beyond compare." She smiled wickedly. "If you two need somewhere to rendezvous," she added as she turned to leave, "you know where you are always welcome."

They danced the rest of night together, barely taking a break to catch their breath and caring little over the tongues that were already beginning to wag concerning them. Finally, at one point during the evening, Michael cut in and, during the dance, he confronted Nancy over their indiscretions.

"It's none of your business, Mick," she replied adamantly. "You're not my father and I won't have you interfering!"

"But have you seen how Benucci's been watchin' you? I'm afraid for the both of you, Nancy. People are goin' to talk and somebody's bound to get hurt," he warned her.

"Mick, that's enough," she exclaimed as she turned and walked off the dance floor. "You and Mother can't seem to get it through your thick skulls that I'm not interested in your opinions on this matter," she replied, annoyed by his intrusion. "I love him, Mick, and nothing is going to change that."

"But Nancy, me dove, you can't spend your entire lives at Laxenburg. One day you have to go back into the real world and then what are you goin' to do?" he pleaded with her.

"We will deal with it when it comes, but for right now, Michael, I'm happy. I'm wondrously, gloriously happy. Please don't rob us of that. If you care for us, you will allow us this time," she begged him.

"All right, Nancy," he conceded, reluctantly. "The good Lord knows ye do have some happiness comin' to you. It's just that I care for you both, and I can't bear the thought of either of you bein' hurt. But if this is how you want it, I'll let it be."

"Thank you, Mick," she said as she took his hand. "I couldn't love you more if you were my own brother. We'll be all right, you'll see." She kissed his cheek and then she made her way to the other side of the dance floor where Mozart waited to lead her in the last waltz.

As Benucci stood watching from the end of the floor, it was all he could take, and he hurled the glass of champagne he held in his hand into the enormous marble fireplace, which stood at the end of the room, shattering the glass into hundreds of pieces. Then he flew out the doors and out of the palace. Those standing nearby muttered amongst themselves over what would illicit such a reaction from someone as mild-mannered and even-tempered as Francesco Benucci, but as Kelly stood nearby, watching the spectacle, he knew that this was only the beginning of the troubles that would result from the forbidden romance between his two dearest friends.

ॐ

The next morning found the lovers wrapped in each another's tender embrace, just as they were the morning before, except on this glorious day, they were afforded the luxury of remaining in one another's arms until they were ready to awaken. After that, they would prepare for a day that would be spent entirely with each other, doing whatever they liked. When they did awaken, they couldn't resist the passionate urge to indulge in a little more lovemaking. Afterwards, Mozart returned to his rooms just long enough for the both of them to dress.

When he returned to retrieve her, he found her dressed for a picnic in a day gown made of soft pastel green cotton with a white organza ruffled fichu that criss-crossed the front of her bodice. Her wide-brimmed straw hat, on which the crown was covered in the same fabric as her gown, was encircled by a wreath of pink, yellow, and green flowers. As they headed out the door, laden with a picnic basket filled with wine, bread, cheeses, cold meats, and fruit, they were greeted by a glorious deep blue sky and a warm, yellow sun peeking out from behind a few puffy white clouds.

After they took a short carriage ride to an outer section of the estate, they walked a short distance and found the perfect spot underneath a clump of chestnut trees. Not far from them was a large pond on which several small rowboats with couples in them drifted lazily by. The bright green manicured lawn was strewn with thousands of tiny white daisies and, along the paths and walkways, there were manicured gardens laden with colorful blossoms, fountains, arched trellises and green hedges. It was a lover's paradise, a land of beauty and indulgence where many a clandestine love affair took place, where the cares and burdens of life in the city were shut out and forgotten if only for the moment.

They unrolled the linen cloth which the cook placed in the basket with the food, and laid it on the ground. Mozart set the basket aside, pulled out one of the bottles of wine and searched for the corkscrew that was packed somewhere in the bottom. As he went about the business of opening the wine, she sat and gazed across the pond, watching the lovers pass by in white row boats, their amorous conversations and playful giggles unknowingly amplified, wafting to her ears by the gentle breeze.

This was her heaven, the only place on earth where she and her lover could exist without the pressures and influence of the outside world staring down upon them—judging their love as illicit, impure, or illegitimate—where they could love one another openly and completely with total abandon, with no fear of consequence or reprisal.

She gave a drawn-out sigh as she allowed her thoughts to drift back to Kelly's warning. We can't stay at Laxenburg forever, she thought as a tinge of melancholy invaded her bliss.

"What are you thinking, meine Liebe," he asked in a tender voice as he seated himself behind her and slipped his arm around her waist.

She removed her hat and set it aside, then took the glass of wine that he handed to her and took a sip as she continued to look out over the pond.

"How I love this place, Wolfgango. It's like heaven. I don't want to go back to Vienna. I want to stay here forever with you." She sighed.

"We're here now, Wanze. And we still have several more days before I have to go back. Let's not waste what time we have worrying about it. That day will come soon enough and when it comes, we'll deal with it," he said as he turned her face toward his and gazed into her eyes.

"Promise me that you will love me forever," she said as she rested her head on his shoulder.

"Ich liebe dich, meine Wanze, für immer und ewig und drei Tagen," he whispered.

"What does that mean?"

"It means, 'I luff you, mine little bug, for ever und alvays und dree days'," he translated as he kissed the dark wisps of hair that lay along the nape of her neck. "We have a lovely picnic and another entire bottle of wine that I don't intend to take back unopened," he said with a playful grin. "I was hoping that I might find a pretty young lady to share it with."

Together they unloaded the basket, and after they filled their plates, they sat on the lawn and ate and drank. Afterward when the wine began to go to his head a little, he laid it in Nancy's soft lap and slept while she picked some of the tiny daisies that were growing on the lawn all around where she was seated. After she picked several, she began to plait them into a chain and weaved the chain into a wreath. After several minutes, Mozart awakened from his peaceful slumber to hear Nancy softly singing her sweet little cavatina from act four. When she came to the part in the aria where she sang the words, "I want to crown your head with roses," she placed the crown of daises upon his brow and then she leaned over and kissed him tenderly. He returned her kiss, lifting his hands and cupping her face, and pulling her toward him. Gently he laid her upon the ground and laid himself on top of her, stroking her cheeks softly with his fingers and brushing her lips. "Du bist so schönn, meine Wanze," he cooed.

He sat up and opened another bottle of wine and poured a glass for each of them and as they sat together under the shade of the chestnut grove, drinking their wine, they talked. They spoke of poetry, philosophy, art, history and, of course, music. When he mentioned his love of Shakespeare and how he might be interested in composing an Italian opera based on one of his comedies, her face lit up with excitement.

"I simply adore Shakespeare," she exclaimed gleefully. "I've memorized all of his sonnets," she said as she went digging through the basket for the little book of sonnets she just happened to pack so that she could read some to him.

Although he spoke some English, they most generally spoke to one another in Italian. However, occasionally, he made a genuine effort to speak English, as he was very interested in the possibility of one day traveling to England to compose for the King's Theater, in London. He had the opportunity to sharpen his English skills when he worked closely with Stephen on his opera and now, with Nancy, the opportunity arose again for him to hone his skills even further.

"Plees," he spoke in English with a heavy German accent, "read some uff dem to me."

"Let me see," she said as she thumbed through the little leather-bound book. "Oh here's a lovely one!"

Let me not to the marriage of true minds
Admit impediments. Love is not love
Which alters when it alteration finds,
Or bends with the remover to remove:
O no! it is an ever-fixed mark
That looks on tempests and is never shaken;
It is the star to every wandering bark,
Whose worth's unknown, although his height be taken.
Love's not Time's fool, though rosy lips and cheeks
Within his bending sickle's compass come:
Love alters not with his brief hours and weeks,
But bears it out even to the edge of doom.
If this be error and upon me proved,
I never writ, nor no man ever loved.

"Dis English is very difficult to unterstant," he said shaking his head as he tried to read some of the lines of the sonnet for himself. "I'm afraid you vill haff to explain it to me," he said, chuckling at himself.

"Well," she began, "it is about love and the marriage of two souls," she said as she pointed to the line where it spoke of the marriage of true minds. "What he is saying here is that when two souls are brought together in love's eternal bond, nothing can or will shake it. See here where he says, *'O no! it is an ever-fixed mark that looks on tempests and is never shaken,'*" she asked him as she pointed to the line. "Ever-fixed means permanent and stable. It is a love that weathers all storms and remains strong. It is true and constant, ever faithful," she explained as she looked into his eyes which suddenly filled with the light of comprehension.

"Yes, I know dis kint uff luff," he whispered. He kissed her softly, pondering the meaning of *'the marriage of true minds'*. "Dis is da luff I haff mit you, Wanze." He peered into her eyes. They sat in silence, both of them fully comprehending the sonnet's profound implications for them and they allowed themselves to be swept up in the moment.

"Please, Wolfgango," she said as she held the book out to him. "I want you to have this. I know all of them by heart."

"Danke. I vill treasure it alvays," he said as he picked one of the tiny daisies and placed it between the pages, marking the place at Sonnet 116. As he slipped the book into the pocket of his waistcoat, he pulled out his watch and looked at the time.

"It's about time for the carriage to arrive to take us back. Perhaps we should pick these things up so that we'll be ready when they come," he said to her as he gave her his hand to help her to her feet.

"Very well," she said smiling. "I'd so completely lost myself in the enjoyment of the day that I forgot all about the time."

"We have to go prepare for your concert this evening."

"Yes, of course. I'd completely forgotten that too," she said as she helped him pick up the linen cloth and fold it.

"Wanze…" He paused. "Please know that no matter what happens I will always love you. Our souls are joined together…" he searched for the words "we have the marriage of true minds."

"It is an ever-fixed mark that looks on tempests and is never shaken," she replied.

"Yes," he said thoughtfully, "an ever-fixed mark."

The remainder of the week passed all too quickly and, as the day of his scheduled return to the city grew nearer, the more time they spent sequestered in her rooms. He promised her that although he was only on the performance schedule for two more concerts for the remainder of the recess, he would try to find a way to carve out a few more days without his wife growing suspicious. Of course, there were always the nights that he could claim that he was going to lodge meeting and might be able to sneak away for a few precious hours, but he would have to leave Laxenburg in time to return to the city before the gates closed, leaving them with very little time in between.

Then there were the issues with Benucci. Since the night of the ball, the gossip flew, and anywhere Mozart was seen with Nancy at Laxenburg, all eyes were upon them. It had already hit the streets of Vienna, where Mozart was sure that Aloysia would hear it and pass it on to Constanze. This would make life at home almost unbearable for him. A dreary melancholy overshadowed their last night at Laxenburg, and their usually tranquil and euphoric lovemaking was invaded with a desperate sense that it was to be their last for perhaps a very long time.

"What's to become of us now," she asked as she lay in his arms dreading the moment when he would be forced to tear himself away from her embrace. They had precious little time before he had to dress and leave to catch the last coach that arrived in Vienna, before the city gates closed.

"We'll be all right, Wanze," he sighed as he drew her in closer, burying his face in her hair. "We'll work it out. We only have an hour left before I leave and I don't want us to spend it like this," he said as he began to kiss and nuzzle her. "Please," he cajoled, "allow us the sweetness of our love without the bitterness of regret."

And so she yielded to his request and gave herself to him once more, with total abandon, giving no thought or worry to what the future might bring.

ᔒᦡᦐᦡᔓ

Elizabeth sat at her writing desk penning yet another letter to her sister, Mary, in England when Antonia entered carrying a post from London.

"It looks like another letter from Herr Stephen, Madame." She curtseyed and handed it to Elizabeth.

"Ah! I've been waiting for this! Thank you, Antonia," she replied as she took the letter and anxiously broke the seal. "Would you close the doors as you leave, please?"

"Ja, Madame."

Elizabeth carefully unfolded the parchment and began to read.

Dearest Mother,

I pray this letter finds both you and Kitten well and enjoying the warmer temperatures that the summer months have afforded. Our weather here has been quite temperate and I have taken advantage of it with an occasional excursion to Bath to take in the waters and the company. Aunt Mary sends her best as do Lord Sheridan and his wife, which leads me to the subject at hand.

I was rather shocked to learn from you that in spite of the fact that Ann has achieved such acclaim in Vienna due to her recent success in Mozart's newest piece, that she has decided to return to England rather than sign on with the Emperor for another four years. Nevertheless, I supposed much of it was due to Kelly's recent decision to return due to his mother's failing health. Assuming that this was true, I have discussed with the management at Covent Garden the possibility of his taking her on, and their response was most enthusiastic. Since our last conversation, they have drawn up the contract and I have taken the liberty of signing it on Ann's behalf. (I have enclosed a copy of it in this post.) Unfortunately, I was only able to sign her on for one year, as they desires to bring her in on a trial basis before hiring her on permanently.

I will return to Vienna at the end of August to fulfill another commission and will stay until Ann's contract it fulfilled at the end of the following February. You will be free to return to England with me then.

Please give Kitten all my dearest affections and many kisses, saving some for yourself.

Your devoted son,
Stephen

"Very good," Elizabeth said aloud, as she opened the enclosed contract and read it over, silently. She had finally pulled it off. At last, after nearly ten years away from her home, her family, and her friends, she would return. She didn't know how she was going to break the news to Nancy, whom she knew would fly into a rage. But it would be short-lived. Once she was used to the idea, Elizabeth knew Nancy would realize that it was for the best for all concerned, including Nancy.

When Stefano Storace first came to London in 1760, Elizabeth was barely fifteen years old. As the proprietor of the Marylebone Pleasure Gardens, Elizabeth's father hired Storace to be the manager of the garden's theater, and it wasn't long before shy, pretty Elizabeth caught his eye. The Truslers were a prominent and respected educated working-class family in London and Elizabeth and her sisters were educated and raised in the fashion of nobility. The family was known as expert bakers and pastry-makers and their pastry shop, located within the gardens, was considered the finest in London. Consequently, when Elizabeth and Stefano were betrothed, she brought with her a fine dowry as well as a sizeable family inheritance.

Elizabeth, although extremely pretty and intelligent, was painfully shy, and although she was highly attracted to her husband's strong, forward, but warm and vivacious personality, whenever it brought her into the forefront, she was barely able to resist hiding behind her fan. Because of her shyness, she didn't understand, or appreciate his love for the stage or the theater, and because she was so close to her home and family, she had no appreciation for his wanderlust nor did she desire to travel or see the world.

When Stephen was born in April of 1762, Elizabeth envisioned a life for her child similar to her own, where he would learn the family trade, marry a local girl and carry on the family business. She was completely shocked and dismayed when she learned that Stefano's ideas and dreams for his children were totally opposite of hers. By the time Ann came along, a little over three years later, it was clear to Elizabeth that her children were destined for a life as theater musicians. They would carry on the family trade all right, but it would be the trade of the Storace family, not the Truslers.

As the children grew, it became apparent that Stephen would be the one whose personality was most like Elizabeth's, and Ann's most similar to her father's. Both English and Italian were spoken in the home and although both Stephen and Ann were bilingual, it was Ann who took best to Italian, later even preferring the Italian pronunciation of her sir name, *sto-rah-chee*, over the Anglicized, *stor-us*. And although Elizabeth loved Ann dearly, and was extremely proud of her talent, she couldn't relate to her daughter's vibrant, friendly personality, the energetic and vivacious girl who didn't know a stranger, and it set up a conflict between them that neither of them could put their finger on. It had been present from the time Ann was a very small child.

Elizabeth continued reading through the contract, almost unable to believe what she read. An emotion of excitement and anticipation she had not allowed herself to feel in years surged through her. When she had finally finished reading both the letter and the contract over twice, she laid them on the desk, as tears pooled in her eyes.

"At last, in only a little over seven months I'll be on my way home to England," she sighed. "This nightmare is nearly over."

Chapter Fourteen

Almost immediately upon the troupe's return from Laxenburg, they were engaged in yet another performance of *Figaro*. Mozart remained at a distance, fearing his presence would only invite more gossip, which was already running rampant among the Viennese theater patrons concerning Nancy's breakup with Benucci. Then within the week, more rumors began to fly concerning Martín y Soler. Over hot chocolate and creamy torts, tongues wagged that as the parts to his new opera, *Una cosa rara*, were passed out among the singers, an uprising took place, led by Benucci, in which several of them refused to sing, claiming that their parts weren't suitable, too short, too long, or too difficult. This seemed to be rooted in Benucci's ever increasing jealousy over Nancy.

Soler was an extremely handsome, talented and arrogant Spanish composer, who when he first arrived in Vienna, months before, quickly scouted out his competition and ascertained that the only one who could clearly give him a run for his money was Mozart. When *Figaro* made it onto the theater docket as the opera to open the new season, Soler was furious and began organizing cabals against the opera as well as against Mozart, himself. Soler went around the city bad-mouthing Mozart and spreading rumors in order to discredit him and turn not only the public against him, but the Burgtheater management as well.

When Soler heard the rumors coming from Laxenburg regarding Mozart and Nancy, he saw it as an opportunity, so when it was announced that his opera was the next on the docket, he formulated a plan. As the parts were passed out, he quietly made suggestive, even forceful and threatening overtures to Nancy, insinuating that if she refused him, he would not only ruin her, but he would ruin Mozart as well. Nancy, intimidated by the terrible memories of John Fisher, felt she had no other choice but to give into Soler's demands, and she prayed that whatever rumors got out about it, wouldn't reach Mozart or that if they did, Mozart would give her the benefit of the doubt and come to her and ask.

The August performance of *Figaro* was nearing, so Mozart requested a private assignation with Nancy in her dressing room immediately afterward. Nancy, who had no idea that he heard the gossip, was taken by complete surprise when he entered and wasted no time in confronting her.

"Wanze, please explain!" he demanded as he shut the door.

"Explain?" she asked in confusion over his apparent distress. "I don't understand."

"Explain the rumors I've heard about you and Soler! Tell me anything, but please tell me that they're not true," he said as he paced in front of her.

She grew pale as the blood drained from her cheeks and her mouth grew so dry that her tongue stuck to it. She felt as if she were going to faint.

"Yes, the rumors are true," she confessed. "But please hear me out, Wolfgango," she pleaded, "for it's not what it appears!"

Hot tears stung his eyes, the hurt and anguish over her infidelity piercing him so deeply that he felt suddenly nauseated.

"How could you?"

She threw herself onto his chest and pleaded for him to listen.

"Please Wolfgango, let me explain!" she cried. "It's not what you're thinking!"

"Then what am I supposed to believe?" he said as he pushed her away.

"Please, I beg you," she said as she fell to the floor weeping. "My love for you has not changed. You must allow me to explain!"

"Very well," he said indignantly, crossing his arms. "Explain how your love for me is unchanged and yet you're engaged in a love affair with my greatest enemy!"

"It's not a love affair. I don't love him!"

"What are you doing with him then? Discussing Shakespeare's sonnets?" he replied sarcastically.

"He began making suggestive overtures to me in front of other members of the troupe when it was announced that his new opera was the next to premiere. I tried to put him off, but he was so insistent. He knew about us and he said that he would ruin you."

She continued to weep. "He was so adamant that he frightened me. All I could think of was Fisher and how he would enforce his way upon me if I didn't comply."

"He didn't…"

"No, no, he didn't," she answered, shaking her head, "but I was frightened that he would if I didn't give in to him. And then I told myself that if I let him have his way with me and the rumors got out about it, then the ones about us would end. I tried to make it bearable by telling myself that I did it to protect you."

She fell into a heap and sobbed. "Please forgive me. I would never hurt you intentionally. I love you!"

"No, no, Wanze," he whispered softly as he knelt beside her and kissed her cheeks. "It is I who must beg your forgiveness. You were only protecting me. I should have allowed you to explain before I accused you."

"I knew you would be hurt, but I had no other choice. I was trapped."

"And I'm not in the position to defend your honor," he said, angry and frustrated by the cruel situation in which Soler had placed them. His inability to protect her left him feeling insignificant and powerless.

"I believe that's what Benucci and the rest tried to do when they refused to sing Soler's opera, but the Emperor stepped in and threatened to fire them if they didn't."

"God, I hate this! Why does it have to be this way? It isn't us, it's everything that conspires against us! Why couldn't I have met you six months earlier? Oh please don't cry any more, Wanze. You're breaking my heart!"

He wrapped himself around her, his sense of futility growing ever stronger. It's my fault, he thought. I should have controlled my passions. I should have never allowed things to go this far.

"I'm afraid that this isn't the only bad news I have, Wolfgango," she said as he handed her his handkerchief to wipe her tears.

"Oh please, Wanze, I don't know how much more I can take."

"I'm so sorry. How I wish I didn't have to tell you this."

"Go on," he said, dread in both his voice and his face.

"It's my mother."

"What has she done now?" he asked, bracing himself for the next blow.

"For months she's been secretly writing to my brother in an effort to convince him to solicit a contract for a position for me in London. As soon as I returned from Laxenburg, I was informed that an agreement was reached with the King's Theater and that when my contract with the Emperor runs out early next year, I am to go back to fulfill a one-year contract with them."

"But that can't be! Is there no way that you can refuse it," he asked, hoping that she had already come up with a plan.

"No," she sighed. "Mother lied to him, and so believing that it was what I wished, Stephen acted on my behalf and signed the contract. It's done. I have to go. But it's only for a year and I'm already negotiating with the Emperor to return to Vienna for the 1788 season," she assured him.

"A whole year?"

"I know, I know, but my hands are tied. I have to go."

He held her closely and stroked her hair. How wonderful she felt in his arms. How could he endure an entire year without her?

"Stephen returns next month to fulfill another commission. I have hopes that perhaps that will curtail his desire to go back to London for a while and that maybe he will change his mind and want to stay in Vienna. But Mother is quite determined to return, so I can't rest my hopes on it too much."

As she spoke, Mozart remembered how his young English pupil, Thomas Attwood, kept suggesting that he go to England to compose an opera for the King's Theater. "What if I were to go with you," he asked, the sudden idea lighting up his expression.

"What do you mean?"

"I mean, go with you to London. I've loved England since I was a small child, when my family traveled there. We lived there for nearly a year and it is very familiar to me. Attwood has been hinting around about the possibility of my going for several months now. They say there's a need for good composers of Italian opera there and Attwood believes he can get me a commission right away," he said with a glimmer of hope.

"But what of Constanze and the children? You can't just abandon them. If you do, you'll never be allowed back in Vienna."

"Of course not. I would never do that. But it's only for a year. Papa and I were away from Mama and Nannerl for over a year during our second tour of Italy. He sent letters and money to support them and everyone got along fine. I could do the same. Constanze has her mother and sisters to take care of her and keep her company. Sophie could move into our apartment; she's there every day anyway."

Although Nancy wasn't sure how Constanze would receive the news that her husband wanted to travel to London with the only woman from whom she felt any serious threat, she agreed that it was worth a try. She knew it was their only hope.

The next morning, after Mozart was up and dressed, he looked in on Constanze, checking to see if the emotional climate was right for him to give her the news. He found her sitting in her favorite chair, quilting some jackets for the new baby's layette. She seemed to be in as affable a mood as she would ever be, so he decided that it was as good a time as any to let her know of his plans.

"Good morning, my love!" he said cheerfully as he kissed her on the cheek. "I trust you slept well last night."

Constanze looked at him and knew immediately that he was up to something, and it probably wasn't good.

"What do you want?"

"I want to give you some important news that will most likely change our lives forever," he announced proudly.

She put her sewing aside, folded her arms across her protruding belly and replied, "Go ahead, change my life. God knows I'm ready for it!"

"Well," he began cautiously, "you remember how Attwood's been trying to talk me into traveling back to London with him and Kelly for quite some time now?"

She nodded with a raised eyebrow.

"Well, I've been giving it some serious consideration and I was recalling how when I was a boy, and my father and I went on our second tour of Italy. We were gone for nearly eighteen months and when we returned we had amassed quite a fortune," he said as he looked at her, checking her response.

"Anyway," he continued, "we had to leave Mama and Nannerl behind during that tour, because it would have been too expensive to take them along. But the whole family agreed that it was worth it after Papa and I came home and were able to move the entire family into that lovely, large house," he said enthusiastically.

"So tell me, husband, where are you going with this?"

He hesitated a moment, dreading his wife's reaction to the news he was about give to her. "I've decided that I'm going to accept Attwood's offer to go with him to London," he announced matter-of-factly. "It will require that I be gone a year, but as I say, I believe that our fortunes will be the better for it."

Constanze sat up straight and thought a moment.

"And who else will be going with you besides Kelly and Attwood?"

"The Storaces," he said reluctantly. "I've just learned that Stephen is returning next month to fulfill another commission with the Emperor and, when he goes back early next year, he will take Nancy and Mrs. Storace with him."

"So Nancy is going back to England and you think that I'm simply going to allow you to get on a coach and go back with her while you leave me here alone to care for our children for an entire year?" Constanze's brown eyes smoldered as her expression turned dark.

"Well, I hadn't thought of it in exactly those terms, Stanzerl."

"Are you mad?" she yelled.

She rose to her feet and went to him, pushing her finger firmly into his chest. "Just in case you're wondering, I've heard the rumors Wolfgang." She began to pace. "Although I have no concern over your little flings now and again, I'm rather disturbed by the news I continually hear about you and Nancy!" she said as her voice raised to a fevered pitch.

"And pray tell what rumors? I suppose that now dancing is a sin! She's my leading lady, for God's sake. We were expected to be seen together! You've been listening to Aloysia again. You know there's a reason why this Scheisse is called gossip, don't you? Besides that, in case you haven't heard, Nancy has now taken up with Soler—my greatest enemy. So even if I was ever tempted, I certainly wouldn't be now, would I?"

"I don't care what excuses you offer to weasel your way out of this, Wolfgang, I'm not letting you go alone with that woman to London!"

Mozart knew that continuing a shouting match with his wife wasn't going to get him anywhere, so he began to bargain with her.

"What if we took you and the children as far as Salzburg and left you with my father while I go on to London? Then, when I'm settled and have a little money saved, I can send for you," he proposed, his voice lowering considerably.

She glared at him and growled. "If you think I'm going to spend even a day cooped up in that house alone with that controlling old man, you're even madder than I thought!"

"Then what about this?" he said calmly. "What if we traveled as far as Salzburg and left the children with Papa, and we go on to London together? Then after four months or so, I would return and get them and bring them back with me," he offered trying to be more reasonable.

Constanze thought for a moment and then she asked, "How long would we be in London?"

"Only about a year. Then we can return home to Vienna, with more money than we'll know how to spend!"

"All right then. Write to your father and ask him if he would be willing to take the children," she said reluctantly. "But I'm not counting on his agreeing, and if he refuses to take them, you're not going," she said as she left him standing alone in the salon.

The following months were almost unbearable for Mozart and Nancy as they awaited news of the fate of his trip to London. After Stephen arrived and it was clear that Elizabeth wasn't going to stay in Vienna a minute longer than she had to, Mozart began to make his plans. He arranged for an English tutor to come to their home twice a week to instruct both him and Constanze. English, Constanze learned, was an extremely difficult language to master and, although her husband was excited to improve upon his already acceptable skills, she was much less enthusiastic as she was drawing nearer her time, and it seemed like entirely too much work for something she wasn't enthusiastic about to begin with.

Mozart decided that he wouldn't write to Leopold until after the baby's arrival, due sometime in mid-October. In the meantime, he proceeded with plans as if everything was going accordingly, for it gave him greater comfort to believe all would go smoothly.

Nancy was too busy with her performance schedule and with keeping up an acceptable front with Soler to worry herself with other concerns. Mozart was sympathetic regarding her difficult position, but as the weeks passed and the affair seemed to linger on, his tolerance began to grow thin. Too many times, when he was finally able to carve out some time to be with her, she couldn't make the arrangements because of Soler's interference, and the few times that they were able to meet, his jealousy would creep in between them, causing them to argue, something which, when it happened, ripped their hearts in two.

Several times the Baroness proved to be a supportive ally, providing for them a secluded sanctuary for one or two days at a time, giving them a respite from the pressures that seemed ever mounting upon them.

It was an unseasonably warm October afternoon when Mozart arrived at the Baroness's estate for another of their long-awaited trysts.

"She's waiting for you. Hurry, now. You don't have much time!"

"Thank you, dearest friend. You have no idea how much this means to us." He took her hand and gave it a grateful squeeze, then he flew down the corridor and out the exit to the garden where he saw Nancy from across the way, seated beneath a large willow tree, examining a music score.

"Nancy!" he called out to her as he ran down the stone pathway, past the lily pond to the secluded corner of the garden where she sat.

"Wolfgango!" She pushed the score from her lap and leapt to her feet. He swept her up into his arms, covering her cheeks and mouth with fervent kisses.

"My God, how long has it been?" he panted as he pulled her soft body into his.

"Too long, my love," she replied breathlessly. "Much too long!"

"I want to take you right here and now," he moaned as his lips found their way over her chin, down her throat and to her soft, round décolletage.

"How long can you stay?" She covered the top of his head with her kisses.

"Only until midnight. I told my wife that I'd be at a Lodge meeting."

"Then let's not waste anymore time here," she said as she took him by the hand and led him across the lawn toward the house.

Once they were inside, he swept her into his arms and carried her up the stairway, into her awaiting bedchamber and laid her gently upon the bed. He spoke to her tenderly as he gazed gently into her face. "Look into my eyes, Wanze," he whispered. "Keep your eyes open. I want you see the love I feel for you. We're one soul. We're different movements of the same concerto."

As afternoon passed into evening and evening into night, they played one another like fine instruments, as if each note were the last. And when they were finally spent, they fell into a deep and contented sleep, safely wrapped inside of each other's tender embrace.

An hour or so later she awakened to find him in the corner of the room, dressing for the trip back to the city. As she sat up in the bed, she spoke to him softly.

"You're leaving now, aren't you," she said quietly as she rested to one side, her thick, dark tresses cascading softly over her shoulder onto her breasts.

"I don't want to leave, Wanze." He climbed back onto the bed and took her gently in his arms. "But I have to."

"I know," she whispered. She began to cry. "When can we see each other again?"

"I don't know. Hopefully soon, but I can't promise…" He kissed her cheek. "Please don't cry, love," he pleaded tenderly, kissing her forehead. "I can't bear your tears."

"I don't know how much longer I can stand this. I feel such a sense of overwhelming dread, as if this were the last time we will ever be together!" She laid her head upon his shoulder.

"Silly little bug," he cooed. "Don't you remember? I'm going to London with you! We'll have lots of time to be together there."

They lingered, wrapped in one another's embrace for several moments before he spoke again. "I must leave now," he said regretfully as he tore himself away from her. "My coach is waiting."

"I love you," she whispered.

"And I love you for ever and always and three days," he said as he left and closed the door behind him.

He was relieved when his coach pulled up to the city gates just prior to their closing, for he'd lingered too long with Nancy. After that, it was only a matter of several minutes before they pulled onto the Schulerstrasse and in front of the gates to his apartment building. He was startled to see that the lights in his apartment were still burning.

As he ran up the narrow stairway to the level of his apartment, he could hear women's voices coming from inside and, as he opened the door, he was met by Constanze's oldest sister, Josepha, who shot him a look which he did not care to name, and exclaimed, "You wicked man! How dare you go off with that woman and leave your wife at a time like this?"

Just then, Sophie came from out of their bedchamber, wiping blood from her hands with a rag.

"What's going on," he asked, panicked by the gruesome sight.

"Your son was born tonight and your wife nearly died!" Josepha spat.

His face grew pale.

"Get out of my way, woman," he said in a low growl, and he turned his attention to Sophie. "How is she?"

"She's just fine," Sophie replied kindly. "She had a harder time with this one than she did with the others."

"She's sleeping now," Josepha added, snarling at him. "Not that you would care!"

"That's enough, Josepha! Why don't you go back and sit with her now and let me talk to Wolfgang alone. And don't you dare upset her by telling her things that she doesn't need to hear!"

Josepha did as Sophie ordered and Sophie pulled Mozart aside and spoke candidly with him.

"Wolfgang, I don't care where you've been, nor do I care with whom, but Constanze knows, so you'd better come up with an excuse, quickly."

Mozart adored Sophie. Of the four Weber sisters, she was the one with the sweetest temperament and she always treated him with the utmost kindness and respect.

"What about the baby?"

"Another boy," she replied, smiling proudly. "I can bring him to you if you'd like to see him."

"Please, Sophie, I would. Thank you."

She left the room and in only a few moments, she returned holding a tiny bundle. As she handed the baby to Mozart, he gazed down into his red, wrinkled face and marveled at the miracle that he held within his arms.

"He's beautiful!" he said as he ran a finger across the baby's soft cheek.

"Of course he is," Sophie replied enthusiastically. "Look at his parents!" She knelt beside him to get a better look at the baby's face.

He waited until daylight before he went in to see his wife, hoping that after she'd had some rest she might be more up to receiving him, and perhaps be in a little better humor. As he knelt beside the bed he noticed that she still looked pale and weary, and a pang of guilt stabbed at his conscience. When he tried to hold her hand, she pulled it from him and turned her face away.

"I saw him last night, Stanze," he said to her softly, "and he's beautiful, just like you."

She said nothing, but kept her face turned.

"Sophie says he's healthy and strong," he continued, trying to elicit a response from her.

There were several moments of strained silence before she finally spoke.

"When did you come in, last night?" she asked in a weak voice.

"It was late. You were already asleep, and I didn't want to disturb you, so I waited."

She turned her face toward him and looked into his eyes. "I know where you were," she said calmly, "and I want you to know I don't have any objections to your little affairs. I never have, for I know how you men are. Physical fidelity means little to me as long as your heart remains faithful. All I ask is that you love only me."

"I do love you, Stanze. You know that," he replied as he took her hand.

"But do you love only me, Wolfgang?" She persisted, forcing him to remain in agonizing silence for several moments, desperately searching for the words she wanted to hear.

"I love you," was all he could say.

That afternoon he wrote to his father, announcing the birth of his new son, who would be baptized Johann Thomas Leopold, and telling him of their plans to travel to England. He made his request, also offering to bring the nurse, as well as to pay him a monthly stipend for their care and feeding. As he sealed the letter he had high hopes that Leopold would accept his request.

In only a few weeks following his birth, little Thomas was seized with a choking, congested cough. Constance sat up night-after-night, holding the baby in an upright position on her shoulder hoping that it would help him breathe easier and ease the choking that only seemed to grow more severe as the days passed. Several times he coughed with such a violent force that she nearly dropped him and they began to fear what seemed inevitable.

Then one night, as it had gotten so bad that Mozart had to put a pillow over his head to muffle the terrifying sounds coming from the salon, he heard a blood-curdling scream. He shot up out of bed and raced into the salon to find Constanze clutching the limp and lifeless infant in her arms.

"Oh God, Wolferl," she cried. "He's stopped breathing! He's turning blue! I can't bear to lose another one! Mein Gott, Wolfgang!" she shrieked hysterically. "Do something! He's dying!"

In a panic, Mozart whisked the baby from her, felt the cold little body go limp in his arms, and knew in an instant that their son was dead.

"He's gone, Stanzerl," he wept, as he held the lifeless child and enveloped Constanze in his embrace. "It's over, Mauschen," he cooed to her tenderly, as she buried her face in his chest and sobbed.

After several stark moments, he finally placed the baby's body back in its mother's arms and spoke again, softly. "I'll get dressed and go get the priest."

Within the same week that little Thomas died, a cold, cruel, and accusing letter arrived from Leopold in which he chastised his son for his selfishness and scolded him for the "senselessness" and "rashness" of his request. He firmly refused to take the children, citing that he was an old man in ill health and accused his son of desiring to bring about his early demise by burdening him with their care

Wracked with a profound grief combined with anger and resentment for his father the likes of which he had never known before, Mozart took Leopold's letter and tossed it into the fire. Then, in a last-ditch effort, he approached Constanze about the possibility of going ahead with the trip and taking little Karl with them all the way to London. He was old enough to make the journey, Mozart felt, and with the nurse along, he wouldn't be difficult to care for. But Constanze, who was grieving the loss of yet another baby, wouldn't hear of putting her only surviving child at risk by taking him on such a long journey across half the continent, as well as across the English Channel, during some of the harshest winter months. So it was with a heavy heart that Mozart had to search for a way to break the news to Nancy.

Leopold Mozart

Chapter Fifteen

*B*y the time his opera opened in late November, Soler had finally tired of his affair with Nancy and turned his attentions to another young actress who was more than willing to oblige him. Nancy was relieved to be able to break the news to Mozart that her attentions were no longer divided; they could spend their last few months together in Vienna free of that particular tension which existed between them. And in only a few weeks they would be on their way together to London, where there would be no threat of gossip or disclosure of their love affair, and where no one would even care.

It was on the night of the November performance of *Figaro* that she had planned to give him the good news. When she entered her dressing room after the final curtain, she was startled to find Mozart already waiting for her, his expression sullen and somber.

"Wolfgango, you're here!" She rushed to embrace him.

"I let myself in several moments ago so that no one would see me," he replied, but as she extended her arms he brushed her aside and turned away.

"What's wrong? Have I done something to upset you?" she asked, confused by his cold reception.

"No, no…" he answered, shaking his head. "I'm sorry, Wanze, but I just don't know how to tell you this."

Nancy dreaded the news that she was about to receive. "Just give it to me like a man, Wolfgango."

He turned slightly, avoiding eye contact with her, fearing that if he looked at her, he would break apart. "I received word from my father last week. It wasn't good."

She shook her head fiercely and whispered out loud, "No, no, no…"

"He has refused to take Karl while my wife and I settle in London," he said as he choked back the tears. "Constanze refuses to leave him here with her mother and she won't allow me to go without her."

Nancy's body shuddered as she grew suddenly weak. She fell to the floor on her knees. "Why, oh why?" she cried. She turned to him suddenly and lashed out, tears gushing from her eyes.

"Why don't you stand up to her? I don't understand. You could easily travel alone and send for her later, and yet you refuse to! You're the man and yet you allow your wife to dictate to you as if she were the husband!"

"It's not that simple!" he snapped, offended by her slap to his masculinity. "I can't leave her right now. She's grieving the loss of her child. I would be an utter cad to travel to a far-off country with my lover and leave her alone at such a time. You of all people should understand her loss. Sometimes I am truly baffled by your callous disregard, Nancy!" Tears of hurt and grief poured down his cheeks.

Silenced by his chastisement, Nancy sat in the floor and continued to weep. Mozart turned away again, unable to bear her tears. For several moments he stood silently until he mustered up the ability to speak.

"I'm a married man," he said softly. "As much as I regret it now, I made a vow to my wife. If I can't give her the full measure of my love, I at least owe her the full measure of my compassion."

He paused as his emotions seized him again. "You own my heart, and believe me when I tell you that on the day you leave to return to London, it will be ripped from me and you will take it with you. It's all I have to give to you. You must be content with that."

He turned to leave, pausing momentarily to run his fingers through her curls, then he left.

The following week Mozart received a letter from Johann von Thun who told him of *Figaro*'s great success in Prague, and who invited him and Constanze to come and spend several weeks with them over the month of January and through most of February, during the Carnival season. They accepted the invitation gladly and began immediately to make travel plans.

Nancy's final appearance in *Figaro* was scheduled for the middle of December, and Mozart attended, desiring to see her one last time as his precious Susanna. During the fourth act, when she sang *Deh vieni non tardar*, Mozart wept silently as he allowed his mind to travel back to the day at Laxenburg when they had picnicked on the lawn near Diana's Temple. He recalled how he fell asleep in her lap as she made the chain out of the tiny daisies that were strewn over the grass, and how she crowned his forehead with it as she sang the line, *ti vola fronte in coronar di rose.*

Nancy's final Viennese concert was scheduled for the eve of her departure and Mozart decided that he would compose an aria, *Ch'io mi scordi di te*, for her to sing as a gift, a personal tribute and farewell, as well as an expression in music of the depth of his feelings for her. He remembered earlier in the year when she'd sung Ilia in *Idomeneo* that she'd mentioned how much she liked the insert aria that he composed for that particular performance, using an obbligato violin. He decided to use the same text as it was entirely appropriate for the occasion and for what he wanted to communicate to both her and the audience. This time, however, he composed it using obbligato piano, which he would play; a duet specifically for and about them. He completed the piece just before Christmas and made plans to present it to her on the day after, as he was invited by Stephen to supper in their apartments. Just before he left his apartment, Mozart entered the aria in his thematic catalog, including a personal inscription: *Für Mlle. Storace und mich* (For Mademoiselle Storace and me).

When he arrived at their apartment, Mozart was greeted warmly by his host and the other guests, which included Michael Kelly, Thomas Attwood and the young Lord Barnard, also known as Harry Vane, who was visiting Vienna on his Grand Tour. He'd met Nancy six months before, after he'd first arrived in the city. He had grown fond of the Storaces and spent a great deal of time with them, and to Elizabeth's delight, chose to be seen all over Vienna escorting Nancy to various social events, as well as attending her performances. The young Lord (who was a year younger than Nancy), found himself rather homesick and desirous of English company upon his arrival in Vienna, and immediately glommed onto the Storaces to fulfill his need for something familiar. Elizabeth saw his attachment as an opportunity to distract Nancy from her attentions to Mozart and so she seized every opportunity to thrust Lord Barnard and Nancy upon one another, ignoring the fact that there was never any possibility of a union between them. If her daughter was going to be anyone's mistress, she much preferred it be with a wealthy young English Lord, than with Mozart.

After supper, they all retired to the salon for a special presentation, for Mozart announced upon his arrival that he had a gift to give Nancy before he left for Prague. He motioned Nancy to step forward and join him at the fortepiano, where he sat, opening the aria. Knowing her excellent sight singing capabilities, he invited her to read through it with him in front of the other guests.

As she quickly leafed through the manuscript, she immediately recognized the text, and turned to him with tears brimming in her eyes. "Wolfgango, you're such an ass," she said as she wiped them. "I can't believe you did this," she whispered.

Mozart smiled sheepishly and replied softly, "I told you I'd make it up to you, Wanze. It's the big aria I promised you." He silently mouthed the words to her in English, "I adore you, little bug." He then played the opening measures of the recitative and she began to sing.

You ask me to forget you?
You advise me calmly to forget you and love another
and want that I still live?
Ah, No! I would rather die!
Come death! I wait for it courageously!
To seek consolation from another,
to give my love to another only fills my heart with dread!
Cruel suggestion! Ah! My despair will kill me.
Do not fear, my love will never be changed.
Faithful I shall always remain.
But my affliction has caused me to falter
and now my soul from grief must flee.
Are you sighing? O woe outpouring?
But all is vain to one who is begging.
O Heaven, I cannot express it!
Pity me, Heaven, see my anguish,
see the grief due to my affection!
Has ever such torment plagued so faithful a heart?
Has such doom or dejection ever beset such a loyal heart?
Hateful galaxies! Vile constellations!
Why should you beset me with such sorrow? Ah, why?

She thought that when he'd composed the role of Susanna, it was the ultimate in his public expression of his affection for her, but now this. Not even the tender, *Deh vieni non tardar*, which they had always considered their special aria, could compare. The music was passionate and tender all at once, and the piano part that he composed for himself to play as a duet with her vocal line, wrapped itself around the vocal melody as a lover wrapping himself around the object of his devotion. She could hardly wait for her concert when they would perform it with the orchestra and she would be able to hear his piano line standing out from the orchestral accompaniment, mingling with hers in a public, musical declaration of what had taken place in their hearts and in their most intimate moments, behind closed doors.

After they finished the last bars, he stood and handed her the manuscript. She read the dedication aloud, *"From your servant and friend..."* and she threw her arms around his neck. He wrapped her in his embrace, the two of them remaining in one another's arms for several moments as the small group of onlookers sat silently and watched, many of them moved to tears by what they had just heard and seen.

Afterward, as everyone sat about the salon and conversed, Mozart took Nancy aside and asked if she would accompany him to the courtyard where they might speak privately. They slipped on their coats and hats and walked out onto the landing and down the stairs to the center courtyard where there was small fountain, and near it some benches.

"Wanze," he began, as he sat, "I know the last time that we spoke I left you with the impression that I was angry," he said, as he took her hands. "I apologize. That isn't what I intended. I simply couldn't bear seeing you in such pain and I didn't know how to comfort you."

"I understand, Wolfgango," she replied softly. "The aria is beautiful." She swallowed hard and tried to change the subject. Tears stung her eyes as she turned her face away and lowered her gaze. She was so weary of tears. It seemed to her that since the night he came to her with the news, all she had done was cry.

A cold December breeze came wafting through the courtyard, kicking up some of the leaves that were still left on the ground from the previous fall. Mozart felt the chill and he wrapped his arms around Nancy's shoulders, pulling her up close to him. "Please don't cry, Wanze," he whispered.

Nancy smiled and wiping her tears with a gloved hand, she turned again to him. "But all is not lost," she said, trying to sound encouraged. "Stephen, Thomas, and I have plans to begin working to obtain a commission for you in London as soon as we arrive. It might take us a little time," she cautioned, "but I promise you we will get it. In the meantime, I still have plans to return to Vienna in a year. Have you forgotten that?" she asked, trying to lift the melancholy that seemed to have overtaken both of them.

"I know, I know..." he replied nodding. "That's what you say, but I can't help but feel this overwhelming sense that after you leave, we'll never lay eyes on one another again," he said as he put his head in her lap. "Oh, Wanze, I don't know what will become of me if I never see you again. Please don't leave me. I can't stand the thought of being without you."

"You know I have to go, Wolfgango," she replied softly. "I have no choice, but I promise you that I'll return. And after I come back, you'll be able to go back with me to London," she said, trying to encourage him.

"I'm leaving for Prague in a little over a week. I won't get back until only a few days before your concert, which means that we have little time left."

"Write to me while you're in Prague." She bent to kiss his cheek. "That way we won't feel so far from one another."

"I'll do that," he replied, managing a smile. "I'll write to you every week and I'll tell you how *Figaro* is doing there."

"My brother's new opera premieres tomorrow. You'll be there won't you," she asked, hoping that perhaps they could arrange to see one another afterward.

"Of course. I wouldn't miss it for the world."

"And you'll be at the Milano afterward?"

"Absolutely." He sat up and took her face in his hands. He pressed his lips to hers and kissed her softly.

"I adore you, Wanze," he whispered.

"And I adore you, Wolfgango," she replied sweetly. "Für immer und ewig und drei Tagen."

⊰⊱

As soon as he arrived in Prague, Mozart did as he promised and wrote a letter, telling her of the journey and how much he already missed her. He wrote of *Figaro*'s great success, but that he wished she could be there to play Susanna, for there would never be another one to his liking, but her. He also wrote that he'd received a commission to write another comic opera in Italian for the National Theater in Prague, and that he was considering Don Juan for its subject. He promised that he would compose a part in it that would be perfect for her and that by the time it opened in Vienna the following year, she would be back and able to take the role.

In her reply she spoke of how her mother, in typical fashion, insisted that she spend every spare minute of her time with Lord Barnard, and of how it seemed to please Elizabeth to no end that his attentions were so focused upon Nancy, who wasn't entirely convinced that he wasn't a fop. He seemed to her to be more interested in Stephen's company, and she found him to be a complete bore, for he knew little or nothing of music aside from his own enjoyment of it.

After supper, on the evenings he dined with them in their apartments, he would predictably saunter over to the fortepiano, and with a limp-wristed gesture, exclaim, "Oh dahling, you simply must sing that new aria from Soler's piece that you performed the other night, for I fall madly in love with you each time I hear you sing it."

They had gone dancing several times at the various balls and parties associated with Vienna's Carnival festivities and each time he had gone home and written to his "ma-MAH" about it. Nancy was completely put off by the fact that he was so attached to his mother that he wrote to her about every detail of every minute they spent together, as if he was trying to convince her that he was happy to spend so much time in a woman's company. Nancy had observed the many occasions when he made eyes at Stephen, and even once or twice the times he had made some obvious passes at Kelly. She was greatly comforted by the fact that Barnard was engaged to his first cousin, Lady Katherine Powlett, and upon their return to England, he would be married within a few months.

Mozart wrote back that he had gathered from Barnard's reputation as a dandy, and from local rumor that he went about "polishing every lamp post" in the city, that he was indeed a fop and that his being seen with Nancy only served to improve his reputation.

On the night Mozart conducted a performance of *Figaro* in Prague, he was given a magnificent ovation. Everywhere he went he heard it, it was played in the streets. People hummed and whistled it, and he was recognized and warmly received throughout the entire city. But despite the festive mood with all of the parties, dances, and activities associated with the carnival season, he wrote to his friend Gottfried von Jacquin that he couldn't find it in himself to dance or make merry, claiming that it was due to his natural shyness and fatigue. However, he knew that he was being overtaken by melancholy and a sense of futility that only seemed to worsen as the time for Nancy's eminent departure drew nearer.

He arrived home in Vienna only two days before her final concert and after a short afternoon rehearsal they performed the aria in the evening in one of the concert halls at the Kärntnertor Theater, which was another one of His Majesty's Imperial theaters. The audience, who seemed to understand the significance of the piece, gave them a warm ovation as they took their bows together with tears streaming from their eyes.

Constanze was in the audience that night, most specifically to hear her husband play one of his piano concertos that Nancy invited him to perform that evening. She was suddenly aware of the fact that during the performance of the aria, the people who sat in the surrounding seats began to stare at her, the women giggling and whispering behind their fans, and the men giving her pathetic side-glances. Constanze was shy anyway, and extremely intimidated by the upper-crust audiences in Vienna's Imperial theaters, and throughout the entire performance she was made quite aware of the fact that something was happening on stage that she didn't understand. The fact that she didn't understand the aria's Italian text only added to her confusion and she was so embarrassed and humiliated that by the end of the concert she was on the verge of tears. Once they arrived home, the confrontation that arose between her husband and her over the evening resulted in his sleeping on the divan in the billiards salon.

Early the next morning, as she sat upon one of the many trunks that were strewn about the salon of her apartment, Nancy gazed out the window into a cold, drizzly, Viennese morning, lost in melancholy reflection. She remembered the girl, only four years before, who sat kicking her feet on the side of the trunk in Venice, the plucky little seventeen-year-old who was ready to take Vienna by storm and whose fondest desire was to meet Mozart and inspire him to compose a memorable role just for her. As she sat, dressed in her dark green wool traveling suit, she held the little King Charles spaniel that Lord Barnard presented to her as a gift for her twenty-first birthday. She stroked his silky, caramel and cream colored fur and sighed as she wondered where the giggling, carefree girl who irritated her mother into near hysterics with her childish antics had gone. She hadn't foreseen this ending. How could she have known that her fondest dreams would become reality, but that in the wake of the reality would be left two broken hearts?

"Kitten," she heard a soft voice behind her speak. "It's nearly time for us to go. Do you have everything?"

She broke from out of her trance and saw Stephen smiling down at her, his gentle and understanding gaze offering the only comfort she felt in her sense of sorrow and regret.

"I think so," she replied as she gracefully extended her hand to him so that he could help her up. She gazed around the salon to see if she left anything behind and to take in its finely appointed elegance one last time. She knew when she set foot in London she would no longer be the prima, the highest paid actress in all of Europe, complete with a luxurious apartment and her own carriage. It had been nearly eight years since she'd left London, and when she returned, no one would even know her name.

"Mother and Michael are waiting for us in the coach," he said, as he took the dog from her and helped her to her feet. "Someone will be here to load our things onto the wagons shortly."

When they arrived at the customs house at the western gate of the city, Michael, Stephen, Elizabeth, and Nancy met up with Thomas Attwood and Lord Barnard. The six of them were to make the journey together from Vienna to Salzburg, where they would stop and spend a day with Mozart's father, Leopold. While there, Nancy was to sing for Archbishop Colloredo and then go on to Paris, where they would part company with Lord Barnard and where Nancy would go to Versailles to sing for Emperor Joseph's youngest sister, Queen Marie Antoinette.

After their papers were put in order, and when their things were loaded onto the coaches, they boarded and began to settle in for the first leg of their journey. As Nancy stepped into Lord Barnard's coach and made ready to take her seat next to him, a cab pulled into the drive and out of it stepped a small man dressed in a black wool greatcoat and a black tricorn. In one hand he carried a small, brown leather-bound book and a letter. His expression was somber, and his eyes were red and swollen from crying.

Michael, who had just emerged from the customs house, saw Mozart as he stepped out of the cab and gestured for him to come over so that he could speak with him.

"Kelly, my friend," Mozart said as he approached him and patted his shoulder. "It looks like I made it just in time."

Michael observed his friend's expression and quickly ascertained its cause.

"It's a mighty cold and gloomy day to be seein' her off, isn't lad?" Michael said as he offered him a drink from his flask.

Mozart graciously declined and began to look around.

"She's there," Kelly said as he pointed toward the first coach, "sittin' next to His Lordship."

Mozart approached the entrance of the coach and found Elizabeth, Stephen, and Nancy, who was sitting, as Kelly said, next to Lord Barnard, her little dog curled up snugly in her lap.

"Mrs. Storace," he addressed Elizabeth, who was seated next to Stephen. "May I have a word in private with your daughter?"

Elizabeth, who still wasn't fond of Mozart, but no longer considered him a threat to her daughter, nodded and gestured toward her. Nancy gently lifted the dog from of her lap and handed him to Elizabeth, then extended her hand to Mozart, who helped her down the step. He led her to the back of the coach, where he pulled the cape of his greatcoat over them to shield them from the freezing drizzle, and so that they could have some privacy.

"Wanze," he began in his broken English, "What vill become of me? I am no gut mitout you. Nuzzing in my life makes any of da sense mitout you."

She wrapped her arms around him as she began to weep.

"Oh, Wolfgango," she said through her tears. "I'm so frightened. I feel such an overwhelming sense of dread, as if I'll never see you again in this life."

"But you vill come back to Wien in von year, ja?" He nodded. "And vhen you come, you vill bring back a commission for me to come to London!"

"Yes, Rosenberg is discussing another contract with the Emperor, but anything can happen," she replied cautiously.

Unable to take the despair any longer, he held her face in his hands and gazed into her eyes. "Ve cannot let our hearts break like dis, Wanze," he said as he pressed his lips to hers. "Ve vill promise each udder dat ve vill meet again in a year. Until den, I promise to write to you von ledder every mont, until ve meet again."

He reached into his pocket and retrieved the book that he brought with him and handed it to her. "Dis is a collection of zonnets by Mr. Shakespeare translated into Italian," he said, managing a smile as she took it from his hand. "I haff been tinking dat I vill compose an opera for you from von of his plays. I've been tinking about Da Tempest. You vould make a wunderbar Miranda, meine Wanze!" He wrapped his arms around her and kissed her one last time. "Addio, angela mia," he whispered.

"Addio, Caro ben mio."

He led her back to the coach and helped her back into her seat, and then he pulled the letter from his pocket and handed it to Elizabeth.

"Please Madame, would you kindly deliver this letter to my father?"

Elizabeth took the letter and nodded. He then turned and gazed upon Nancy's face one last time as he silently shut the door.

As the two coaches pulled out of the customs area, Nancy turned to look at Mozart from the tiny rear window. He stood in the middle of the road, his shoulders sagging from the weight of the sense of loneliness and futility that had seized him, and his hat drooped as the freezing rain fell relentlessly upon him.

Kärntnertor Theater

Chapter Sixteen

*I*t was a cold and dreary three-day trek through the snow and ice as the coaches made their way across the countryside to Amstetten, where the travelers stopped the first night, then to Frankenmarkt and across the Maria Plain into Salzburg. Nancy sat quietly the entire time, her dog curled upon her lap, and blankly stared out the window at the snow-covered rooftops of the quaint houses and churches that dotted the countryside along the way. As much as she tried to erase it from her memory, she couldn't forget the sight of Mozart standing in the middle of the road, drenched and forlorn in the freezing drizzle as the coach pulled through the gate from Vienna. Occasionally she reached up to wipe a single tear that made its way down her cheek as the melancholy scene replayed itself over and over in her thoughts. Several times, upon noticing her tears, Harry reached across and took one of her hands and gave it a gentle, sympathetic squeeze. Everyone knew what troubled her, yet all were at a loss at how to offer her comfort. Elizabeth, who was notably excited that they were finally on their way home, grew weary and impatient with Nancy's moodiness and, shortly before they rounded the corner into Salzburg, she ordered her daughter to end her pining and sighing before they were greeted by their host.

The coaches pulled into the Hannibalplatz, in front of the residence of Leopold Mozart, in the late afternoon. The elder Mozart greeted his English guests with all the congenial hospitality that he could muster for a sixty seven-year-old man who suffered with dropsy and gout. He was baffled by the great amount of luggage that had to be unloaded from the coach, especially for such a short stay, and all the fuss distressed him to the point that he was finally forced to sit and rest for several moments before he could show his guests to their quarters. They would dine with him that evening and then they would go to the Residenz where they would meet the Prince Archbishop Colloredo, and where Nancy was scheduled to sing.

Once everyone was settled in the Mozart home, a large, sprawling place with a large ballroom that housed many musical instruments and portraits, Leopold took Nancy's arm and led her through the salons. He took her to music room to show her the numerous curio cabinets filled with trinkets and memorabilia of Wolfgang's childhood, and the various tours that had made the Mozarts famous all over Europe.

As they stopped in front of a large, ornately painted cabinet, Leopold pulled a small, brass key from out of the pocket of his waistcoat and unlocked it. Displayed prominently among the many trinkets—pen cases, snuff boxes, sashes, and medals—was the medal, sash, sword, and spurs which had been awarded to young Wolfgang by the Pope, bestowing upon him the title, Ritter von Mozart. Leopold reached carefully past the display and pulled out a small book that lay near the front.

"This is a sacred libretto that I purchased many years ago and gave to Wolfgang to study when he was a child," he said proudly as he opened the book. "You will notice that I stamped it with my seal." He showed Nancy where it was clearly stamped on the inside cover in brown ink. "Now if you will look in the back," he said opening it to the back cover, "you will see where my son decided that his initials should be stamped in it too."

Nancy smiled and ran her finger across the place where the young boy had scribbled his initials, one on top of the other, "WM", with fancy scrolling between to connect the two letters.

"It has little more than sentimental value now," Leopold said as he too, ran his fingers across the letters, "but one day, perhaps many years from now, it will be worth a great deal."

As he continued to show her about the music room, they stopped at a large painting, a portrait of the entire Mozart family.

"Alas, my poor wife was already deceased before this portrait was painted," he said as his voice trailed off.

Anna Maria Mozart's face was depicted in the painting as a portrait hanging on the wall behind the rest of the family. Wolfgang and Nannerl were seated at the fortepiano while Leopold stood behind it. "My son was twenty-five at the time. It was just before he ran off to Vienna and married that Weber girl," he said bitterly. He paused as Nancy lowered her eyes and replied softly.

"Please pardon me, sir, but your son has seen much success in Vienna, and I for one am grateful, for had he not been there, I would never have had the opportunity to know him."

Impressed by Nancy's candor, Leopold thought, What a foolish son I have! If only he had waited, he could have had her.

"Your son has made quite the name for himself in Vienna, and in Prague, with his newest opera," Nancy continued, speaking of *Figaro*'s, success. "And I have plans to return to Vienna next year and sing in yet another one of his operas," she announced confidently. "Perhaps after that I shall be able to obtain a commission for him to compose an opera for the London stage."

"Wolfgang was always fond of England," Leopold replied, hearing Nancy's affection for Wolfgang in her voice. "I regret that I was unable to care for his children, Signora Storace, but understand that I am getting old and I haven't been well. And then there is the cost of such a trip. How would he manage such expenses, only to arrive in London with no sure prospects for employment? Wolfgang can be rather impetuous with his requests. I simply couldn't agree to it under the circumstances."

Nancy recalled the afternoon when Wolfgang came to her dressing room and gave her the bitter news concerning Leopold's refusal. She had felt anger and animosity for the old man, but standing with him there, she was filled with an understanding and affection for him that she couldn't name. She could see the resemblance between Wolfgang and his father, especially in the eyes and the mouth, and when he smiled, his whole face lit up, just like Wolfgang's.

"Come now," Leopold said as he smiled and took Nancy's arm, "I do believe it is time for supper, and then we must be off to the Residenz for your concert. I'm so looking forward to hearing you sing, Signora. Wolfgang has often written very highly of your abilities and, as I'm sure you're well aware, he is not the most generous of critics."

The concert went surprisingly well, considering Nancy's melancholy and fatigue from the journey. The Archbishop greeted her and all of the English guests warmly and seemed to thoroughly enjoy their being there. The next morning they were up early to take in all the sights that Salzburg had to offer, with Leopold acting as their guide and escort throughout the small city. He took them to St. Peter's where both he and Wolfgang had been employed by the Archbishop and where Wolfgang had served as composer, organist, and choirmaster before he made his infamous break from Colloredo's service. Afterward he served them lunch, then Nancy performed a private concert in the Mozart's ballroom for Leopold and some of his closest friends. By midnight the group had their luggage loaded upon the coaches and they went, once again, on their way.

It had been close to two months since Nancy and all of Mozart's English friends had left Vienna. A letter from Stephen arrived at the end of March announcing their safe arrival in London and giving their new address as number 23 Howland Street. He assured Mozart that they would be in contact as soon as possible and that as soon as they were settled, they would begin to work toward gaining a commission for him. A month later, Nancy received a letter from Vienna, addressed to her personally.

Meine Liebe, meine Hertze!

I compose this Lied as I think of you, and I wonder if your heart beats still true for me. I can't not forget you, Wanze, for I feel you yet each day with me here. O, tell me that true you remain even though far apart we are.

> *The angels of God weep when lovers part!*
> *How shall I be able to live,*
> *o maid, without you?*
> *A stranger to all joy,*
> *I shall live, henceforth to suffer!*
> *And you? Perhaps forever*
> *Louisa will forget me!*
> *And you? Perhaps forever*
> *Louisa will forget me!*
> *I cannot forget her!*
> *Her song, O Lord! her song!*
> *While she sang, all the worlds*
> *toppled in my midst!*
> *My ear and heart resounded*
> *with sweet, perplexing alarm!*
> *And you? Perhaps forever*
> *Louisa will forget me!*

I pray that I shall receive soon word from you. Please address all personal correspondence care of the Hungarian Crown Kaffeehaus. And one last request, dearest Wanze—as my personal correspondence is intended for you only, I ask that each letter from me be destroyed as it is received and read.

I remain, ever your devoted
Wolfgang

Upon receiving Mozart's letter, Nancy sent one immediately in return.

My dearest Wolfgango,

I cannot describe how my heart leapt in my bosom when your letter arrived! As I opened it, I prayed that it would contain news of your continued affections, and my fervent prayers were answered! I have not forgotten you. Indeed my affections have only grown in their intensity since my departure from Vienna. How I long to see your smile, my dearest one, for the last memory I have is of your sad and forlorn figure standing in the rain as my coach departed.

Soon, my love, very soon, we shall see one another again. I have only just received a letter from Rosenberg which states that he is negotiating the terms with His Majesty for my return next season. Once the final arrangements can be made, I should be back in Vienna by the next January. That is only a little over nine months away, my love, which seems forever, I know. However, it is not long considering that three months have already passed since we last saw one another. Until then, I shall continue my correspondence with you, as promised and remain ever true in my affections.

Faithfully yours,
Nancy

Nancy opened at the King's Theatre in Paisiello's *Gli schiavi per amore,* in which she played the part of an American slave. In attendance at her debut was the Prince of Wales. When he came again on the following night, he arrived before the beginning of the overture, which was considered a great compliment. An even greater compliment was paid to her by the Prince when he was in attendance at a third performance only two days later. Nancy knew that the Royal approval could get her far when it came time to appeal to His Highness regarding Mozart's commission. Her experience with Zinzendorf in Vienna over Stephen's commission could prove beneficial when approaching the Prince Regent on Mozart's behalf, something she no longer reviled or feared but viewed simply as a tool necessary for a woman in obtaining whatever it was she wanted.

After the performance on the second night, Nancy joined Lord Barnard for a late supper. Having just returned from an extended stay in

Paris, he knew that his days of escorting Nancy out and about were over as he would be expected to call upon his fiancé and escort her to all major society functions.

"I envy you, you know," he said quietly as he crossed one leg over the other and sipped his wine.

"You envy me? Good God, Harry, whatever for?"

"You're free. You love your work and you're loved for the work you do. You're witty, intelligent, extremely talented, and you could have any man you want any time you want. But I, well, my life has been chosen for me," he said as he picked up his pipe and lit it. "I must do my duty, marry the woman my father chose for me, sire an heir, and serve my King and country."

Nancy sighed as she fingered the stem of her wine glass. "My life is more complicated than you think, Harry. I have expectations and family obligations to live up to, as well. There are commitments that can't be broken, and men who cannot be had no matter how desperately I might desire them."

"Ah, I see. Then you're still in love with him?"

Nancy sat silently and stared into her glass.

"You don't have to answer that, dahling. I understand, and I don't blame you. He's a lovely man." He blew a smoke ring into the air and watched her as she contemplated a reply.

"We both live in cages." She sighed. "Yours just happens to be lined with velvet. We're both consigned to our fates with little choice than to swallow them down and like it." She smiled at him then. "I'll miss you, Harry. You've been a dear friend."

"We have had a jolly good time, haven't we, Nan? I'll miss you, too, but I'll be seeing you. I'll still have my box at the theater you know, and all you need do is look up from your place on stage and I'll be there waving my kerchief at you," he said with a wink.

The following September, Harry married his first cousin, the Lady Catherine Powlett and began his service in the House of Lords the following January. They never associated with one another again.

Chapter Seventeen

*I*mmediately following Nancy's departure from Vienna, Mozart's life seemed to fall apart. The melancholy that began to overtake him after Leopold's refusal to take the children led to a depression that only deepened with each passing week. As he had promised her, Mozart wrote to Nancy on a monthly basis, sometimes twice a month if the separation he felt from her grew unbearable. In late June she received an especially distressing letter from him informing her of his father's death in May, only about six weeks after she had been the elder Mozart's guest in Salzburg.

The following October, Mozart traveled with his wife to Prague to conduct the premiere of his newest opera, *Don Giovanni*. He had written to Nancy months earlier that he had composed the part of Zerlina especially with her in mind, and sent her a copy of the score so that when she returned for the 1788 season, she would have it ready for the Viennese premiere. Six weeks after their return from Prague, Constanze gave birth to their first daughter, Theresa, whom Mozart affectionately called Thresl. Shortly after, Mozart received a letter from Nancy that delivered yet another devastating blow.

My dearest love,

I cannot describe to you the anguish I feel as I write this letter. O my love, how will we bear it?

Over the course of the last several weeks, Count Rosenberg and I have written back and forth, negotiating my contract for next season. It seems that the escalating war with Turkey has drained His Majesty's coffers and, although he wishes me to return, he simply cannot afford it and, rather than withdrawing his invitation, he has offered me a salary which is half of what I was receiving when I left Vienna earlier this year. I cannot afford to return under such conditions and have therefore withdrawn.

I cannot express the grief I feel as I write this letter to you, my love. I promised you that I would return in one year and now I have broken that promise. Please know my heart is breaking and that I can only beg your forgiveness.

Tearfully,
Nancy

Don Giovanni's Viennese premiere in May of 1788 was a miserable failure, and only strengthened Mozart's resolve to obtain a London commission. With the ongoing recession, things seemed to be going from bad to worse for Vienna's musicians and, finally, in October, the Kärntnertor Theater closed, forcing Aloysia and other local Viennese singers out of work. Mozart continued to write to Thomas Attwood as well as to Stephen and Nancy, who were in ongoing negotiations with The Prince of Wales, who was then the acting regent due to his father, King George III's, chronic illness. However, the wheels turned slowly as England too was embroiled in her own financial struggles following the loss of the American colonies a few years earlier.

Mozart wrote another distressing letter to Nancy in the summer, filled with grief over the loss of yet another child. The daughter whom Mozart had come to adore and upon whom he doted night and day was suddenly taken ill with a severe intestinal blockage and died at the age of only six months.

Finally, in an effort to encourage the bringing of Italian comic opera to the London stage, Stephen wrote to Francesco Benucci and invited him to come sing a series of concerts with Nancy that included the music of both Mozart and Salieri, including several pieces from *Figaro* and *Don Giovanni*. It was a joyful reunion when Stephen and Nancy met Benucci at the coach station in London. Upon seeing him, Nancy ran toward Benucci with open arms as he swept her up in his embrace.

"Bella Anna, how I've missed you!"

"And I you, Caro," Nancy replied as he planted kisses on both of her cheeks.

"Mozart sends his fondest greetings to you all, and most especially to you, Anna," he said with a knowing grin and a twinkle in his eye.

Nancy sensed that with this gesture all was forgiven where Benucci was concerned.

The concerts were a huge success, the audiences greatly taken with Mozart's music, and Benucci was prepared to return to Vienna with news that a London commission would soon follow. However, on the day before his scheduled departure, the King's Theater, the theater for which Mozart was to be commissioned to compose, burned to the ground and Benucci was forced to return with a discouraging report that the long-awaited commission would be further delayed.

It was the summer of 1789 when Antonio Salieri, who was being awarded a medal of service from Emperor Joseph, chose to conduct a revival performance of *Le Nozze di Figaro*. Word was passed back and forth of the possibility of bringing Nancy back to Vienna for the opening three performances, but she was engaged in a production of Stephen's new opera, *The Doctor and the Apothecary*, which was to premiere at the same time. It was a sullen and discouraged Mozart who refused to allow the new singer, Adriana Ferrarese del Bene, the mistress of Lorenzo Da Ponte, to sing the arias that he'd composed for Nancy in the original production. He instructed Da Ponte to write a new text for which he would compose a completely new aria that would contain none of the tenderness or the passion of the original. Mozart later wrote to Nancy that he refused to hear Da Ponte's slut singing their aria and vowed that as long as he lived, he would never again hear anyone but Nancy sing the role.

In mid-October, Constanze entered into confinement with another pregnancy. This one had been especially difficult and had been complicated by the fact that she developed and infection in her foot which ulcerated, forcing her to spend several weeks at the spa in Baden while it was being treated.

As she sat chatting with Aloysia over the latest gossip, Nancy's name was brought up in conjunction with the *Figaro* revival, which was meeting with huge success in Vienna.

"You must have been relieved to see her go, Stanze," Aloysia said nonchalantly. "It was no secret that she was after your husband."

"There were rumors to that effect, I know," Constanze answered softly, "but I never took them seriously. I know Wolferl has had his little affairs with all kinds of women, including Nancy Storace. He's a very desirable man. Women love him." She sighed. "But he always comes home to me."

Aloysia looked up from the gossip paper she had been reading and looked her sister in the eye. "Then you must not be privy to what went on between them at Laxenburg that summer," she said coldly.

"What are you talking about?"

"I'm talking about the last summer that Nancy was in Vienna, during the run of *Figaro*. You can't tell me you didn't know. They were seen everywhere together. And he was seen slipping in and out of her apartments nearly every night for a solid week! Why, everyone knew he was in love with her. It was far more than a 'little affair', Stanze, and everyone seemed to know it but you."

Constanze flushed as her stomach began to twist up in knots. "You lie!" she shouted. "You're just saying those things because you're jealous and you're trying to be mean again!" Hot tears poured from her eyes as she stood and limped toward the entry, her foot still sore and tender. "I think you should leave, now, Sister. I'm not feeling well and I need to lie down."

"He's still in love with her, you know. All this time he's been working for a commission in London, he's been trying to fix it so that he can go there by himself and leave you in Vienna. Don't be a fool, Constanze!"

"I want you to leave now," Constanze shouted as she pointed toward the door. "Leave and don't ever set foot in my home again!"

Aloysia found her cloak and hat and put them on and headed for the door, but when she got there she turned to Constanze once more. "Mark my words, Constanze. He's going to try to get back to her. I'm telling you this because I care about you and your children. I'm warning you, don't let him out of your sight or you'll never see him again."

A month later, Constanze gave birth to another baby girl. They named her Anna, and had her baptized as quickly as possible for she was extremely weak and they knew she wouldn't survive the night. She died within an hour after her birth.

⊰⊱

In early autumn, Mozart was presented with a commission from the Emperor for another comic opera in Italian entitled, *Così fan tutte*, another plot about unfaithful lovers, full of bait-and-switch, and masked identities. Once again, Mozart chose Da Ponte to write the libretto and included a part that would be ideal for Nancy, hoping that, should a commission from London arrive, he might be able to bring the score with him and persuade a London impresario to produce it with Nancy singing the role of the devious little maid, Despina.

Earlier, the Emperor had returned from the Turkish front in ill health and, by the end of the year, he was dying of consumption. This was another blow to the musicians in Vienna, for Emperor Joseph had been known throughout Europe as a great patron and supporter of the arts, most especially music, and the Hapsburg who would take his place, Leopold II, had little or no interest in the arts.

By the time *Così* premiered, Emperor Joseph was too ill to attend, never seeing the last opera that he had commissioned from Mozart. He died the following February. Vienna's musicians marked his death as the beginning of the end. For Mozart, it meant that a commission from London was more crucial than ever, for although he amassed large amounts of money, he had large debts that accompanied his fortunes and work was becoming harder and harder to find. He tried, with little success, to obtain students as his debts began to oppress him.

After baby Anna's death, a deep melancholy and sense of dissatisfaction seemed to settle upon the Mozarts. Aloysia's cruel revelation to Constanze had cut her to the quick and left her suspicious and distrustful of her husband and as a result, she nagged him, taking on an angry, shrewish edge that provoked many an argument that devolved into shouting matches between them. The servants referred to them as "the battling Mozarts" and noted that Constanze, when she wasn't at the spa in Baden where she had taken to spending weeks at a time, slept in a separate room on the opposite end of the apartment.

As Mozart's financial tensions escalated, so did the tensions in the marriage. Over the course of only three years they moved a total of five different times, each time believing that new accommodations might help ease financial burdens. But the increasing debts mounted so quickly that Mozart found himself constantly writing to his friend and fellow freemason, the moneylender Michael Puchburg, for loans, some for substantial amounts.

Mozart continued his correspondence with his friends in England, never giving up hope that he would soon receive the elusive commission. He continued to write to Nancy privately, although the frequency of his letters diminished considerably. Some letters were simply newsy correspondence between good friends and others were more impassioned, expressing frustration at the fates that always seemed to come between them. Always, he professed his undying devotion.

By the fall of 1790 he became so frustrated over his deteriorating position in Vienna and the dismal prospects for any future work that he took an impulsive step and decided to embark upon an unprecedented German tour to attend the coronation of Leopold II. Although he had not been commissioned to compose any work for the event, nor had he been invited to perform, he told Constanze that he believed that the

215

opportunity to perform would be opened to him once the new Emperor heard that he was there. Then he did something that made absolutely no sense to her—he pawned the silver and used the money to purchase an expensive coach with four horses, rather than hire a coach or take a public transport, which was his usual custom.

"But I don't understand," Constanze said as she stood in bewilderment watching her husband map the route to Frankfurt. "Why did you feel it necessary to buy a coach rather than hire one? It's so much more expensive this way!"

Mozart sat in silence, ignoring his wife's interrogation and continued to mark the map.

"Wolfgang, answer me!" she demanded.

"Stille, Weib! I don't have to explain anything. I simply want my own coach…" He hesitated a moment, "…to make a better impression. Besides, I don't wish to travel in a hired one this trip. They're too cramped and uncomfortable."

"Who's going with you," she asked, remembering Aloysia's warning the year before. The route, from what she saw, looked like a straight shot to Calais, and from there to London.

"No one. I'm going by myself."

"No, Wolfgang, you're not," she insisted. "It's not safe. There are all manner of highwaymen and thieves on the roads looking for luxurious coaches like yours. You could be robbed, or worse, killed," she said, pretending to be concerned mostly for his safety.

He ignored her and stood suddenly, going to the desk where he kept his money. "Here's the key to the strong box. I'm leaving you with enough money to pay the household expenses for several months." He pulled out a small bag filled with coins and handed it to her. "I want you to take this to Puchburg after I leave. This is what I owe him."

Constanze stood in stunned silence. He had everything planned. He was leaving her and going to London; she knew it.

"I've also made arrangements for you to move to a smaller, less expensive apartment while I'm away. It's closer to your mother and to all of the places you need to go," he said as he handed her a copy of the lease. "Süssmayr will be here with the movers to load all of our furniture and belongings at the end of the month. It has all been arranged."

Franz Süssmayr was Mozart's newest pupil, a young man who came to Vienna to study with Mozart several months before. He had become a good friend to both Mozart and Constanze and Mozart trusted him with her safety and that of their son, Karl. Several times he sent Süssmayr along with Constanze to Baden, not only to ensure her safety but to keep a watchful eye on her as word was getting back to him of improprieties on her part where a certain young Lieutenant was concerned.

"Why isn't Süssmayr going with you?"

"He's staying here in Vienna with you while I'm away—to take care of you, of course."

The next day, after Mozart was up and out of the apartment, Constanze took a carriage to the home of her older sister Josepha, asking to speak with both her and her husband, Franz Hofer. Franz, an affable, gentle, and soft-spoken man, reminded Constanze very much of her long-deceased father, Fridolin, and Constanze was fond of him.

"Wolfgang has planned a sudden tour of Germany. He insists on going alone and I strongly suspect that he is making plans to steer his coach, at some point along the way toward Calais, and then on to London."

"He's leaving you for that Storace woman," Josepha exclaimed, wide-eyed. "I knew it!"

"Hush, Josepha," Franz chided. "You know no such thing." He then turned to Constanze and spoke to her softly. "Why do you suspect this of him, my dear?"

Constanze swallowed hard as the tears drizzled down her cheeks. "Josepha is right. He's in love with that Storace woman. He has been for a long time. He wanted to go to London with her when she left Vienna several years ago, and since then he's been trying to gain a commission from the Prince Regent of England to compose an Italian opera for the London theater. All this time I've known it was happening, but I chose to believe that the affair was nothing serious, and that Wolfgang always came home because he loved me."

She swallowed again, and wiped her tears. "Now I realize that I was being played for a fool. He loves her and he'll stop at nothing to be with her."

"And what is it that you want me to do?"

"I've come to ask you if you would go with him, not only to keep him company, but to see to it that he returns home."

"This is quite an accusation to be making of your husband, Constanze," Franz said with a condescending frown. "You'd best be quite sure of what you're asking of me, for not only is he my brother-in-law, but he's a fellow freemason, and for me to act out of suspicion of a brother is a serious matter indeed."

"I understand," Constanze said, lowering her head, "but I would sincerely appreciate your help in this matter. I don't know what would happen to me or to our son if he were to abandon us."

"I don't believe for one second that he's capable of such a terrible thing and I'm ashamed of both of you for suspecting him, but if it will put you at ease, I am more than willing to do as you ask."

When Constanze returned home she found Mozart going through his papers, making sure all was in order for the trip.

"I've just come from Josepha's," she announced as she walked through the door. "I asked Franz if he would travel with you on this tour. He agreed that it was dangerous for you to go alone and said he would be happy to go along."

"You did what?" Mozart exclaimed, incensed that his wife went behind his back.

"I just told you. Franz is going."

"You did this without consulting me?"

"You wouldn't listen to reason, Wolfgang. I don't want you going alone. It's too dangerous."

"And what if I refuse?"

"Then you're not going," she said, emphatically. "That's my final word."

Mozart knew Constanze was serious by her expression. The manner in which she set her jaw said it all. He also knew that if he pressed the issue, he would most likely give everything away. She'd won; he'd have to come up with a different plan.

A week later, Mozart set off with his brother-in-law on what would amount to an immensely expensive and fruitless two-and-a-half month journey. When they arrived in Frankfurt, Mozart was ignored by the Emperor and received no invitations to perform at the events surrounding the coronation. However, he didn't allow this disappointment to disturb him too much, for the real reason for the journey was still to come and he still had high hopes for its success, despite the fact that Constanze had thrown a rock into the works.

While in Frankfurt Mozart sold his coach for a good price and, when the coronation festivities were finished, he and Franz took a market boat to Mainz, a trip that was designed to save money, and which was highly suspect in Franz's eyes. Once they arrived in Mainz, it was Mozart's plan to lose his brother-in-law by booking him on a public coach back to Vienna while Mozart booked himself on a coach to Calais and then onto a ship to London. With the sale of the coach and horses, Mozart had enough money to book passage across the English Channel and still have plenty left over for lodgings in London.

His plan would have succeeded had it not been for the fact that on the morning that they arrived at the station to purchase their tickets, he was suffering from a bad cold. He was so distracted by his condition that he was careless about concealing the itinerary from his brother-in-law, and when Franz noticed that there was one person booked for Vienna and another for Calais, he pulled Mozart aside.

"It's true then, what your wife suspected," he said, disappointed.

"I don't know what you mean."

"Constanze feared that you would attempt to travel on to Calais and then to London without telling her. That's why she asked me to go along with you. Please tell me that this isn't what you've been planning."

Mozart sat quietly, his eyes downcast. He sniffed a couple of times and blew his nose, but said nothing.

"Wolfgang, you have a wife and a son, and you have an obligation. I understand that these are difficult to meet sometimes, but I appeal to your honor to do the right thing. Please don't abandon them. You'll never forgive yourself if you do."

Mozart continued to sit quietly. Tears welled in his eyes as he thought of Nancy, who was only just across the channel. He was closer to seeing her than he had been in years, but Franz's words pierced his soul, challenging him to do the right thing and return to his family. He choked back the tears and pretended that his eyes watered due to the cold in his head. As he wiped them with his handkerchief, he looked at Franz and offered a weak smile. He stood slowly and went to the counter to purchase their tickets.

Aloysia Weber Lange

Chapter Eighteen

On the way home, Mozart decided to make a stop in Munich, thinking that he might be able to make up for some of his financial losses with some performances there. He was well-known and liked in Munich, mostly due to the tour he had taken with his student and brother freemason, Prince Karl Lichnowsky, the year before, and he thought it might prove fruitful, once again. He also knew that he would need some time to cool down before he encountered Constanze.

On the final leg of the journey home Mozart remained sullen and silent, his anger and sense of betrayal over his situation ever-mounting with each passing day. He resented his brother-in-law's intrusion into his private life and the idea that Constanze put Hofer up to it enraged him. It was like having his father's spies lurking around the corner all over again. By the time they arrived home, his outrage over the situation reached the point of explosion.

When he walked through the door of the new apartment, he instructed the servants to take his luggage into his bedchamber and then leave him alone so that he could have a word with his wife. He entered the salon to find Constanze reclining comfortably on a settee, looking a little drawn and pale. He knew what that meant, for Constanze, who was robustly healthy when she wasn't pregnant, was very energetic and disliked lying around the apartment doing nothing. This could only mean one thing.

"Well, I see you decided to come home, my darling," she said with all the vitriolic sarcasm she could muster.

Mozart glared at her, then turned and looked around the salon for the entrance to the bedroom when he saw one of the servants exiting the room. As he made his way toward the door, Constanze rose to follow him.

"Aren't you going to speak to me? No kiss on the cheek, or a 'How I've missed you, my love?'"

Trying to control his temper, he held his hand up to silence her.

"I warn you, woman, do not provoke me!" he spat.

"You were going to do it, weren't you? You were going to leave us for her. Well, you'll be pleased to know that now your fondest wishes have been granted."

"What are you talking about?"

She went to the secretary and opened a drawer from which she retrieved a letter addressed to her husband.

"This arrived while you were away. It's from London," she said as she thrust it toward him.

Mozart took the letter from her hand, seeing that it was from Johann Salomon, the German impresario who resided and worked in London and acted as his agent. He broke the seal and began to read.

"I've been commissioned to compose two Italian operas for the 1791 season at the King's Theater in Covent Garden."

"Ah, see there, my darling, the fates have finally smiled upon you and your little British whore. She can now be yours with the blessings of the English Crown."

Enraged by his wife's sarcasm, he dropped the letter and grabbed her by both of her shoulders and pulled her toward him, speaking to her through clenched teeth.

"You will not speak to me like that ever again," he hissed. "You will remember that I am your husband, and I will not tolerate such disrespect from you!"

"And I suppose that I'm to be forced to tolerate your infidelity as a sign of that respect!"

He let go of her and thrust his finger at the barely protruding mound on her belly. "And who are you to bring up the question of fidelity, unless by some slim chance that is mine? I don't recall sharing your bed in recent months, Madam!"

"So why are you here and not in London, with her?" she sneered.

"You know why I'm here. You went to Hofer. How dare you?" he shouted as he paced angrily. "You set the trap and he caught me in it. You're just like your mother! And now you've fixed it to where now that I actually have a legitimate reason to go to London, I can't. If word of this gets out to my Masonic brothers through him, I'm ruined. You may have destroyed all of my chances for gaining employment in both London and Vienna!"

He continued to pace, his face red with rage, while Constanze stood silently. He had been angry with her before, but never in the years that she knew him had she witnessed anything like this.

"What a stupid thing you've done! Do you see what your vindictiveness has wrought for you now? What will you do if I can no longer get work? I left you with a nice apartment and enough money to support you for up to four months while I got set up in London. I had every intention of continuing that support for the rest of your life. But now…" He threw his hands in the air, his anger and frustration resurging, and turning toward the wall he hit it with his fist. "Damn it, Constanze," he shouted, "I have half a mind to send you and that little bastard you're carrying packing to your mother!"

Flying into a panic, Constanze he threw herself onto him, begging and pleading. "Mein Gott! Bitte nein, Wolferl! Es tut mir leid!" she pleaded. "Please don't send me to Mama's! I'll do anything you ask, but please, not that! My family would never let me live it down!"

As she fell into a heap on the floor in front of him, weeping, Mozart felt for her plight, but he couldn't bring himself to take her into his arms. He was still too angry. He paced for several moments, all the while muttering to himself. Finally he stopped and looked at Constanze, who was still curled up on the floor, sobbing.

"Stop crying. You know I won't do that, nor will I leave you," he said softly, but without emotion. "I'll stay here and we'll make the best of it. I'll figure something out."

He knew that there was no way that he could accept the commission under the present circumstances, for to do so would mean that any doors to him in Vienna would be closed forever. Hofer would go to their lodge and, being bound by oath, he would be forced to reveal what had transpired with Mozart in Mainz. The keeping of one's oaths was sacred in freemasonry and should word get out that he attempted to abandon his wife and children, it might travel to the London lodges as well and he would be blackballed there, too. His hands were tied and he had little choice but to do what he felt he was forced to do.

"We must never speak of this again," he said, breaking the long silence. "I will go to Hofer and apologize for my moment of weakness and ask his forgiveness, and I'll plead with him not to share this with our lodge."

He paused for a few moments to compose himself and then he continued.

"You must go to your sisters, especially Aloysia, and make it very clear that all gossip regarding Nancy and me must end now, and that if they hear any gossip from anyone else, they must do their best to quell it. Make it clear to them how very crucial this is and that if they fail, your ruin will be the result. I will give this child my name and all that goes with it. Nothing further will be said regarding its parentage if you swear to me that you will cut off all contact with the real father. I will hear no more of your improprieties with that Lieutenant at the spa," he spoke sternly.

"I swear to you," Constanze replied, drying her eyes with her apron.

"I will write to Salomon and make up an excuse—I'll tell him that a trip to London is out of the question right now because it is too expensive and I fear losing my Viennese contacts, and that perhaps I can do it in another year or so."

He cleared his throat.

"There have been some letters," he confessed. "I asked her to destroy them, but I can't guarantee that she has. There could be some trouble when I cut off contact—when she realizes that it is over between us." He could hardly speak the words.

"We'll take things as they come, Wolfgang," Constanze replied. "I promise I'll do everything you ask, only please tell me that you still love me."

When he couldn't answer, he turned and went into the other room.

Over the next several days, Mozart agonized over the letter that he was forced to write to Nancy. His affections hadn't changed, but the fates had spoken, so it was with a heart heavy with grief that he wrote to her one last time.

> *My own Love, my Treasure, my Heart!*
>
> *How I languish in the writing of this letter. Truly, there are no words to express the grief in my heart for what I must tell you, so I will come straight to the point and, as I have requested before, I make my most fervent plea that this be destroyed after you have read it.*
>
> *It is with much sorrow and regret that I must inform you that I will not be accepting the commission that I know you, your brother, and Thomas Attwood have worked so assiduously to obtain on my behalf. I cannot express the gratitude I have for you all and for your diligence*

in this matter. However, there are circumstances beyond my control which compel me to decline, despite everything within me that shouts otherwise.

This brings me to another, even more painful matter: O Wanze, how can I bear to write the words? What cruel fate has brought us to this point? Again, I shall not tarry but shall come quickly to the point. This will be my last letter to you, my dearest love, not because my affections for you have diminished for, on the contrary, they have only grown deeper and more impassioned since last we saw one another, but because circumstances in my situation have developed to the place where, for the preservation of my reputation, my work, and my family, our affair must end. And although we will never see one another again in this life, my soul will always yearn for you. I vow to you my undying love for all eternity, whatever that is. I vow that whatever happens in this universe, I shall always find you and love you. You will never be alone. Whoever else may have my body, you will own my heart. Farewell, angela mia.

Forever,
Tuo Wolfgango

Over the course of the following months the Mozarts made a concerted effort to improve the conditions of their marriage, although the hurt and distrust that had existed between them for so long still remained beneath the surface. Constanze continued to spend weeks, even months at a time in Baden, even though her health had improved considerably and her pregnancy was the easiest and most healthy pregnancy she ever experienced. And although his debts continued to be a burden, Mozart began to experience financial increase in amounts that he hadn't experienced in several years.

Occasionally, during quiet moments of reflection, or when he took long walks by the pond with Karl at the Prater, he thought of Nancy and his heart ached. He never received word from her after his final letter and he often wondered if she still loved him as he did her.

A son was born to Constanze while she was at the spa in late July and, because Mozart was not in attendance, the child was baptized Franz Xaver, after Franz Süssmayr, who was with her in Baden, acting as her chaperone. Later, to avoid the threat of gossip, Constanze added the suffix, W.A. Mozart, Jr. to the child's name.

"The morning post has arrived, Signora," the maid said to Nancy as she sat at her desk going over her accounts.

"Thank you," Nancy replied. "Just lay them over here on the desk."

After she finished the day's business, she turned to the stack of letters. On the top was one written in a familiar hand. It was from Vienna!

As she picked it up, she brought it to her nose and took in the scent that lingered on it. Ah! How she loved his scent—the aroma of cologne made from West Indian spices mingled with his pipe tobacco.

It won't be long now, she thought. He should have received Saloman's letter regarding the commission by now. Perhaps he mentioned it in this!

Anxiously, she broke open the seal and unfolded it. As she read the first line, tears poured down her cheeks.

"Oh Wolfgango, no! How can this be?" she exclaimed aloud. "After all we've been through…after we came so close…he's ending it now?"

Bitterly, she folded the letter and started to rip it apart, but after second thought, she decided to lay it on the desk while she retrieved the others that he wrote to her over the years, from out of the bottom drawer.

He asked me to destroy these as I read them, she thought as she wiped the tears that still streamed from her eyes. I couldn't bring myself to do it…but now…

She took his last letter and placed it on the stack with the others, and then tied the bundle together with a crimson cord. She went to the hearth and held the stack over the fire, intending to drop them in. She began to sob.

"No, I refuse," she said aloud. "It can't be over! I won't accept this," she exclaimed as she pulled them away.

She went to her desk and searched through the drawers where she found a small, wooden box, covered with ornate carvings. She placed the letters in the box and locked it, and then she tucked it away in a bottom drawer.

"I won't give up now, Wolfgango," she said resolutely. "No matter what it takes, I'll find a way. We'll be together again, my love."

Suddenly she remembered the aria—the last piece he composed for her. She went to the cabinet where she stored all of her music scores and pulled out one of the narrow drawers. "There it is," she exclaimed as she picked up the manuscript, which she hadn't touched since the day she packed it, just before her final concert in Vienna.

Flashes of the day of her departure went through her mind. It had been almost more than either of them could bear. She still had nightmares of the scene of him standing alone in middle of the road, the freezing rain pouring down upon him like tears. As the coach pulled out, she could see him standing there, and as they drew further and further away, he fell into a dark abyss. She awakened in terror each time she reached that point in the dream, her heart pounding wildly in her bosom.

She went to her fortepiano and sat in front of it, spreading the score out across the lid so she could read the orchestral reductions. She played the opening bars—the intro to the recitative—and then she sang.

Ch'io mi scordi di te? Che a lui mi doni puoi consigliarmi?
E puoi voler ch'io viva – Ah no!

She stood defiantly and shouted, "Wolfgango, you're such an ass! I can't believe you've done this!" She glanced further into the score and read the text of the bravura section.

Do not fear, my love will never be changed.
Faithful I shall always remain.
But my affliction has caused me to falter
and now my soul from grief must flee.
Are you sighing? O woe outpouring?
But all is vain to one who is begging.
O Heaven, I cannot express it!
Pity me, Heaven, see my anguish,
see the grief due to my affection!
Has ever such torment plagued so faithful a heart…

Afterword

Let me first state that it has never been my intention to present Constanze Mozart in a negative light. She was a woman of her times caught in a patriarchal system that limited her to the role of wife and mother and little else. In that world a woman was a virgin, a wife and mother, or a whore, and marriage, especially in Roman Catholic Europe, was not what we know and understand marriage to be today. Women were raised to fulfill certain roles and most often a woman's role was to make her husband's life easier and to present him with heirs to carry on his name. And without exception, married or not, women existed for the pleasure of men.

In this story I have presented two women in Mozart's life who he loved, each for very different reasons. Each of them fulfilled needs in his life that the other could not fill, and each loved him in a way that only she could. So it is very important for us then, to remove the filters of our modern understanding of marriage and the role of women in modern western society before we can understand the difficult place in which these three people found themselves.

If Nancy Storace was so important to Mozart, then why have we not heard of her? When I began my research on her over ten years ago, I asked myself this question. Several Mozart biographers including Georg Nissen and Joseph Lange mention that Mozart had an "emotional attachment" to Nancy, which, in eighteenth century terms meant an affection of the heart. And the great Mozart historian and biographer, Alfred Einstein, even went as far as to say that Mozart loved Nancy, and that the great concert aria, *C'hio mi scordi di te...Non temer amato bene, K. 505*, he composed as a farewell gift for her was a declaration in music of his love for her. Einstein makes his disdain for Constanze very clear in his Mozart biography, *Mozart: His Character, His Work*, and adds that Nancy was much better suited for Mozart in temperament, education, and status. It has only been the more recent biographers who have chosen to minimize the role and influence that Nancy had in Mozart's life, most often in an effort to accentuate the relationship between Mozart and his wife, and bring Constanze back into a more favorable light. To one, Constanze is the end-all and be-all of love interests to Mozart, and Nancy, nothing more than a minor fling, and to the other, Nancy is the great love of whom fate and circumstances deprived him, and Constanze is little more than an air-headed spend-thrift who didn't understand her eccentric, genius husband. Through my research I've found both views to be extreme and that the truth probably lies somewhere in-between. Again, we have to look within the historical and cultural context of these peoples' lives and events and look beyond the surface facts and our own cultural biases to what would be most likely true for them.

After years of combing through Mozart biographies, memoirs of Mozart's and Nancy Storace's contemporaries, websites, numerous articles, online forums, BBC transcripts, and one fairly recent, complete biography on Nancy Storace, it became clear to me that a piece of the Mozart story was missing, leaving a number of questions about the latter years of Mozart's life unanswered. Why did Mozart pawn the family silver to buy a coach and four to go on that last German tour for which he had no invitation or commission? Why did Constanze, in the last two years of Mozart's life, spend so much time in Baden, separated from her husband? Why did Mozart write a letter to her while she was at the spa, telling her that he had heard rumors of her amorous adventures, begging her to be discrete? Why was Constanze not at home when she gave birth to her last child, and why was Mozart not present when the child was born? Why did she, only after her husband's death, give the child the name Wolfgang, Jr.? Why do none of Constanze's letters to her husband survive? How did Georg Nissen know of the letters that Mozart wrote to Nancy, and why did he want to confiscate them? And most importantly, why did Nancy save the letters that Mozart wrote to her only to destroy them just before her death, twenty-six years after his?

Two things convinced me that there had been a massive cover-up of the relationship between Mozart and Nancy orchestrated by Mozart, Constanze, Constanze's second husband, Georg Nissen, as well as Nancy, herself. First, when my partner, S. K. Waller, and I began to collaborate on the parts about Mozart and Nancy in her novel entitled, *Night Music: The Memoirs of Wolfgang Amadè Mozart*, we put together a timeline of their lives and found that the opportunities for such a love affair were ample, and that the situations in which they found themselves would easily lend to it. The fact that Nancy was educated in a fashion unlike any other woman performer of her day would have been extremely attractive to Mozart and knowing his character and personality, she would have been irresistible to him. Nothing that I have written in this novel is outside the realms of possibility, and in much of what I have written there is a very strong possibility that it happened in the very fashion in which I described it. I was very careful to stick to the documented events in these two people's lives, even in my conjecture.

Second, it wasn't until very recently that I learned that there had been an inquest into Nancy's death in which her maid testified about the two "German men" who showed up at Nancy's door inquiring about the "letters from Vienna". The maid testified that when they demanded she hand over the letters to them that Nancy "railed" at them and threw them out of her house. On the evening of that very same day, she suffered the last in a series of strokes and died a few days later. The letters from Mozart (presumably), were never found, but her son, Spencer Harris Braham, years later wrote to Nancy's good friend, the English architect, John Soane, that Nancy had destroyed them.

I believe that in an effort to protect their reputations, both living and posthumously, Mozart and Constanze began the cover-up in such a manner as I have described in this novel. Then after Mozart's death, Constanze continued to try and boost her own reputation, which was directly tied to her husband's, in order to garner the sympathy of the court so that she could receive the yearly widow's stipend that would help sustain her and her two children. When Nissen came into the picture, he saw financial opportunity in being the first to write Mozart's biography.

Knowing that there was much evidence that would sully Mozart's reputation in the form of letters, Nissen decided to use his diplomatic connections to confiscate any letters that might serve as evidence against the cleaned-up and sanitized Mozart he wished to present, thus the two German men that Nancy's maid testified about in the inquest into Nancy's death. In an effort to keep the only thing of Mozart she had left, sacred, Nancy destroyed the letters, leaving history to wonder what had transpired between them.

Since this book is not a scholarly work, but rather a piece of historical fiction based on actual people and events in history, I have chosen to forego the inclusion of a formal bibliography and/or footnotes as, again, I felt it would be too cumbersome for my readers and would bog the story down. In light of that, however, I would like to acknowledge some of my major resources:

Anderson, Emily, editor, *The Letters of Mozart and His Family*
Brace, Geoffrey, *Anna Susanna: Anna Storace Mozart's Original Susanna*

Carr, Francis, *Mozart & Constanze*

Clive, Peter, *Mozart & His Circle*

Da Ponte, Lorenzo, *Memoirs*

Einstein, Alfred, *Mozart: His Character, His Work*

Gutman, Robert W., *Mozart: A Cultural Biography*

Hildesheimer, Wolfgang, *Mozart*

Kelly, Michael, *Reminisces*

Landon, H.C. Robbins, *Mozart's Last Year*

Mersmann, Hans, editor, *Letters of Wolfgang Amadeus Mozart*

Selby, Agnes, *Constanze: Mozart's Beloved*

Waller, SK, *Night Music: The Memoirs of Wolfgang Amadè Mozart*

Finally, I would like to thank several people who have been instrumental in my efforts in the research and writing of this novel. First, I would like to thank Geoffrey Brace, the author of *Anna Susanna: Anna Storace, Mozart's Original Susanna*, which is the only complete biography written about Nancy Storace. I don't believe that Mr. Brace will agree with the conclusions that I have drawn regarding Mozart and Nancy's relationship, but without his work, I wouldn't have had such a complete and detailed picture of Nancy's life and career, and therefore, it has been invaluable to me.

Many thanks go to the people who have supported and contributed to the editing and reviewing of the original manuscript: my partner, Steph Waller, who served as my chief editor (and who also contributed large portions of the research, writing, and ideas in this novel), and Deni Hall, a dear friend who contributed her editing expertise. Thanks also go to Kathy Handyside, Jessica Jewett, Nellie Kampmann, and Juliana Brandon who have served as readers and reviewers.

Many thanks go to Dr. Allen Scott, who was the chair of my graduate committee, and who has since become one of my dearest friends. Dr. Scott was the one who encouraged me to write my master's thesis on the life and work of Nancy Storace and her relationship to Mozart. And although he would have preferred that this piece be a scholarly work, without his encouragement and friendship, this book would never have been written.

To Larry Weinstein goes my deepest appreciation for his belief in the beauty and veracity of this story. Without his insight Nancy and Wolfgang's story might never have been told.

Last, but certainly not least, my heartfelt thanks go to my beloved Steph, who is the love of my life, the inspiration for every word I write, and who is the very heart and soul of this beautiful story. Ich liebe dich für immer und ewig und drei Tagen.

K. Lynette Erwin
2009

The End of Book One

When Love Won't Die

The Continuing Story

K. Lynette Erwin

Alla Breve Books

MMXI

Dedicated to those who have loved and lost, and loved again.

Foreword

*H*istorians, whether professionals or serious amateurs, become so partly because they see the compelling, human stories in what others see as dry facts and figures (names, dates, and places). In addition, not many can tell the stories of these figures in such a way that they are brought to life for the layperson. For this reason, it is especially rewarding when a reader discovers a story, whether objectively factual or novelized, written in such a way that he or she is drawn into the inner life of the historical characters.

Another trait of the historian is a combination of curiosity and dedication—the kind of curiosity that keeps you asking more and more questions and the dedication to pursue the answers no matter where they lead. Ms Erwin's curiosity about the life and career of Nancy Storace led her to spend thirteen years in satisfying it. *So Faithful a Heart* is the result of her intellectual journey in pursuit of a woman who obviously played a significant role in Mozart's life and career.

In the first book, Ms Erwin created such a compelling character in Nancy Storace that I wanted to know about her life after leaving Vienna. In the second book, she satisfied my curiosity. Book one primarily recounts the significant events of the young singer's life and career up to 1786, when she returned to her native England. In book two, we see how Storace comes to terms with and integrates those experiences into a complex and passionate adult personality. She grows into a strong woman, not because she lacks weaknesses but because she has them. Mozart remains a living presence in her life, and the development of Storace's character is intertwined with her struggles to find a place for him in her heart while still allowing room for present concerns and present loves.

Writing historical fiction is a tricky endeavor. The genre's greatest challenge is to remain true to the objective historical events that can be verified through extant documents and recorded eyewitness accounts while filling in the blank spaces in such a way that the result is an intellectually comfortable and plausible story. Ms Erwin deftly meets this challenge by telling Storace's story as an inner drama in which the historical facts serve as catalysts for the heroine's self-actualization and character growth.

It is my hope, as I am sure that it also is Ms Erwin's hope, that after reading *So Faithful a Heart* the reader will return to Mozart with a deeper understanding of his world, the significant people in it, and ultimately to a deeper insight into his music. Music is, after all, a human art, and whatever affects the human affects the art.

Allen Scott, Ph.D., Musicology
Autumn 2011

Prologue

London Courtroom, Late 1817

"*If* it pleases the Court, I call Signora Storace's chambermaid, Miss Emma Walthen," a robed and wigged lawyer called out over the hushed chamber.

As young Miss Walthen made her way to the front, a murmur was heard across the courtroom as those in attendance speculated over the testimony they were about to hear. After taking the oath, the maid took her place before the judge for questioning.

"Please state your full name for the Court."

"Emma Eugenia Walthen," the maid replied. As a young woman born of humble circumstances, with little or no formal education, she felt a bit intimidated by the court trappings and protocol.

"You will have to speak a little louder, Miss Walthen, so that the Court can hear you."

"I'm sorry, guv'na. I'm just a bit shy," she replied, clearing her throat. "EMMA EUGENIA WALTHEN," she shouted. "There. Was that better, guv'na?"

The people in the room burst into laughter as Miss Walthen looked about, confused as to what she said that would illicit such a reaction.

"Please, would you tell us of the events that took place on 19 July, 1817, just prior to Signora Storace's final illness?"

"Well, it started out as any ordinary day," the maid began. "Madam was sitting in the drawing room at her desk, reading what appeared to be some old letters."

"How do you know they were letters?"

"They had addresses on them."

"How do you know? Did you see them?"

"I did. When Madam went to the drawing room, she left the door wide open. As I passed by the doorway I peeked me head in, just to have a look-see. Madam hadn't been well and we were all a bit nervous about her condition, so I looked in on her every chance I could."

"What happened after that?"

"I went about me business and several minutes later, I heard someone knockin' on the door."

"Did you answer?"

"I did, yes."

"Who was there?"

"They was two men. They was dressed all fine like and spoke English, but with queer accents."

"What did they say?"

"They wanted to speak to Signora Storace."

"Did they say why?"

"No, sir. Only that they wished to speak with her."

"What did you do then?"

"I excused meself and went to the drawing room to speak to Madam."

"What did you tell her?"

"I said that there were two German men who wished to speak to her."

"What made you think they were German?"

"Well, guv'na, ya see, I have me a cousin who's German and when he goes ta speak, he sounds like them two gentlemen did."

More laughter broke out through the courtroom as the maid looked about, once again confused.

"How did Signora Storace respond?"

"She asked me if I was sure they was German. I told her that they sounded German to me, and then she said for me to show them in."

"After you showed them in, what did you do?"

"Madam sent me to fetch the tea."

"So you didn't hear the beginning of their conversation with Signora Storace?"

"No, sir. I was in the kitchen with the cook."

"And how long were you with the cook?"

"Only a few minutes, I reckon. It was time for tea anyway, and the cook had already put the kettle on the boil. I only asked that she set the tray with two more cups and some extra biscuits."

"When you returned to the drawing room with the tray, what were they discussing?"

"Some letters. It seems that Madam had some that they wanted."

"Do you know who the letters were from?"

"No guv'na, but something was said about the letters being from Vienna."

"Vienna? Why Vienna?"

"Why, Madam was a very popular singer in Vienna back in the old days, she was quite a lovely woman and had the gents' eyes, she did!"

"So you're saying the letters they wanted were from a gentleman in Vienna? A lover, perhaps?"

"I can't say. I only know what I heard the gentlemen and Madam talkin' about. I never heard who the letters was from."

"Did the signora indeed have the letters in question?"

"She wouldn't say one way or another. She just kept insistin' that even if she had the letters, she wouldn't sell them because they would be of too personal a nature."

"Did the men threaten the signora in any way?"

"Yes, sir, they did," she said, wide-eyed. "They insisted that she hand the letters over straight away, or else they'd be forced to get a warrant to take them legal like."

"And how did she respond to this threat?"

"She got spittin' mad, she did. I can't recall when I've seen her so cross, not even when her and Mr. Braham got into a row. She railed and cursed at them, and ordered them to leave the house."

"Did they obey her order?"

"No, guv'na. She called me into the room and told me to show them the door. When they refused to leave, she grabbed them by the arms and showed them out herself. I opened the front door and she shoved them out onto the step, shouting at them."

"What did she shout at them?"

"I don't rightly believe I can repeat such words in genteel company, sir. It wouldn't be proper." She leaned into the lawyer and whispered, "She called them bloody bastards."

Again, laughter broke out in the courtroom.

"What did she do after that?"

"She slammed the door right in their faces and then she nearly fainted dead away. Her face was as purple as a turnip and her eyes was poppin' outta their sockets, they were. She called for me to get her smelling salts."

"And what happened next?"

She paused, trying to remember.

"Well, she fainted for several minutes. I sat down next to her until I was certain she was fit to be moved, then I helped her up and took her back into the drawing room, and helped her lie down on the settee."

"Continue," the lawyer said.

"I sat with her until she insisted that she was all right and ordered me to go on about me business. So I went out to the stables to report to Mr. Spencer what happened. After that, he decided to come back to the house to check on her to see if she was all right."

"Did she move herself from the chair at that point?"

"No, sir. Not while I was in the room. I left after she was settled, and it wasn't until several minutes later that I smelled something like old paper burnin' in the fire. It was strange, too, because it was a very warm day and I couldn't imagine why Madam would have lit the fire."

"Did she burn the letters?"

"I wouldn't know. All I can say was what I seen, heard and smelled, and that was something what smelled like burnin' paper."

"Did you ever again see the letters that you said you saw her reading earlier that day?"

"No guv'na, I didn't. They just seemed to vanish into thin air."

Chapter One
London, September 1791

It was a typical day at Richard Brinsley Sheridan's theater in Drury Lane. The morning was filled with rehearsals for the new up-and-coming productions that lasted into the early afternoon. Afterwards, the cast and crew broke for a three-hour lunch while the sets were placed for that evening's performance. Costumes hung in dressing rooms and stagehands swept the theater floor and dusted the seats. Then, at six in the evening, the cast arrived to begin the nightly routine of putting on make-up and getting into costume before the eight-fifteen curtain.

"Good evening, Signora Storace," the make-up assistant said as she ushered Nancy to her seat in front of the mirror. "Hold your head still for just a moment, please, while I tie your hair into this cap."

Pulling Nancy's long, dark tresses back from her face, she plaited her thick hair into a single braid and wound it into a circle on the back of her head. After covering everything in a thin muslin cap, she pulled the drawstrings taut so that it fit neatly without any gaps, and tied it.

"Are we ready now?" Nancy said with her characteristic cheerful smile.

"I think we are, Signora. Now, look up!" the assistant instructed as she applied the base to Nancy's skin. After the make-up was set, she penciled the definitions around the eyes, applied cheek and lip rouge and then a fine dusting of powder.

Finally, she took a wig from of its stand and placed it on Nancy's head, tucking in bits of the cap that peeked out-until they the wig fit snugly.

"All right, signora, you can change your clothes now."

Nancy went behind the screen and slipped into her costume for Act I, and then stepped out so that her assistant could lace the bodice up the back.

Nancy went to a full-length mirror for a final look, her assistant following behind to make sure there were no loose threads hanging or hems sagging. She handed Nancy her fan, her only prop in the first scene, and sent her out the door.

"Break a leg!" she said in the theatrical tradition of wishing an actor or actress good luck. "You'll be wonderful, as always, I'm sure."

"Thank you, Eleanor." She headed into the hall and made her way to the stage.

Just as she turned the corner to the stage wings, she heard the orchestra tuning. She could tell from the din of voices murmuring through the heavy curtain that once again the theater was packed.

She heard Michael Kelly's Irish brogue behind her as he whispered something to the stage manager and the orchestra began the overture.

"Places for scene one!" the stage manager called out softly.

Nancy shook her limbs and stretched her neck to loosen up before she walked on to sing her opening duet with Kelly. Only seconds before the orchestra finished the overture, the curtain rose over the massive proscenium as Nancy and Kelly walked briskly out onto stage to take their places.

The audience broke into applause. It was sometimes difficult for Nancy and Kelly to hear their orchestra cues over all the clapping, so Stephen always reminded the instrumentalists to play a little louder at that point.

They reached their spots on stage in perfect sync with the music and together, the magnificent Signora Anna Storace and the stupendous Mr. Michael Kelly opened their mouths to sing the first measures of the night's performance and to thrill their London audience once again.

ஐ௮

Since Nancy and her brother Stephen made the break from the King's Theater at Covent Garden a few years before to join forces with Sheridan, along with their old and good friend Michael Kelly and the popular English actress Ann Crouch, they had risen to the ranks of stardom throughout London. Nancy was excited to perform in the same theater with such notables as Sarah Siddons and John Bannister. Stephen became wildly popular as both a composer and a producer of a new form of English musical theater, which he derived from the German Singspiel after his months of study with Mozart, in Vienna. He was at Covent Garden when his first production of *The Doctor and the Apothecary* (which he adapted for the English stage from a production he saw in Vienna), became extremely popular. The English audience quickly embraced the new style and Sheridan saw its popularity as a way to bring in fresh audiences. When Stephen, Nancy, and Kelly were handed lucrative offers form Sheridan, the three made the break from the Italian-dominated King's Theater to Drury Lane with amazing ease.

After the move, Stephen and Nancy continued to work alongside Thomas Attwood and Wolfgang Mozart's agent in London, Johann Salomon, to gain a commission at Covent Garden for Mozart. Sharing a fevered correspondence with the composer, they obtained copies of his latest works and performed various pieces from them in their own productions. Their tireless efforts were finally rewarded with a commission from His Highness The Prince of Wales, for Mozart to compose two Italian comedies for the King's Theater. In late 1790, however, Mozart turned it down for reasons that he did not explain. Nancy, who had been involved in a passionate love affair with Mozart at the time she left Vienna in early 1787, had high hopes for the affair's renewal. She was bitterly disappointed with his refusal.

Over the previous years, they kept in personal contact, writing letters which expressed the passions that they kept alive, despite the distance. They hoped to re-consummate those affections when they reunited, but it wasn't long after he refused the commission that Nancy received his last personal letter to her, telling of his undying devotion but sadly spelling out the necessity of why he must end their relationship.

> *O Wanze, how can I bear to write the words? What cruel fate has brought us to this point? Again, I shall not tarry but shall come quickly to the point. This will be my last letter to you, my dearest love, not because my affections for you have diminished for, on the contrary, they have only grown deeper and more impassioned since last we saw one another, but because circumstances in my situation have developed to the place where, for the preservation of my reputation, my work, and my family, our affair must end...*

"No I refuse to believe it," she exclaimed through her tears as she folded the letter and laid it on the stack with the others. "He can't mean this. We've worked too hard and come too close for him to give up on us now!"

She picked the letter up to and read the last paragraph again.

> *...And although we will never see one another again in this life, my soul will always yearn for you. I vow to you my undying love for all eternity, whatever that is. I vow that whatever happens in this universe, I shall always find you and love you. You will never be alone. Whoever else may have my body, you will own my heart. Farewell, angela mia...*

"I know him. He won't be able to live with this decision. This isn't the end... It can't be—I won't let it be."

Full of bitter feelings, Nancy gathered up all the letters and tied them in a bundle; her intention was to grant his request and destroy them.

How could he ask me to do this, she thought as she held them over the fire. They're all I have left of him. Holding them there for only a few seconds, she pulled them back.

No, I refuse, she thought as she turned away.

She went to her desk and put them inside a wooden box, which she locked in the bottom drawer.

A year later, still grieving over the ending of their love affair, she came up with one last-ditch effort to bring Mozart to London by mentioning the possibility of producing *The Marriage of Figaro* at Sheridan's theater, a production in which she would sing the role of Susanna, the role she had created five years earlier in Vienna. They could invite Mozart to conduct the first three performances and perhaps, then, they could entice him to stay and compose more operas for their theater.

"It's certainly worth asking, don't you think, Richard?" Stephen presented the proposal at the director's meeting that was called to discuss the idea.

Sheridan, who was fashionably rotund, always wore a somber and calculating expression when facts and figures of any venture played foremost in his mind.

"Well, it depends entirely upon the cost," he said. "What do you propose we offer him as recompense?"

"Standard commission, travel expenses, and lodgings would be reasonable, I should think."

"Hm... Lodgings included?"

Stephen glanced at Kelly and rolled his eyes. This was typical of Sheridan—the cheapskate.

"All right then," Stephen replied impatiently, "he can lodge with me at my flat."

"What about commission based on percentage of house take?" Sheridan offered.

"Be realistic, Richard," Kelly said. "We've no idea what the house take will be. Give the man a standard commission. Tis only right. After all, he is the composer!"

"This stands to be quite a profitable venture, Sheridan," said Mrs. Crouch. "A Viennese composer coming to London to conduct one of his own Italian comedies in our theater? That's something that even Covent Garden didn't achieve."

Sheridan slumped in his chair and thought for a moment, the calculations whizzing furiously through his mind. Finally, he took a deep breath and slowly exhaled.

"Very well, then. Mrs. Crouch, you write the necessary letters. And I want to see all the figures in writing before anything is signed or delivered! Do you understand?"

"Of course. I'll make them available to everyone before I send anything," she said as she grinned at Stephen and Kelly.

Drury Lane

Chapter Two
Freihaus Theater, Vienna, October 1791

"That backdrop needs to come down faster," Mozart ordered from the center of the theater. "And Papageno, make sure you come in on the correct beat at the entrance of that phrase! You're two beats behind. How many times do we have to go over it, God damn it? The opening's tomorrow!"

"Entschuldigen Sie mich, Herr Mozart," a page whispered from behind as he handed him a letter. "It's from Herr Salomon. I've been instructed to wait for your reply."

Mozart opened it and read.

> *I've been informed that you are soon to receive a letter from London regarding an invitation to conduct the London premiere of Le Nozze di Figaro in Sheridan's theater in Covent Garden. I strongly urge you to seriously consider this invitation, Mozart, as after your refusal of the last commission from The King's Theater, this may well be your last chance to get to England.*

"Take a fifteen minute break," Mozart shouted to the cast on stage. He sat forward and ran his fingers through his hair. "I have to give him an answer now?"

"Yes, Herr Mozart. That's what he requested."

Mozart sighed and thought a moment.

"Tell him that I can't possibly make a decision at this precise minute. I've got a show opening tomorrow, for Christ's sake!" He ran his palm across his forehead. His head ached. "Tell him when I receive the letter I'll seriously consider it, when I know all the details."

"Ja, Mein Herr," the page replied. "Guten Tag."

I can't think about London right now, he thought. I have too much at stake here—too many things finally going well.

Life had suddenly taken a good turn for him. After the birth of his youngest son in July, he and Constanze seemed to be getting along better than before; even though she still spent what he felt was an inordinate amount of time at the spa in Baden. Expensive as it was to maintain two households, as well as sending their oldest son Karl to that costly boarding school, the money was starting to roll in. Between this new opera, which he was sure would be a great success, and a commission for a Requiem Mass for which he had already received some pay, he had also obtained a new post as Kapellmeister at St. Stephen's cathedral. Stanze was most certainly happy about that. Finally, a steady post which brought with it a steady income, meager as it was.

And what would he tell Constanze? London? They promised nearly a year ago never to speak of London—of her—again. The matter was settled, the letters written and he put that all behind him. Or had he? True, he never spoke of her again. He never even mentioned her name in passing, but that didn't keep him from thinking of her. Although she rarely entered his thoughts directly, she was always there. Her presence was often felt, especially on his long walks with little Karl through the Prater. Once, he even allowed his thoughts to drift back to that glorious summer in Laxenburg, where they were able to freely indulge their passions and declare their undying love. The promise of Paradise—those days seemed so far away now.

He leaned back in the seat and closed his eyes, allowing his mind to drift back to one of those luscious mornings at Laxenburg when he awakened in her bed. They had a game they played with one another to help him with his English and her with German.

"Sagst du auf englisch, 'Ich liebe dich,'" he asked.

"I love you," Nancy whispered as she took his face in her hands and drew his mouth to hers. She kissed him deeply. "How do you say in German, 'Make love to me'?"

"Mach Liebe mit mir," he sighed as he enveloped her in his arms and held her body close to his, returning her ardent kisses.

Ah, Nancy, he thought. We were never meant to be. A single tear made its way down his cheek. He wiped it away. I can't think on this now. I don't have time. I'll think on it later, when the letter arrives.

It was a busy year. The entire first part of the 1791 season was filled with concerts with Joseph Haydn, who was in London through Johann Salomon, the same agent who worked with Mozart. Nancy sang in a concert in which Haydn premiered his 96th Symphony (affectionately known as the *Surprise Symphony*), and sang the premiere of his English cantata, *Ariadne*. In July she was invited to Oxford to see Haydn awarded an honorary doctorate of music. It was a three-day occasion marked with another of his oratorios, *The Seasons*.

Nancy and Haydn became dear friends and he often spoke of Mozart, recalling the days when she was in Vienna with her brother, and of the friendship they shared there. When he learned that Mozart was invited to conduct a London premiere of *Figaro*, he was delighted and hopeful that Mozart would accept the invitation. He knew of Stephen's deep devotion for and friendship with Mozart. He also knew there was something deeper in Nancy's regard for his friend than a warm professional relationship. He saw the sparkle in her eyes and the blush on her cheeks whenever they spoke of him.

"Not to worry mein klienes Singvogel," he said. "If I know that little man, he'll move hell and high water to get to you. It's not over yet." His brown eyes danced. "I was at your last concert in Vienna. I heard it in the aria he composed for you. I saw it in his eyes. He can't stay away from you, Nancy. And who can blame him?"

She blushed and looked away.

"If only I were half my age, he'd have some competition," he said with a wink.

The spring months filled with the music of Haydn were followed by a summer of performances with Sheridan's theater. Ironically the summer season was moved to the newly re-built King's Theater in Covent Garden as only a few months before, Sheridan's theater on Drury Lane burned to the ground, taking many original copies of most of Stephen's earlier works with it.

In a frantic rush to meet the needs of an ardent public, Stephen rescheduled three of his surviving operas to be performed along with an adaptation of Salieri's comic opera, *La grotta di Trofonio*, which was the piece Nancy sang upon her return to the stage in 1785 in Vienna, after her extended illness.

Accustomed to a busy schedule, Nancy never complained. She wasn't the type to sit out of a performance over a cold, or any complaint, for that matter, so it was only when she made an exit from the stage that Stephen noticed she didn't look well.

"Kitten, are you ill?"

"I'm fine—just a bit tired. I think the schedule's been a little much lately with the move and all. I'll be all right. You know me, I always pull through."

He grinned and smacked her on the bum with a rolled-up score.

"I wish I had ten more like you. I don't know what I'd do without you, Kitten. You know that don't you?"

"I do. And you'd best not forget it," she said with a grin.

It was difficult for Stephen to admit that his success was so completely attached to his sister's. As a man, it was a bitter pill to swallow. If only he were as naturally gifted as his friend Mozart, perhaps he could stand on his own better. But as it was, he was grateful that he had Nancy.

Music wasn't his true passion. He would rather have been an artist—a painter—but it was their father who'd insisted on pressing him towards a career in music, starting him with lessons on the keyboard and violin when he was very young. He took to the violin, but composition didn't come as easily. He was a solid and consistent composer—Mozart said that—but even he knew that his pieces were a strange mixture of the banal and the inspired and he was grateful that his London audiences didn't know the difference.

He recalled as a twelve-year-old boy when Stefano sent him to study composition at the music conservatory in Naples, how homesick he'd grown for his family and friends, and even for London. He hated life at the conservatory and he hated formal musical study. It wasn't long before he found comfort in the company of a fellow Englishman, a painter by the name of Thomas Jones, a man who was twenty years his senior. Jones came to Italy to paint the beautiful landscapes there and he took Stephen in as a companion and apprentice. It wasn't long before the conservatory wrote a letter to Stefano, telling him of Stephen's truancy and of some trouble that Stephen had gotten into while in Jones' company. It was only after receiving the letter that Stefano decided that it would be a good time to launch young Nancy's Italian singing career as well as take care of the trouble with his son and his friend.

Stefano never spoke of the nature of the trouble and Nancy dared not ask, for apparently it was something very serious—serious enough to cause her father to uproot their whole family, including their mother Elizabeth from her family and friends in London, the only home she had ever known.

Elizabeth begged her husband to leave her and Nancy behind. She insisted that Nancy was too young to start a singing career (an idea that was corroborated by Nancy's singing teachers, Venanzio Rauzzini and Antonio Sacchini). Still, Stefano was insistent and, despite the intense protests from all around, he set sail with his family for Naples when Nancy was only twelve years old.

Upon their arrival Stefano found the trouble to be worse than he had expected. He immediately removed Stephen out of the conservatory and took his son's studies back into his own hands. Stephen was nearly an adult and there was no time to lose if he was to undo the damage that Jones' influence had already had upon him.

Stephen, who was of a quiet and sensitive nature, but who was easily influenced by men like Jones, resented his father's intrusion. He never forgave his father for shaming him only to force him back into a profession that he secretly despised. Even Stephen's eventual success and overwhelming popularity with the London public couldn't extinguish the resentment that burned in him.

But who was he to complain? He was a wealthy and successful man who was held in great esteem by the theater-goers as well as the general public, so perhaps Nancy was indeed as dependent on him as he was her. After all, in the end, he knew that it was always the composer who would be remembered over the performer. Composers were immortal; singers, by the very nature of the voice's dependence upon the ever deteriorating body, were not.

Stephen Storace

Chapter Three

*O*pening night of Die Zauberflöte was every bit the success that Mozart had hoped it would be and to add to that, his partner and librettist Emmanuel Schikenader reported that the first week's house takes were double any he had ever had in the theater's history. Mozart celebrated by attending every performance, often enjoying having his friends and colleagues accompany him. On one occasion he was accompanied by his friend and fellow composer, Antonio Salieri and Salieri's mistress, the famed Viennese singer, Catarina Cavalieri.

Dizzy with his success, Mozart began to make plans for the future. Believing that money was no longer an issue, he thought about the offer that Salomon told him was coming and began devising a way that he could take a sabbatical from his newly-appointed post with St. Stephan's. He wasn't scheduled to take over the post until the beginning of the following year, so he didn't know how he could leave it so soon. He feared he would have to stay on for at least a year before he could ask for a sabbatical. The question was if Sheridan would wait that long. Mozart knew from his correspondence with Stephen that Sheridan wasn't known for being the most patient of impresarios. Dominant, controlling and calculating of nature, as well as possessing a fiery temper (as demonstrated often with his outbursts as a member of the House of Lords), Sheridan was definitely going to be difficult to please.

As he sat in his favorite tavern sipping beer and contemplating his future, he allowed his thoughts to wander, thinking again of London and the woman who could be waiting for him there.

Does she still love me? How could she after I insisted that it had to be over between us? She's too passionate to be without a lover. How could I expect her to carry a torch for me for the rest of her life?

Eternal love was a romantic notion from which only poets and playwrights profited. For everyone else it was something too unrealistic to be attainable. Marriage was the only permanent bond. The Church said it, so it must be true—a sacrament, eternal, lasting and forever.

He reached for his handkerchief and wiped the beads of sweat that ran down his face. Eternity spent with Constanze? He couldn't imagine it. That wouldn't be heaven, he thought. That would be sheer hell. Perhaps I should remain in purgatory.

Constanze was at the spa again. He couldn't help but wonder why she continued to go there, knowing how expensive it was. She didn't seem to care that every trip she made there plunged him deeper and deeper into debt, forcing him to work night and day composing, seeking work and commissions just to keep up. They were by no means poor—far from it—but the debts were still oppressive. Even the financial success of Flute and the steady income from a new post wasn't enough to keep up with all the debts she racked up.

As he took another sip of beer, he felt ill. Suddenly seized by intense nausea and cramping, he clutched his belly. As it overtook him, he clapped his hand to his mouth as he felt the urge to vomit. He ran to the door, waving off the tavern proprietor, who had been observing him from behind the bar. He staggered out, barely making it before he turned towards the wall of the tavern and vomited.

He looked up, down the block towards his apartment building. Could he make it without getting sick again? His feet felt suddenly heavy and swollen inside of his boots.

What is wrong with me? I can't get sick now! Too many things to do. Too many people depending on me.

He made his way across the cobbled street, leaning against the buildings.

If I can lean against the walls, I think I can manage to make my way...

Another wave seized him. He clutched his stomach, retching. The pain was excruciating. Suddenly the cramping gave way to an intense urge to defecate.

I can't shit myself. I won't shit myself. Mein Gott, what is wrong?

Through a feverish blur, he finally saw the entrance to his building, so he shuffled as quickly as he could, struggling to hold his foul excrements at bay. Finally, he made it to the doorway when a man passed him on the street and saw his condition and helped him inside and up the stairway to his apartment, where only the maid and the cook were home to receive him.

ॐ

"Ladies and gentleman, the necessary letters have been sent," announced Mrs. Crouch to the gathering of theater executives and patrons.

Stephen and Nancy turned to one another and smiled. Surely Mozart would accept this proposal.

Although she managed to keep her affections for Mozart secret, she couldn't help but allow them to vent a little at the prospect of his coming to London to conduct the very opera which had ignited their deepest passions for one another. It couldn't be more perfect.

It's going to happen this time. I just know it!

Fearing her giddiness would give her away, she sat on her hands and said nothing, biting her lip in nervous anticipation while she listened to Mrs. Crouch lay out the details of the proposal. Her thoughts were suddenly transported back to that summer at Emperor Joseph's summer estate in Laxenburg.

Diana's Temple. She could remember every detail as if it had only been the night before. The deep night sky filled with stars and Mozart's shadow in the moonlight, waiting for her under the massive baroque pavilion. She closed her eyes and felt herself in his arms, felt his lips searching for hers, making their way to her chin, down her throat, and to the soft rounds of her bosom.

"Oh my love, my very heart," he whispered as he covered her face with kisses. "I thought I'd lost you. I feared I'd taken too long—that you'd grown weary of waiting."

"I would've waited forever, Wolfgango, for there's no one I love as you," she exclaimed as she held him closely.

"I've fallen in love with you, Nancy. I'll say aloud that I adore you," he declared defiantly. "I've been afraid of allowing myself the joy of this emotion, fearing the consequences of such affections, but it only tore me apart and made my longing for you even deeper. Right or wrong, I can't put aside what I feel any longer, Wanze. Right and wrong be damned; I've made my choice."

She let an unconscious sigh escape and hearing it, Stephen elbowed her in the ribs, waking her out of her reverie.

"What in heaven's name is the matter with you?" he whispered. "Why are you falling asleep?"

"I wasn't asleep. I was just… thinking, trying to remember the music. Susanna is a huge role, you know."

"I know you. You'll remember. You don't forget anything," he whispered as he turned his attention back to the discussion.

After the meeting ended, everyone gathered for some punch and refreshments. The room was filled with excited chatter about the upcoming season and the anticipation of Mozart's arrival. Nancy stood in a corner, alone with her thoughts and memories. Suddenly she felt dizzy. Closing her eyes, she thought it must be another bout of fatigue, but when she opened them again, the room started spinning. She reached for a chair, but she felt her knees give way and she fell to the floor.

When she opened her eyes again, she was home, in her bed.

"What happened," she asked, as she tried to sit up.

Elizabeth and Stephen were in the corner of the room discussing something with her doctor.

"You fainted," Elizabeth replied. "You passed out on the floor at the theater. Don't you remember?"

"The last thing I remember was the room spinning, and then I woke up here," she said, perplexed.

"How are you feeling now," Dr. Roberts asked.

"A little tired. That's all. It's nothing serious is it?"

The doctor glanced at Stephen and Elizabeth. Neither of them spoke.

"I'm afraid, Signora, that it may be quite serious. Excuse me for intruding upon a painful and intimate subject, but when you were in Vienna…"

He cleared his throat. "During your marriage to John Fisher, did you suffer any head injuries?"

Nancy stared at her hands which lay folded in her lap. She fiddled with the lace on the edge of the sheets.

"Again, I apologize for bringing up such a painful event, but it's important that I know. I hope you understand," he said with noted compassion.

"Yes. He boxed my ears and slapped me so hard that my head nearly snapped off of my neck," she said, bitterly. "Why? What has that to do with what happened tonight?"

"Whenever the head is battered about in such a manner, the brain is slammed against the skull. It can be bruised and often lacerated and will bleed. In your case, the bruise or laceration was partially healed, allowing you to live a normal life...up to this point." He hesitated again. "You could die, Signora Storace."

Nancy sat in stunned silence. She looked to the corner of the room where her mother and brother anxiously awaited the prognosis.

"Is there anything to be done?"

"It's a surgical procedure. I've already discussed it with your mother and brother, but I must discuss it with you and obtain your consent before I will proceed with it."

"What is it? How is it done?"

The doctor cleared his throat again. "I will have to bore a hole in your skull, about the size of a walnut, so the blood may drain from out of your head. It's extremely dangerous and the procedure itself could be fatal."

"Is there nothing else? Can't I be bled instead?"

"I'm afraid not. It needs to be done immediately, signora."

Nancy looked again to her mother and Stephen. "What do you say," she asked, hoping they would object.

"Kitten," Stephen replied. "It sounds like it's the only way. If it's not done tonight you could die."

"But I feel fine. I'm not even dizzy."

"The bleeding will continue and you will fall into a coma and die," the doctor said.

"How long will that take?"

"An hour, a day, a week—no one can be sure."

She fell silent, deep in thought. "No, I'm not ready," she replied firmly.

"But Ann, didn't you hear the doctor?" Elizabeth said. "You could die in an hour if you don't have this procedure."

"And I could die in an hour if I do!" Nancy snapped back. "I feel fine now, and I'm not willing to take the risk!"

"Ann, you must..." Elizabeth pleaded.

Nancy pulled Elizabeth into her arms and held her tightly. "Mother, please..." she begged. "If you love me, don't ask me to do this."

"Very well, then," the doctor sighed. "But if her condition worsens, I'm to be notified at once. Do you understand, Mrs. Storace?"

"Dr. Roberts, we appreciate everything you've done on my sister's behalf," Stephen interrupted, "and if the condition does worsen we will send for you immediately. The maid will see you out now. Thank you, again, Doctor," he said as he ushered him out the door.

Nancy fell back onto her pillow and rubbed her forehead with her fingers. "Well, I'm not sure I believe all this silliness about dying. I'm just tired, that's all. All I need is a good night's rest and some peace. You can count on me being back tomorrow, Stephen."

"Ann, you can't..."

"Mother, I think it is best we leave her now," Stephen said, taking Elizabeth by the shoulders and directing her to the door. "We'll send Harriet in to watch over you as you sleep tonight."

Nancy started to object but was cut short.

"Don't say me nay on this one, Kitten, for it will be done," Stephen insisted. "Now, good night." He blew her a kiss. "We shall see you in the morning."

Anna "Nancy" Storace

Chapter Four

Vienna and London, December 1791

*M*ozart sat in his bed, propped up by several large pillows. On his lap lay his lap desk and spread upon it, a large manuscript. For the moment the nausea had subsided and his head was clear enough for him to work.

I must finish as much of this as I possibly can. It will bring more money in for Constanze and the babies.

He began to weep. How could it be? How could he die now? Not now. Things had only just begun to turn for him. He had work, more now than ever before and there was this new prospect in London. And Nancy. How he loved her, still. He would never see her again.

Lacrimosa dies illa...Qua resurget ex favilla...Judicandus homo reus...

"Tearful will be that day on which from the ashes for judgment, the guilty man shall rise..." he whispered.

After the tavern incident, the doctors committed him to his bed. His sister-in-law Sophie came to care for him as Constanze was still in Baden. She had to be summoned for the doctors said that he only had weeks to live. Since her return she hadn't been in his room more than two or three times to sit with him, comfort him, or talk with him. Instead, it was Sophie who nursed him and gave him the tenderness that he so needed in his waning hours.

"I am the guilty man rising from the ashes for judgment," he said to himself. "Only it isn't God who judges me, but my wife and family. This is my Requiem. I compose this for me. Forgive me. Oh, dear God, forgive me."

Constanze sat and stared blankly out the window onto the passersby below. Seven-year-old Karl played on the floor with the little tin soldiers that Franz Süssmayr gave to him as a present—something to help divert his attention from the fact that his father lay dying in the next room.

This was not at all the way she pictured it would be when just over nine years ago she stood in front of one of the lesser altars at St. Stephan's and took the vows of marital fidelity, honor, and obedience. He promised to make her happy, wealthy, and secure. After all, he was the most popular composer in Vienna! Instead, she was left with the painful memories of four dead children and the burden of two to raise and support on her own, a mountain of debt (that could easily land her in debtor's prison if she couldn't find a way to pay it off), and a husband who would most likely die with another woman's name written on his heart.

The resentment she felt was almost overwhelming, but still she had to pretend to be overcome with grief. Pretending was something she was never good at. Her mother and sisters wondered why they hadn't seen her cry. She had no tears to shed; they were all shed when she realized that his love for her was gone and that he only remained with her out of duty as well as fear for his reputation and loss of livelihood.

He lay swollen and languishing in his bedchamber and as her youngest sister carefully and tenderly nursed him in his last hours, Constanze plotted her revenge. No one will know, she thought. No one will ever believe that he loved anyone else but me. He'll die, and then I'll tell his story and I'll bury that woman with him. No one will even remember her name.

∞☙

It had been nearly three weeks since the ordeal which brought with it the news that she might be dying, but still Nancy refused the treatment that could save her. She claimed she was much better and went about her daily activities as normally as possible. However, when she started fainting on stage during her performances, she was ordered immediately back to bed.

"I'm afraid she's no better," Dr. Roberts said. "In fact, she's worse."

"She'll never consent," Stephen replied.

"Then we shall have to do it after she faints and can't withhold consent. At that point, Mr. Storace, your consent shall be all that is required."

"Won't it be too late by then?"

"Most likely, but it's our only alternative."

ဆာငလ

"How much longer, Dr. Closset," Sophie asked.

"Only hours—a day at the most. He's getting weaker. We bled him, and that seemed to help give him a little more strength."

"What shall I tell Constanze?"

"Tell her that if she cares for her husband, that if she ever cared for the poor man, she will make peace with him now. There is very little time."

ဆာငလ

"Stephen, hurry," Elizabeth exclaimed. "Send for the doctor. She has a fever and she's growing delirious."

ဆာငလ

Mozart lay unconscious in Sophie's arms. His body was so swollen that she barely recognized his face. Only a couple of hours before, he'd looked up into her eyes and with tears in his own, he'd smiled and said, "I die now."

Suddenly, she saw his cheeks puff and he blew out in a rhythmical beat. She believed he was trying to create the sounds of the tympani in *The Magic Flute*, but it was really only the signal that death had come.

> "On the very eve of his death, had the score of the Requiem brought
> to his bed, and himself (it was two o'clock in the afternoon) sang the
> alto part; Schack, the family friend, sang the soprano line, as he had
> always previously done, Hofer, Mozart's brother-in-law, took the
> tenor, Gerl, later a bass singer at the Mannheim Theater, the bass.
> They were at the first bars of the Lacrimosa when Mozart began to
> weep bitterly, laid the score on one side, and eleven hours later, at one

o'clock in the morning (of 5 December 1791, as is well known), departed this life." (Benedikt Schack, the first Tamino in *Die Zauberflöte*)

ဆင္ကၠ

"She's delirious, Doctor. She slips in and out of consciousness," Stephen said.

"She has a fever. I'm afraid if it goes any higher, she won't survive. It's up to you, Mr. Storace. If I'm going to do it, it must be done immediately."

Stephen gazed down at his dying sister, then over to his mother, who sat in a chair in the corner of the room, weeping.

Her life is in my hands. What do I do, he wondered. He sighed then and reluctantly gave his consent.

ဆင္ကၠ

The room was familiar—soothing sights, sounds, smells, textures. Nancy sat at her dressing table applying her makeup for the night's performance when she heard a soft knock on the door.

"Wolfgango, you're here! I knew you would come. You don't know how I've missed you."

"Only as much as I've missed you."

"Come, let us fly from here. Yes, take me to Laxenburg! Deh vieni non tardar! Incoronar di rose."

"Not now, meine Wanze. It's not time for us yet. I can't stay long; I only wished to see you once more before I leave."

"But where are you going, Wolfgango? Please, let me go with you!"

"You can't come yet. You have to stay for now, but I promise I'll come for you. Love doesn't die, Wanze. Our love won't die. I'll come back to you when the time is right. Until then, farewell, angela mia!"

ဆင္ကၠ

A loving breath from our beloved will grant sweet solace to the heart...
From the aria "Un aura amorosa" from *Cosi fan tutte* by W. A. Mozart

Wolfgang A. Mozart

Chapter Five
London, January 1792

"Mr. Kelly," the page whispered. "I'm sorry to disturb you, sir, but I have an urgent message from a Mr. Haydn."

"Thank ye, lad," Kelly replied as he stood from his seat in his theater box and handed the page a farthing. He quickly made his way to the lobby where he opened the message.

"Oh, dear sweet Mother of Jesus," he exclaimed as he crossed himself. "It can't be! Say it's not so!"

It had only been three weeks since Nancy's ordeal, which very nearly robbed her of her life. Amazingly, her recovery was going very well and she was slowly feeling her strength and vitality return. Her recovery was speeded along by her knowledge that the invitation for Mozart to come to London had to have arrived by then. It was close. She could feel his very presence surrounding her. Why, even while she was lost in a deep coma on the night of the operation, she dreamed he came to her in her theater dressing room. She took it as a sign that she was to fight to live through the ordeal and recover quickly, for in the dream he promised he'd come for her.

"Ann, are you awake?" her mother called through the door as she knocked upon it, softly.

"Yes, Mother. You can come in. The door's open."

Quietly, Elizabeth entered Nancy's room to see her lounging comfortably on a settee, where she'd been inventing the scene in her mind of the passionate reunion—of him taking her in his arms and holding her there forever. It was so real Nancy could almost feel his breath.

"Ann," Elizabeth said, sounding a bit shaken. "Michael's here. He has something he needs to tell you."

"It's awfully late. Did he say what it was?"

Elizabeth nodded. "He did, but I think he should be the one to tell you."

"All right then." Nancy sighed, perplexed by her mother's strange behavior. "Send him in."

He entered to see her in her favorite chair, the wound left in her skull by the surgeon only three weeks before neatly concealed beneath a fashionable, yellow, silk turban. She looked remarkably well for a woman who had only recently experienced a close brush with death.

"Have a seat, Mick," she said, gesturing to the settee. "What brings you here at this hour?"

"I've just received news from Vienna."

"Ah! Then Wolfgango got the invitation!" She perked up at this news, the color instantly returning to her cheeks.

"Yes, Nancy," Michael replied. "The invitation arrived, but…"

"So what did he say? Will he come?"

"No, Nancy, I'm afraid not." He knelt beside her.

"Why not? What's his reason this time," she asked, dismayed.

Tears pooled in his eyes and his chin quivered. "He can't come, Nancy, because…"

"Mick, what is it? Why can't he come?" She sensed the bitterness of the news she was about to receive and flew into a panic. "Why are you crying, Mick? Please tell me what's happened!"

"Oh, me darlin' dove," he said as he buried his head in her lap and wept. "He's dead, Nancy. He died three weeks ago on the very same night we nearly lost you."

"It can't be! Who told you this?"

"I just received word from Haydn. It arrived this evenin' as I was attendin' the theater. I rushed over immediately to tell ya."

Nancy stared past him in shock. "Does Stephen know," she asked, flatly.

"I assume Haydn has written to him as well, I guess. I don't know." He was so overcome with emotion that by this time he could hardly speak.

"Dear God…" She whispered as she ran her fingers through his thick blonde curls, a tear making its way down her cheek. "Would you mind leaving me now? I'm not feeling well, and I need to be alone."

"Certainly, me dove," he said as he raised his head and pulled his handkerchief from his waistcoat to wipe his eyes. "You know where I am if you need anything—anything at all," he assured her.

"Yes, thank you, Mick." She managed to look at him and smile.

After he shut the door, Nancy sat for a few moments and allowed the bitter news to sink in. How was she to bear up under this? What fates were so cruel that she be handed such a cheated lot? Suddenly she opened her mouth and released a mournful wail.

"Oh, God, no! Please, God. It can't be!" She fell from her chair onto the floor, wailing and sobbing. Managing to rise to her feet, she staggered to her vanity table and cried out again.

"You promised me, Wolfgango! You promised me you'd come back! How could you die? Oh, God, he's dead! He's dead!" she wailed.

Then with one great sweep of her arm she cleared the tabletop of its contents. Powder and rouge boxes, perfume bottles and trinkets all went crashing to the floor.

She fell on her knees and continued to sob, burying her face in her hands, then she slowly crawled to the bed where she clung to one of the posters and grabbed at the curtain pulling it down on top of her. She wrapped herself up in it and continued to weep, crying and heaving until at long last she exhausted her tears and fell into a deep sleep on the floor by her bed.

≫〇≪

"Good morning, Kitten," Stephen crowed cheerfully. He carried the breakfast tray to the table and as he set it down, he turned to his sister, who was awake but lingering in her bed.

The four months since Nancy's operation had been touch and go. Her recovery was slow due to what Dr. Roberts believed to be a reticence on her part to live. Following the operation she regained consciousness and her recovery progressed at a pleasing pace until Michael Kelly arrived three weeks later with the news of Mozart's death. None of them received the news well, and all were deeply grieved, but Nancy seemed to take it harder than anyone. Stephen wished that he had been there when Michael told her, for he would have suggested that Nancy's condition was still too delicate and that it should wait until she recovered her strength more completely.

"You're up and about awfully damned early," Nancy moaned, rolling over as Stephen drew the curtains to allow in the sunlight.

"For God's sake Stephen, it's too early, and my bloody head is pounding."

Stephen ignored her complaint and went about his business. "Our Auntie sent over some of those breakfast scones you love so much. I thought you'd enjoy one with your coffee. And after you're up and about, I thought I'd bring your nephew over for a short visit. You've not seen him since before your operation and, since the wife brought him with her into town a few days ago, I thought it would be a good time for a visit."

Just shortly after they'd returned home from Vienna, Stephen married Mary Hall, the daughter of his godfather, John Hall. She was pregnant when they married and several months later gave birth to their son, Brinsley, who was named for Richard Brinsley Sheridan. Shortly after the wedding, Stephen moved his little family to a different flat on Howland Street, just down the way from Nancy and their mother. Then, not too long after the baby was born, Stephen bought a country home in Hayes, Middlesex, where his wife resided with their son. Stephen, who much preferred life in the city and who felt he needed to be closer to the theater, took a smaller flat on Percy Street, which he shared with his friend and librettist, Prince Hoare. Nancy always thought it to be a strange arrangement and wondered why Stephen was so content to be mostly separated from his wife, who seemed amiable and pleasant enough. Nancy adored little Brinsley, and his visits always served to cheer her.

"I'm too tired. Perhaps tomorrow."

"Mary's going back to the country tomorrow, Kitten. Now up with you, and have some breakfast. The good doctor fears you're not getting proper nourishment and it may be part of the reason you're not recovering as quickly as you should be."

"I'm not hungry."

"Kitten, what's the matter?" He sighed. "It's been months now. You survived the most perilous part of it and you should be doing much better than this. We're all quite worried."

Tears welled in her eyes.

"What if you travel back to the country with Mary tomorrow? You love the countryside, and all the gardens. Remember back in Vienna when you recovered from your ordeal at Baroness Waldstädten's estate? Mother wrote that the fresh country air did you good."

"I don't want to go into the country." She began to cry, so he pulled her into his arms.

"Oh, sweet Kitten, what have I said? What' troubling you? Can't I make it better?"

"There's nothing you can do."

She snuggled up and allowed him to hold her. His arms felt warm and safe. It didn't matter that it was her brother, she hadn't been held like that by a man in such a long time and she lingered in his embrace. She needed a man like her brother, especially now.

"Everyone misses you, Kitten. You should see the numbers of cards and letters that are delivered to the theater every day, all asking about you and wishing you well. People love you, darling."

"I simply don't care anymore, Stephen. It hurts too much to care."

"Oh, Kitten, please don't say that. There's always a reason to go on caring about life. This simply isn't like you. You're always the one telling me what a sorry disposition I possess concerning such matters, now look at you."

She let her head droop a little off his shoulder and hiccupped several times. What choice did she have? She could continue to languish in bed in grief and despair, or she could decide to move on with her life. It was obvious she wasn't going to die at this point no matter how much she wanted to. Her brother was right. This wasn't like her at all.

"Perhaps you're right," she said as she finally pulled out of his arms and wiped her eyes with her sleeve. "A visit to the country might do me some good after all. I'll enjoy sweet Mary's company and I do adore that impish little son of yours." A smile crept upon her lips.

For the first time since this all began, Stephen saw a little sparkle return to her eyes.

"Now, will you get out of that bed, sit in your chair and have some breakfast with me?"

"All right," she agreed.

ಜೋಜ

Nancy spent a month in the country with her sister-in-law and nephew and as her brother suggested, it seemed to be just the medicine she needed to complete her recovery. Although the grief she felt for her loss remained buried deep within, she was able to face life again and the prospects that the rest of it would be lived without her precious Wolfgango.

She returned to London near the end of May to make her comeback to the stage in her brother's opera, *The Siege of Belgrade*. London's favorite diva was greeted with thunderous applause and bouquets of flowers tossed at her feet from the audience.

Nancy's unrelenting performance schedule began once again and she engaged in a whirlwind of concerts, stage performances, and oratorio performances that had her singing throughout London and in various cities and counties all across southern England.

Since her old teacher and friend Venanzio Rauzzini relocated to Bath several years before, she and Stephen were often invited to visit and perform concerts for the wealthy theater patrons and nobility who frequented the old Roman city, which was famous for its mineral baths and spas. While in Bath, the Storaces hobnobbed with some of England's most noted, respected and wealthy men and women, including the famous architect Sir John Soane, Lord Barrymore, Lord and Lady Hamilton, and many other famous and fashionable personages. They were frequently seen at the most fashionable parties, dances, and soirees in Bath's Royal Crescent and their fame spread beyond London's theater patrons. The demands for their talents brought them into the salons of England's most noted gentry, nobility, and royalty.

"Mr. Soane," Nancy exclaimed when their eyes met across the crowded room at a party given by the Barrymores in their opulent home on the Crescent. "I hoped I would see you here," she said as he made his way to her. She extended her hand. "How did you enjoy our little concert this evening?"

"It was absolutely marvelous, as usual," Soane exclaimed as he took her hand and politely kissed her cheeks.

Soane secretly fell in love with Nancy from afar when she was a sixteen year-old girl on the stage in Pergola, Italy while he was on his early Italian architectural tours.

"And you even performed my favorite piece!"

"Indeed. And which one would that be, Mr. Soane?"

"Oh, it's that darling little ditty from your brother's version of that German piece that he picked up while you two were in Vienna, *The Doctor and The Apothecary*."

"*How Mistaken is the Lover?*"

"That's the one! Delightful little number, and you sang it in such a coquettish fashion that I daresay you had every gentleman in the room falling at your feet, including me." He laughed.

"You're too flattering, Mr. Soane," she replied, blushing. "But I'm most certainly glad it pleased."

"Oh, it pleased. Quite effectively, in fact, as I glanced across the room and saw Lady Barrymore give her husband a sound smack with her fan when she caught him gazing at you too intently."

"I'm sure you exaggerate, Mr. Soane." Nancy laughed.

"Indeed not," he replied playfully. "I'm an architect and I'm quite exacting in all things, including my observations on such matters."

ಬಿೞ

It was the late fall of 1794, during one of their visits to Bath, and Rauzzini was excited to introduce Nancy and Stephen to a young pupil of his, a tenor by the name of John Braham. Eleven years Nancy's junior, Braham had been orphaned as a child and was forced to sell pencils to keep from starving. He was also a descant singer in the Great Synagogue in London and his lilting, lyrical voice had caught the attention of a Jewish opera singer by the name of Michaele Leoni. Leoni introduced Braham to a wealthy Jewish family who were patrons of his theater in Covent Garden, by the name of Goldsmid. The Goldsmids took him in to raise and, later, sent Braham to Bath to study with Rauzzini.

Braham, who was short and stocky and possessed a thick mop of curly, black hair, couldn't act to save his life, but the sweetness, fullness, and richness of his tone made up for any lack in his acting style. It was reported that the first time that Lady Hamilton ever heard him sing, she was so overcome that she suffered a fit of hysterics and had to be escorted from the theater.

Nancy and Stephen first met Braham at a concert in which Nancy was invited by Rauzzini to sing some duets with him. Anxious to show Braham off and have him seen on the same stage as the wildly popular Anna Storace, Rauzzini thought it was a good way to launch the tenor's stage career and make the public sit up and take notice.

"Signora Storace," Rauzzini said. "It is my greatest pleasure to introduce one of the finest young talents I have ever known, Mr. John Braham. Mr. Braham, this is the magnificent Signora Anna Storace. The

Signora was of course, one of my students many years ago and has risen to be one of my greatest successes. I'm very proud of her."

"Mr. Braham," Nancy acknowledged with a nod of her head.

"Signora," Braham replied with a low bow, planting a kiss on the back of her extended hand. "It is a tremendous honor. Of course, no introductions are needed as I have long been your greatest admirer. I must confess that I fell in love the moment I laid eyes on you in a production of your brother's *No Song, No Supper*. At the mere suggestion of our performing this concert together, I was nearly overcome. Ah!" he sighed, "I'm besieged with tender emotions at the mere touch of your hand!"

Nancy had to hold back her intense amusement at the young fellow's overly-effusive remonstrations. How long could he have been her greatest admirer? Good God, how old was the boy, anyway, seventeen? She wasn't impressed. She had many male admirers, among them a number of silly, lovesick boys just like Braham.

The impression was made, however, at the first rehearsal and the following concert when he opened his mouth to sing. She'd never heard anything like it before. It had to be one of the sweetest sounds on earth. Indeed, Rauzzini was correct in his assessment regarding Braham being one of the finest young talents he had ever known. It was a sheer pleasure to perform with him.

"My God, Kitten, I've never heard such an incredible voice! He's absolutely miraculous! So what say you of bringing the lad to London to cut his teeth in our theater," Stephen asked as they traveled the road back to London.

"Well, certainly there's no question that he's up to the task, vocally. And oh, what an absolute joy to sing along side such a voice! My only concern is with his acting abilities. He seems quite stilted, and he often makes up for that with melodramatic sentimentality and over embellishment."

Stephen smiled as he looked out the window over the passing countryside. He began to chuckle.

"What?" Nancy questioned. "What do you find so amusing?"

"Mozart would have loved him. I'm referring, of course, to the 'melodramatic sentimentality' part of your assessment. He seemed ever so fond of that in his tenors. I mean Kelly, for the love of God!"

Nancy laughed. "Indeed. He would have," she exclaimed. "I'll never forget the time when Kelly launched into that dreadfully awful sentimental and completely inappropriate embellishment in that Handel piece at one of Mozart's little home concerts. Do you remember?"

Stephen nodded, smiling.

"Well you know Wolfgango, not being extremely familiar with Handel thought it was only too magnificent, all the while you and I sat in the back row, cringing."

Stephen laughed. "He really was one to completely lose himself in a sentimental phrase." Suddenly, his expression grew serious as he gazed back out the window. "I miss that chap, you know. I miss him quite a lot. I don't know why, but lately, I've felt his presence a great deal, as if his spirit were here watching over." Tears welled in his eyes.

"I know. I miss him too, Stephen. I can hardly speak of him without being reduced to tears," she said, trying to hold back her own emotions. "I think you're right about him being close. For some reason, and I don't know exactly why, since my last ordeal, I've sensed his presence. I've always found it rather odd that he passed on that very night."

"Indeed," he replied, nodding.

"And it's probably no secret to you, either, that there were some tender affections expressed between us, although I've never spoken of them, really. But since he's gone now…"

They both remained silent for a while until Stephen spoke up again.

"Kitten, I need to ask you something. Of course, you don't have to answer. I mean, if I'm intruding on something too personal, well, please forgive me."

"You know there is very little I would keep from you, Stephen."

"I know." He swallowed hard.

"Go ahead. Ask. If I don't wish to answer, I simply won't." She smiled as she dabbed her eyes with her handkerchief.

"I know there were many things that went on in Vienna of which I knew nothing. I always sensed that you and Mother kept certain things from me, and I wasn't quite sure why." He hesitated. "But now that you've brought it up…"

"Go on, then."

"The baby."

"Yes? What about her," Nancy asked, perplexed.

"She wasn't Fisher's child, was she?"

She turned and stared out the window as the tears poured down her cheeks again.

"Please forgive me if this is too painful for you, Kitten. You know I never wish to hurt you."

"I know what you're asking, so to save you some time and misery I'll tell you. No, the child wasn't Fisher's. Does that satisfy you?"

"You're angry with me."

"No, I'm not. I'm simply confused as to why you would bring this subject up now."

"Now? You mean now when we're discussing Mozart?"

Nancy glared at Stephen. "How dare you insinuate…"

"I'm not insinuating anything Ann, I'm simply asking."

"Why? Why do you need to know who the father was? Does it really matter? The child is dead and for that matter, so is her father."

There were several more moments of tense silence before Stephen spoke again. "Then it was him, wasn't it?"

Nancy diverted her gaze.

"I'm so sorry, Kitten. I didn't mean to hurt you."

"Then why did you persist? Why was it so important to you? Are you jealous?"

Stephen looked stunned. He turned away and stared out the window, then looked back again at his sister, who couldn't believe what she had just said.

He *is* jealous, she thought. *Oh dear God, Stephen, you can't have been. You were in love with him?*

Stephen didn't answer, but turned to stare once more out the window.

Suddenly it all made sense—the wife and son who lived estranged in the country, the flat in the city with his friend, Mr. Hoare, his flirtations with Lord Barnard in Vienna years ago, and even the trouble he got into as a young man with that Welsh painter in Italy.

"My God, Stephen."

Frontispiece for *The Siege of Belgrade*
by Stephen Storace

Chapter Six
London, December 1794

After the revelation which left her stunned, Nancy finally accepted that this was most likely the way that Stephen had been bent for his entire life. How could this be? She was grieved and saddened, but more than anything else, she was frightened. Still, she did her best to deny that they'd ever had the conversation in the first place and that this deep, dark secret had ever come between them. She would do well in her denial until Mr. Hoare would come strolling into the theater—he and his foppish mannerisms and his obvious fawning on Stephen. He was careless and too obvious, and she secretly resented him for putting her brother in danger. Was she the only one who noticed it, or had everyone else always known and never said anything? Of course they never mentioned it. What was she thinking? It was something that everyone knew happened, but it simply wasn't discussed, and it certainly never happened in one's own family.

And then there was the issue regarding Mozart. It did make sense, though. Stephen had always worshipped him to the point of being overenthusiastic in his esteem for him. Still, she never dreamed that she would had ever had to compete with her brother over the affections of a lover, and for him to know that her dead child was Mozart's only made the wound deeper. She didn't know how to reconcile it. Perhaps it was something that would always be between them. Nancy loved Stephen more than any other person on earth and to have this come between them left her with unspeakable grief and loneliness.

Still, there was work to be done and more shows to be staged. Nancy was far too busy helping her brother make the new Drury Lane Theater a success to keep her mind occupied with personal matters. Stephen was in the midst of staging several newer works, but it was always the older ones that seemed to draw the larger crowds. She sang with Kelly in several more productions of *The Haunted Tower* as well as *The Siege of Belgrade*. All the while, Stephen worked feverishly on new pieces, which he was determined to make every bit as successful as his earlier works.

One day he called Nancy into his study, where he sat looking over an old libretto that he came across—one that he found in his father, Stefano's library.

"Look at this, Kitten."

"What is it?"

"It's one of Papa's old librettos—*Dido and Aeneas*."

"Thinking about improving on Purcell now, are we?"

"No," he said with a wink. "We're already better than Purcell. Now we're setting our sites on Mozart."

Nancy raised an eyebrow. "Oh really? We *are* ambitious."

"Seriously though, this looks intriguing. Of course I'd have to have Prince bring the libretto up to date."

"It's a serious piece. It's been a while since you've composed opera seria."

"I know, but it's such a fabulous story and with the witches and demons, it could be spectacular! And it wouldn't be seria, exactly. I'd do it in the Singspiel style—spoken dialogue and all—but the subject and story would be serious rather than comedic."

"And who would sing Dido," Nancy asked as she leaned into him, batting her eyelashes.

"Oh, I don't know. I was thinking about Elizabeth Billington," he replied with a grin. "She'd make the perfect Dido. What do you think?"

Nancy's eyebrows furrowed.

"Don't like that idea? Hm. Then how about Sarah Siddons?"

"Wonderful actress, but she doesn't sing," Nancy replied as she folded her arms.

"Oh no, not true," he exclaimed, wide-eyed. "Why just the other day I heard her singing some lovely little ditties in her dressing room."

He spoke in a womanly, high-pitched, sing-song voice, imitating. "'Oh, dear, John! Why you're ever so...Oh...Oh...Oh my!'" He shot her a devilish grin. "Then she started singing duets with someone that went something like this: 'Oh, God. Oh, God! Oh...dear...Gaaaaaawd!'" He fought to keep a serious face. "Don't know who the composer was, sadly, but the counterpoint and voice leading were rather good."

Nancy burst into a fit laughter.

"I think Miss Siddons has missed her true calling. Really," Stephen concluded.

Dido, Queen of Carthage opened to an expectant audience, but it wasn't received with the enthusiasm that Stephen's comedies garnered. The critics were harsh, and it failed within the first month's run. Nancy was bitterly disappointed over its failure, and claimed that the London critics were boorish and lacked the sophisticated taste necessary to appreciate it. For the rest of her life she regarded *Dido* as Stephen's finest work.

Despite *Dido*'s dismal failure, letters and offers continued to pour in from neighboring areas and theaters—offers for Stephen and Nancy to come and perform. Nancy was in charge of keeping up with all of the correspondence—accepting or rejecting of offers and the recording and filing of all letters and invitations—as she seemed to have a keen mind for such things. Stephen relied not only on her talents on stage, but also her sharp mind and natural instincts for the business of the stage as well.

One afternoon as Nancy sat at the desk in Stephen's salon going about the business of filing the most recent correspondence, she came upon a yellowed letter written in a familiar hand. She picked it up and upon closer observation she saw that it was a letter from Mozart, written to Stephen and Thomas Attwood at the time that they were all working hard to obtain a commission for him to compose an opera for the King's Theater.

"What is this doing out," she wondered aloud.

She allowed a smile to curl her lips as she carefully unfolded the letter and read. His written English was never as good as his spoken, yet he insisted on writing to them in English, rather than Italian, which was also a common language among them.

Don't never forget your true and faithful friend...

She continued to read the letter which was mostly a personal expression of thanks to all of them for their tireless efforts on his behalf. Still it was from him, and seeing the words written in his own hand, in his so-familiar broken English was comforting and it made Nancy feel as if he weren't so far away after all.

She heard Stephen's voice calling out to her as he came through the front door. "Kitten?"

"In here filing some of these most recent letters."

"Oh, there you are," Stephen said cheerfully as he stepped through the open salon doors. He walked to the desk and picked up a pile of letters and started rummaging through them.

"So how many are we rejecting this week?" He chuckled. The enjoyment of such fabulous success was one of his not-so guilty pleasures.

"Too many, I'm afraid, but there comes a point when we can only spread ourselves so thin, and I do believe that we've reached it."

"A good place to be, actually."

"Indeed, but it's difficult when I have to turn down so many worthy charity events. Still, we can only attend so many." She shrugged, shaking her head. "I only hope that they won't be offended and will invite us again for another season on the chance that we'll accept the next go-around."

"What's this," Stephen asked as he noticed the open letter lying on the desk beside the others.

"Just an old letter."

"What's it doing out?"

"I don't know, Stephen. I found it lying here with the others."

"Did you read it?"

"Well, yes. When I saw that it was an old letter from Mozart, I was naturally curious," she replied defensively, wondering what was behind Stephen's questions.

"It wasn't addressed to you, was it?"

"Well, no, but when I saw that it was also addressed to Thomas Attwood, I assumed—"

"You assumed that it was all right for you to read someone else's personal correspondence?"

"What is the matter with you? It wasn't personal in the least. In fact, it could easily have contained my name in the address considering the subject. Why are you reacting so?"

"The point is that it wasn't addressed to you, and therefore you had no business reading it," Stephen shouted.

Suddenly, Nancy remembered the conversation that they'd had in the coach on the way back from Bath.

"He wasn't your lover, Stephen," she spoke through clinched teeth.

"How dare you!"

"How dare *I*? You're standing there overreacting to something completely innocent on my part, and you ask that?"

She walked around to the front of the desk.

"Do you really want to read some letters from Mozart, Stephen? Do you?" She began to pace. "Because if you do, I have plenty of them. They're locked in a box in my desk. Do you want to read them?"

He remained silent, his eyes lowered.

"I think you should. Then perhaps we can clear up between us who his lover really was." She stopped and glared at him. "The letters are addressed to me and me only, and they contain sentiments that leave little to the imagination. Perhaps they would serve to shatter this little fantasy that you seem to have going on in your head!"

Nancy walked out through the French doors into the entry to retrieve her cloak and called to him.

"From now on you can have someone else take care of correspondence. Perhaps your dainty little friend, Mr. Hoare, could do it for you. That is, unless you're afraid he'll read all those personal sentiments from your dead lover!" She paused a moment to tie her bonnet. "By the way, I'm taking a week off to drive to Hayes to visit your wife and son for Christmas. They've been feeling rather neglected lately and I thought a visit from family was needed in order to cheer them. I'm telling you because you'll have to get my understudy to fill in. Good day."

⁝⁞

"How good of you to come, Ann," Mary exclaimed as Nancy stepped into the entry of her sister-in-law's home.

"Brinsley," she called up the stairway. "Your Auntie Ann is here! Do hurry, darling! She's ever so anxious to see you." Mary took Nancy by the arm and escorted her into the salon where she and little Brinsley had only just finished decorating the mantle and the windows with fresh pine boughs and sprigs of holly. The finely appointed cottage was warm with the glow of candlelight and the fire blazing in the hearth.

Mary was a lovely, petite woman with the delicate bone structure, porcelain skin and chiseled features that were so fashionable at the time and so very attractive to the men. Her strawberry blonde hair was braided and coiffed in the new Grecian style and she wore the newest frocks which were higher in the waist and flowed straight to the floor in a diaphanous fashion. When she spoke, her voice was as delicate as her appearance. Mary was always polite and amiable, and Nancy admired her lady-like ways and appearance, often wishing she could be more like her.

Mary, in turn, admired Nancy for her talent, wit, and spirited ways and was always anxious to hear the latest gossip from London. She was proud of the success that her husband and Nancy enjoyed together and sat listening, wide-eyed, as Nancy recounted the trips to Bath and of the fashionable soirees in the fashionable homes attended by all the fashionable people on the Royal Crescent.

Any other woman, Nancy thought, would be resentful of a husband who traveled all over to such noted and luxurious locations and not take her along. What man in his right mind, with such a lovely and refined woman for a wife, would refuse to show her off?

"How have you been faring, Ann? The last I heard from Stephen, he wrote that you were all quite busy and he was fearful that your health might not hold up."

"Oh, don't worry about me," Nancy replied, laughing. "It's that silly brother of mine who concerns me. He burns the mid-night oil working until all hours of the morning, and then is up at eight o'clock for a morning rehearsal. And when he isn't rehearsing a new piece or composing one, he's conducting a performance, or leading some meeting with the patrons, or planning the next road trip."

"Oh, dear," Mary said as she folded her hands in her lap. "Then perhaps I have been remiss in chiding him so harshly over his long absences of late. I didn't realize…"

"Of course not, Mary. He's your husband. You have every right to want to see and be near him. I simply don't understand why he doesn't invite you and Brinsley to spend more time with him in London."

"Oh, I dislike the city terribly. It's too crowded, dirty, and stuffy for me. I much prefer the quiet solitude of the country. It's a much better environment for our son, and we're both happier here. It's just that we do miss Stephen so. Brinsley needs his father, more now than ever and…"

Nancy reached over and took Mary's hand.

"I understand. Perhaps I can talk to him and persuade him to take some more time away to be with you and little Brinsley. I don't think he realizes how neglected you feel. You know men, only thinking in the moment."

"Thank you, Ann. You and Mother Storace are always so good to me. I hope you know how very much I appreciate your kindness. You're the sister I never had."

As Mary poured some tea, seven-year-old Brinsley came bounding down the stairs and into the salon.

"Auntie Ann! I'm so glad to see you! Did you bring me a surprise from London?"

"Brinsley Sheridan Storace!" Mary scolded, "Mind your manners, young man! Now give your Auntie a kiss and, before you go asking for presents, you ask her how she is faring."

Brinsley leaned over and planted a wet kiss on Nancy's cheek. "How are you faring Auntie Ann? Now, what did you bring me?"

Nancy laughed, took him in her arms, and squeezed him tightly. "Have you been a good boy?"

"Why of course, Auntie. I'm always a good boy."

"Do you mind your Mama?"

He looked over at Mary who sat smiling proudly. "Most of the time," she replied.

Brinsley, who was the spitting image of his father, looked back into Nancy's face with his huge dark eyes and echoed his mother. "Most of the time."

"That's fair enough!" She leaned over and whispered something into his ear. Brinsley's eyes grew wide and his mouth fell open.

"Oh, Auntie Ann, you didn't!"

"I most certainly did," Nancy replied. "Now, mind you, it's from both your Papa and me."

"May I go and see it now?" He looked over at Mary, who sat confused.

"What is it you're going to see?"

"A pony! Auntie Ann and Papa got me a pony!"

"Oh, Ann," Mary exclaimed, "He has wanted one for some time now!"

"I know, but we were afraid that he wasn't old enough. I think now, as long as there is someone with him to supervise, he should be fine."

"Run now, and get your coat and hat," Mary said. "Martin will be in the stables tending to the other horses. He'll take you to your pony."

"Oh, thank you! Thank you, Auntie Ann!"

Little Brinsley bounded back up the stairs to be helped by the maid with his coat and hat and before long he flew back down and out the door towards the stables where his new pony awaited him.

Chapter Seven
London, 1795

"Nancy!" Stephen called to his sister, who stood on the corner of the stage discussing a blocking maneuver with Kelly.

"Can it wait a moment? I'm in the middle of something."

"Yes, of course," he said, waving it off. "Go on, I'll wait." Stephen leaned against the stage and continued to read the letter that he had just received from Bath. It had been a little less than a year since he and Nancy had traveled there to meet Rauzzini's newest singing pupil.

A moment later, Nancy made her way off the stage and down to the front where she found Stephen still reading the letter.

"What is it?"

"It seems our young tenor is ready for his debut."

Nancy looked confused. "Young tenor? I'm afraid I'm not following you. What young tenor?"

"Don't you remember? The one we met in Bath last November—the little Jewish one with the creamy-smooth voice who over-embellished everything."

"Oh, yes, of course! How could I forget? The lovesick boy who has 'long been my greatest admirer'." Nancy laughed, recalling the moment they were introduced. "I do admit, however, that his is one of the finest voices I've ever heard. John Braham was his name, if I recall correctly."

"Indeed. It seems that Rauzzini is ready to release him into the world, and has asked me if I might have a place for him in our theater."

"Well, there's no question that we have a place for him. The question is whether or not Sheridan will be willing to pay him."

"Never mind Sheridan; I can work around the stingy bastard. My biggest question is in what piece shall I debut him? I don't have any open tenor slots at the current moment and I don't want him understudying Kelly. He's too good to understudy. He's ready to go now, and if we don't offer him something soon, someone else most certainly shall."

"How long would it take to compose a new piece for him?"

"Damn it, Kitten, I don't know. I have so many new pieces on the table right now. Besides, my new pieces just aren't faring as well as the old ones. People are still beating down the doors to see *No Song, No Supper*, and it looks as if *My Grandmother* is going to be right up there with it. They just don't seem as interested in my newer ones."

"But those are two of Kelly's best shows. You can't take Kelly out and replace him with Braham. That wouldn't be right."

"I wouldn't dream of replacing Kelly. You know I wouldn't do that. I just don't know, but I've got to find a way to work this out," he said as he rubbed his chin and stared at the letter.

"Whatever you decide, Stephen, I'm behind you. It's up to you," she said as she patted his back and made her way back to the stage to begin the second half of the rehearsal.

৪୦৫୪

"Now, where did I put it?" Nancy said to herself as she looked all over her dressing table for the necklace she'd taken off before she'd changed into costume. "I thought I'd laid it right here."

When she didn't find it in the spot where she believed she'd left it, she opened her jewelry box and began to search in there. It wasn't lying on the first shelf, so she slipped her fingers through the ribbon loops on the sides to lift out the top tray, revealing the contents in the lower level. There on the very bottom, she noticed, peeking out from underneath several other pieces of jewelry a small red velvet box tied with one of Mozart's black satin cue ribbons. Recognizing it immediately, she retrieved it and held it in front of her.

"Oh, my God," she exclaimed. "I'd forgotten all about these!"

She untied the ribbon, which was one his favorites, and opened the box to reveal an exquisite pair of garnet earrings, the very ones he gave to her as a token of his deepest affections on their first night together at Laxenburg.

He promised that he would have me dripping in garnets, she remembered as she smiled, looking into the mirror to slip them into her earlobes.

"How beautiful they are!" she said aloud. "How could I have forgotten them?"

As she sat in front of the mirror turning her head back and forth, allowing the soft light to catch the numerous facets in the stones, she remembered the night she wore them for the first time—the night of the Emperor's opening ball at Laxenburg. Mozart was her escort, for as she was the star of his opera *The Marriage of Figaro*, which had just opened the new season, it was expected that he would be at her side.

He hadn't seen her when she'd entered the room, for he was standing at the window, his hands clasped behind his back, peering out into the night recalling the events of the evening before at Diana's Temple, when under the very same sky, he declared his undying affection for her.

"Wolfgango," she spoke his name sweetly.

As he turned, he saw what he believed to be one of the loveliest, most exquisite sights he'd ever beheld. There she stood all dressed in blue and pink, with flowers in her hair, her charming dark eyes peering into him from over her fan.

He took her hand and twirled her slowly so that he could look at her from all sides. "My darling, you are enchanting!" He was unable to take his eyes off of her. "I shall be the proudest peacock at the ball!"

"I'm wearing your earrings," she said as she tipped her head to one side, making them sparkle as they caught the light.

"Indeed, you are, and they look exquisite against your skin." He took her by the waist and pulled her in close. "I have half a mind to skip the dance and take you to bed this instant and ravish you, except that it would be an utter shame not to show you off."

Nancy buried her face in her hands, weeping. The memories were still too vivid, too real. "I can't take this, Wolfgango!" she cried. "How could you have left me here all alone?"

୫୦୯୪

Stephen was late, which wouldn't normally have been a problem except for the fact that they were staging a brand new piece and Stephen and Mr. Hoare had all of the copies of the new score with them. Kelly kept pulling out his watch, pacing back and forth.

"Where the hell is he?" he fretted. "We were supposed ta be startin' this rehearsal half an hour ago!"

"I'm quite sure he'll be here soon, Kelly," Nancy said, trying to soothe his Irish temper.

"We're on a tight schedule here and that damned librettist, Colman, has been breathin' down me bloody neck for over a week now. We don't have time to be waistin'."

Suddenly, Hoare entered, looking a bit hurried and upset.

"Ah! Mister Hoare! Nice ye could make it ta rehearsal. We've all been a sittin' here waitin' and in the meantime, we've been payin' an entire cast for the last half hour ta do nuthin' but sit on their bloody arses! Now, where's the goddamned scores?"

"I apologize, Mr. Kelly, but we ran into some difficulties this morning. I've brought the scores and if you will give me a few moments to get them sorted out, I'll have them passed out as soon as possible."

"Where's Storace?"

"Well, we need to talk about that, Mr. Kelly," Hoare said as he lowered his gaze and looked around the room. When his eyes met Nancy's, he motioned for her to come over. He pulled Nancy and Kelly aside and began to speak candidly.

"I'm not wishing to alarm you, but I believe, Signora Storace, that your brother may be very ill."

"What do you mean?"

"Well, for the past two weeks he has awakened every morning with a severe headache. They started out not too badly and by the middle of the day, they were gone. We weren't alarmed at first. Thought perhaps he was working too long into the night and was suffering from eyestrain." He hesitated a moment.

Sensing that the news they were about to receive was going to be bad, Kelly put his arm around Nancy and drew her in close.

"Then, beginning earlier this week, they got worse," Hoare continued. "He started vomiting. Sometimes he'd wake up so nauseous that as soon as he'd lift his head off the pillow he would start."

"Have you summoned a doctor," asked Kelly.

"No, not yet. I mean, not until this morning. That's the reason I was late getting here with the scores. This morning when he awakened he said that in addition to the blinding headache and nausea, he was having trouble hearing, so I sent the maid immediately to fetch Dr. Roberts. Then, as soon as she came back with the doctor, Stephen insisted that I gather the scores and bring them here."

"Oh, dear God." Nancy nearly fell to the floor, but Kelly held her up and led her to a nearby chair. How much more could she take?

"I'm sorry to have to be the bearer of bad tidings," Hoare said, "but I just didn't know what else to do."

Kelly placed his hand on Hoare's shoulders. "You've done just fine, Prince. Thank you. Now, ya go back and see what's happenin' with Mr. Storace and the good doctor, and Signora Storace and I'll be on our way shortly."

Hoare looked over at Nancy who sat, looking weary. "I'm so sorry, Signora."

"It'll be all right, Prince," Nancy said, calmly. "It's probably nothing serious. We'll wait to hear what Dr. Roberts has to say. Now, you run along. We'll be there soon."

When Nancy and Kelly arrived at Stephen's flat, they found that the doctor was waiting with grim news that Stephen was most likely suffering from a brain tumor. Dr. Roberts had no idea how long he had to live—perhaps only a few months—but there was little doubt that he would die.

Nancy sat stunned as she listened to the doctor give his prognosis. How could this be? Not her brother—her best friend and the only person in this world who she trusted completely. I've got to hold myself together, she thought. This isn't the time for tears. Everyone is going to depend on me now.

"He should be allowed to live as normal a life as possible, until he can no longer function," the doctor instructed, "Bed rest won't serve to prolong his life." He turned to Nancy and asked, "Where are his wife and son?"

"They're at home, in the country."

"She should be summoned. He needs her now."

"I'll write the letter immediately," Nancy replied, nodding in agreement.

"And your mother? Where is she?"

"She still lives with me, Dr. Roberts. I'll go home immediately and tell her."

"Is Stephen the only surviving male in the family?"

"Yes, sir," Nancy replied. "In the most immediate family, that is."

"Is there a male who will be responsible for you and your mother?"

Nancy gave the doctor a sheepish grin. "No, I don't suppose there is. But don't worry about us. I should think that I'm man enough for the job."

"Indeed, Signora Storace." The doctor smiled and placed his hand on her shoulder. "Indeed, I believe you are."

"May I go in and see him?"

"Of course. He's perfectly able to receive visitors at any time. I've given him a little laudanum for the pain, but he's still awake. I'm sure he'd welcome your company."

Nancy entered Stephen's bedchamber where he lay comfortably, propped up by several pillows. When he saw her he smiled. "Hello Kitten," he said warmly.

"How are you feeling?" She drew near his bed and took a chair near him.

"A little rough, but from what the doctor says, it sounds like it's only going to get rougher, so I'd better enjoy the easy time while I have it."

"Oh, Stephen," Nancy said as tears welled in her eyes, "I'm so sorry. This was supposed to be me, not you. Why you?"

"Why anyone, Kitten? I don't know. Why do any of us have to get sick and die? It's just a part of life—a bargain we strike the moment we're born. When it's our time, it's our time. That's all there is to it." He paused for a moment and then he took her by the hand. "Would you do something for me, Kitten?"

"Of course, Stephen," she replied. "Anything."

"Would you go to Mary and ask her come and to bring Brinsley? I need to be with her, and with my son."

"Of course. I'll write her as soon as I get home."

"Tell her that it's my only and last request."

"Of course, Stephen. I'm sure she'll be only too happy to honor it."

CRW

"I'm sorry, Ann," Mary said quietly as she lowered her head. "I know he needs me, but I can't come right now. You must think me a terrible wife."

Nancy wrote to Mary two weeks earlier, informing her of the doctor's grim prognosis. She expected to receive word that she would come and bring little Brinsley within the week, but instead, there was no reply. Thinking that perhaps Mary had not received her letter, she decided to drive out to inform her personally. Perhaps this is how it should have been in the first place. Nancy wasn't sure. She had always been the one on the other side of such situations.

"But Mary, it's his last request," Nancy pleaded. "He said that he needed to be with both you and his son. How could you not honor your dying husband's last request? This simply isn't like you."

"No, Ann," Mary replied firmly. "I'm sorry, but I just can't."

"Is it Brinsley? Are you afraid for him to see his father ill? If that be the case, then he is most welcome to stay with Mother and me. She would most certainly enjoy his company and I can't say that I couldn't use a little cheering up, myself. You know how we both adore him."

"No, thank you, Ann. Sincerely, but it's not Brinsley." Mary's eyes filled with tears.

"Well, what is it then? Oh, dear Mary, please tell me." Nancy moved next to Mary on the settee and put her arms around her.

"I can't even speak of it," Mary said through her tears.

"Speak of what? I don't understand."

Mary pointed to a small secretary in the corner of the room. "Over there. A letter. It explains everything."

Nancy walked to the secretary and picked up a letter that was folded neatly and laying on top of another letter which Mary started to write to Stephen. "Is this the one?"

"Yes," Mary replied, nodding. "Read it."

It was from a man in London. Nancy didn't recognize the name. Perhaps a family friend, or relative of Mary's whom Nancy didn't know.

"It's from my cousin Albert, who was in London only a few months ago."

My dearest cousin,

I don't even know how to begin this letter, but I have been made privy to a situation regarding your husband Stephen Storace, which I thought most important that you should know.

I was out and about late one evening as I returned to my guesthouse after a night at the theater. I must confess that the house where I stayed, being one of the less expensive lodgings in the city, was only a few streets over from a street which is rumored to have as one of its houses, a house of ill repute. To put a finer point on it, a male house of ill repute, or as some call it, a Molly house. As I walked by, I happened to glance over and saw two gentlemen, who I thought looked familiar, entering the house together. I turned around and went back to examine the men more closely. When I did so, I was shocked and dismayed at what I saw. Standing there, waiting for the door to be opened to them, were your husband and his flat mate, Prince Hoare. I called to them, "Hey you gentlemen there! Do I know you?" Upon hearing my call, they quickly ran down the street and out of sight.

I cannot claim to know what their intentions were on entering such a place, but the thought sickened me to the point that I nearly vomited then and there, right on the street…

Nancy couldn't finish reading the rest, as her eyes were filled with hot, stinging tears.

"I'm so sorry, Ann. I didn't want to tell you. I know how you love your brother so."

Nancy made her way back to the settee and sat. "No, no," Nancy said, "I'm the one who's sorry."

"What do you mean? You can't tell me you already knew!"

"Yes, I knew."

Mary sat quietly for several moments, searching for the right words. Finally, as she choked back more tears, she asked, "How long have you known?"

"A little over a year. He unwittingly shared something that led me to the obvious conclusions. You know Stephen. He simply can't keep things from me, no matter how hard he tries."

"What did you say?"

"What could I say? I was as shocked and dismayed as you," she replied as her lips began to quiver. Nancy suddenly put her hand over her mouth and sobbed, her chest heaving so heavily that it rendered her unable to speak.

"Oh, dear God, Ann," Mary said as she took Nancy in her arms and laid her head in her lap.

Finally, someone else knew. Finally, Nancy could allow her feelings to vent. All the grief, fear, anguish, anger, and loathing that she pent up inside of her for over a year came pouring forth. How could he do this to her, to his wife, to his son, and to their mother?

The weeping continued until finally, Mary leaned over and laid her face on Nancy's and as they cried their tears mingled into one great river down Nancy's cheeks—woman tears, healing tears. When they'd shed all the tears they possibly could, Nancy sat up, pulled out her handkerchief and dried her eyes.

"Who else knows of this besides us," she asked, fearing that the cousin had gone to Mary's father, John Hall.

"No one that I know of. Bertie threatened to go to Papa with it, but I begged him not to, promising him that I would write a letter to Stephen to try and clear up what I believed to be a case of mistaken identity." She sighed. "But in my heart, I knew he was right. There was too much evidence on my own part to support it."

"I understand."

"Yes, I'm sure you do. Anyway, I had only just started writing a letter to Stephen when I received yours informing me of his illness. Well, I didn't see the point in finishing it after that."

"No, I agree, there would be none."

"What is to be done, now," Mary asked.

Nancy's head was pounding by this time and her swollen eyes stung. "I don't know, Mary. I wasn't prepared for this." She began to pace across the room rubbing her pounding temples with the tips of her fingers. "We must behave as if everything is normal. We can't…"

Mary cut Nancy short. "If what you're saying means that I must pretend to be the dutiful, grieving, wife, then, no, you're asking too much of me, Ann. You're the actress in the family; not I."

"Mother won't understand."

"I'm sorry, but I can't. Please don't force me to be unkind about this. I feel for you, and you know I love you as dearly as my own blood sister, but I cannot be forced in this situation. You cannot know the anger and betrayal I'm feeling right now."

"Of course," Nancy replied. "I understand. Please forgive me."

"I'll make my excuses to the family. I'll write to Mother Storace and tell her that Brinsley is too young to understand what is happening to his father and that I don't feel that taking him from his home is the best thing for him. She'll either accept it or she won't, but I have no other alternative."

Ɑⵑⵍⵓ

As the year waned, Stephen's condition worsened and by the beginning of the next year, he was so ill that he was confined to his rooms. Nancy worked at a feverish pace to keep up with all the demands of the theater, often working in Stephen's stead when he was too ill to attend rehearsals. She even served as his transcriptionist when he needed to compose, but when his eyesight was too dim, or he was too nauseated to sit up in order to do it himself. She would sit by his bedside with a small desk in her lap, the manuscript lying on top, and write every note down as it was dictated to her.

"Which bar are we coming up on now," Stephen asked, his head pounding so hard that his ears rang.

"Bar eight," she replied. "Remember? We're at the next phrase now."

"I'm so sorry, Kitten." He burst into tears of frustration. "The pain's so intense that I just can't concentrate."

Nancy laid the manuscript aside and leaned over the bed and took his hand.

"Oh, Stephen," she said through her own tears. "It's all right. You don't have to do this, you know. You need to rest. Just rest now."

"Why won't she come, Kitten?" he sobbed. "I need to see her so badly—to tell her..."

"To tell her what?"

"To tell her how very sorry I am. To tell her that I tried my best, and how much I wanted to be a good husband and father, but I simply didn't know how to be."

"Of course you wanted to be a good husband and father. You're a good man. You have a good heart. You're the kindest, best person I know," she said as the tears rolled down her cheeks. "I'm sure Mary understands that."

"No, she doesn't. She hates me. She harbors nothing but contempt for me."

"That's not true, Stephen. I know that's simply not true," Nancy replied adamantly. "Mary's not like that. I know her too well."

"You know her better than I, Ann. How could I have done this to her? A good man wouldn't have abandoned such a beautiful, kind, and gentle woman as I have Mary."

"She'll forgive. In time, she'll forgive you…as the pain lessens."

"And my son? Will he?"

"Of course he will. He loves you and he's too young to know anything else but the affection and admiration he feels for his father."

"I simply can't die in peace without their knowing how I loved them and how I wanted nothing more than to be what they needed and expected of me."

"I'll tell them, Stephen. They'll know. I promise you, I'll tell them."

John Braham arrived in London the following January and created a splash among the city's music patrons in several concerts and recitals around town. Despite Stephen's desperately ill health, he insisted on composing an opera for him and began work on a piece entitled, *Mahmoud, Prince of Persia*, but despite his persistence and overwhelming desire to see it to it's fruition, he was unable to finish the piece before the tumor overtook him and he was forced to put it down and take completely to his bed.

"Thank you, Mr. Braham, for meeting with me on such short notice."

"You're most welcome, Signora Storace. It is my honor, indeed."

"I'm sure that you are well aware of my brother Stephen Storace's condition, and were he able at this point, it would be him who would be meeting with you concerning this matter."

"Certainly, signora. I understand."

Nancy looked up from the desk and choked back a tear. She gave him a nervous smile and then cleared her throat. "Excuse me, Mr. Braham, but this is most difficult." She paused for a moment and then went on.

"I'm sure you're also well aware that since we met a little over a year ago, my brother has been determined to have you as part of his theater, and to that end he began composing a piece especially for you. Unfortunately, he is now too ill to complete it."

"What is it that you wish for me to do?"

"Here's the situation, Mr. Braham. My brother is married, with a young son. When he passes away, they will be left in need so it is my intention to give a benefit performance of this opera and, if you will accept, to have you sing the part in it that has been composed for you."

"But you said that it is unfinished."

"Indeed, it is unfinished. However, Mr. Michael Kelly and Mr. Thomas Attwood have agreed to finish it together in Mr. Storace's stead." She paused again to compose her herself.

"We would be most honored and pleased if you would accept this offer, Mr. Braham. It was my brother's firm intention for you to sing this part, and I would love to be able to give him a dying wish as well as have you participate in such a worthy cause on behalf of my sister-in-law and her son."

"It would be both an honor and a pleasure, Signora Storace. Thank you."

"Good, then. It's agreed." She smiled, offering her hand for him to shake. Instead, he turned it over and placed a soft kiss on the back. Nancy blushed and, as she pulled her hand away, she looked down at the papers on the desk. "I'll have all the proper documents and agreements drawn up immediately. As soon as those are complete, we'll be in touch."

"Indeed, Signora Storace. It has been a distinct honor and a pleasure to meet you again. I'm only sorry that it had to be under such distressing circumstances."

She looked up and smiled. "Good day, Mr. Braham."

"Good day, signora."

Nancy kept up a strong appearance in spite of the fact that her brother's illness was distressing and that she was the one to whom everyone looked to for strength and comfort. Even Prince, for whom she had secretly held so much animosity, looked to her, relying on her seemingly unwavering strength and, in those last months and weeks she developed an affection for him that even she didn't understand.

"Good afternoon, Prince," Nancy said as she gave him a warm embrace. "How is my brother doing today?"

"Not so well, Nancy. Those headaches just get worse and worse and the nausea is extremely difficult to control. He can't eat, he can't sleep…" He began to tear up.

"You're exhausted, Prince. You're not taking good care of yourself, either. Here, I brought over some of Auntie Mary's bread and some of her wonderful scones," she said as she handed him a large basket filled with two loaves of soft, freshly baked bread and warm cinnamon scones filled with currants and raisins. "You need to eat better, to keep your strength up."

He lifted the basket to his nose and drew in a deep breath. "Ah! Your Aunt Mary bakes the best scones!"

"I know," Nancy replied with a wink, "and I have the hips to prove it."

"Thank you, Nancy. You don't know how much I appreciate everything you do to help," he said as the tears returned.

"It's all right, Prince." She gave him a warm embrace. "We both love him, very much. You're a dear friend and you're taking such good care of him. It's the least I can do."

A new show, *The Iron Chest*, with music composed by Stephen, opened in early March, but he was so ill that he had to be carried to the last rehearsals wrapped in blankets. By the opening, his illness had advanced to the point that he was completely blind, and couldn't attend the performance. Two days after the opening, Nancy was summoned, along with their mother, to come and sit by his side, for death was imminent.

"He can't see or hear you," Prince warned as he led Nancy and Elizabeth to his room. "He mostly sleeps. Dr. Roberts has ordered laudanum for the pain."

He opened the door and escorted them in. Two, large comfortable chairs were placed near the bed, one at the head and another at the foot. Nancy took the one at the head, for Elizabeth didn't feel that she could endure watching him in his last moments. After she was seated, Nancy leaned in and looked at Stephen while he slept.

"He looks so peaceful," she whispered to Prince.

"He's resting well now. The laudanum helps, of course. If you'll take his hand he'll feel it and know you're here."

She reached across the covers and took hold of Stephen's hand and squeezed it. She felt him squeeze in return and then he opened his eyes.

"He's awake!"

"Yes, he is, but remember that he can't see or hear you. Put his hand to your face and let him feel it. It's the only way he has to recognize you."

Nancy did as Prince instructed. Stephen felt her nose and mouth and across her cheeks, and when he reached her thick, wavy hair, he smiled. He recognized her.

"Yes, Stephen, I'm here," she said, as she took his hand in both of hers and squeezed it.

She placed his fingertips upon her lips and mouthed the words, "I love you."

"I love you, too Kitten," he spoke aloud.

Tears ran down her cheeks. He felt them as they flowed onto his fingers.

"Don't cry," he said. "All is well…all forgiven."

"Yes, all forgiven," she mouthed in return.

Finally she broke down. "I just can't be strong any longer, Stephen. I've been so strong through it all, but now I just can't do it any more. Please don't leave me! You're all I have left. You're the only reason I have to live. What will I do without you?"

She laid her head down and wept. Stephen could feel the bed quiver as she cried, so he placed his hand on her head and stroked her hair. Finally, she pulled herself up onto the bed and lay beside him, laying her head upon his chest as she did so many years ago with her father when he lay dying. Stephen wrapped her in his arms and held her there and in a few moments they were both asleep.

In memory of
A life devoted to the study of Musical Science and
Shorten'd by Unremitted application and anxiety in the
Attainment of its object
This marble is erected in the Name of
STEPHEN STORACE
Whose professional talents commanded publick applause
Whose private virtues ensur'd domestic affection.
He died March 16, 1796, aged 34, and is interr'd under
this Church.

Silent his lyre, or wak'd to heav'nly strains
Clos'd his short scene of chequered joys and pains
Belov'd and grateful as the notes he sung
His name still trembles on Affection's tongue,
Still in our bosoms hold its wonted part
And strikes the chords which vibrate the heart.

P.H. (Prince Hoare)
This marble is put up by a tender mother and
an affectionate sister.

Chapter Eight

Sheridan's theater, London, May 1796

The theater was filled with thunderous applause and wild cheers as the young tenor took his final bows. He extended his hand to the right wing and out came Nancy, who made her way to center stage and curtsied. The audience jumped to their feet and began to whoop and shout as they threw flowers, silk fans, handkerchiefs, ribbons, and bouquets at the couple's feet.

Stephen's final opera, *Mahmoud, Prince of Persia*, was given sixteen times in only two months and in that short time span, young John Braham became the most popular singer in all of London. With tutoring and coaching from Nancy, his stilted acting improved, although he still relied heavily on melodrama and over-embellishment. It was something they would have to continue to work on. Still, the sheer beauty of the voice, along with his impeccable technique served him well, and the London audiences packed into the theater for every one of his performances.

Together, they exited stage right and, as they turned to the left and down the hallway to their dressing rooms, Braham caught Nancy by the elbow and swung her around, facing him. He gazed into her eyes for a moment, then kissed her tenderly on each cheek.

"Thank you, signora, for everything. There simply aren't enough words to express my gratitude."

Nancy, who was a little taken aback by his rather familiar advance, took his hands, which were wrapped tightly about her waist, and held them in hers.

"You're most welcome, Mr. Braham," she said warmly. "You have been amazing, utterly amazing, and I'm so very proud of you." She let go and turned to go to her dressing room when he stopped her short.

"Signora?"

"Yes," she replied as she turned to face him.

"It would be a distinct honor and would give me great pleasure if you would join me for supper tonight." He bowed. He was a charming little man despite being a bit cocky and forward and he reminded her greatly of Mozart in that respect.

"Thank you, Mr. Braham."

"Shall I pick you up at your dressing room door, say, in an hour?"

"Yes, that will give me plenty of time. Thank you."

"Until then," he said as he took her hand and kissed it.

"Until then, Mr. Braham."

Over the weeks and months since Stephen's death, Nancy immersed herself in her work. It helped keep her mind occupied and off of how desperately she grieved. The current production, being a benefit for Stephen's widow and son, helped tremendously and she felt she could perhaps atone for Stephen's neglect of his family by making sure that they weren't left in need. The production was a huge success, thanks to the sensational young tenor. Mary and little Brinsley would receive a large portion of the take, which would sustain them for years to come.

And then there was young Mr. Braham, whom Nancy immediately took in as her protégé, working with his acting, stage presence, and coaching him on the various aspects of stage gesturing. Acting, for Braham, was as unnatural as breathing water. It could be rather frustrating for Nancy for whom acting came easily, probably more easily than singing, and who sometimes lacked the patience required to repeat an action over and over until Braham got it. Often, she would simply give up and go on. Still, he was improving slowly but surely, and there was no doubt that his singing was impeccable.

He seemed to look up to her a great deal, hanging on her every word and watching her every move as she demonstrated the various gestures. He was extremely polite and most charming, and his dark eyes would dance with delight whenever she drew him near and placed his hands on her waist to demonstrate a stage action. He was no doubt dazzled by her reputation and success, and at times it seemed he was beginning to develop a boyish crush on her.

"For Christ's sake, I'm eleven years older than the boy," she whispered to Kelly, who often stood in the wings and noticed the amorous attentions she received from Braham.

"Perhaps the lad's fond of grayer, plumper women," Kelly replied.

"I'm *not* gray! Perhaps a little more filled out around the waist and rounded in the hips…" Nancy placed her hands on her hips and then held them up to see how wide apart they were. "Well, a lot more rounded in the hips." She chuckled. "But that's what success will do to a girl."

"Yes indeed, me dove. Tis a good thing, success is. Fills one's supper plate ta overflowin'," Kelly said as he leaned back and patted his protruding belly.

"So tell me, old friend, what should I do about my amorous little tenor?"

"Ah, give the lad some time to get over bein' star-struck. He'll come out of it soon enough. He's destined for stardom himself. Won't be long before the young ladies will be a-swoonin' at his feet. He'll have his pick then."

"Let's do hope," Nancy replied, bewildered. "Let's do hope, indeed."

The 1795/96 season ended in May as a huge success despite the illness and death of Stephen Storace. The house takes for *Mahmoud* alone were phenomenal and Nancy expected that she would soon hear that Mary had received her portion and that it was enough to keep her and her son comfortable for years to come. However, at the end of July, Nancy received a distressing letter from Mary stating that the amount that Sheridan sent was quite insufficient. In fact, it was so insufficient that she didn't know if it would last her out the year.

"Twelve pounds!" Nancy shouted as she slammed the letter down on Sheridan's desk. "Twelve bloody, goddamned pounds to last her the rest of her life? What is the meaning of this, Sheridan?"

"It's business, Nancy. I had debts. They had to be paid first," he replied, nonchalantly. "I gave her what was left."

"God damn you, Sheridan! What a bloody cheat you are! A bloody, goddamned, sodding swindler!"

"Come now, Nancy, be reasonable—"

"Reasonable? The child is your godson, for Christ's sake and you cheat him out of the money left to him from his father's last work? You're beyond despicable."

"There's nothing I could do about it. I…"

"Well, there's certainly something I can do, you buggering bastard! I quit! You hear that? I'm tendering my resignation effective today! We'll just see how you fare without me!"

"Hmph! We'll see what theater will hire you now, you fat old cow!"

Nancy grabbed the letter from off of Sheridan's desk and stomped out, fuming.

"Rest assured, you'll be hearing from my lawyer!" As she slammed the door, she suddenly ran into Braham, who had been standing in the hallway for some time. "God, you scared me!"

"I'm sorry, Signora Storace. I was coming to meet with Sheridan about next season when I heard, well, I couldn't help but hear…"

"How much did you hear, Mr. Braham?"

"Nearly all of it, I'm afraid. Oh, Signora, are you really quitting?"

"I'm afraid so, Mr. Braham. I simply can't tolerate…that cheating bastard!" She shouted loudly enough for Sheridan to hear her from the other side of the door, then she burst into tears.

He took her in his arms and laid her head upon his shoulder. "I know how upsetting this must be for you. How could he do such a terrible thing?"

"And to his own godson!"

"Especially to his own godson. There, there, please don't cry. I can hardly stand to see a lady cry, especially one as lovely as you."

Nancy pointed towards Sheridan's door. "He called me a fat old cow." She sobbed even harder.

"A beautiful lady such as you? How dare he?"

"You don't think I'm a cow, do you, Mr. Braham?"

"Why of course not! You're one of the loveliest ladies I've ever had the joy to lay eyes upon! Why, haven't you noticed how I gaze at you?" He hesitated a moment. "Where will you go now? What will you do?"

"Oh, I have so many offers and engagements here in London, as well as in Bath, that I can't possibly take them all," she said as he handed her his handkerchief.

"Take me with you, signora. I want to come with you as your singing partner. I'll resign today, right now. That is, if you'll take me."

"Oh, you can't possibly mean that, Mr. Braham. You've only just begun here and—"

"I do mean it. I'm quite serious. I want to come with you."

"I don't know what to say."

"Say yes."

Nancy hiccupped and looked up.

"There now, dry those tears," he said tenderly. "You don't need that old sod anyway. You're better than him. *We're* better than him. Now, what do you say?"

"Alright then, I say yes, Mr. Braham."

℘℘℘

6 January, 1797
My dearest Mary,

I write to you today to inform you that Mr. Braham and I have settled in nicely here in Bath and that we are already meeting with much success and acclaim. It has been a whirlwind of concerts, soirees, charity events and the such.

Please forgive the impropriety of the following mention, but I should like to inform you that I have taken it upon myself to have several of your husband's scores recopied and have offered them to sell for several pounds a piece. All of the proceeds from their sale will be given to you forthwith. It is my hope that this will, in part, make amends for the deplorable manner in which Mr. Sheridan cheated you and Brinsley out of what was rightfully yours.

Mr. Braham and I will return to London in April to begin the spring opera season in late May. Mr. Kelly, who is now in charge at both Drury Lane as well as the King's Theatre has engaged us in two productions there. In the between, I hope to drive out to the country for a short visit with you and Brinsley. In the meantime, give him hugs and kisses from his Auntie Ann and I will remain your ever true, affectionate, and loyal sister,

Ann S. Storace

The split from Sheridan did nothing to Nancy's and Braham's popularity. In fact, after the winter in Bath, where they concertized and hobnobbed with all of the gentry and nobility who wintered there, they returned to London in the spring just as popular as they ever were.

Sheridan, on the other hand, didn't fare so well. After Nancy and Braham's resignations came a succession of resignations from several of his top managers and players. They were all fed up with his mismanagement and cheating, and it wasn't long before Sheridan had to give over the management of his theater to Michael Kelly, who took the role on with ease.

Upon their return to London, Nancy and Braham were met again with a whirlwind of productions and concerts, performing operatic excerpts at concerts in both Drury Lane and Covent Garden recital rooms, concerts at the Freemason Hall and Tottenham Court, Willis's Rooms and Hanover Square. Then there were the numerous charity events and the annual Handel commemoration festival in which Nancy had sung every year for ten years and to which Braham was introduced.

The couple's success threw them together both professionally and socially and, for the first time since her days in Vienna, Nancy began to enjoy a rich and active social life. With Braham as her escort, she found herself at numerous parties, soirees, balls and dances and she was often seen on his arm in the various pleasure gardens, as well as at other public assemblies and events.

"So however did you score that handsome, young devil," Nancy's friend and colleague Ann Crouch whispered to her one day as they strolled together with Kelly and Braham through the gardens at Vauxhall.

Despite her being a married woman, Ann had been involved in an affair with Kelly for many years, and the two of them lived together quite openly without, it seemed, much criticism from the public. That sort of thing was to be expected from actors.

"I don't know that I have necessarily, scored him," Nancy whispered in return. "I think it was more like I inherited him." She giggled.

"Well, I would certainly regard it as a huge score on my part if I were you. Oh, my," she exclaimed, "Just look at him! Young, handsome, obviously smitten with you, and then when he opens that mouth to sing, oh, dear Nancy, I wouldn't object to having the fellow sing to me in my bed!"

৪০০৪

"I have to say that I've never seen house takes as good as these," Kelly exclaimed to Nancy as he went over the books from the previous month.

"Ye and Mr. Braham can be credited for that, I must say."

"Thank you, Kelly," Nancy replied with a broad smile.

"And on a personal note, I will add that I've not seen ye this happy for a long time. Not since, well, since those last couple of years in Vienna."

"What do you mean?"

"That blush on yer cheek, the twinkle in yer eye. Yer youthful glow, me darlin' dove. Everyone sees it."

"Whom do you mean by everyone?"

"Come now, Nancy, ye can't pretend that ye haven't heard the gossip that's floatin' about!"

"What gossip?"

"Surely ye can't believe that tongues weren't a-goin' ta be waggin' about it now, can ye?"

"Wagging about *what*?"

"Why, ye and Mr. Braham, of course."

"Mr. Braham and me? What about us? We're professional partners. What gossip can one find in that?"

"Ah, but you've frequently been seen in places in far more than a professional capacity, me dove."

"It's all a part of the act, Kelly, you know that. People expect us to be together at social events."

Kelly nodded. "Aye, jest like ye were expected ta be seen with Mozart at the openin' ball at Laxenburg and, I might add, dance every dance with him. Of course, I understand perfectly."

"How dare you! I can't believe you would throw that back at me in such a fashion!"

"Same thing, wasn't it?"

"You know it was different, Kelly, and I'm cut to the quick that you would even make the comparison."

"Then yer not in love with Braham?"

"Of course I'm not! He's a mere boy—my protégé and professional partner. Again, how dare you!"

"I meant no offense, Nancy. I'm simply lookin' out fer yer best interests."

"I appreciate your concern, Kelly, but as usual, your looking out for my best interests most generally involves meddling into areas that aren't any of your concern."

"I simply felt that in the absence of your brother—"

"What is it with you men?" Nancy interrupted. "Why do you think that a woman must always be looked after by a man? Why must a woman's success always be hinged on a man's, and why must that man always be a relative or a lover?"

"Again, I'm sorry Nancy, I didn't mean…"

"I can look out for myself, God damn it! I don't need you, or my brother, or some lover to do the job for me!"

Kelly was taken aback by her reactions. "I'll be more careful to keep me tongue in me stupid head from now on, Nancy. Again, I apologize."

"I think you'd be most wise to do so," Nancy said as she turned to leave. "Good day, Kelly."

John Braham

Chapter Nine

London, June 1797

30 November 1790

…This brings me to another, even more painful matter: O, Wanze, how can I bear to write the words? What cruel fate has brought us to this point? Again, I shall not tarry but shall come quickly to the point. This will be my last letter to you, my dearest love, not because my affections for you have diminished for, on the contrary, they have only grown deeper and more impassioned since last we saw one another, but because circumstances in my situation have developed to the place where, for the preservation of my reputation, my work, and my family, our affair must end. And although we will never see one another again in this life, my soul will always yearn for you. I vow to you my undying love for all eternity, whatever that is. I vow that whatever happens in this universe, I shall always find you and love you. You will never be alone. Whoever else may have my body, you will own my heart. Farewell, angela mia.

Forever,
Tuo Wolfgango

As Nancy read the letter, tears fell from her cheeks onto the yellowed parchment, causing the ink to run in places. She lifted it to her nose, trying to make out if there was any of his scent left. She could still detect a little tobacco, but the cologne had long since faded away. Ten years it had been—over ten long years since that day in Vienna at the Karinthian Gate when she last saw him, held him, kissed him—longer than that even since they last made love.

She closed her eyes and lifted the letter to her nostrils once more. She breathed in deeply, remembering his scent, taking in everything that lingered on the paper.

"Ah, there you are meine Wanze. I've been waiting for you. It's been far too long, you know."

He took her in his arms and tenderly kissed her mouth. She felt his warm, moist breath linger upon her chin, her throat, and then upon her bosom as he kissed the tender cleavage.

"I've missed you, Wolfgango. How I've missed you."

"Sh…" he whispered as he placed his finger to her mouth. "Don't speak. Feel, only feel."

He swept her up into his arms and carried her to the bed where he carefully unlaced her bodice, revealing the object of his desire. Soft, wet brushes of the lips and tongue gave way to impassioned kisses, soft coos, and intense urges to be filled completely. Cries of ecstasy gave way to quiet breaths dissipating into soft, deep, contented slumber.

"Ann. Ann, dearest…"

Nancy felt someone gently tapping her on the shoulder. She awakened and looked up to find Braham standing in front of her.

"What are you doing here," she asked, surprised.

"I'm sorry. I didn't mean to startle you."

"Who let you in?"

"Your mother. I thought she announced me, but apparently she didn't."

"It's all right, John. She may have and I was simply too deep in my thoughts to hear." Nancy looked down at the letter in her hand and folded it. "Excuse me a moment while I finish here."

"Certainly," Braham replied as he moved to the other side of the room.

Nancy carefully placed the letter into a box and shut the lid. Then she placed the box in the bottom drawer of her desk and locked it.

"I received the message that you wanted to speak with me," he said as she made her way to the settee, inviting him to have a seat beside her.

"Yes, yes. I would like to speak with you," she replied, still trying to clear her head of the fog from her reverie.

"I do hope it's nothing serious. You're not upset with me, are you?"

"Oh, no, of course not. Nothing like that, although it is rather serious business, I think."

She hesitated, then rubbed her eyes. "Please do excuse me. I was very deep in thought when you came in and I can't quite seem to shake myself out of it."

"Should I come again at another time?"

"Oh, no, please," she said with a smile. "Please, do sit back down, John. It's just that I was a little addled there for a moment. No, I really do need to speak with you, for it concerns you personally."

"Me, personally?"

"Indeed. I was going over in my mind just the other day, remembering my travels to Italy as a young girl, and remembering..."

"Remembering?"

"Yes, remembering what a tremendous experience it was for me. I don't mean just the travel, which was thrilling all by itself, but about what a tremendous learning experience it was for me and how it helped me to get my feet wet and hone my skills as a performer."

"And?"

"Well, it started me to thinking about you and how here you are, nearly twenty-one years of age and you've not even been out of southern England. By the time I was your age, I had been employed by the Emperor of Austria for over four years as his prima buffa."

"Does my lack of experience show that badly?" Braham asked, looking dejected.

"No, of course not, but your inexperience does limit you greatly, especially in the world of Italian opera. You've done mostly English comic opera with a little Italian seria interspersed here and there, but nothing to speak of, really. You need more training, but England is pitifully lacking where Italian comic opera is concerned. That's why Stephen and I worked so very hard to try and bring Mozart to England several years ago." She hesitated and thought a moment.

"Do go on," Braham urged.

"Well, then, there is all this mess over some silly gossip."

"Gossip? Whatever are you talking about?"

"The gossip that's apparently going around over us."

Braham sat up and grinned from ear to ear. "Oh that," he said, beaming. "That doesn't bother me in the least. In fact, I think it's quite flattering."

"Then you've heard it?"

"Well of course I have," he said proudly. "Excuse me for saying so, but being thought of as the lover of the most beautiful and talented actress in all of London doesn't dishonor me whatsoever."

"Well, excuse me for saying so, but it does me," she replied indignantly. "No insult to you, but I am eleven years your senior and although we are seen together in a social capacity and I am seen on your arm at various functions does not mean that we are privately lovers, and I resent the implication that it is so."

Braham's countenance fell. "I'm sorry, signora. I didn't, well, I didn't know that."

"Oh, John, you don't have go back to the formal titles. Please. I'm sorry; I didn't mean it as a personal insult."

"I understand," he replied as he lowered his eyes.

"Oh, now you're going to make me feel terrible."

"It's only that after we've spent so much time together and have been seen with one another publicly, I was hoping…"

"I understand, John, but at this juncture I feel it best that the relationship remain as it is: a warm, personal friendship and professional partnership."

"All right," Braham consented, with a grin. "For now."

Nancy continued, laying out the details of the whole adventure along with her travel plans, places where they would perform, noted teachers with whom he would study, as well as addressing his desire to learn more about composition.

"So, when do we leave," Braham asked, after she finished her presentation.

"Oh, not so fast, dear boy, not so fast! First I have to arrange the financing, which won't be an easy feat by any means. That should take at least a month, and then another month for planning. Hm. I think we could safely say by sometime mid-August. How does that sound?"

"Very good," he replied.

"Good, then. We'll meet to discuss it as things come up, and in the meantime, I'll start to arrange the financing."

"Thank you, again, Ann, and I don't care how loudly you protest, it is still an honor to be seen out and about with the prettiest actress in London."

Nancy relished the opportunity to travel abroad once again. It had been over ten years since she, Stephen, and their mother left Vienna after nearly nine years abroad in Italy and Austria. She was ready to get out of England for a while and this was the perfect opportunity for young Braham to cut his teeth on Italian opera and find some new teachers to work with his stage technique, which was still pitifully lacking. And perhaps, too, they could quell the gossip that persisted by being out of sight for a while.

This trip, however, was going to present some dangerous challenges. To get to Italy from England one had to travel through France, and France was in the throes of a nasty revolution. Only five years before, they had beheaded their king, and now they had a new revolutionary government called the *Directoire executif*. Under the new "Directory" government France had gained a tremendous amount of military power and, under the leadership of a young general by the name of Bonaparte, it was waging war all over Europe. England was in Bonaparte's sites as one of his prime targets, and relations between the two countries were hostile since France had recently declared war on them.

Also in the back of Nancy's mind was Vienna. It was her sincerest wish that while they were on the continent they would have the opportunity to travel there. Venice was most definitely in the plans so Vienna, being so close, wouldn't be out of the question. She didn't know what was in it for Braham, but for her there were many memories, and perhaps a demon or two that needed slaying.

Arrangements for financing came through with ease and the couple was set to leave in the middle of August as Nancy had anticipated. After one last engagement in Birmingham, their bags and boxes were loaded onto the ship, ready to cross the English Channel to Calais.

"Now you be keepin' yerself safe while in France," Kelly instructed as he took Nancy's face in his hands and kissed her tenderly on the forehead.

"I will, Mick. We'll be just fine. We don't plan to be there long anyway."

"Mr. Braham!"

"Yes, Mr. Kelly," Braham replied.

"I'm expectin' ye ta keep a good eye out fer this fine lady. Take care of her," Kelly said as he shook Braham's hand. He leaned in and spoke softly, but loudly enough that Nancy could hear, "although she claims to be one of those new independent women who don't need a man ta look after her," he said with a wink.

"I will, Mr. Kelly. Rest assured, I won't let her out of my sight."

"Good, then," Kelly replied.

He turned once again to Nancy and with a tear in his eye, he took her into his arms.

"Seriously now, me darlin' dove, do be safe. Ya know how I adore ya. I'm going ta miss ya somethin' terrible."

"I'll write often," she promised.

"Please do."

"And please do take good care of my family. I will miss them so, especially Mary and little Brinsley."

"I suspect that when ye return, 'little' Brinsley won't be so little anymore."

"I suspect you're right," she replied with a smile.

Suddenly they heard the ship's bell and the call, "All aboard!"

"Well, now, I suspect it's time for us to get aboard ship," Braham said as he took Nancy's arm and pulled her to his side.

"Good bye, Mr. Kelly," Braham said as he shook Kelly's hand.

"Adieu, mon amis. Godspeed to ya both."

Michael Kelly

Chapter Ten

Calais, France, August 1797

26 August, 1797, Calais
My dear Kelly,

Mr. Braham and I arrived late last week in Calais, we were put immediately under house arrest for lacking of passports. To add insult to injury, we were accused, of all things, of being British spies! Of course I assured them that this was not the case, but that we were simply performers on our way to Italy by way of Paris and that our intentions were in no way hostile. We are now awaiting papers from Paris giving us permission to travel on. In the meantime, we are being treated with the greatest of amiability and hospitality. We have been given the finest lodgings and are permitted to attend the theater and move about the city at our own leisure.

I shall continue to send word as we continue our journey, and shall send you my address as soon as lodgings are secured in Paris. Until then, I remain your loving and faithful friend,

A. Storace
"Nancy"

"Ah! Look here, John," Nancy exclaimed. "Our passports have arrived!"

"Finally," said Braham, quietly.

It was hot and the salty breeze which came in through the open casements off the Dover Straight didn't seem to cool things off any better. Braham sat staring out the window dressed in nothing but his shirtsleeves and breeches. The three weeks since they'd arrived in Calais seemed to drag on endlessly. With little to do but attend the theater and frequent the local brew houses, he was about to go mad, and it made him irritable.

Nancy handed him his passport.

"It's in French."

"Well, of course it is. It came from Paris."

"I neither read nor speak French," he said impatiently.

"Another thing which we shall have to remedy." She opened her own passport and began to read.

"Oh, so me lady also speaks fluent French," he said sarcastically as he rose, slamming down his passport. "Is there something, *anything*, which Madame Goddess Sophia doesn't know?"

"Whatever is the matter with you?"

"Nothing. I'm just sick and tired of waiting around. I'm bored stiff."

"Well, my dear boy, you shall have plenty to occupy yourself soon, for now that we have our passports, we will be off to Paris tomorrow."

He turned, glaring at her.

"What is it now?" she demanded, growing impatient with his foul mood.

"That's another thing. I'm sick to death of you calling me a boy. I'm not a boy, Ann. I'm a man, and I resent your constantly treating me as a child!"

"Why you're barely twenty-one," she replied, astonished by his sudden outburst.

"And I was nineteen when you first met me. That was three years ago. I was a boy then, but I'm not now. So I'd appreciate it if you'd stop treating me like one."

"I'm sorry, I didn't realize..."

"It's condescending and disrespectful," he continued.

Nancy put down her passport and went to him. Looking into his eyes, she took his hand in hers. "Please forgive me, John. I can be overbearing at times, and I simply forget myself. I'll try and not do it again. I can't bear it that you're angry with me."

"I'm not angry," he replied, still bristling.

"But I've hurt you. I'm sorry."

"I'm very fond of you, Ann. Very fond of you indeed, and when you treat me like a child it makes me feel as if there's a sort of distance between us. It makes me uncomfortable—like I don't know where I stand."

80

"I don't know quite what you're saying."

"For a while, for many months, in fact, I looked up to you. I was your protégé and I gladly accepted that role. But after we returned from Bath, and we started appearing with one another socially, well, I…" He hesitated.

"You what, John?"

"I had hoped that your feelings towards me would change and that you would see me more as your partner and your equal. I've developed feelings for you, Ann—affectionate feelings—and I was hoping that they would be returned by now."

She removed her hands from his grasp and lowered her eyes. "I don't know what to say."

"Say you feel for me what I do for you."

"What are you feeling?"

"I love you, Ann."

She closed her eyes and rubbed her forehead. "You don't know what you're asking of me. I'm very fond of you, John, but—"

"But you don't love me."

"No, not in that way."

"Could you ever love me?"

"It's not that simple, I—"

"Please forgive me for pressing you. It's just that I had to get this out. It has been building in me until I felt I was about to explode, and now that we're on this journey together…"

"I know. I understand. Can you give me some time? I mean, to think on it?"

"Of course I can. It will wait. I shall wait forever if I have to."

"Thank you," she said quietly, and she turned towards the door. "Have your bags packed and ready to load on the coach by sunup tomorrow. We'll be leaving for Paris early."

"I shall. Good afternoon, Ann."

"Good afternoon, John."

Their arrival in the French capital was marked with more political upheaval, for on the very day they entered the city, a coup d'état was staged by the Directory, which annulled many of the elections that had been held in the various departments. The people were furious and the streets were in a riotous uproar. They were both notably shaken as they stepped from their coach at the customs house. While their bags were transferred to their carriage for transport to their lodgings, Nancy, who shivered from sheer terror, slipped her arm through Braham's, clinging to him for security. Of course he didn't object in the least, and he played along as her gallant protector. When at last they reached their hotel, it was late in the afternoon and Nancy was exhausted not only from the trip, but from the terrifying experience of making their way through the angry French mob.

As they walked into the lobby of their hotel, Nancy fainted and Braham took charge of the situation, demanding they be taken to their rooms immediately. The sheer forcefulness of Braham's insistence was enough to intimidate the proprietor into granting his request, and Braham lifted her into his arms, following the valet up the stairs.

"Ann, darling," he said softly as he laid her upon a settee. "Please wake up. We're here now, and you're safe."

Nancy began to stir. "Where are we," she asked faintly as she looked around the room.

"We're here in our hotel. In Paris."

As her eyes cleared, she could make out the details of the salon, which was one of the most luxurious she had ever seen.

"Good God, look at this place," she exclaimed as she sat up, looking around.

Above her head, suspended from the delicately frescoed ceiling, was an ornate crystal chandelier and across the room stood a large, ornate marble fireplace with a gilt column on either side. Displayed above it hung an enormous mirror that reflected the entire room, making it seem much larger than it actually was. The furniture was upholstered in fine, pastel silks and satins and the floors were of inlaid mahogany. Appropriately, the bedchambers were furnished with equal opulence.

"Yes, indeed," Braham replied as he, too, marveled at the salon's magnificence. "No doubt it used to belong to some unfortunate bastard of the ancient regime who has long since lost his head."

"What happened?" Nancy asked as she turned her attention back to the situation.

"You fainted just as we entered the hotel."

"How did I get here?"

"I carried you. How are you feeling now?"

"Better. That was an experience I certainly don't wish to repeat," she said as she rubbed her temples with the tips of her fingers.

"Nor I," he agreed removing his hat and coat and throwing them across a nearby chair. He ran his fingers through his hair as he continued to look around. Suddenly, he noticed Nancy massaging her head. "Do you have a headache?"

"Oh, it's nothing," she replied, dismissively. "I always get them whenever I'm upset or distressed for any reason. It's most likely due to an old head injury from my Vienna days."

"Where does it hurt?"

"Here, right up front."

Braham seated himself beside her on the settee. "Here, lay your head down."

As she lay back down, he grabbed a nearby cushion and placed it in his lap.

"Now, close your eyes." He began to gently massage her temples.

"Mm…that feels so good…"

"Excellent. Now, just relax." He continued the massage until she fell into an exhausted slumber and, when she was sleeping deeply enough that he felt she wouldn't awaken, he took her in his arms and carried her into her bedchamber and laid her on the bed. "Good night, sweet angel," he said, and he planted a kiss upon her lips. "Tomorrow will be an easier day."

The next morning they were both up early so that they could go about the business of settling into Paris. As they planned on staying around a month, they set out to meet the local impresarios in the nearby theaters, and offer their services.

Their hotel was only a short walk from Théâtre de la République, the most fashionable theater in Paris. All of the Directory's elite frequented it, and it was known as *l'endroit à être*, the "place to be", among the citizens.

Nancy soon discovered that this was a completely different city than the Paris she'd visited ten years earlier when she'd performed at Versailles for Emperor Joseph's youngest sister, Queen Marie Antoinette. She shuddered to think of poor Queen Marie and the horrible fate of her and her children. Nancy thought her remarkably charming and kind—much like her older brother. She was grateful that Emperor Joseph had already passed before his sister's execution, for it surely would have broken his heart.

Most notably missing was the Bastille, the prison which loomed large over the city and had been stormed (by just such an angry mob as what they encountered the day before), the guards carried out, killed, and their heads mounted on pikes and carried throughout the city. In subsequent years, the people dismantled the Bastille stone by stone until it lay in ruins. They sold the stones as mementos of that fateful day in July of 1789 and used the proceeds to finance the Revolution.

Another noted change was in the social climate of the city. There were fewer somber faces, and music and dancing filled the streets. Women in transparent muslin gowns with no undergarments beneath and dandies in narrow, striped breeches and brightly-colored waistcoats paraded shamelessly. Casinos, dance halls, hotels, theatres, cafés and magnificent public gardens lined the sidewalks. Gone were the seriousness and oppression of the theocratic feudal system, and the Catholic religion that created it, making way for Enlightenment ideals of the new secular, democratic Republic—an atmosphere in which the arts and self-expression thrived.

As they walked down the street together, Braham's mouth literally dropped open whenever they came upon one of the scantily clad women or some *incroyable* wearing an outrageous hat. Things seemed to have settled down very quickly from only the day before, as if the outrage of the takeover by the newest coup was satiated by a day of mass street demonstrations and public displays of anger. Suddenly, it was business as usual.

Entering the theater, they were greeted by a neatly-dressed man who inquired as to the nature of their business.

"Bonjour, Cityoen. Je voudrais parler au directeur du théâtre, s'il vous plait," Nancy said.

The man gestured for them to follow him and after only a short wait, they were escorted into a large, brilliantly lit office which was every bit as opulent as their rooms back at the hotel—nothing like the stuffy, dusty old offices in which their theater directors back in London were forced to work. Braham couldn't stop gazing around the room in complete awe.

"Bonjour, Mademoiselle Storace. I am most pleased to see that you and Monsieur Braham have arrived safely in Paris. I hear you experienced some difficulties in Calais. Some silly business over passports, and being British spies?"

Marguerite Brunet, known by her theatrical name, Mademoiselle Montansier was the owner/director of the Théâtre de la République, which she purchased with the large sum of money that was given to her as recompense for her false arrest and imprisonment by the Terror on charges that she conspired with Queen Marie Antoinette to set fire to the neighboring French National Library. Once acquitted, she took the money and purchased the theater as well as established the first comedic opera troupe in Paris. A middle-aged woman with sparkling dark eyes and dark hair that was grayed at the temples, she was happy to finally see Nancy and Braham sitting in her office, for she'd anxiously awaited their arrival since Nancy first wrote to her several months before of their plans to come to Paris.

"Indeed, Citizeness Montansier," Nancy said. "It seems they were quite overzealous in their desire to drum up some excitement. I do believe the poor soldiers were bored."

"Very possible," Mlle. Montansier replied. "And please, call me Mademoiselle. All this 'Citizen this' and 'Citizeness that' is far too cold and impersonal for my tastes. The rules are much looser now that we've gotten past the Terror."

"Oui, Mademoiselle. Merci."

"So you and Monsieur Braham would like to perform in our theater, oui? What is your specialty?"

"We specialize in Italian opera as well as oratorio and art song. Monsieur Braham and I have made quite a name together in England, singing programs of opera duets in recitals and concerts."

"Bon! Just what I've been looking for! We are so miserably bereft of good Italian opera in Paris. All we seem to find are performers who sing only French opera comique. But it is Italian opera buffa that our audiences most desire. When can you start?"

"Why immediately. As soon as possible."

"Very good, then," Mlle. Montansier replied. "You may start rehearsing immediately. I have an opening in the schedule in early October. Will that give you enough time to rest and get your voices into shape?"

"Oui, merci, Mademoiselle. Ample time, I'm quite sure."

ଈଓଔ

"So what does it say," Braham inquired anxiously.

Nancy sat lounging in her nightdress, eating breakfast and reading the reviews that had just come out on their debut at the Théâtre de la République.

"Overall, it's good. Not as good as I had hoped, but for the most part we were well received," she said as she picked up a sweet, plump blackberry and popped it into her mouth. "They seemed quite pleased with my singing. Of course, there was the titter over the curtsy at the end of my first number. I should have known, but after Mlle. Montansier's lax attitude regarding the use of titles, I only assumed that it would extend to that as well."

"The French! You never know with them. They're so inconsistent," he scoffed. "What did they say about me?"

Nancy sighed. "Well, it says here that they quite enjoyed your last number, that it was your best performance all evening."

"That's all they said?"

"Well, no."

"Well, what else?"

"I'm not sure you want to hear it, John."

"Why? Is it bad?"

"It's not exactly bad, but it's not good, either." She took a deep breath. "They said you sounded tired and out of breath, that your technique sagged in some of the melismatic passages, and they were highly critical of your acting, that it was too stiff and contrived."

"Bloody French," he exclaimed as he pounded his fist on the fireplace mantle.

"You were tired and nervous, John. It was your first performance on foreign soil. French audiences aren't easy. Give yourself some credit."

"I'm inexperienced," he said sarcastically.

"Well, yes, you are. You'll do better next time."

"Hmph! If there is a next time."

"Don't be such a defeatist. Of course there'll be a next time. Mlle. Montansier already has us booked for three more performances and I've received word from two more theaters that wish to book us as well."

"Because of you. You're the only reason."

Nancy put down the paper and frowned. "What a nasty little sourpuss you are this morning!"

"Well, what of it?"

She arose to her feet and went to the fireplace, where Braham leaned against the mantle, holding his head in his hands.

"What is the matter, John?"

"I don't like it here," he whined.

"What is it that you don't like?"

"I don't like the French, for one thing, and I can't speak the bloody language."

"But you're doing beautifully with your French! Why, I've been very surprised at how quickly you're picking it up," she said, gently grasping his forearm.

He broke from her grasp, paced to an arched window and stared out over the street below.

"You must be patient with yourself, John. It's your first time abroad, in a mostly hostile nation. You aren't familiar with the customs, the language, the food—"

"No, that's not it."

"What is it then? Please tell me. I'm trying to understand."

He turned and looked at Nancy, who had come to stand in the window beside him. The sun morning shone through the sheer fabric of her nightdress, revealing every curve of her voluptuous figure.

"It's you! God damn it, Ann, it's you!"

"Me? What are you talking about?"

"Well, look at you standing there! You know I'm in love with you and you strut around here dressed like one of those French whores wearing that see-through gown. I can hardly stand it! Why are you so cruel?"

She glanced down at herself.

"I didn't even think. I assumed... I mean, you've seen women making quick changes backstage so many times by now that it didn't even dawn on me that this would bother you."

"I'm not in love with them."

She sighed. "Oh, John..."

"Ann, please…" He put his arms around her waist and pulled her close. "Please let me show you how much I adore you."

Panicked by Braham's sudden advance, she tried to pull away. Visions of her estranged husband John Fisher and the violent ways he had of enforcing his will upon her flooded her mind.

"John, please don't force me!" she cried.

Stunned by her panic, he let go.

"Of course I wouldn't force myself on you, Ann. I'm not a brute."

She fell into a heap on the floor in front of him, sobbing, and he knelt beside her, stroking her hair.

"Oh, Ann," he cooed softly, "whatever have I done?" He sat down beside her and scooped her up into his arms. "Please tell me, sweet angel. Tell me what's wrong. You don't know how I long to make it all better for you."

He held her in his arms and rocked her, comforting her until her sobbing ceased. Then, as he bent his head to kiss her cheek, she turned her face to his and allowed him to kiss her mouth.

A surge of warmth passed through her, a sensation she hadn't experienced in far too long. As she wrapped her arms around his neck, his kisses grew more impassioned and she met them with her own.

He passed his hand over her body, feeling her curves and contours through the thin fabric of her nightdress. "How soft and beautiful you are," he whispered.

Their urges mounted and before long their bodies were intertwined. Impassioned kisses, soft cries and excited breaths melted into an intense desire for complete union. Willingly, ever so softly, she surrendered herself to him.

How mistaken is the lover,
Who on words builds hopes of bliss,
Who fondly thinks we love discover,
If perchance we answer "yes".

From *The Doctor & the Apothecary* by
Stephen Storace, 1788

Chapter Eleven

Paris, March 1798

As the weeks passed into a month and one month into six, Nancy and Braham found that what they planned as only a short stay in Paris turned out to be much longer. Despite their less than stellar debut, their popularity soared among the Paris elite in a very short time. Within only a few weeks after they'd opened at the Théâtre de la République, they performed for Napoleon Bonaparte and his new wife, Josephine Beaumarchais, impressing the couple so much that they returned several times specifically to see Nancy and Braham perform, not only at the Théâtre de la République, but also at the Elysée Bourbon. In a very short period of time, Mlle. Montansier began to make offers for them to stay and direct a new Italian opera company. They declined, however, fearing they would be arrested and imprisoned by the French government should hostilities between their two countries grow even worse.

After his and Nancy's first amorous encounter, Braham's entire attitude regarding Paris and the French underwent a complete transformation. Suddenly, Paris was the most beautiful city he had ever seen, and the "bloody French" became some of the most intelligent and enlightened people he had ever encountered. Even his desire to learn the language was heightened and within only a few weeks, he was conversing as fluently as Nancy. He began to enjoy going to the casinos and frequenting the various salons, conversing and hobnobbing with the Directory elite. Jerome Bonaparte, the younger brother of Napoleon, became one of Braham's closest friends and the two of them spent many an evening together gambling, and talking politics and philosophy.

Braham was proud to have Nancy on his arm on the evenings they went out to the casinos, or to attend a performance in one of the many theaters. It was clear from the way that they were received, the couple was extremely popular and the elite found it fashionable and prestigious to have them seated with them in their boxes at the theater, or at the casino tables.

Most often, on the nights when they weren't performing, they would return late from the evening's entertainments to indulge in a little lovemaking. Braham began to feel more secure with Nancy's feelings for him. Even if he hadn't won her heart completely, she was still generous and tender with her affections. From what he could see, she never flirted with any of the elite and powerful men with whom they associated, and that only served to heighten his sense of security.

"Good evening, love," Braham sang cheerfully as he came in from a night at the casino. "What on earth are you doing up this late? I thought you came home with another one of your headaches."

"I did," Nancy replied, "but when I returned, I was handed this." She held up a letter.

"Who is it from?"

"It's from Mother. She's frightened, John."

"Frightened? Of what?"

"It seems that word is spreading across London that a French invasion is imminent. She says that they're predicting it within the month."

"Dear God, are you sure?"

"That's what she wrote in her letter. She writes that she's hearing the news from some very reliable sources." She closed her eyes and rubbed her forehead. "I wrote to Mary this evening, asking if she would allow Mother to come and stay with her in the country. She'll be much safer there than in London should there be an invasion."

Braham saw Nancy rubbing her head, so he slipped in behind and took over for her. "Do you think we need to return home?"

"I've seriously thought about that. I just don't know. Really, what could we do if we did return?" She sighed. "Ooh... That feels so good. Where did you learn to do that?"

"I'd say from my mum, but she died when I was eight, so I don't quite remember. I think I was born knowing how." He smiled, and kissed the top of her head. "Is there something we could do from here?" he asked, brainstorming.

"What do you mean?"

"Well, we do have the ears of the Bonaparte brothers. Of course, I'm not saying that we could walk up to the general himself and say, 'Excuse me, Général, Sir, but in light of our friendship, it would be rather shitty of you to invade our country, so I'm asking you to reconsider.'"

Nancy laughed.

"But on second thought," he added, "it might be a splendid idea. It would certainly be bold, would it not? I think Bonaparte would actually piss himself."

"Yes," she agreed. "Piss himself laughing! But, then again…" The wheels began to turn as she tried to think of ways that they could ingratiate themselves with the Général.

"What are you thinking," Braham asked, half afraid of how she would answer.

"I'm thinking about how loyal the Général is regarding his friends. Seriously, John, you're onto something. It's much harder to think of someone as your enemy when they have proven to be your friend. If you know someone in a more intimate capacity…"

"You can't be serious, Ann."

"I'm quite serious."

He thought on it a moment. He wasn't sure just exactly what she had in mind, but he trusted her instincts and experience.

"Well, why not?" he conceded. "There's little else we can do, so we might as well give it a go."

The next evening, as they entered the casino, there sat the Général at one of the card tables. He saw them as they came in, so he gestured for them to join him. He invited Nancy to sit next to him as Braham took his seat to her right.

"Bonsoir, Général," Nancy said, as he arose politely to take her hand as she was seated.

"Bonsoir, Cityoenne Storace. You're looking quite lovely tonight."

"And where is your beautiful wife," Braham inquired.

"She decided to attend the theatre instead. Something about too much smoke and noise in the casino," he said, chuckling. "She prefers quieter, more refined entertainments."

"Indeed," Nancy replied with a pretty smile. "I do hope she is well."

"Oui, she's quite well, merci." He allowed his gaze to drift to Nancy's bosom. "Shall I deal both of you in?"

"Oui, merci beaucoup," Braham answered.

As the first round of bets was placed, they picked up their cards and settled in for the hand. Polite conversation was exchanged and as the champagne flowed, they grew looser and more relaxed, playing hand after hand.

"Lady Luck is with the Général tonight," Nancy exclaimed when Bonaparte won the third hand in a row. "What is his secret," she asked flirtatiously.

"Perhaps it's the lovely lady seated next to me," he replied with a smile.

The champagne having gone to her head a little, Nancy felt a bit more at ease with herself. Her conversation with the Général was marked with humorous chit-chatting, polite niceties and mild flirtation and, soon, she felt at ease enough to lay her hand on his thigh. He gave no response except to smile from one corner of his mouth. She saw this as a signal that he liked what she did, so she took another liberty by gently massaging it.

As the evening progressed, she observed as he ate from the plate of various fruits and cheeses that was placed just in front of them, taking note of which ones he chose most frequently. She broke off a morsel of one of the cheeses that seemed to be his favorite and held it up to his mouth, offering to feed it to him. Braham saw this gesture out of the corner of his eye and gave her a gentle kick. She kicked back as if to say, "Leave me alone. I know what I'm doing." Bonaparte glanced at her and smiled, and allowed her to place the bite into his mouth.

"Mm… Delicious, oui?" she said with a seductive giggle.

Then she picked a ripe, pitted cherry from off of the plate and gently flicked it into her mouth with the end of her tongue. She rolled it around for just a bit before she chewed it delicately, and swallowed. Then she brushed the tip of her tongue over her lips to get the last drops of juice. When she noticed Bonaparte watching her intensely, she asked, "Would The Général like one, too?"

He nodded, so she picked another cherry from the plate and placed it on his tongue, wiping the corners of his mouth with the tips of her fingers.

The flirtations continued, and as the champagne produced its desired effect, she gently ran her hand up his thigh to his groin. Finally, after several minutes of stroking and massaging, the Général leaned over and whispered something in her ear, then he got up and politely excused himself. Nancy smiled and, after waiting for a discrete amount of time, she excused herself as well. As she passed behind Braham's chair, he slipped his hand to the back and brushed her skirt.

He carried on polite conversation with the rest of the people at the table, pretending not to be concerned about what everyone knew was happening in another room and, after what to him felt like forever, they returned—the Général first and then Nancy. After she took her seat, Braham placed his arm around her shoulders and drew her in close. She could sense from his demeanor that he wasn't pleased.

During the entire ride home, Braham was uncharacteristically silent. Finally, as they entered their rooms at the hotel, he spoke. "What the bloody hell do you think you were doing back there, Ann?"

"Exactly what I appeared to be doing. I thought it was clear last night when we discussed it."

"Discussed what?

"Ingratiating ourselves to the Général, of course."

"Yes, but I didn't expect, well, I'm stunned and hurt. I thought that when we, I mean, when you started giving your affections to me that—"

"It's nothing, John. Surely you don't believe that there are any affections attached to it on either of our parts."

He sighed and appeared unsure.

She turned to him and spoke matter-of-factly.

"I have a supple throat and a flexible tongue. They are the tools of my livelihood and I can also use them to get what I want in a man's world. They have served me well both on and off stage. I have now been honored to use them in the diplomatic service of His Majesty and my country."

From that evening, each time they encountered the Général in a social setting, it was the same. Discrete flirtations followed by Nancy and Bonaparte excusing themselves to return in half an hour or so. When, finally one night, they didn't return to the tables, Braham's patience with the situation reached its limit. He left the casino in a huff and looked for a tavern where he could have a beer or two to soothe his wounded pride.

Nancy didn't return to their rooms at the hotel until early in the morning and as she entered the salon, she could hear a young woman's laughter coming from Braham's bedchamber.

"The ungrateful little shit," she thought as she walked past his door to her own chamber. "We sleep together a few times and he thinks he possesses me now?"

She went into her bedchamber and threw her cloak over a chair, looking around the finely appointed room. "I provide these expensive lodgings and this is how he thanks me? By bringing in his slut?"

The next morning she was up early, sitting in the salon enjoying her morning coffee and reading the most recent theatrical reviews, when out of his room came Braham, along with the young woman whose laughter Nancy heard the night before.

"Why, good morning, darling," Nancy greeted him cheerfully. "And who, might I ask, is your lovely friend?"

Looking a little weary and hung-over, as well as surprised to find Nancy in the salon, Braham gestured towards the young woman standing beside him.

"Ann, this is Collette. Collette, Mademoiselle Storace."

Collette, a young, pretty, dark-eyed, dark-haired chambermaid, smiled broadly and gave Nancy a polite head gesture. "O, mais oui, I have heard so very much about you, Mademoiselle." She giggled in girlish fashion. "I, too, want to be a singer and an actress," she exclaimed.

"Well, mon cheri," Nancy replied, "you are most certainly pretty enough."

"Oui, merci," she exclaimed.

"Let me ask you, dear, do you read music?"

Braham stood aside, looking quite uncomfortable with the situation.

"Oh, no, Mademoiselle, but Monsieur Braham says he is more than happy to give me singing lessons," she said with a broad smile. "He says I have a beautiful voice!"

"Oh, really? Well isn't that nice of him?" Nancy replied as she glared at Braham. "Pray, do you speak Italian?"

"No, Mademoiselle, only French,"

"Tsk, tsk," Nancy clucked. "Well, I suppose Monsieur Braham will have to give you lessons in Italian as well."

"That would be wonderful, indeed. Perhaps then I could learn to read," she exclaimed, wide-eyed.

"Oui," Nancy replied as she picked up her coffee cup and took a sip.

"Well, now," Braham interrupted, "I think that Collette should be on her way."

"Oui," Nancy agreed. "I'm quite sure her maman must be frantic."

As Braham showed Collette to the door, Nancy went back to her reading. When he closed it, he turned in place and watched for Nancy's reaction.

"Tres charmant," she said without looking up from her paper.

"Yes, and quite pretty, too," Braham replied nervously. He went to the credenza, poured himself a cup of coffee and sat down.

"Mais oui!" she replied, mocking the girl's high-pitched voice. Et *tres* intelligent! Good God, John, how old is she? Thirteen?"

"Fifteen."

"Practically an old woman. Afraid she'll end up a spinster, I'm sure."

He said nothing in reply. They sat together in the salon drinking their coffee, saying nothing for several minutes until Nancy made a slight gesture in the direction of the fireplace.

"Oh, I nearly forgot."

"What's that?" He was relieved that she finally broke the silence.

"Over there on the mantle. It's for you," she said as she continued to read.

She pointed to a piece of folded paper. Braham sat his coffee cup on the table and went to the fireplace. He picked up the paper, opened it and began to read.

"What's this," he asked, confused.

"It's an itemized invoice for your part of the expenses for this trip, thus far."

"What do you mean, my part of the expenses? I thought, well, I assumed—"

"You assumed what?"

"Nothing was ever mentioned about expenses, so I assumed—"

"Oh," Nancy said, as she put down her paper. "You assumed that I would be paying."

"I suppose I did." He looked back down at the invoice and his eyes grew wide.

"Good God! Look at this! I don't have money for all this."

"Hm," Nancy replied. "How much money do you have?"

He ran his hands through his hair, blushing. "I only have what I've made since we've been in Paris, and I've, well, we've spent many nights in the casinos and—"

"And you've lost most of it."

"Yes," he confessed.

"Oh, dear," she said as she got up from her seat and went to where he stood. "Don't you have a bank account in England?"

"Well, of course I do. I'm carrying my letter of credit, but at the rate we're going now, my account will be demolished before we're even out of Paris." He paced, glancing at the invoice and nervously running his hand through his hair. "What the hell am I going to do?"

"I suppose you could make some money giving singing lessons to Collette."

He sighed and rolled his eyes in embarrassment and frustration.

She let him stew in his reaction for a few moments, then she reached for the paper and took it from his hand. Looking at it and then into his eyes, she ripped it in half and threw it into the fireplace. She gave him a tender kiss and said, "It was just reminder, that's all."

In the following weeks, it became clear that Napoleon had decided against an invasion of England, and instead turned his sites upon Egypt. Nancy felt it was safe for her and Braham to move on, so, after eight months in Paris—seven more than she planned—they packed their bags and prepared to move on to their next destination.

From Paris they went to Florence, Italy, a city that Nancy knew to be in the control of the Coalition, which included England. From there they could navigate in and around the rest of the country, depending on where the heat of the hostility was focused at the time. With Napoleon concentrating on Egypt, perhaps things in Italy would cool down a bit. It was abundantly clear, however, that their journey was going to get riskier as they went, and they braced themselves for the possibility that they might eventually have to turn around and go back to England at a moment's notice.

Napoleon Bonaparte

Chapter Twelve

On the road to Toulon, May 1798

18 January 1788

A great melancholy seized me, Wanze, when I read your last letter informing me that negotiations between you and His Majesty, the Emperor, had fallen through. I was in the midst of counting the days until your return, believing that it would be soon that I would be holding you again in my arms.

In light of this bitter news, it becomes even more imperative that we find a way for me to come to England. Already I have begun the sketches for a new opera based on Shakespeare's The Tempest, as I said I would. The part of Miranda, of course, will be composed for you as was Susanna in Figaro. Perhaps, too, after I have spent a year or so in London, we—you and I—could make an Italian tour together, for I am of the utmost confidence that we should be well-received by the Italians, who haughtily believe that they are the only ones who produce great opera. We certainly could teach them differently, could we not?

Until that time when I do hold you once again, know that you remain ever in my heart, and I remain your faithful and affectionate servant,

Tuo Wolfgango

As the coach rocked and rattled along the dusty road to Tulon, Nancy stared out the window as Braham, who sat in the opposite seat with his feet propped up, slept.

"However does he manage to sleep in the coach like that?" she wondered. Each time they hit a bump, it rattled her teeth so fiercely that she swore she had broken one or two. At least for now, she had the money to hire a private coach, but by the end of the trip they would most likely end up in a crowded post coach, which was even bumpier, more cramped, and more uncomfortable.

The journey to Florence was long—three weeks, possibly a month, depending on the weather and road conditions. Once they reached the port city of Toulon, there was no telling what the conditions would be like on the Mediterranean. When they reached Toulon, they would book passage on a ship to Livorno and then travel again by coach to Florence.

She turned her gaze upon Braham, who was still sleeping soundly. I should have been making this trip with Wolfgango, she thought, remembering a letter he wrote to her many years ago, suggesting a tour of Italy for the two of them. I wonder if he snored as loudly in a coach as John does. She let a quiet sigh escape as she turned to look back out the window at the passing French countryside. Rows of vineyards lined the rolling hills, red poppies dotted the fields, and cattle grazed the green pastures—so different from the noisy, dusty, crowded city.

She remembered how much Mozart said he hated Paris. "The French! Basta! Such pigs," he would exclaim. His attitude towards the French was very much like Braham's was when they first arrived in Paris. But this—the countryside—was so quaint and beautiful, with no noisy, rude, people to spoil it. Wolfgang would have loved this. No one could hate this. But then, she had always loved the country. When I retire from the stage, she thought, perhaps I'll build a chateau in France and have my own vineyard.

Suddenly, Braham awakened, stretching his arms and legs and opening his mouth with a yawn like a bear coming out of hibernation. How such a small man could suddenly take up so much space was absolutely baffling to her.

"Have you been awake all this time," he asked as he sat upright.

"Oh, yes," she replied. "I can't ever sleep in a coach."

"What have you been doing?"

"Looking out at this beautiful countryside and thinking how nice it would be to have a home and a vineyard here." She sighed and looked out again. "Wouldn't you love to live in a place like this, John?"

Braham glanced out the window for a few seconds and then shrugged. "Meh," he grunted. "Nothing to do but stand in the pasture with the cows. I prefer the city. Always have."

"Oh, I love the city, don't take me wrong, but sometimes I simply have to get away from it." She thought for moment before she spoke again. "I learned that about myself years ago after Mozart whisked me off to a country estate belonging to a Baroness with whom he was friends. He took me there to recover from the…" she hesitated. "To recover from the wounds I sustained when my husband…" She fell silent when she realized that this was the first time that she had ever spoken about that night with John Fisher.

"When your husband what?" he asked, urging her to continue.

"When he beat me," she said, embarrassed.

"He what?"

"He beat me. He nearly killed me, in fact. Emperor Joseph banished him because he feared that Fisher might rob him of his prima buffa."

Braham shook his head in amazement. "I'm speechless, Ann. I had no idea you went through anything like that."

"You knew that I was married and that I still am."

"Yes, but I didn't know the circumstances surrounding your estrangement."

"Well, now you know." She took a deep breath. "Anyway, it was while I stayed with the Baroness that I fell in love with the country, and I was determined that one day, when I retire from the stage, I shall own a cottage in the English countryside, and have gardens filled with fragrant roses." She looked up and smiled.

Braham moved from his seat and sat down beside her, taking her in his arms.

"There, there, my sweet angel," he said as he drew her close. "Of course you'll have your home in the country, if that's what you want. I'm going to be richer than the king himself, and I shall give you anything your heart desires!"

She buried her face in his chest.

"Don't worry, my love. I promise I'll take care of you for the rest of your life."

The drive to Toulon took nearly a week and when they finally arrived, they were met with one of the most stunning demonstrations of French naval power they had ever witnessed. The streets were literally choked with uniformed men, nearly all of them dressed in naval attire. Once they reached the harbor, they saw what must have been nearly the entire French fleet. There were guns, ammunition and supplies all loaded into ships that were ready to set sail for Egypt, where Napoleon planned to stage the next campaign in his war against England.

"Bloody hell," Braham exclaimed wide-eyed.

"Imagine what would have happened had these ships been bound for England," Nancy said as she gazed in amazement at the scope of it all. "I can't pretend that I had even a small part in changing Bonaparte's mind, but if I did, thank God."

Braham shrugged. "Nah, he would have met up with Nelson, and bloody Horatio would have stopped him for damned sure."

Nancy smiled. "Yes, I think that's what Bonaparte was afraid of, too. He's a remarkably intelligent and calculating man. He'll wait for his best opportunity—forever if he has to," she said, recalling the many hours she sat and played chess with the Général. "Failure is not a word in his vocabulary. He may well rule the world one day."

"Perhaps it's a good thing that I finally learned to speak French. It may come in handy in the near future." Braham chuckled nervously.

ഇൗൽ

Three weeks later, when they finally arrived in Coalition-controlled Florence, Nancy felt a sense of sudden relief. Finally, they stood on friendly soil. She hadn't realized what a strain living eight months in an enemy country was on her until she felt the tension melt away just moments after their coach pulled up to the customs house near the city gates. As they handed the official their passports, he smiled and spoke to them in English, with a heavy Italian accent.

"Welcome to Florence, Signora Storace and Signore Braham. We look forward to seeing you both on our stage."

"Grazie, Signore," Braham replied. "Si felici di essere Firenze!"

"Ah! So you speak Italian," the official exclaimed.

"Si," Nancy said. "Entrambi noi!"

"Forgive me, but most of the English I have encountered speak only English and French, so I assumed that you would be like them."

"No offense taken," Nancy said, smiling. It certainly was good to be among friends again.

Nancy and Braham were scheduled to sing at the Pergola Theatre in their serious opera season with two productions—Moneta's *Le furie d'Orete* and Basili's *Il ritorno d'Ulisse*, and it was there that Braham met Italy's premiere tenor, Giacomo Davide, who was regarded as Europe's finest.

Nancy was determined to engage Braham in lessons with Davide, as she wished to refine his sentimental, overtly Jewish style and bring him to a more classical approach in his technique and ornamentations. Who else to help her accomplish this but Europe's greatest classical tenor? After Braham spent several weeks under Davide's tutelage, Nancy inquired as to his progress.

"There is no doubt he possesses a great, natural gift," Davide said. "But he possesses not a shred of integrity where singing is concerned."

"What do you mean," Nancy asked.

"I am quite familiar with his teacher in Bath—Rauzzini. I know Signore Braham has been taught well, for Rauzzini is among the best, but he refuses to employ the skills that he has been taught, preferring to resort to what is easiest and most natural for him."

"Of course, you're right," she agreed, recalling how long she'd worked with him on his acting techniques, and the frustration she experienced when he still resorted to the same stilted style he'd always used.

"The problem is the fact that his voice is so naturally beautiful and his audience is drawn in so completely, they don't know that his technique is at times deplorable. He cheats and no one cares."

"And neither does he, for it still serves him well."

"Si, signora," replied Davide.

"What can be done, then?"

Davide shrugged. "If the man has no integrity, nothing can be done. I can teach singing," he said, "but I cannot teach integrity. That, one is either born with, or not." He sighed. "It is a shame, however, for the man could be regarded as Europe's finest tenor—after me, of course," he added with a wink.

After they finished the summer/fall season in Florence, Braham and Nancy traveled north to Milan, where, despite the fact it had recently fallen to the French, Braham had been invited to sing opposite another English singer, Elizabeth Billington, who was an old colleague of Nancy's.

During the trip up to Milan, they were met once again with the reality of war, for as they drew nearer the city, the sights they encountered were sobering and terrifying: burned-out farm houses and barns, rotted carcasses of dead animals left lying on the ground, ravaged fields, broken trees, and the occasional dead soldiers still left along the side of the road, their eye sockets sunken and hollow. How things had changed since the last time she'd traveled this route, when she was only a girl.

"I hate war," she said as she stared out the coach window at the devastation. "If I had a son, I would not allow him to go to war, for what purpose does it serve?"

Braham drew his window shade so that he couldn't see any more.

"Why it's the grand and glorious Révolution! Liberté! Égalité! Fraternité!" He sighed. "Bloody bullshit is what it is. It lines the pockets of the rich and powerful. That's its only purpose."

She thought about Mozart and the fact that they might have been touring Italy together if all had gone as they had hoped. She wondered how he would feel about it all, especially now that the Revolution had spread beyond the Enlightenment's ideals of liberty and equality, and evolved into wars of conquest under Napoleon and the French Directory government.

Once they reached Milan and settled into their rooms, Nancy was anxious to get to the theater to see Elizabeth Billington, for it had been several years since they were associated, as Elizabeth, like Nancy, split from Sheridan's theater just shortly after Stephen's death and began her tour of Italy.

"Nancy, dearest," Elizabeth exclaimed as the two embraced one another. "How good it is to see you."

"And you, as well, Lizzie," Nancy said as she squeezed her friend tightly. "You do remember Mr. Braham."

"Of course I do," Elizabeth replied as she extended her hand.

Braham took her hand and politely kissed it. "Miss Billington," he said, nodding. "I'm so looking forward to our work together."

"So am I, Mr. Braham. So you've seen the theater?"

"Oh yes, Signora Storace has shown me around. She's still very familiar with it, even after all the years it has been since she last performed here."

"Good, then. We start rehearsing tomorrow, if that is fine with you."

"Indeed, Miss Billington. I'm looking forward to it. Signora Storace has told me many good things about you."

"Well, I take that as a great compliment coming from her. She's the best in the business!"

The next day, Braham began rehearsals for a production of Naolini's *Il trionfo di Clelia*. Nancy had already told him that Elizabeth Billington was one of the very best, and that he could learn much from her. Braham sat in on Elizabeth's private rehearsals and coaching sessions. Nancy coached him to listen particularly to her embellishments and ornamentations, for she considered them the utmost in artistry, taste, and style. She encouraged him to incorporate a similar style into his own embellishments.

After two weeks of rehearsal, opening night arrived and Nancy was anxious to see how much Braham had gleaned from the time he had spent in rehearsal with Elizabeth. As he moved into stage position for his first aria, she watched in great anticipation, hoping that he had benefitted from his exposure to one of the world's premier sopranos. He began very well and sang through the first and second sections beautifully, but when he began the da capo, the repeat of the first section where the singer is free to ornament and embellish according to their own taste and skills, he launched into an exact copy of one of Billington's own roulades. Nancy felt the color rush from her cheeks and had it not been for the fact that she always carried her smelling salts, she would have fainted.

After the performance, she rushed from the theater as fast as she could, backstage to Elizabeth's dressing room, where she pounded on the door and begged Elizabeth to let her in. When Elizabeth finally opened the door, it was apparent that she had been crying as her stage make-up was smeared and blotchy, and her were eyes red and swollen.

"The bloody little thief!" Elizabeth shouted as she paced in front of Nancy.

"I am so very sorry, Elizabeth. I can't express to you how very sorry..."

"You can't tell me you didn't know he was going to do this," Elizabeth accused.

"Of course I didn't know! I'm cut to the quick by such an accusation! We've been dear friends far too long to—"

"Yes, but a friend is often too easily trumped by a lover," Elizabeth snapped.

"Come now, Lizzie. You know me better than that," Nancy pleaded. "You know my integrity when it comes to our profession. That alone should relieve you of any misgivings over my involvement in this. And regarding loyalty, I hope you've always known that I am the most loyal of friends and that I should never allow my romantic attachments to compromise that."

"Then why would he do such a thing?"

"I do confess that I encouraged him to listen and learn from you. You're one of the best in the profession, and I felt that he learned all he could from me. But I would never have said that it was all right for him to copy your ornamentations to the exact note."

Elizabeth stopped pacing and went to her dressing table. Picking up a handkerchief, she looked into the mirror and began to wipe the smeared make-up from off of her face. "Well, perhaps you need to teach your little protégé, or lover, or whatever it is you consider him, that if he's going to plagiarize another singer's work, it's best that he not do it with said singer standing in the wings on the same stage."

"He shall receive a thorough lesson on it from me, I assure you. Please, dear Lizzie, will you forgive me?"

"Of course I forgive you, Nancy." She smiled and then turned from the mirror, extending her arms for an embrace. "We've been friends far too long to allow even this to come between us."

Nancy felt a sense of deep relief as she wrapped her arms around Elizabeth's waist and hugged her tightly.

"But mind you," Elizabeth warned. "After this run is over, I'll never share the stage with that little bastard again."

After Braham changed out of make-up and costume and back into his street clothes, he and Nancy rode together to a local café, where the other actors and people associated with the theater planned to meet after the performance. Nancy sat silently, staring out the window.

"You didn't say how you liked my performance tonight, darling," Braham said. "Were you not pleased?"

"How could I be pleased John, with a performance that nearly destroyed a friendship between me and one of my most esteemed colleagues?"

"I don't know what you mean," he replied, astonished.

"I mean that you stood there in your opening aria and, without a shred of remorse or shame, copied note-for-note, one of Elizabeth's roulades. How could you, John?"

"But I didn't know that—"

"Oh, please, you can't tell me that you had no idea that what you were committing was thievery! I nearly fainted on the spot when I heard it. Poor Elizabeth was frantic, believing that I had somehow put you up to it. I had to convince her that I had nothing whatsoever to do with it. Why, I've never been so embarrassed in my entire life!"

Braham sat in dejected silence. "I didn't mean to offend anyone," he finally said.

"You have no integrity, John. You're extremely talented, but you're lazy, and because of your laziness, you'll take the easiest, most expedient route to success. Now you've damaged a long-time relationship with a dear friend, and I don't know if I can ever forgive you for that."

"I'm sorry, Ann. I really didn't mean for this to happen."

She sighed. "If you're truly sorry, you will go to Elizabeth and apologize personally."

"I promise, I shall."

"Good enough," she replied. "We'll not speak on the subject again."

Elizabeth Billington

Chapter Thirteen
Liverno, Italy, August 1799

26 June 1789

I beg of you, dearest Wanze, do not compromise your integrity on my behalf, for it has always been the steadfast holding to what you believe to be right that is the quality I love in you the most. You are the dearest, truest, and most loyal of friends, but if for the sake of bringing me to London you must lower your standards, I would much rather I never lay eyes upon you again than to suffer the knowledge that you were compromised for my sake.

Please know that I love you, and keep that knowledge in your heart. Until that time when we meet again, I remain ever your devoted,

Wolfgango

*A*s Nancy had requested, Braham went to Elizabeth and asked her forgiveness for his indiscretion and, fortunately, the incident didn't serve to damage Nancy's relationship with her. But, true to her word, Elizabeth refused to ever sing again with Braham.

They sang another season in Milan and upon its completion they intended to set out for Naples, but tensions were far too high in that region, so they traveled back towards the southwest, to Liverno where there was a large Coalition stronghold. It was there Lord Admiral Horatio Nelson and his mistress, Emma Hamilton resided while Nelson waited for his next opportunity to confront the French navy.

Nelson, who by that time was already a legendary hero among the British, presented a strong, slender, confident figure. He had once been considered dashingly handsome, but his years of naval combat robbed him of an eye as well as an arm, and had left his face scarred and somewhat disfigured. He had a wickedly naughty sense of humor, however, and he was known for his contagious, musical laughter. It was clear from the way his good eye danced and sparkled whenever Emma entered a room, that he absolutely adored her.

"So, Mr. Braham," Nelson chimed, "I've heard that while you were in Paris, you and your lovely lady were seen in frequent company with Bonaparte."

They had been invited to dine with Lord Nelson and his mistress, and provide the entertainment for the company, which included Elizabeth Billington (who introduced them to Nelson), as well as the Queen of Naples, who was another sister of Emperor Joseph II and Marie Antoinette, and whom Nelson brought to safety in Liverno when Napoleon's armies began to lay siege on the city.

"Yes we were, Your Grace," Braham replied. "However, it was actually Signora Storace who spent the greater amount of time with him. I was fonder of his brother Jerome's company." He glanced at Nancy who sat glaring at him. "I found him to be a much more pleasant chap than his brother, and much easier to engage in conversation. But Signora Storace seemed to have a special 'touch' with Napoleon," he added, as he cleared his throat.

Nelson turned to Nancy, who sat next to Emma. "So, tell us, Signora, what type of man is he?"

Nancy politely put her fork down, dotted the corners of her mouth with her napkin and laid it neatly back into her lap.

"He's a quiet and thoughtful man, Your Grace," she replied as she gave Braham a sharp kick under the table. "Quite intelligent and extremely calculating, yet there seems to run deep within him a curiously tender heart."

"So the man has a soft spot," he said as he reached for Emma's hand and gave it a gentle squeeze.

"Yes he has, Your Grace. He quite adores his son. He also considers his army as his own children, and they love him for it. As a result, I do believe that they would do almost anything for him."

"I hear his soldiers call him 'The Petite Commander'," Emma said, giggling.

"Indeed, they do," Nancy replied, "but only as a term of endearment. He chooses personal guards who stand much taller than himself, which gives him the reputation of being short of stature, which in reality, he is not."

"What would you consider his greatest strengths?" Nelson continued, intent on learning more about his foe.

"He has tremendous resolve. He won't be deterred and his opinions are not easily swayed, especially when he is convinced that he is right. He is a man of tremendous conviction and integrity," she said as she looked at Braham.

"He can be rather arrogant on that point, can he not?"

Nancy smiled. "I do suppose, Your Grace that one could see it as arrogance, but having known the man in a social capacity, I see it as a mask."

"A mask? For what, pray tell?"

"For his insecurities and weaknesses," she answered.

"Ah, yes," Nelson replied, nodding. "'Tis the man's arrogance that could eventually be his undoing, for, despite the appearance, the attitude doesn't indicate confidence, but reveals a streak of insecurity." He pondered this for a moment, then he asked, "And how did you learn all of this about him, Signora?"

Braham began to squirm.

"Chess, Your Grace," Nancy answered, smiling.

"Chess?"

"Indeed, Your Grace, chess. I've found that everything that can be known about a man is revealed in his chess game."

Nelson laughed and then slapped the table, bellowing, "God damn it Braham, where the bloody hell did you find this woman? She's a bleedin' military genius! By George, I'm going to slap her into a uniform and give her a commission in my navy!"

"She is a rare catch, to be sure, Your Grace," Braham replied. He took Nancy by the hand and leaned in close, giving her a kiss on the cheek. "Now that I know her secret I shall have to be much more cautious the next time we play chess, or she'll be learning more about me than I care to reveal," he said as he chuckled nervously.

After they finished supper, the men retired to the salon for their pipes and brandy while the women took a leisurely stroll out onto the terrace, where Nancy and Emma leaned over the railing to watch the ships as they floated in and out of the harbor. Dusk had settled on the bay. A gentle evening breeze cooled their faces as they gazed out onto the red and amber sunset casting its glow upon the ships, their red, white, and blue Union Jacks flying high above the masts, tinged with a subtle orange hue.

Her Majesty the Queen of Naples and Elizabeth Billington sat on the other side of the terrace next to a potted palm tree, conversing and sharing stories and gossip while Emma's two little Yorkshire terriers romped and played.

"This has to be my favorite time of day," Emma mused. She threw her head back and took a deep breath, drawing in the salty air that blew in off the Mediterranean. "Little wonder Nelson loves the sea. The air is so refreshing this time of evening!"

Emma Hamilton was quite possibly the most beautiful woman that Nancy had ever laid eyes upon. With her pale, creamy complexion, light auburn hair and deep blue eyes, she was like Helen of Troy, possessing the face that launched a thousand ships. At least it was clear to Nancy that she had launched Admiral Nelson's ship and that it would never find harbor anywhere else but in Emma's snow white bosom.

"What a lovely little man, your John Braham," Emma said, her eyes dancing. "Wherever did you find him?"

"Oh, we met several years ago when Stephen and I were in Bath. He was then a student of my old singing teacher."

"Oh, yes, yes, I remember. The old Italian castrato. What's his name?"

"Rauzzini," Nancy answered.

"Of course. Rauzzini," Emma repeated. "Braham is quite young, is he not?"

Nancy nodded and smiled. "Quite. That is to say he's much younger than me." She laughed a little. "And I'm not sure that I'm entirely comfortable with that."

"But he seems quite devoted, despite the disparity in your ages," Emma replied.

Nancy didn't answer, but stood looking out over the distance. Emma observed Nancy's reticence and continued to gently press her for more information.

"Ah, I detect that devotion isn't shared by you for him," Emma said softly.

"No, it is not," she sighed, "for my heart has long been given to someone else."

"Then why is that someone else not here with you?"

Nancy attempted a smile. "He was supposed to be."

"Then where is he," Emma asked as she slipped an arm around Nancy's waist.

"Dead. He died several years ago, quite suddenly."

"Oh, Nancy, I'm so sorry. Well, I don't even know what to say. You poor, poor dear," she said as she laid her head upon Nancy's shoulder. "I can't even imagine what would happen to me if…" She choked back a tear. "Well I can't even speak it now can I?"

"Yes, I know, Emma. Don't…don't speak it. Don't even think it."

"I don't believe that I could ever love again if that should happen," Emma said.

Nancy nodded. "That's the problem. You do love. Your heart continues to love, but it's empty. There's a hole left there that no one and nothing else can fill. They're dead, but the love won't die."

"But isn't that a good thing? Isn't a love like that meant to be forever?"

"I don't honestly know, Emma. I know it hurts like hell, and sometimes I wish it would just bloody go away and leave me alone."

Emma drew Nancy closer to her side and held her there as they watched the sun continue to fall until it was no more and the black Mediterranean night sky lit up with stars. Then she pointed to the brightest one and said, "There! Right up there he is, Nancy. He's smiling at you."

Rest gently, my dear love,
sleep until your good fortune wakes;
there, I shall give you my portrait,
see how kindly it smiles at you.
Gentle dreams, rock him to sleep,
and may the images in his dreams of love
become reality at last.

Ruhe sanft mein holdes leben, from *Zaide* by W. A. Mozart

Lord Admiral Horatio Nelson

Chapter Fourteen
Venice, Italy, March 1800

Nancy stared into the mirror and ran her hands across her cheeks. As she pulled up the corners of her eyes with her fingertips, she let out a sigh of frustration. "There's no denying it," she said to Braham, who had just finished his coffee and had settled in to read the morning reviews. "I'm getting old."

At the age of thirty-four she was beginning to see the effects of the already full and active life she had led. A few wrinkles and lines began to form around her eyes and she started to accumulate some extra weight around her hips and thighs, typical of her Italian heritage. Her beautiful, long, wavy, dark brown tresses were as full and luxurious as they ever were, however, and her dark eyes were still large and expressive.

"What do you mean you're getting old?" he said with a devilish grin. He put his paper down and got up and to stand behind her. Wrapping his arms around her waist, he began to nibble and kiss the back of her neck and behind her ears. "You don't look old, and you certainly didn't act old last night!"

Nancy giggled as she squirmed from out of his embrace. "Oh you're just silly," she said, "but I'm grateful that even at such a young age, your eyesight is failing."

Braham laughed and gave her a playful smack on the backside. "Well, my eyesight may be failing, but not so badly that I'm unable to read these wonderful reviews of our performance! You should read these, my love," he said as he picked the paper up and showed Nancy the article. "We've taken Venice by storm!"

"Let me see!" She took the paper from him and read. "Look at this," she exclaimed. "They loved you and they're clamoring for us to stay for another season!"

She folded the paper and turned to him. "Congratulations, John. You've done it. You've nearly completed your first successful Italian tour," she said, beaming with pride.

Braham grinned broadly and strutted around the room, puffed up like a peacock. "I did it," he exclaimed as he flung his arm into the air in a foppish gesture and followed through with a fanciful bow. "I've performed for princes, kings and queens, arrogant and ambitious little French generals and one-eyed admirals, and have lived to tell about it!" They both burst into laughter as he took her in his arms and squeezed her tightly. "And I couldn't have done any of it without this lovely lady, to whom I am eternally grateful," he said as he lifted her chin and gave her a tender kiss.

"It was my pleasure, John. You deserved the opportunity and I'm honored to have been the one who could give it to you."

His expression suddenly went somber.

"Honored? Your pleasure?" He repeated her words back to her. "Your passion is overwhelming, Ann," he said indignantly as he moved back to the settee.

"I don't know what you mean." She was confused by his sudden change of humor.

"What is wrong with me, Ann? Why am I not good enough for you?"

"I don't understand what you're asking, John. There's nothing wrong with you. And why would you ever believe that I don't think you're good enough?"

"Is it the difference in our ages? Or perhaps it's the fact that I'm just a poor Jewish orphan whom they found out on the streets of London selling pencils!"

"What are you talking about," she asked, astonished.

"I'm simply not good enough for you, that's it. You and your high and mighty theatrical-legend family and your noblewoman's upbringing and education!"

"John! What is wrong?"

"I'm in love with you, Ann! I have been in love with you from the moment I laid eyes on you, and yet, in spite of everything I do to win you, you remain distant." He paced to a window and looked out as Nancy stood silently, waiting for him to continue.

"In London, it was my age. Then, when we were in Paris, you weren't ready. Then, once we arrived in Italy, suddenly I was getting lectures about my laziness and lack of integrity, and how I wasn't meeting up to your standards. I've done everything I know to do to please you, to make you happy and make myself worthy, but you still reject me."

"I'm not rejecting you," she finally said. "It's not that simple. You do make me happy. I'm very proud of you and I have grown to love you dearly but—"

"But you're still not in love with me."

"No, John, I'm not," Nancy said, impatiently. "Why can't you understand and accept that? It's not you, your failings, or successes. It's my feelings. I can't make myself feel something that isn't there."

"But what is it you need that I've not given to you? Name it and it's yours! I'll give you anything you want."

"Do you hear yourself? What do you expect of me? There's nothing you can do and nothing you can give me that will make me love you in the way you wish to be loved."

"Are you in love with someone else?"

Nancy turned away, stunned by his audacity. How dare he ask such a personal question? She felt her face flush and her eyes well with tears, but instead of giving her feelings away by replying defensively, she decided to tell him the truth.

"There was someone, yes," she said at last. "But it's over. It's been over for years."

"How long ago?"

"It's been nearly fifteen years. A long time ago."

"When you were in Vienna?"

She turned to face him. "It doesn't matter anymore, John! It was long ago and far away and it has nothing to do with what is happening between you and me at this very moment."

"I don't believe you. I think you're still in love with him."

"That will be quite enough from you, Mr. Braham!" Nancy had finally lost her patience with the whole conversation. "I was nearly ready to concede to the idea that perhaps my holding onto something that has long since passed away could be what has kept me from giving my affections to you completely, but your stubborn and, might I add, insensitive and childish persistence of the matter has hardened my heart against you! You say you love me? Then if you love me half as much as you claim, you will cease your pursuit of this and leave my presence until I've had time to cool my temper! Then, perhaps we may discuss this later in a more reasonable fashion."

Braham's dark eyes smoldered as he bowed to her politely. "As you wish, Madame," he said as he stormed to his bedchamber, slamming the door.

Over the following week tensions ran high as the couple barely spoke to one another except to say, good morning, or to exchange polite niceties here and there.

"John," Nancy said, one morning while they sat having their breakfast and reading the morning reviews. "John," could you put the paper down for just a moment? I have something to say to you."

He looked up with a raised eyebrow, fearing that he was about to receive another tongue-lashing, and wondering from where it would come this time.

"It's nothing bad, John. Just put the paper down and look at me, please."

Silently, he laid the paper aside and, as he folded his hands on the table in front of him, he looked straight into her eyes.

"I just want to apologize to you for losing my temper last week. I was feeling pressed and I've not yet learned how to govern my passions when I'm in such situations. Anyway, what I said to you wasn't necessarily out of line, but the way in which I said it most certainly was. I can't bear this distance between us any longer, so I'm extending the olive branch and humbly asking for your forgiveness."

"So does it change how you feel about me?"

"Well, no, John, it doesn't. It only means that if we're going to continue working as partners then we shall have to come to an amiable understanding of one another's position in this matter and allow each other some room. As it is, I can't just change my feelings. Feelings aren't like that. But if you will be patient and give me the time and distance I require, you might find better success."

Looking down at his hands, he remained silent. It wasn't exactly what he wanted to hear.

"I know that what I'm asking of you is difficult, if not impossible, for you as a man," she continued. "Men and women are not alike in matters of the heart, John, but please, I value our friendship and our successful partnership above all. All I'm asking is for some time."

He nodded. "All's forgiven. And forgive me for my impatience. If time is what you need, then I'm willing to give it in whatever measure you require. I agree with you regarding our friendship, as well as the partnership. Those are the most important things right now."

"Thank you, John," she said as she reached over and took his hand. "You don't know what this means to me."

Giving in to audience demands, they agreed to stay for another season in Venice and ended their Italian tour with great success in the late spring of 1801. All the goals that Nancy had set for Braham were accomplished, and they both sensed that the time was right for their return to England. As Nancy planned, their return route would be by way of Vienna and Trieste, and then on to Hamburg where they would stay a week or so to give a few performances before traveling on home.

Their arrival in Vienna was marked by a heavy rainstorm that had settled in over the city. It was late in the evening and quite dark, so they couldn't see much when they passed through the gates. This was just fine with Nancy, who was still haunted by the scene of Mozart standing in the road in front of the customs house when she'd left Vienna fourteen years before, and who didn't wish to relive it in her mind.

She'd slept so soundly during the night that it wasn't until she was awakened by the sunlight streaming in from outside that she noticed that the rain had stopped. When she got up and went to the window, she could clearly see the city spread out before her. The familiar sight of the spires of St. Stephan's cathedral and the chatter and noises of the bustling Graben below made her smile.

"German," she said aloud to herself. "How long has it been since I've heard German spoken?" She wasn't sure if she even remembered enough to speak it.

She turned to look at the clock hanging on the wall opposite her bed and saw that it was still rather early. He won't be up for at least another two hours, she thought. That gives me plenty of time. She dressed as quickly as she could and then she scribbled a note to Braham and left it on a table by the settee in the common salon before heading out the door.

As she walked along the Graben, which was one of the most fashionable streets in the city, she took in the familiar sights, sounds, and smells. How many times had she walked this way with Mozart, Benucci, or even Kelly, stopping at an outdoor café for a glass of wine or cider? She giggled as she remembered the time when Mozart, Kelly and she sat together at a café table after a Sunday morning rehearsal of *Figaro*. They watched as the local prostitutes walked by on their way to the cathedral to confess their sins as the two men pointed to various ones, trying to guess which nobleman they had serviced the night before.

Coming to the Trattnerhof, she had to stop and gaze at it for a moment. Mozart and Constanze lived in an apartment there for a few years. How many games of chess had she played with him in the ground floor casino? They were too numerous to even count. It was during one of those chess games that he'd expressed his concern over her engagement to John Fisher and how he had heard the rumors of what a brute he was. After that, he walked her around the corner to the Burgtheater to retrieve a score that she left in her dressing room and in the quiet, empty backstage he'd made love to her for the first time. She had to laugh a little when she recalled recently telling Lord Nelson that everything that could be known about a man was revealed in his chess game. She learned everything she needed to know about Mozart by playing chess with him, for in that he revealed that he had fallen in love with her.

Finally, she rounded the corner into the Michalerplatz, and there it stood. The center of her entire life in Vienna was located in that circle of buildings. There stood the Hofburg, the royal palace in which Emperor Joseph II, her employer at that time, resided, and next to it, the Burgtheater, where she reigned for five years as the Italian Opera Company's prima buffa. Almost directly across from the theater was St. Michael's Church, where several times she ran inside seeking asylum from another one of Fisher's beatings. And down a narrow street not far from St. Michael's was the building in which she resided, in one of the most luxurious apartments she had ever seen.

She walked past the entrance of the theater and on to the palace gates, where she encountered one of the guards. She handed him her passport as well as a letter of introduction and asked for entrance into the Redoutensaal, a large palatial hall where she knew Haydn was giving a dress rehearsal of his oratorio, *The Seasons*, the piece she premiered for him in London ten years before. Once she was let in, she was escorted by another guard to the hall's entrance. He opened the door for her and allowed her to slip in quietly, as the rehearsal was already in progress. Facing the musicians on the stage, Haydn didn't see or hear her as she silently slipped in and found a seat near the back.

For nearly half an hour she listened, recalling the days when she sang the soprano solo at the English premiere of the same work in Oxford. She smiled, remembering what a warm, personal and professional relationship they had developed during his years in London, and how upon his departure, he embraced her and gave her an affectionate kiss on the cheek, telling her how much he would miss her.

When the rehearsal came to a close, and the musicians began to scatter and depart, Nancy stood and made her way to the front where Haydn spoke to one of the violinists about a section in the score where there had been some confusion. Then, as he finished his conversation and turned to make his way to the back exit, he saw her standing there.

"Anna! Why Anna Storace, is that really you?"

"Indeed, it is, Papa Haydn," she replied, beaming.

He threw his arms open and she ran into them, wrapping herself around him.

"Mein kleiner Singvogel, what a soothing sight for these tired old eyes," he exclaimed.

"Und wie ist Ihre Gesundheit, Papa?"

"Ach! I'm old," he replied. "How good can one's health be when one is so old?"

"Oh, Papa, it's so very good to see you again," she said as she slipped her arm through his and began to walk with him to the exit.

"And you, too, my dear," he exclaimed. "Whatever has brought you back to Vienna?"

"I'm just passing through, really, on my way back to London after an extended tour of Italy with a young partner."

"Really? And who would that young partner be," Haydn asked curiously.

"He's a young tenor who joined our company just before Stephen died."

Haydn stopped walking and turned to her. "Your brother is gone? I'm so very sorry, Anna, I had not heard. Oh dear, he was very young was he not?"

"Yes. He fell ill just shortly after you left London and left us a few months later. He was only thirty-four."

"Oh dear, dear. Even younger than…" He hesitated for a moment. "Well, he was even younger than our dear friend, Mozart."

"Yes," she said softly, nodding. "Which is partially why I've come to see you, Papa."

"Go on," he said as he took her arm and began to walk again.

"It's about Mozart. I was wondering if you could do me a great favor."

"And what would that be, meinen Liebchen," he asked with a smile.

Unbeknownst to Nancy, Haydn knew of the love that Mozart had for her. Mozart shared with him in strictest confidence many of the details of their love affair. Haydn knew it was Mozart's fondest hope to be able to travel with Nancy when she returned to England so that he could stay there with her.

"I don't quite know how to ask this really, but…"

"Let's sit down, shall we?" Haydn suggested as he gestured towards a row of chairs.

After they seated themselves Nancy gathered up her nerve and went on.

"I'm sure you must recall that when we all learned of Mozart's unexpected death, I was recovering from a near brush with death myself," she explained. "Mozart was a very dear friend, dearer to me than anyone knew, really, and when I learned of his death, I was quite literally devastated."

Haydn couldn't help but smile as she struggled with the request that she was about to make of him, and he longed to tell her that he knew everything. But of course, propriety kept him from doing so. As she continued to speak, his mind filled with pictures of the first time that Mozart had spoken to him of the affair.

"Oh, Papa! I must tell you that I am so in love! Never have I experienced a feeling like this in my entire life!"

Mozart was such an effusive little man, he thought. But, oh dear, he had never seen him act like that over any woman until Nancy. This was no fly-by-night affair. Mozart's affections for this woman were genuine and deep.

"So I was wondering, Papa" Nancy continued, pulling him from his thoughts. "Knowing the friendship and esteem that you two held for one another, if you would do me the honor of driving me to the cemetery and escorting me to his final resting place so that I may pay him my respects."

Haydn leaned in closely and enveloped her hands in his. "My very dearest Anna, as honor and propriety forbids me to speak more than this, I will say to you that he held you in the highest esteem, and I am quite sure that at the very moment of his death, it was you, he took with him in his heart."

As tears welled in their eyes, he spoke with a quivering voice, "It would my greatest honor and pleasure to accompany you to visit his grave."

When Nancy returned to their lodgings on the Graben, she found Braham up and dressed and ready for the sight-seeing tour of Vienna that she had promised they would take together. He didn't even ask where she had been, or why, but cheerfully gave her his arm as they exited their rooms, descended the stairway and walked out of the building.

As they walked the city's streets she took him to the Michalerplatz and showed him the Hofburg, the Burgtheater, and the building where she had lived. Then they walked a short distance to the Stephansplatz, where she showed him the magnificent St. Stephan's Cathedral, and then just down the Domgasse, to the building where Mozart lived when he composed *The Marriage of Figaro*. She told him of the many private parties and soirees that she and Stephen had attended there and how Stephen played violin in the performances of Mozart's newest string quartets. Interested in hearing about Nancy's life in Vienna all those years ago, he hung on her every word in complete awe and fascination.

Early the next morning, Nancy got up and dressed herself in mourning black. When Haydn arrived in his carriage to take her to St. Marx, she asked if they could stop by a flower cart where she could purchase some violets. Haydn, who was more than happy to oblige, informed the driver and even offered to make the purchase himself.

On the drive out to St. Marx, he explained to her that several years before Mozart's death, Emperor Joseph decreed that there were to be no more burials within the city walls for reasons of health and to protect the city's water supply. He also decreed that bodies were to be buried without embalming, and in shared graves, so no one was sure exactly where Mozart was buried, only the general vicinity. He told her he would do his best to take her to the most likely spot.

When at last they pulled up in front of the cemetery gates, Nancy pulled the black veil attached to her bonnet down over her face and took Haydn's hand to be helped from the carriage. Silently, with Nancy on his arm as she clutched the bouquet of violets in her hand, he led her through the gates and up a long, narrow path lined with trees. They walked the path for several feet before they reached a clearing to the left.

"There," he said, pointing. "It's over in there somewhere."

He took her by the arm again and led her off the path toward the area he had indicated. When they got there, they stopped and he looked around some more. "It's one of these," he said. "It has to be, for I was told that this is where they buried most of the people who died within the same week that he did."

He lifted the veil from her face to kiss her cheek as a father would do with a bride, then stepped back. "I'll leave you two alone," he whispered.

As Haydn backed away from her, she stood looking down at the three or four communal graves that lay at her feet. She waited a moment until one just to her right called to her. She knelt down softly in front of it and whispered, "Wolfgango, is that you calling, my love?"

"Yes, it's me, Wanze. I'm so glad you came. I've missed you."

"Papa Haydn brought me," she said with tears in her eyes.

"I know. He's such a dear friend. He knows about us, you know. I told him. I simply couldn't hold it in. I had to tell someone."

Nancy laughed a little and said, "I kind of suspected that."

There was a moment of silence and then she spoke again. "I've come to tell you good-bye Wolfgango. I've held onto you for so long, for so many years and now it's, well…"

"I know, Wanze. It's holding you back. It's keeping you from your happiness."

"But I love you so much," she said as she began to sob.

"I know. And I love you, too—more than I could ever adequately express, but it's time for you to let go now. I want you to be happy again. You don't have to stop loving, for the love we share for one another will never die, Wanze. Only the body dies. My love for you follows you wherever you go."

"Wolfgango, my love, my very heart!" she cried out as she threw herself prostrate on the grave, her body heaving as the tears flowed freely and the mournful cries of grief arose from out of her bosom so fiercely that she was overcome.

As Haydn stood back observing the scene, he couldn't help but weep, the tears running down his cheeks in rivers to his chin. How he had loved that little man, and now that same love was extended to the one whom Mozart esteemed as his beloved.

Her eyes kept pouring tears and the sobs grew deeper and harder until she felt they would rip her in two. She lay on Mozart's grave for what seemed like hours. When the tears finally ceased, she sat up, pulling herself to her knees. She took out her handkerchief and wiped the remaining tears from of her cheeks and then she placed the violets, which were still clutched in her hand, on the grave.

At last, she leaned over and kissed the ground, whispering, "Addio, mio Caro. Addio, mio Tesoro. Ich liebe dich für immer und ewig und drei Tagen."

She rose to her feet and went to where Haydn stood and, as he gave her his arm, she said, "It's done now. We can go."

If you will weep then by my grave,
and mourn my ashes,
then, o friends, I will appear to you,
bringing a breath of Heaven.

Shed for me a tear, my beloved,
and pluck for me a violet from my grave;
and let your tender eye
look gently down on me.

Dedicate a tear to me, and oh!
Do not be ashamed to do so.
In my diadem it will become
the fairest pearl.

From the Lied, *Abendempfindung,* by W. A. Mozart

Franz Joseph "Papa" Haydn

Chapter Fifteen
Vienna, Austria, June 1801

*W*hen Nancy returned to their lodgings, she found Braham dressed and waiting for her so that they could spend the rest of the day enjoying the Prater. However, when he saw her dressed in mourning clothes, he was not only curious, but concerned.

"What's all this," he asked as he fingered her black crepe gown.

Nancy untied her bonnet and laid it in a nearby chair. "I was visiting the cemetery this morning, the grave of an old friend who died several years ago." She tried to appear unshaken and detached.

"Did you go alone? You didn't have to, you know. I would gladly have accompanied you."

"Thank you, John, but it wasn't necessary for you to have to get up so early for that. Joseph Haydn was happy to accompany me. We were mutual friends. He hadn't been there in a while and wanted to go."

"Joseph Haydn? You mean that old composer who came to London a few years back? The one everyone called Papa?"

"Yes," she replied, nodding. "That's the one."

"You know him?"

"Of course I know him," she said, as she turned her back to him so that he could unlace her bodice. "We met when I was here, but our professional association grew to its peak during the years he spent in London. I sang in just about every oratorio he premiered."

Braham thought a moment and then he asked, "Wasn't he also a good friend of Mozart's?"

By this time Nancy had moved into her bedchamber so that she could change into something more suitable for a picnic.

"Yes, he was. They were the dearest of friends."

"So is that where you went together this morning—to visit Mozart's grave?" He waited for an answer, but there was none. Only silence. Perhaps she didn't hear him. "I say," he called out again. "Was it Mozart's grave you visited this morning?"

When she didn't answer the second time, he decided to let it drop and moved on to another subject.

"Have you heard the scuttle about this young composer named Beethoven?" he called.

Nancy emerged from her bedchamber having changed into a fresh pink muslin gown, and slipping on a pair of ear bobs.

When Braham saw her out of the corner of his eye, he looked up and said, "Well I do say, that looks much better. That mourning garb was rather dismal, don't you think?"

"What was it you were saying before?"

"Oh, yes, well I wondered if you had heard anything about this new composer called Beethoven. I hear he's making quite a splash here in Vienna."

"Yes, I have. In fact I read something just yesterday in the paper." She moved about the room, searching. "Ah! Here it is," she said as she picked up the paper and began to translate the German for him. "It says that there's a concert in the Augsburg Palace hall this evening featuring a performance of his First Symphony." She turned to him. "Would you like to go?"

"I would, very much," he said, smiling. He stood for a moment gazing at her face and noticed that it had changed somehow. He couldn't put a finger on what it was that was different. She was lighter, perhaps, and there was a sparkle in her eyes and a blush on her cheek that he hadn't seen before.

"You're looking rather charming this morning, Ann. I don't know if it's the pink in your dress, or that pretty new ribbon you're wearing in your hair, but you look young and happy." He leaned in and gave her a sweet peck on the lips. "Are we ready to go now?"

"Yes, I believe we are," she said with a smile as she took his arm.

When they arrived at the Prater, Braham was impressed with how very similar it was to the Vauxhall and Marylebone pleasure gardens in London. As soon as they found a spot for their picnic, they ordered the carriage driver to stop. Braham retrieved the picnic basket and the rug that they brought for ground cover and they walked to a spot where several trees stood in a group.

"This looks like the perfect spot." He sat the basket down and bent over to unroll the rug.

Nancy looked out over the surroundings. "I'd forgotten how beautiful it is here."

Early June in the Prater was one of the most beautiful times of the year. The tree-lined walkways and paths were lush with foliage and the lawns were soft, green, and plush from the April and May rains. There were hedge mazes, perennial gardens filled with bulb flowers, ponds with boats, horse racing, and a lane lined with cafes, casinos, stands serving Italian ices, and a various sundry of shops and eateries. Nancy went there several times with Stephen and Kelly, as well as Lord Barnard, but never had she gone in early June, for that was always the time of year when she and the entire Italian Opera Company were assigned to accompany the Emperor to his summer estate at Laxenburg.

Braham finished setting up their spot and began poking through the picnic basket. Nancy turned to see him holding a large, plump strawberry. Not realizing that he was being watched, he popped the whole thing into his mouth at once and the sweet, red juice dripped from his mouth to his chin. Nancy laughed out loud and knelt down to retrieve a napkin to wipe off the juice before it could fall onto his white cravat.

"Well, I must say that was one bloody strawberry, was it not?" he said as he laughed at himself.

"Yes, well, I should have warned you about that," she said. "They grow their strawberries quite large here." She handed him the napkin so that he could wipe his fingers.

After they finished their picnic, they strolled over to the stands where the horse races were about to begin. Placing their bets, they walked to the fence and stood with the crowd that gathered there to watch the race.

As the riders lined up their mounts for the race, Braham hoisted Nancy up onto the first rung of the fence so that she could get a better view, and then climbed up beside her. She had placed her bet on horse Number 9, as that was her lucky number and Braham on horse Number 4. When the signal was given for the start, the horses shot out in a flash, the ground rumbling so fiercely beneath them that they felt the violent vibrations through the rung.

As the horses speeded by, Braham put his fist in the air and called out, "Come on, Four! Pour it on, pour it on!"

The wind created by the powerful steeds as they speeded past was so fearsome that Nancy had to place her hand on her bonnet to prevent it from blowing off.

When Braham's horse began to lag behind he called out, "Move it, you sodding piece of shit!"

As the horses cleared the first turn, Nancy could barely see through the trees that her horse was ahead, so she began to cheer him on. "Run faster, Number Nine! Run faster! Go! Get it out there!"

As soon as the horses were out of sight, Braham jumped down off the fence and grabbed Nancy to help her down. Then they both took off in the direction of their carriage so that they could drive over to the finish line as the horses made their way through the winding course.

The finish line wasn't too far over the bend, so they arrived in plenty of time to see as the horses passed by. As they stood and waited, Nancy said breathlessly, "I'd forgotten how much I loved the races! It reminds me of when I was a girl and I went with Papa to the ones at Marylebone."

Smiling, Braham put his arm around her shoulders and gave her an affectionate squeeze.

They didn't have to wait long before they heard the rumbling sound of hooves clearing the bend just a half a mile to their left and, only a few moments later, they saw them emerge into the clearing, their heads bobbing up and down rhythmically, enveloped in a massive cloud of dust.

Braham leaned forward to see which horse was out ahead and called out, "It's Number Four! Bloody hell, it's Four!"

Nancy began to jump up and down in excitement, cheering Braham's horse on as it made its way to the finish line.

"Pour it on, God damn it! You can do it!" Braham called out, shaking his fist. "Come on, boy, just a little more to go!"

As the riders approached the finish line, they cropped their mounts, urging them to move ahead of the fray and, in an instant, Number Four pulled out ahead by a half. Seeing this, Nancy shouted, "He's ahead! Number Four's ahead!"

As they sped past the line, Number Four clearly won. Excited, Braham grabbed Nancy by the waist, hoisting her into the air, cheering and shouting.

"He did it! Damn it all, he won!" When he put her down, he wrapped her in his arms and planted a big, wet kiss on her mouth.

"Luck was with me today," he exclaimed. "I haven't won a race in I don't know how long. It's all because of you, Ann. You're my good luck charm!" He smiled and kissed her again.

After Braham collected his winnings, they took a stroll along the promenade so that Nancy could take him to the various shops, and where they could stop to enjoy some Italian ice. Then they loaded into their carriage to head back to their lodgings on the Graben. Once they arrived at the hotel, they changed into proper attire for the evening's concert at the Augsburg Palace.

As their carriage pulled up to the palace entrance, Braham was stunned by the sheer magnificence of the homes which had belonged to some of Europe's wealthiest princes. Being an orphan from the streets, he had never seen such opulence. Even the luxurious palaces in London and Bath in which he had performed on several occasions, couldn't compare, for England's royalty, being longtime separated from the Pope, didn't benefit from the conspicuous wealth of the Catholic Church.

When they entered the palace, they were escorted into the great hall, where the concert was to take place. Nancy looked about the sea of unfamiliar faces to see if there was somebody, anybody, she recognized. It wasn't long before she saw a man speaking with two other gentlemen and a young woman.

"Antonio! My God, that's Antonio Salieri," she exclaimed aloud.

Salieri turned around to see who had called him. When his eyes met Nancy's, he broke out into a smile and he hurriedly made his way to where she and Braham stood. Throwing open his arms, he exclaimed, "Anna Storace! Dio nel cielo è così buono vederlo!" He kissed her on both cheeks, embracing her fondly. "Dear God, Anna, how long has it been?" He drew away and took both of her hands in his.

"Too long, Signore Salieri. Far too long," she exclaimed.

"Ah, please, we're long-time colleagues and friends, Anna. Please call me Antonio. I must say, after all these years you still look absolutely stunning."

"And her singing is still every bit as stunning, as well," said Braham.

"And may I ask who your fine escort is?"

"Antonio, this is John Braham, one of the finest English tenors that London has ever produced," she said, proudly. "Mr. Braham, this is Antonio Salieri, a dear friend and colleague of mine."

The two men lowered their heads and shook hands in a gentlemanly fashion.

"Mr. Braham and I have been touring the continent for the better part of the last five years, and we are now on our final journey home. Since we were in Venice, I had no good reason not to stop in Vienna for a visit and to show him this magnificent city."

"I am quite familiar with several of your works, signore," Braham said. "In fact, just before we left England I heard Signora Storace sing in *La grotto di Trofonio*. Of course, as always, she was magnificent," he said as he slipped his arm around Nancy's waist.

"Yes, I'm sure she was. The role of Ophelia was composed especially for her," Salieri replied, proudly.

"So what do you know of this Beethoven," Nancy asked, curious to know if Salieri knew him personally.

"He's a genius. Every bit the genius that Mozart was, but much more somber about it," he said with a chuckle. "He was one of my students for several years, before he went to Haydn."

"Is that so?" Braham said, impressed. "I've heard he's creating quite a stir here in Vienna."

"That he is. He's the beginning of a new generation of musicians— not from the old school like Haydn and me, or even Mozart for that matter—but a new generation of composers that have been brought up in the midst of great political and social revolution. The music is quite different, very new. He premiered this symphony a little over a year ago, and it was published earlier this year."

"We're looking extremely forward to tonight's concert," Nancy exclaimed.

"Good, then," Salieri said. "Perhaps you'll join me for some champagne at the Milano afterwards? We can catch up with one another and I can learn more about your fine young tenor, here."

"It would be a pleasure, Antonio. Grazie," Nancy said.

"Excellent. I'll see you there," he said as he kissed her hand and excused himself.

Soon after they took their seats, the orchestra began to tune, the varying tones of the strings, oboes, flutes and horns rising above the din of muted voices filling the great hall. A few moments later, Beethoven entered, a handsome, serious-looking young man of thirty, and took a seat near the front. As the concert master stood to conduct the orchestra in the symphony's opening bars, the audience fell silent.

Nancy was intrigued by the piece's opening, for the symphony was supposed to be in C major, but it started out with a sequence of tonic to dominant chords in other relative keys that eventually led the listener to the tonic key of C. Very clever, she thought, we're in for a treat! Salieri was right, this music was new, yet at the same time she could hear the resemblances to both Haydn and Mozart.

Braham sat mesmerized by the new sounds, a smile curling his lips whenever he heard a passage that particularly pleased him. He spent the entire evening leaned forward on the edge of his seat, his elbows resting on his knees as he listened intently and considered every note that fell upon his ear.

As in the opening movement, the symphony's finale started unusually—an opening chord followed by a succession of scales in the violins that led the listener into the piece. The finale was stirring and energetic, in the end leaving Braham and Nancy craving more.

"Indeed," Braham exclaimed when the concert was over, "this Beethoven is among the greatest! I'm only too anxious to hear what he has for us in the future!"

Their remaining weeks in Vienna were spent visiting various other palaces and sights: Schönbrunn Palace, the beautiful Laxenburg estate which held within it some of Nancy's happiest memories of her years in Vienna, as well as the beautiful countryside village of Klosterneuburg and its surrounding vineyards.

Soon, it was time for them to be thinking of returning home, but as hostilities had continued to build between France and England during the years they spent in Italy, it was clear that their return could not be through France, but rather, they would be forced to take the longer, more difficult route north through Prague and on to Hamburg.

Ludwig van Beethoven, at age 30

Chapter Sixteen

Prague, July 1801

7 July, 1801
Dearest Kelly,

Mr. Braham and I have arrived safely in Prague, after spending several weeks in Vienna. I cannot express to you what a joy it was to return to that magnificent city and see the places that had been home to some of our earliest triumphs. The city in and of itself has changed very little. However, there were very few persons with which you and I were associated, left. I did see Papa Haydn and was able to spend a good amount of time with him, and I bumped into our good friend, Antonio Salieri (at a concert by a young German composer by the name of Ludwig van Beethoven, with whom we, Braham and I, were very impressed), and he invited us to sit with him at his table at the Milano afterwards. How many recollections do you have of doing just that very thing after our performances? Salieri seemed quite well and I spent a wonderful evening getting reacquainted and reminiscing, as well as acquainting him with Mr. Braham.

I write also to inform you that we will be returning to London by way of the North Sea from Hamburg, as our return via Calais is now completely out of the question. We expect to arrive in Hamburg in a month and then back in London by early September. We plan to spend three months on holiday before we return to the stage.

I pray that this finds you well, and you know that I look forward to seeing you very soon. Until then, I remain your "darlin' dove",

A. Storace
"Nancy"

Of all of the cities to which they had traveled, none held quite the appeal to Braham as Prague, for as France, Italy, and Austria were to the European Catholics, Prague was to the Jews. Housing one of the largest Jewish centers of population in Europe, as well as one of the most ancient and revered Synagogues in central Europe, Prague had always been on Braham's list of the cities he most wanted to see.

As a young Jewish orphan, Braham began his life as a singer in the Great Synagogue in London, where he received his earliest vocal training and where he began his career singing descants. His Jewish heritage was boldly apparent not only in his singing, but in his appearance, something that wasn't always to his advantage. Because of his "overt Jewishness", Braham worked hard to make his singing so sweet and so appealing to his audiences that they were charmed into dropping their anti-Semitic leanings long enough to listen, and fall in love with him. On the other hand, it was also because of his earliest training in the Synagogue that he had a tendency towards over-embellishment and melodrama, something he was never able to completely overcome and for which he was often severely criticized.

After he'd reached adulthood, Braham remained culturally and religiously loyal to his Jewish heritage, often supporting Jewish charities and causes for which Nancy had no objections or misgivings whatsoever. Still, despite this dedication to his heritage, insecurity and self-consciousness always lurked beneath the surface due to the vast anti-Semitic attitudes that prevailed in European society.

As soon as they secured their lodgings, Braham took a carriage to the Jewish quarter, where, in the center stood the Great Synagogue of Prague. Approaching the entrance to the Synagogue, he removed his hat and pulled his kippah from out of his coat pocket, placing it on his head.

Entering the synagogue, he was awestruck by the sight before him. Over the entryway was carved twelve vines with twelve bunches of grapes, representing the twelve tribes of Israel. Upon entering, there stood four bays with a total of twelve narrow Gothic lancet windows, again representing the twelve tribes. Two large pillars, aligned east and west, supported the bays and between the pillars stood the bimah—a tall platform from which the Torah was read. The narrow lancet windows directed their light towards the bimah, which stood as the focal point of the sanctuary.

He stood looking up at the tall Gothic ceilings and architecture, very similar to what he had seen in Europe's cathedrals, but at the same time containing its own unique Jewish characteristics.

"Guter Nachmittag, mein Sohn. Mag ich Ihnen helfen?" a rabbi said.

"Buon pomerriggo, rabbino. Prego, parlate italiano?" Braham asked.

"Sì, un poco," the bearded rabbi replied with a warm smile.

"Grazi, rabbino."

"So, my son, how may I help you?"

"I am from London, a singer," Braham answered.

"Sì, and what has brought you all the way to Prague?" the rabbi asked.

"I've been on tour of France and Italy and have just come to Prague by way of Vienna."

"Ah! Vienna, such a beautiful city," the rabbi said, nodding.

"Indeed, it is," Braham agreed. "But I have always longed to see Prague and most especially this beautiful Synagogue."

"And you said that you are a singer?"

"Sì, rabbino," Braham answered.

"Were you trained in the Synagogue?"

"Sì rabbino, I was. I was orphaned at a very young age. A wealthy Jewish family took me in and when they heard I had a voice for singing, they took me to the Great Synagogue in London, where I trained as a descant singer."

"So how long will you be in Prague?"

"Only a week or so. We will be leaving for Hamburg soon."

"We?"

"Sì, rabbino," Braham said. "Another singer—a woman, and myself. We've been touring together."

"Would you like to sing here, in our Synagogue?"

"Ah! Sì, rabbino! It would be such an honor!"

"How about this coming Sabbath?"

"O, sì," Braham exclaimed, "I must hurry now and tell my partner about this," he said as he started to make his way to the exit.

"But wait," the rabbi called out, "I don't even know your name!"

"Braham," he replied. "My name is John Braham."

"Then I will see you tomorrow Signore John Braham from London," the rabbi said, "and we shall go over the Sabbath service together."

"Grazie, rabbino. Grazie molto," Braham exclaimed as he darted for the door.

Rabbi Jakub was excited to have the young singer from London participate in the next Sabbath service. Braham would sing a prayer, a praise to God for the protection and abundance that he has provided for his people. He was so elated that he could hardly contain himself until the next Sabbath.

When Saturday finally arrived, Braham was up early, getting ready for the service and going over the words of the text so that he wouldn't stumble over any of the Hebrew. It had been years since he'd done any singing of this sort, and he was a bit anxious.

"You'll do beautifully, John," Nancy assured him as she sat at her dressing table putting the finishing touches to her hair. She, of course, was going. She told him that she wouldn't miss it for the world, although she had never in her life attended Synagogue.

"Now, you do understand that you'll have to sit in a separate room off to the side, along with the other women, don't you?" he reminded her.

"Yes, I understand," she said. "But will I be able to see you?"

"Oh, yes, of course. You'll see and hear everything."

For the occasion, Nancy chose a modest gown of peach silk with three-quarter length sleeves and a cream-colored fichu tucked in at the neckline. Her bonnet was the same color as her gown and had a sheer, chiffon veil that draped down over her face, thus meeting the requirements for a woman's head and face to be covered while in the Synagogue.

"Will this do," she asked as she stepped from her bedchamber into the salon, where Braham was reading the Hebrew text aloud from his prayer book.

He looked up and saw her standing there, slipping on her little white gloves.

"Oh, dear, " he said.

"What," she asked, confused. "Is there something wrong?"

"That simply won't do at all," he said as he laid his book down and made his way over to her.

"Why? Is it not modest enough?" she asked, crestfallen.

He put his arms around her waist and drew her to him. "It's plenty modest, but you're simply too pretty wearing it. You look like an Italian ice standing there in your delicious peach frock and all I want to do is eat you. I won't be able to concentrate on my Hebrew, knowing that you're sitting there in the other room looking so sweet."

"Oh, you silly little man," she exclaimed as she smacked him on the backside with her fan. "Is that all you think about? Here you are about to give the prayer in one of the most important Synagogues in Europe and you're making over me!"

"Making over you helps calm my nerves," he confessed. "You're a very pretty and pleasant distraction."

"Well, it's a good thing you'll be wearing your prayer shawl," she said as she gave his shawl a tug. "It shall serve to cover the fact that you're so distracted."

When they arrived at the Synagogue, Rabbi Jakub greeted them both and showed Nancy where she was to sit. He then escorted Braham to a seat close to the bimah. Since his prayer was a text from the Torah, he would climb up the steps and deliver it from there.

The room where the women sat was situated outside the main sanctuary with little windows looking in. Inside were several rows of small pews, the ones furthest to the front being mostly occupied by women who were members of the most prominent Jewish families in Prague. Rabbi Jakub, however, made it clear that one of the front pews was to be reserved for the special singer's guest, so Nancy was assured a place where she could both see and hear everything that went on during the service.

The service was divided up into several parts, very like the Catholic Mass, or what was even more familiar to Nancy, the formal mass of the Church of England. The Jewish Sabbath service consisted of praising God for his attributes, followed by the Blessings, then the recitation of the Psalms, the Shema (which was the giving of the commandments), the Amidah, or eighteen silent prayers given by the congregation while standing, the reading from the Torah, the Sermon and, finally, another Blessing.

Braham would participate in several of the various parts of the service, starting at the beginning with the opening prayer of Praise.

When the time came, Braham arose from his seat and climbed the steps to the bimah. Nancy sat anxiously, peering through one of the little windows at the small figure of a man dressed in a formal black suit wearing his blue satin kippah and prayer shawl made of white silk, embroidered with two large blue stars of David with gold tassels dangling from each corner. Strapped to his forehead was a small black box containing little scrolls with scriptures, called a Tephillin, indicating that he had been ceremonially cleansed before ascending to the bimah to recite the prayer.

"Ma yakar hasd'kha Elohim…" he began in plain chant. "Yirv'yun mi-deshen beitekha, v'nahal adanekha tashkem."

With the next phrase he embellished the chant by adding passing tones and some trills. "Ki im'kha m'kor hayim…"

In a thoughtful gesture, he provided Nancy with a page of translations that he wrote out especially for her.

> *How precious is your kindness, O God! People take refuge in the shadow of Your wings. They are sated from the abundance of Your house, and from the stream of Your delights You give them to drink. For with You is the source of life; by Your light shall we see light. Extend Your kindness to those who know You, and Your righteousness to the upright of heart.*

He sang through the entire chant once, then beginning it again, he started with the same modal melody and added numerous passing tones, turns, and embellishments very similar to the way they would perform a da capo aria in the Italian style.

Nancy listened intently to the voice that she had heard so many times before, lilting out over the congregation, charming and wooing them with its purity and sweetness, but never had she heard it sound quite like this. It had the same beauty, but with an added mood of melancholy tinged with deep passion and devotion. Her heart pounded within her bosom and she felt the tiny hairs on her arms stand on end as tears welled in her eyes.

This is the most beautiful music in the world, she thought. It's the voice of God.

Suddenly it all came together. The reason he sang in the manner in which he did, with what she and many others had judged as over-embellished and melodramatic was because this was who he really was. He couldn't separate himself from what was at the very core of his being, nor, she decided, should he have to. In that moment, Braham revealed his heart and in turn, she opened hers to him. At long last she could say she loved him.

By the end of the service, she was completely overwhelmed and, as she stood outside the Synagogue waiting for him to come out, she took out her handkerchief so that she could dry her tears before Braham could see that she had been crying.

After he spoke with Rabbi Jakob and several members of the congregation who wished to thank and congratulate him, Braham made his way back to Nancy.

"Well, what did you think," he asked, anxious for her opinion.

She looked into his eyes and said, "It was the most beautiful thing I've ever heard in my life, John. I've never been quite so moved by anything."

"You're serious?"

"Quite. It was awe inspiring. I was moved to tears."

He smiled broadly and hugged her, then he whispered in her ear, "Thank you, Ann. You don't know what that means to me."

She responded by turning her face and giving him a tender kiss on the cheek. "Come now, darling," she said as she took him by the hand. "Let's go back to our rooms, for I've something to tell you that you've been waiting for some time to hear."

When they returned to their rooms, she asked him to sit beside her on the settee.

"So what is it you need to tell me?"

Nancy sighed, and sat for a moment gathering her thoughts.

"Is it bad? Have I done something wrong?"

"Oh, no, no, no," she said as she placed her hand on his knee to reassure him. "No, quite the contrary. On the other hand, well, I hope you receive it as good news, although considering the way I've put you off and kept myself at such a distance, I'm not exactly sure how you may feel now."

"Feel about what?"

"I don't know if you remember the argument we had when we were in Venice. It's been well over a year ago, and I'm not sure you men remember such things as we women do."

Braham chuckled, then said, "I'm not quite certain, but think I do recall the one you're referring to."

"We've had our share, have we not?" she said with a smile. "Anyway, I don't know if you recall how it ended."

"Now, that I do recall," he said with certainty. "You were quite angry with me. You barely spoke for a week afterwards."

"Yes, I know, but I was very confused and afraid."

"Afraid? What on earth were you afraid of," he asked, perplexed.

"I was afraid of letting go of something—something that was holding me back from seeing what I truly needed to see and from feeling what I needed to feel." She hesitated another moment as she tried to think of the right words.

"Things began to change when we were in Vienna. I'm not sure you even noticed, but while we were there, I began to experience life again and to allow myself to feel happiness—to actually enjoy life as I haven't enjoyed it in years."

"Yes, I noticed," he replied. "Something changed in you, almost overnight," he said as he took her by the hand. "What is it you're trying to say, Ann?"

"Today when we were at the Synagogue, well, I confess I really didn't know what to expect. But then, when you began the opening prayer, I was completely taken in by the beauty of it, by your singing…by you. It happened then."

"What happened?"

"I saw you. For the first time I truly saw you, and I liked what I saw. Indeed, I loved what I saw and…" She lowered her gaze, afraid to see his reaction to what she was about to reveal. "What I'm trying to say is that I've fallen in love with you, John."

Her confession was met with silence, so she looked up into his eyes so that he could see that her affections were genuine.

"I love you."

He sat in complete silence for a few moments, taking in her confession and allowing the words to sink in. Then he took her face in his hands and kissed her.

"Finally," he replied in a hushed voice. "I love you, my beautiful Ann. I love you so very, very much."

He slid his hands behind her head and held it in them as he lightly brushed her lips with whisper kisses and in only a few seconds his fingers were groping to find the pins and combs which held her hair neatly in place. One by one, he found them, and he pulled them out of place, allowing her thick chocolate brown tresses to fall in waves over her shoulders and down her back.

"I'm still craving that Italian ice," he said as he gave her fichu a gentle tug, removing it from around her neck and revealing her smooth, firm cleavage. He kissed the tops of her breasts. "Mm… Peach. My favorite."

"Is this allowed on the Sabbath," she asked as she removed his kippah and ran her fingers through his thick, black curls.

"It's not work, is it?" he said with an impish grin.

"Oh, but what of all those laws forbidding fornication?"

"Ah, yes. Death to fornicators. By stoning, no less," he said as he pulled the neckline of her gown open and peeked in. He sighed. "Ah, but at least I die a happy man!"

He kissed her mouth, her chin, and down her soft, supple, throat. Then, lifting her into his arms, he carried her to her chamber where he laid her gently upon the bed. She wrapped her arms around him and kissed him deeply, passionately, until it left her nearly breathless.

"Love me, John. Love me as you've never loved me before," she whispered.

He lifted her skirt to her waist and laid himself upon her, feeling her gentle movements as she softly opened herself to him. After a few tense, but pleasurable moments, he was inside of her, moving with her and allowing their mutual pleasure to mount ever so gradually.

"I love you, Ann. I loved you the moment I laid eyes on you," he cooed.

Tears of joy poured down her cheeks. How long had it been since she felt such utter elation, pleasure, and tender affection in the act of love? Her heart was broken for far too long. It was time for healing.

Suddenly, they were both overcome and in the same moment they cried out as they melted into one another. In that moment, they, at long last, became one.

ഇ൞ൽ

A week later they were on the long road to Hamburg. As Nancy anticipated, they were forced to make the trip by post coach, as what was left of most of the rest of their money would be needed to secure new permanent housing when they arrived home in London. Fortunately, Braham didn't mind sharing his seat with Nancy, keeping his arm wrapped securely around her shoulders and cradling her head affectionately when she drifted off to sleep.

Nancy felt safe in his arms. At last she was able to exhale after the nightmare marriage to John Fisher and the torrid, bittersweet love affair with Mozart that ended in complete heartbreak. Everything was going to be just fine now.

When they reached Hamburg at the beginning of August, they discovered that their arrival was anticipated and that they were scheduled to give a concert for Prince Charles of Hesse. Exhausted from the long, arduous journey from Prague, they'd hoped for some time to rest before having to board a river barge for the North Sea coast, where they would board ship for their journey back home to London. Reluctantly, they agreed to perform the concert despite their fatigue.

"Ann," Braham called as he rapped on the door of her dressing room. "Ann are you all right, darling? It's almost time to start."

Nancy opened the door and beckoned for him to enter.

"I'm not sure, John," she said as she clutched her belly. She looked quite pale and little beads of perspiration dotted her cheeks and forehead. "I think I may have eaten something that didn't agree with me, in one of those deplorable inns."

"Here, sit down," he said gesturing towards the settee. "Would a sip of wine help," he asked as he saw a glass sitting on her dressing table from which she had already been drinking.

She turned her face away and raised her hand. "Oh, no, please. That's what started it."

"Can you go on?"

She chuckled. "Of course I can go on. I *always* go on."

"Yes, indeed you do, my love," he said as he kissed her on the nose. "It's one of the things I love the most about you." He started for the door and then turned around and looked again. She didn't look well at all. "Are you sure, love? We really don't have to do this if you're ill."

"I'll be fine," she said as she took a deep breath. "You run on, now. I'll meet you in the wings in just a couple of minutes."

"Are you sure?"

"Yes, quite sure," she said as she mustered up a smile.

Although both of them lacked the energy to perform at their peak, they managed to give a decent enough concert and amazingly they received favorable reviews from the local critics who described the event as "Ein sehr brillantes Konzert."

A few days later they boarded a river barge for the coast and finally, after five long years abroad, they were on the ship home.

That I should forget you?
That you could advise me to give myself to him?
And would you wish me to live still?
My life would be much worse than death…

From the concert aria *Ch'io mi scordi di te…non temer amato bene*
Composed for Anna "Nancy" Storace
December, 1786, by W. A. Mozart

Chapter Seventeen
London, September 1801

At last they were home. As their ship sailed into port, Nancy felt a sense of relief and gratitude to be in her own country, among her own people, her friends, and family. The feeling was completely different from the last time she'd returned from a long trip abroad with her mother and Stephen, for this time she had no heartbreak or regrets. This time she was on the arm of the man she loved.

Their most pressing concern was to find a new home in which they could reside together as a couple. They were able to secure a flat on the prestigious and fashionable Leicester Square and, after all was arranged for their furnishings to be delivered, they took off for a long recuperative holiday on the southern coast, where they would spend a few months in Margate and Brighton, and then travel on to Bath.

They spent their first days in Margate, sleeping late, enjoying late brunches, followed by early afternoon walks along the beach and then returning to their lodgings to indulge in a little late afternoon lovemaking. There were no schedules, no performances, and nothing that they absolutely had to do but indulge themselves in rest and in one another's company. The only thing that put a bit of a damper on their enjoyment was the fact that Nancy was still plagued by an occasional bout of upset stomach and nausea. Some days it was worse than others, and on other days it wasn't there at all. At first she believed that she had caught a distemper from eating bad food in one of the roadside inns where they stopped just before reaching Hamburg, but when the condition persisted after they arrived home several weeks later, she began to suspect something entirely different.

"Are you feeling ill again this morning, darling?" Braham called to her, concerned that her condition was growing serious.

He put down his paper and went into the bedchamber, where she stood behind the screen retching into a chamber pot.

"Perhaps we should send for a doctor. I don't like this at all. It's been going on far too long, now."

"No, that isn't necessary, my love," she said as she wiped her mouth with a soft cloth. She made her way back to the bed and crawled in. She rolled over onto her right side and propped her head up on a soft pillow, which seemed to help somewhat.

"Well, I think it's quite necessary. I'm worried."

"There's no reason to be worried, John. This is perfectly normal."

"Normal? It's normal for you to be ill nearly every day for two solid months?"

"It is when I'm going to have a baby," she said, smiling.

His eyes grew wide and his mouth fell open. "A what?" he exclaimed.

"I said that you're going to be a papa, Mr. Braham."

"I'm what?" he repeated to make sure he heard her correctly.

"I'm going to have your child," she said as she sat up and held her hand out to him.

Stunned by the news, he walked to her in a near trance, crawled upon the bed and sat beside her.

"Are you sure?"

"Quite sure," she said taking his hand.

"Whe— whe…" he stammered, "I mean, when?"

"Sometime around late April or early May, I'm figuring," she said, calculating the most likely time it could have happened. "I'd say it occurred just before we left Prague."

"And you're fine? Nothing's wrong?" He was still stunned.

"Of course not," she assured him. "I'm just a little ill. It shall pass in time."

"And the baby? It's all right?"

"Yes, it's just fine."

"Is it a girl or a boy?" he asked, revealing his complete ignorance regarding such matters. Men weren't educated about these things. It was women's business.

Nancy laughed. "We won't know that until it's born, you silly man."

Braham had to laugh at himself for not realizing the obvious. "Well of course not. What am I thinking? I'm just so stunned."

He took both of her hands in his and gave her a tender kiss. "Oh, Ann, a baby. I'm going to be a papa! You're giving me a child."

"Then you're happy?"

"Well, of course I am," he exclaimed. "Who wouldn't be? I'm going to have a son, someone with my name!"

"We don't know that yet, John. It could just as easily be a daughter."

"And that would be equally as nice," he assured her.

Suddenly his expression grew somber.

"What's the matter? What are you thinking now?"

"My mother. She, well…"

"What about her," Nancy asked, softly.

"She died in childbirth. I had a younger brother. He died too."

"Oh, John…"

"Papa died not too long after that. His heart was broken." His eyes filled with tears as he recalled the events that had made him an orphan. He had never really spoken of it to her in detail. "I can't lose you, too, Ann. I can't go through losing everyone I love like that again."

"Look at me," she said. "I shall be fine and so shall the baby. You won't lose us."

"Do you promise me?"

"I promise. I love you, John. Don't be afraid."

"All right," he said, trusting her. His eyes traveled down her body until they stopped at the place where the baby grew inside of her, and he reached over to touch it. "May I?" he asked politely.

"Of course," she replied, as she took his hand and placed it on her belly. "You can't feel anything yet. It's still very tiny, but in a few months you'll be able to feel it move."

When he felt the warm, soft mound, he smiled. "I'm going to have a son."

As the weeks passed, Nancy's pregnancy was quite noticeable, and as she told Braham it would, the sickness that tainted the first several weeks passed and she developed a healthy, youthful glow.

Braham was charmed by his pretty, pregnant wife (although the union wasn't consecrated, they esteemed and referred to one another as husband and wife), and as her belly grew, so did his infatuation with the whole idea of being a father.

For Nancy, it was a dream-come-true; nothing like her first pregnancy when the father, no matter how he may have desired to, couldn't even acknowledge that the child was his. He couldn't rejoice with her at the first quickening, or lay with her at night and wrap his arms around her ever-growing belly and fall asleep holding her and his unborn child close to him.

"Quick, John," Nancy exclaimed as she felt the baby kick. "It's moving again. Come over here and perhaps you'll feel it." For some time she felt the infant's movements, but each time she called him over, it stopped.

"Here, put your hand right there and press down a little," she said as she took his hand and directed it to a spot just on the lower, right side. "I'm sure that's a foot," she said, smiling.

He did as she instructed and almost instantly he felt a little kick. His eyes widened.

"Did you feel that?"

"I think, a little," he said, grinning. "Let me try it again. Perhaps I can feel more."

He applied a little more pressure and sure enough it happened a second time, this time even stronger than the first.

"Oh yes, indeed, I felt that one! What a strong little fellow he is!"

"He's telling his papa, hello," she said, beaming. "'Good day, Papa! I do hope you're faring well. Mama tells me that you're ever so handsome and that you're the greatest singer in all the world! I hope one day to be as fine a singer as my Papa!'"

By the beginning of December it was time for them to think about getting back home to London, for in the last week of the month they were to begin a new season with the Royal Theater at Covent Garden. Despite her advancing pregnancy, Nancy was on the schedule, along with Braham, right up until the baby was due. If all went well with the birth, she could return six weeks later after her confinement.

Reluctantly, they packed their bags, wishing that their holiday could go on forever. On the day before their departure, after being out and about town, Braham returned to their lodgings to find Nancy packing a few last minute things into her trunk. She didn't hear him come in, so he stole a quiet moment to watch through the doorway as she went about her business, her rosy cheeks firm and youthful, and her thick, dark, hair healthy and shining.

"Good evening, my love," he said as he broke the trance and stepped through the door. He gave her a peck on the cheek, then took off his greatcoat and hat, and hung them in the armoire.

"Good evening, darling. You've been out a while. Where did you go?"

"Oh, I've been over and about. I called on Signore Rauzzini to let him know that we are leaving tomorrow, and to thank him for the lovely time we spent with him and the Lord and Lady Crenshaw the other evening. He seemed ever so sad that we were leaving and he expressed that he wished that we could stay longer."

"Indeed, so do I," Nancy pined. "Oh, well," she said as she shrugged. "Duty calls us back to the stage."

"Indeed it does, and my bank account calls for another deposit," Braham said with a grin.

He went over by the bed, where she neatly folded some gowns to pack into her trunk. Standing behind her, he pulled a small box from his waistcoat and then wrapped his arms around her, presenting the box in his open palm.

"I have a present for you, darling."

Nancy smiled and turned her head. "What is this?"

"Go on," he said, grinning proudly. "Open it."

She took the box from his hand and opened it to find a beautiful gold band inlayed with several ocean blue gemstones.

"It's a wedding band," she said, feeling a bit perplexed.

"Yes," he replied. "I know that we can't actually be wed, by reason of the fact that you're still legally married to Fisher, but that doesn't mean that in our hearts we're not husband and wife. Plus," he added, "I didn't want you going back to London in your obvious condition only to be stigmatized by the fact that you're not married to the child's father."

"Oh, John," she said as she threw her arms around his neck. "How very thoughtful of you."

"Do you like it?" he asked anxiously. "I do hope it fits. Here, let me slip it on your finger."

"Oh, I love it. It's absolutely perfect," she exclaimed. "What are these lovely stones," she asked as she held out her left hand.

"They're aquamarine. My birthstone," he said proudly as he slipped the ring on her finger and held it there. "The jeweler also told me that aquamarine is the Zodiac stone of Scorpio, which is, of course, your sign, and it represents beauty, honesty, loyalty, and happiness." He kissed her and then added, "Please wear this, Mrs. Braham, in honor of the vow I have made to love, honor and cherish you for the rest of your life."

"I don't know what to say," she said with tears in her eyes.

"Say you love me. Say you'll be my wife."

"Oh, of course I love you, and yes, I'll be your wife."

"Good, then," he said as he patted her belly. "Now that this little fellow's finally gotten his parents to the altar, I'm sure he's feeling better about things. Don't you imagine that's so?"

"I'm quite sure," she agreed.

Immediately upon their return to London, they were engaged in rehearsals for their first production. Because Nancy felt particularly healthy and energetic, there were no issues with regards to her continuing to work throughout the entire duration. The only issue that came up was when Braham saw a copy of the playbill a week before they opened.

"Thank you so much for the wonderful rehearsal, ladies and gentlemen," the director called to the cast members on stage. "That's all for today!"

As Nancy made her way off stage, she saw Braham standing, waiting in the wings and holding a copy of the new playbill. His expression was grim as he appeared to read.

"Hello, darling," Nancy said as she took his hand and gave him a kiss on the cheek. He absent-mindedly returned the gesture as he continued to read the paper.

"What's that," she asked, leaning over to see.

"It's a copy of the new playbill."

He didn't look pleased.

"Is there a problem?"

"You tell me," he said as she shoved it into her grasp.

Nancy read it over, but couldn't see anything amiss. "Is there something wrong with it?"

"Look at your name," he grumbled.

Nancy looked again, still confused. "What about it? It looks perfectly fine to me."

"Signora Anna Storace," he read.

"Yes, that's my name," Nancy said, not sure where he was going with it.

"What about Mrs. Ann Braham?"

"What are you going on about, John? You know I can't be billed as Mrs. Braham. We're not legally wed and you know I'm still married to John Fisher."

"You're using my name in society."

"That's different. That's all about appearances. But professionally I can't use it and I refuse to be identified as Mrs. Fisher," she said indignantly. "Besides, we've always been billed together like this. Why do you have a problem with it now?" She shoved the playbill back at him.

"I have a problem with it because in polite society we are now recognized as a married couple. Very few people even know that we're not consecrated, and even those who do know still refer to us as Mr. and Mrs. John Braham."

"John, let me make this very clear to you," she said firmly. "I have been recognized for my entire professional life as either Signorina or Signora Anna Storace. It is how my public knows me. I love you, and I regard you as my husband with all the respect and honor due that title, but I absolutely refuse to compromise on this issue."

"Then you won't have this changed?"

"No, John, I will not," she said as she walked away.

Their first appearance at the Royal Theater after their return to London was a great success. They continued on, both together, as well as billed separately, for as Nancy always preferred the Italian opera buffa roles, Braham was happiest in the more serious Italian opera seria, where he could indulge his more lavish embellishments with less fear of being so severely criticized. However, if the audience or occasion called for it, he was just as happy to appear in the less demanding oratorios and English comedies. His flexibility made him extremely popular and always in demand, despite his ethnic drawbacks.

As a couple, they were unusually accepted within the upper echelons of society and even admired for the devotion and commitment that they displayed one for the other, and the quite obvious fact that Nancy was with child didn't present any complications or close any doors to them whatsoever.

By the time she'd reached her final month, Nancy had grown quite large, and it was rather uncomfortable, especially for her back. She found it difficult to sleep at night and she would toss and turn relentlessly, forcing Braham to sleep in the other bedchamber. At other times, when he could afford to go without sleep himself, he would lay in bed with her and gently massage her lower back until she drifted off.

"That feels so good," she whined. "Thank you, darling."

"I'm glad it helps," he replied sympathetically. "I can only imagine how uncomfortable it must be for you."

"I don't know many husbands who would be so obliging. You're quite rare, Mr. Braham."

He smiled as he brushed the hair away from her face. "I know. Now try and get some sleep."

When her time drew near, they sent for Nancy's sister-in-law, Mary, to attend the birth. Even though she remarried the in the previous year to the Rev. John Kennedy, Mary and Nancy remained close. It was comforting for Nancy to know that Mary would be there to help her through the labor and delivery along with the midwife. Also in the back of Nancy's mind were memories of the last time she gave birth, when her mother attended. She never forgave her for whisking the infant from her arms and giving her to a foundling home. And although the circumstances surrounding this baby were completely different, Nancy vowed that Elizabeth would never be present again when she gave birth.

It happened on stage one night as Nancy and Braham gave their final curtain call. As they exited the stage holding hands, she spoke into his ear, "It's time."

"Time for what?"

"Time to get me home to have our baby," she said, smiling.

Braham's eye's widened and his voice trembled as he spoke. "Now? Right this very minute?"

"Oh, no. We have plenty of time," she assured him. "I only just started feeling the pains in the middle of Act II. There's no rush. Go take off your make-up and change your clothes."

"You're sure?"

"Yes, I'm sure."

"You certainly do take this calmly," he said as he ran to his dressing room. "I'll meet you outside in a few minutes, love! Don't worry. We'll have you home as quickly as possible."

She blew him a kiss as he closed the door. "No rush, darling. I'm fine."

When they arrived home from the theater earlier than usual, Mary knew instinctively that Nancy must have gone into labor during the performance.

"How far apart are the pains," she asked as she helped Nancy off with her coat and hat.

"I would venture about five minutes," Nancy said, guessing. "I'm not quite sure."

"How bad are they?"

"Not bad at all at this point," but they're growing stronger each time. "I got through my Act II aria in the middle of one."

Braham shook his head in amazement. "I didn't even know! That's just bloody impressive, Ann. Goddamned bloody impressive!"

Mary took him by the shoulders. "It might be best for you to wait in the salon. And you might send for some male company," she suggested. "This could take a little while."

Braham followed Mary's suggestion and sent word to Thomas Harris, who was the manager of the Royal Theater. He, as well as Michael Kelly, had been chosen as child's godfathers. As soon as Kelly got word, he dashed out the door with two bottles of fine Irish whiskey from his private stash tucked under his arms. Harris, too, was more than happy to wait with his friend, and together, Harris and Kelly vowed to keep Braham thoroughly distracted from what was happening in the other room.

"Well, I think we've finally gotten the men settled in for the duration, now," Mary said as she closed the door to Nancy's bedchamber.

"Good," Nancy said with a sigh. "Thank you for suggesting company. I don't know that John could sit out there all alone through this. He's as nervous as a cat."

"First-time fathers always are. I remember your brother when Brinsley was born," she said with a smile. "Oh, dear, he was fairly hanging from the ceiling."

"Yes, well, he had been through it already with me, but I don't think that was quite the same as having his own. Oh, dear," she suddenly exclaimed. "Here comes another one."

"Try to breathe through it," Mary instructed as she dabbed Nancy's forehead with a cool, damp cloth.

When the pain subsided, Mary took Nancy by the hand and smiled. "You did well with that one. It appeared to be much stronger than the one before it."

"Yes, I think it was," she agreed. She started to look a little concerned.

"It shall be all right, Ann," Mary said, sensing her anxiety. You'll handle each one as they come. Try not to think about it too much."

"Just keep talking to me, Mary. It helps keep my mind off of it."

In the other room, Kelly and Harris had Braham engaged in a game of faro, which, as long as his money could hold out, Kelly intended to keep going until the moment the child was born.

"What the hell do they do in there, anyway," Braham asked Harris, who was already a father three times over.

"Bloody hell if I should know," Harris replied. "My wife and her sisters wouldn't let me within a hundred feet of the door when she gave birth to mine."

"It surely is quiet," Braham remarked.

"It won't stay that way for long," Harris replied. "Pretty soon there'll be lots of screamin' comin' from outta that room."

"We'll get ya good 'n drunk before that time comes, boyo," Kelly said as he gave Braham's back a good slap. "Then ye won't even notice it."

"Not too drunk," Braham exclaimed. "I want to be good and alert when the baby comes. I can't miss the birth of my first child because I'm passed out!"

"Alright, then," Kelly said. "Slow and steady, Mr. Harris. Pour it slow and steady."

∞∞∞

"Oh, God, Mary, that one was strong," Nancy exclaimed, panting.

"You did beautifully, Ann. You're doing so well."

"How much longer do you think it will be?"

"Not much," Mary replied as she went to the bowl to wring out the cloth and soak it with fresh, cool water. "In fact, it might be time to send for the midwife."

"Oh, really? That close?" Nancy seemed relieved.

She had started to show signs of fatigue, which concerned Mary a little. After all, Nancy was thirty-six years old—rather old for giving birth—and it had been sixteen years since she'd had her first and only child. Still, she was encouraged by the fact that Nancy's pregnancy had been such a healthy one.

"I'll have the maid send for her now. Are you all right, Ann?"

"I'm bloody exhausted," Nancy replied. She was growing weaker, Mary could tell.

She opened the door. "Abby! Come quickly," she called.

The maid, who was sitting in a chair near the doorway, waiting to be of service at a moment's notice, jumped to her feet.

"Go and get the midwife, and quickly," Mary said. "It's very important, Abby. When you get there, tell her to hurry—that Mrs. Braham isn't doing well at all."

"Yes, ma'am," Abby replied as she made a scramble for the entry.

Mary closed the door and turned back to Nancy who was perspiring profusely and looking drawn and pale.

"I'm not feeling so well, Mary," she said, frightened. "I think something's wrong."

"You're just having a harder time with this one, Ann," Mary replied as she wiped Nancy's brow again. "I've sent Abby for the midwife. She'll be here soon and she'll know what to do."

⬥

"Ye've got yerself a darlin' woman in there, I hope ye know, Mr. Braham," Kelly slurred as he pointed towards the salon entry.

Kelly and Harris were both rather drunk by this point, but Braham, sensing that something wasn't going right, stopped drinking at a certain point so that he could keep alert to what was happening with his wife and child in the next room.

"I thought you said there was supposed to be a lot of screaming and carrying on by now," Braham said with a note of concern in his voice.

"Perhaps she's havin' an easy go of it," Harris replied. "Sometimes they do that."

"No," Braham said, shaking his head. "I know Ann. She'd be cursing a blue streak by now, blaming me and God and the entire world for getting her into this." He looked anxiously in the direction of her chamber. "Something's not right."

In just that instant, Abby came flying through the entry with the midwife, who hurried straight for Nancy's room and slammed the door.

Braham went to the door and knocked softly. Mary poked her head out and saw that it was Braham. Seeing the panicked look in his eyes, she stepped out, closing the door behind her.

"What's wrong, Mary?" he asked, nearly in tears. "Something's not right. I can feel it."

She put her arm around his waist and gently led him away from the door.

"She's having a hard time, John. She's older, you know, and giving birth is a painful, tiring thing for a woman. But she'll be fine," she said calmly, trying to reassure him. "The midwife's here now, and she'll do everything to see that both Ann and the baby are well."

She took his hands and peered into his face. "You're a good husband, John Braham," she said. "Ann has needed someone like you for a long time. So don't worry, she's waited this long for you—she's not going to leave you now."

Abby put her head out the door. "Mrs. Kennedy! The midwife needs you to come in here straight away!"

"I have to go," she said. "Go back to your gentlemen friends. I'll be out again shortly."

Reluctantly, Braham let go of his grasp and allowed her to return to Nancy's chamber.

What if Mary's wrong? he thought. What if I do lose her? I couldn't bear that, not again. His worst fears were coming true. It's all my fault. I did this to her. If she dies it will be my fault.

"Hurry, Mrs. Kennedy. Get that cloth and go up and lay her head in yer lap and sponge her forehead real good, like. She's gone and fainted on us," the midwife said. Mary did as she was ordered.

"Now, talk to her and try and get her awake. The baby's stuck and if she's not awake enough to push it out, they'll both die!"

"Ann! Ann!" Mary called, "You've got to wake up now. Come on, Ann. You're almost finished, now. Wake up!"

"Hurry, Mrs. Kennedy! Get her awake now! Don't be so gentile about it, woman! Smack her on the cheeks if ye have to, but make her wake up!"

Mary did what the midwife said and after a few minutes of firm coaxing Nancy finally opened her eyes.

"Where am I?" she asked, a bit confused.

"Yer here tryin' ta get this wee one out," the midwife said. "You've got ta stay awake, Mrs. Braham. Stay awake now and help me, all right?"

"Yes," she said as she took a deep breath to clear her head. "I'm awake now."

"You're almost there," the midwife said as she stuck a rough hand deep into Nancy's body, feeling the position of the baby's head. "Just a few more strong pushes and it's out, Mrs. Braham."

"I understand," Nancy said weakly.

"But you can't go a faintin' on me again! Ye hear?"

"You can do it, Ann," Mary encouraged her.

"Now, when ya feel another pain, I want ya ta bear down as hard as ye can."

Nancy nodded in reply.

"Tell us when ya feel the pain a comin' on," the midwife instructed.

"Now… It's coming now!"

"Good, now bear down."

Nancy did as she was instructed and bore down as hard as she could, but she was so weak that her legs began to tremble and she started to cry.

"I can't do it," she cried, tears rolling down her cheeks. "I'm too exhausted."

"God damn it, Mrs. Braham, yes you can!" the midwife scolded. "I know ye well! I've seen ya on stage many times. Yer one hell of a strong woman so don't tell me ye can't do it.! Now, PUSH!"

Nancy took a deep breath and bore down again, clenching her fists and her teeth with all the strength she could muster.

"That's the style," the midwife exclaimed. "That's the style! Now give us one more like that, and I think we can get the head out."

❧☙

"What the hell's going on in there?" John said as he paced the room. "Why isn't someone telling me what's happening?"

Kelly stood and went to him. "She'll be fine, John. I know Nancy, and she's a fighter. She'll be just fine."

"Mary says she's not doing well."

"She isn't young, John," Harris replied. "But she's strong—she's very strong."

Suddenly they heard a woman's loud cry, followed by the wail of a newly born infant. Harris jumped to his feet as Braham and Kelly made a rush for the salon entry. As they entered the hall, they saw Mary coming out of the room.

She looked at Braham and smiled. "It's a little boy, John. You have a son," she said, beaming.

"And Ann? Oh God, what about Ann?"

"She's all right. She's weak and exhausted, but the midwife says that after some rest she'll be just fine."

"May I see her now," he asked as he darted for the door.

Mary grabbed him by the arm. "No, John. Not just yet. The midwife is cleaning her up and getting the baby cleaned up as well. You'll get to see her soon enough."

"Are you going back in?"

"Yes," Mary said nodding. "Do you want me to tell her something for you?"

"Just tell her that I love her and thank her for giving me a son."

"I'll most certainly tell her. And she told me to tell you that she loves you."

As Mary went back, Braham turned to Kelly who stood behind him, grinning from ear to ear.

"I told ye that ye had one darlin' of a woman in there, John. Congratulations, boyo. You're a papa!"

After they spent several minutes congratulating the new father, Kelly and Harris poured one last round of whisky for everyone and drank a toast to the new addition to the Braham household, as well as to the mother, and then they were on their way out the door. Braham, who was exhausted from the worry and strain of it all, unbuttoned his waistcoat, pulled out his shirttails and plopped down on the settee to wait for Mary to come and tell him that it was all right to go into Nancy's room.

"John." He heard a soft voice calling him. "John, wake up," he heard the voice say as he felt a gentle hand shaking him.

"You can go in and see your wife now," Mary said softly.

He sat up and rubbed his eyes with his palms. "How long have I been asleep?"

"A while," Mary replied. "I thought it best to let you sleep. Ann fell asleep soon after we finished cleaning her up, so I didn't see the point in waking you."

"How is she?"

"She's still very tired, but she's doing well. She's awake now if you'd like to go in and see her."

"Oh, indeed, yes, I would!"

He jumped up from the settee and dashed to the door of her room and knocked gently.

"Come in," he heard Nancy call out in a weak voice.

When he opened the door, he saw her propped up by several pillows in the bed. She looked pale and drawn, but her eyes had a sparkle and she greeted him with the most beautiful smile he'd ever seen.

"Come and take a look at your new son," she said, beaming. She looked so natural sitting there, cradling her baby in her arms. Motherhood already agreed with her.

He sat on the bed beside her, peering into the red, wrinkled face of his infant son and his head of black, wispy curls.

"Look at all the hair," he exclaimed.

"He looks just like you, John," Nancy said, proudly.

"He's beautiful, just like his mother." He looked up into her face and leaned over to kiss her. "Are you sure you're all right? You look so pale."

"I'm fine—just tired, that's all. Give me a few weeks to rest and I'll be as good as new," she assured him.

"May I hold him?"

"Of course you may," Nancy replied as she placed the baby in his arms. "Now, just be careful to keep your arm under his head. His neck isn't yet strong enough to support it."

As he held the infant, Braham slipped his little finger through the baby's tiny fingers, marveling at how very small and delicate they were.

"He's absolutely perfect," he said in a hushed voice. "I just can't believe I have a son."

"You do, Mr. Braham. He's all yours."

"Thank you, Ann. Thank you for giving me a beautiful son."

Mr. and Mrs. John Braham
proudly announce the birth of their son,
William Spencer Harris Braham.
Born 3 May, in the year of our Lord,
Eighteen-hundred and two,
in London, England.

Chapter Eighteen
London, 3 May 1805

"Look, Mummy! Look at the ship that Cousin Brinsley gave me for my birthday," little Spencer exclaimed as he held the toy battleship in front of his mother.

"Yes, darling, I see!" Nancy said in animated reply. "Oh, Brinsley, what a thoughtful gift. You know how he adores anything having to do with ships. Thank you."

"You're welcome Auntie Ann," Brinsley replied, smiling at his little cousin who walked in a circle around the terrace, rocking and rolling the ship, pretending that it was tossing on the ocean waves. "Later, I'll walk him over to the fountain in the square and help him launch it."

Spencer stood up straight, puffed out his little chest and spoke in as stern and gruff a voice as he could muster. "I'm the heroic Lord Admiral Horatio Nelson! Beware, you scurvy Frenchmen, for I shall blow your ships to kingdom come!"

Everyone clapped and cheered as Spencer made a low bow.

"Precocious little fellow, is he not? It's clear to see he has his parents' theatrical blood running in his veins," John Soane exclaimed. "Bravo, young man, Bravo!"

It was Spencer Braham's third birthday and friends and family were gathered at the Braham home in Leicester Square to celebrate the occasion. Among the gathering were Spencer's grandmother Elizabeth Storace, the Rev. and Mrs. John Kennedy, and Mary's seventeen year-old son Brinsley Storace, Mr. and Mrs. Thomas Harris, Michael Kelly, and the noted architect and family friend Mr. John Soane, and his wife.

"He also has his father's love for politics," Nancy said as she laid her hand on Braham's knee. "John's been teaching him some of the songs that he's composed for the various political rallies and events for which he sings, and Spencer's taken to them quite readily."

"Been doing a lot of those, have you John," Harris asked.

"I have lately," Braham replied. "Especially since Nelson's been in pursuit of the French in the West Indies."

"Damned blockade runners," Soane said. "I can't believe the French slipped past Nelson at Toulon again."

"Bah! He'll catch up with them," Braham said, confidently.

"And when he does," Kelly chimed in, "it'll be a sad day for Villeneuve, for bloody sure!"

Mary leaned into Nancy. "I think all men love politics, especially British men." She laughed, noting how little it took to get the men going on the topic.

"Yes, and they all have an opinion whether they know anything about the subject or not," Nancy added, grinning.

It had been a trying past few years for Great Britain and their national hero, Lord Admiral Nelson. In July 1803, from his flagship HMS Victory, he spent an entire year-and-a-half enforcing the blockade of the French fleet at Toulon, but in January of 1805, the French, under the command of Admiral Pierre-Charles Villeneuve, eluded the British. Nelson chased Villeneuve into the Mediterranean until he learned that the French were blown back into Toulon. They managed to escape for the second time through the Straight of Gibraltar, heading for the West Indies. Everyone was on pins and needles waiting to hear any news of Nelson's catching up to the French fleet and engaging them in battle.

Shortly before Nancy and Braham left Venice for Vienna, Nelson and Emma Hamilton had traveled the exact same route from Florence to Vienna, through Prague and then up through Hamburg and the North Sea back to London. It was after his return to London that Nelson's wife, Fanny, gave him an ultimatum to make a choice between her or his mistress. Nelson chose Emma and after that, never lived with his wife again. Emma was pregnant with Nelson's child and their daughter, Horatia was born in January of 1801. The couple made their home in Merton, as Nelson intended to retire there.

On occasion, Braham and Nancy took a drive down to Merton to visit Emma as Nelson had been called away once again to the Baltic. They enjoyed their visits with her tremendously and Emma and Nancy developed a warm and close friendship.

Life was good for the happy couple. They had a bright, healthy son, two brilliantly successful careers, a noted and respected standing within society, many dear and respected friends, and between them they had accumulated a tremendous amount of wealth.

"Look at this, John," Nancy exclaimed as she sat at her desk, going over their financial accounts and statements. "Look at these totals. We've reached our goal!"

"Our goal for what?"

"Do you remember last year when we said that we were beginning to feel a little cramped in this rented flat and that we'd like to make it a goal to afford our own home?"

"Yes, I vaguely recall that conversation."

"Well, we've done it!" Nancy announced with a broad grin.

"Let me look at that," he said as she turned the ledger so that he could read the figures.

"Yes, indeed, I believe you're right, darling," he said with noted triumph in his voice. "Oh, yes, this is very, very good."

"I think we can do it, now, don't you?"

"Indeed, I think we can and should," he said with a grin.

Within two months, they moved into a sumptuous townhome located at 96 Russell Street in fashionable and prestigious Camden Town, surrounded by some of the wealthiest members of London society. Nancy spared no expense in decorating the home, filling it with the most luxurious and elegant furnishings, carpeting, draperies, and art pieces that money could buy. Soon, the home would be filled with the laughter and music of fetes, soirees, and private parties, attended by London's highest society echelon.

Around the same time, they also made the decision to return to Drury Lane, to the delight of Michael Kelly who was still struggling to manage Sheridan's theater. Their first performance there was in Stephen's piece, *The Siege of Belgrade,* which met with great success. However, their excitement was overshadowed the very next morning with the news that broke out in the London papers of another great triumph coupled with an even greater tragedy.

"Ann! Ann!" Braham shouted as he flew through the door. He had been out and about early and heard the news. Everyone was talking about it in the streets and all were stunned, many—even men—were crying. He ran into the salon and picked up the morning paper, which still lay on the table unread, and ran up the stairs to search for Nancy.

He found her in her bedchamber, sitting at her vanity, leisurely drinking her morning coffee while her hair was being dressed for the day.

"What is it John, what's all the commotion?"

"Ann, you're not going to believe this," he panted as he held the paper up, revealing the headlines.

ADMIRAL NELSON TRIUMPHS AT TRAFALGAR
In the most glorious naval VICTORY *in* HISTORY
but
LOSES HIS OWN LIFE!

Nancy's eyes widened as she read the tragic headline. "Oh, my God," she said as her heart rose into her throat. "We've lost him! I can't believe we've lost him!"

Braham sank onto the settee, and began to read the article.

"It says that he was hit early in the battle, but survived for several hours, waiting to hear the news of the victory. His last words were, 'Thank God I've done my duty to God and Country'," Braham read aloud as tears welled in his eyes.

"What of poor Emma and little Horatia?" Nancy lamented. "What will they do now?"

"I don't know," Braham replied. "Society forgave Nelson for his indiscretions, for they loved him dearly. It won't be so readily given to his mistress and bastard child, I fear."

The next day, Nancy sent word to Emma Hamilton at Merton, asking if she could come to express her sympathy and give her condolences. Emma sent a favorable reply, so at the end of the week, Nancy and Braham drove down to Merton together.

They were greeted by one of the servants who showed them into the salon, where Emma sat waiting for them. The minute she laid eyes upon them, she stood, crying, and threw out her arms for an embrace.

"Oh, my darling, Emma," Nancy said, as she took her in her arms. "We're so very sorry. I can't even express the sorrow that has gripped our hearts for you and little Horatia."

Braham waited politely as Nancy expressed her condolences and, when Emma turned to him, he embraced her, kissing the top of her head and telling her how very sorry he was. After their long embraces, Emma invited them to sit with her and talk.

"I'm told," she began, as she dabbed her eyes with her handkerchief, "that one of Nelson's last requests was for me to be taken care of."

"Well, of course, it would have been," Nancy replied. "He adored you, Emma. You know that."

"That may be true, but if that horrible wife of his has anything to say in the matter, I'll be left in the cold, along with my child."

"Surely that won't be the case," Nancy said. "Surely someone will see to it that his last wishes are honored."

"You have no idea, Nancy, what it's like to be the other woman. You may be loved and adored by him and he may even have transferred his full affections to you from the wife. He may also have every good intention regarding your well-being in the event of his demise, but in the end, no one will recognize that, or respect it, for propriety, yea, posterity demands that you be forgotten."

Although Emma had no way of knowing, Nancy's heart was stabbed by Emma's words. Of course she could easily sympathize with Emma's plight, but sitting there in front of Braham she could say nothing. She sat in complete silence as tears rolled down her cheeks, recalling the words of Mozart's last letter to her.

> *This will be my last letter to you, my dearest love, not because my affections for you have diminished for, on the contrary, they have only grown deeper and more impassioned since last we saw one another, but because circumstances in my situation have developed to the place where, for the preservation of my reputation, my work, and my family, our affair must end...*

Emma looked at Braham, who sat in silence listening as the women conversed.

"You live a charmed life, Ann. Look at you sitting there with the man you love, surrounded by your family and friends in such wealth and security. Don't take that for granted, for it is too easily lost." She began to weep.

Nancy went to her again and took her in her arms. "I'm so very sorry, Emma. I don't know what else to say."

Almost immediately after the news broke of Nelson's death, the area theaters, both in Covent Garden as well as Drury Lane, began to stage tribute productions in honor and memory of Great Britain's fallen hero. Covent Garden's was the first. Staged within days of the news, *Nelson's Glory* was criticized for its haste and lack of sufficient preparation. Braham collaborated with the stage manager at Drury Lane to produce a piece entitled, *The Victory and Death of Lord Nelson*, and because they took more time in its creation and rehearsals, it was well received by both the audience and the critics.

"The morning post has arrived, sir," the maid announced to Braham who sat at his desk and going over some accounts. "Do you wish to take it now, or would you like for me to leave it in your box?"

"Thank you, Abby, I'll take it now," he said.

She handed him the stack of letters, curtsied politely and left.

As he shuffled through the stack, Braham noticed one that was addressed to him from the family of Admiral Nelson, so he broke the seal on it first, and read.

"Oh, my God, Ann, you've got to come and read this!"

"Mrs. Braham left for the theater only a few moments ago, sir," Abby said as she stepped back into the room.

"Thank you, Abby. Would you send word to the stableman for me, please? Have him get my carriage ready to leave as soon as possible."

"Yes, Mr. Braham."

When he arrived at the theater, Braham found Nancy, Kelly, and Ellison the stage manager discussing some issues regarding the coming season.

"Look at this!" he called out to them as he entered through one of the stage wings and crossed to where they stood. His face was covered with a huge grin as he held up the letter he had brought.

"What is it?" Kelly asked.

"It's an invitation!"

"For what?" Nancy asked as she put her hand out to take the letter from him.

"Look! Read it!"

Nancy took the letter and read. "It's an invitation for John to sing at Lord Nelson's funeral!"

"Blimey," said Ellison. "You've jolly well hit the big time now."

"Tis the greatest, honor, John, me boy," Kelly said, slapping Braham on the back. "Congratulations."

"Oh, John, I'm so proud of you," Nancy exclaimed as she threw her arms around his neck and kissed him.

"The funeral takes place early next month. That gives me plenty of time to prepare," he said, thinking ahead. "Oh, God, this will be largest audience for which I've ever sung!" he said nervously, pondering the full implication of the great honor which had been bestowed upon him by the Nelson family.

"Yer up to it, John," Kelly replied. "Yer just the man fer the occasion. Again, congratulations."

On 9 January, 1806, the day of Nelson's funeral arrived. Homes and business throughout London were decorated with garlands, wreaths, portraits, anchors, and monograms. As Nelson's casket was driven in procession along the route to St. Paul's Cathedral, mourners lined the way, weeping, and tossing flowers and wreaths. It was one of the greatest spectacles London had ever seen.

The dome of St. Paul's was filled to capacity by the funeral guests, which included thirty-two admirals, over a hundred captains, and ten-thousand soldiers who also participated in the procession. The captured flags of both the French and Spanish ships hung from the dome's ceiling and the casket sat on a dais in the center of the dome, surrounded by Nelson's family, closest friends, and fellow officers. Nancy sat close to the front with Braham, who was given a seat as an honored guest of the Nelson family. Emma Hamilton was denied the right to attend.

When it came time for his part in the four-hour service, Braham took his place and, with all the beauty, dignity, and elegance he could muster, he sang out over the black sea of mourners. If there had been a dry eye before, there wasn't one left by the time Braham finished, for so tender, so moving was his rendition that none, not even the crustiest, most sea-worn admiral could fail to be touched. It was Braham's finest moment.

Emma Hamilton quickly exhausted the small pension left to her by her husband, Sir William Hamilton. Although Nelson willed his estate to his brother, Alfred Nelson, he left Merton Place to Emma, who used up her meager pension on upkeep of the estate. The instructions that Nelson gave to the government to provide for Emma and Horatia were ignored and the money was instead awarded to his brother. Several years later, Emma spent a year in debtor's prison with Horatia, then escaped to

France where she turned to drink and died in poverty of amoebic dysentery in Calais, in 1815.

Earlier, in 1807, Lady Hamilton attended a soiree held by the Brahams and, for several years thereafter, they remained in close touch. Braham and Nancy were grieved over the cruel fate to which poor Emma finally succumbed.

For pity's sake, do search for
My husband, my beloved.
Poor me, I live in pain –
Without him I cannot be.

Text from the aria, Per pieta, deh, ricercate,
from *L'incontro inaspettato*
By Vincenzo Rhighini
Originally sung by Catarina Cavalieri,
the beloved mistress of Antonio Salieri.

Emma Hamilton

Chapter Nineteen

London, August, 1806

12 August, 1788

...My only regret in life will be having married too hastily. If only I had not allowed myself to be pressured by the likes of Frau Weber, who like a spider, wove me into her devious plans to capture me for one of her daughters, and ensnared me there. If only I had waited six months—I shall go to my grave lamenting that decision.

Your devoted and ever faithful,
Wolfgango

*I*f the Brahams were an unconventional couple by the standards of English propriety of the day, they certainly weren't regarded publically as such. They were invited as guests, as well as entertainers, in the homes of London's most respected, most honored, and most elite and in turn, received the same aforementioned persons in their home on many occasions. By all accounts, their union was regarded as legitimate as any that were consecrated.

On occasion it seemed to bother Braham, more than Nancy, that they could not be legally wed, but knowing the arrangement that still existed between Nancy and her legal husband, John Fisher, there was no point in pursuing it.

At one point, just shortly after Nancy returned from Vienna in 1787, Fisher, who lived in Ireland at the time, engaged his lawyers to demand from her an annual alimony payment of ten pounds for the privilege of his "staying away". Nancy's lawyer saw this as the blackmail it was and invoked the recognition of the banishment edict issued by Emperor Joseph II of Austria upon the courts in London. Fisher was so intimidated by this action that he backed down from his threats and never bothered Nancy again.

It was a lovely summer afternoon and Nancy, who always loved sitting in her garden when she had the opportunity, was on the terrace taking in the fragrances of her roses, foxglove, and the various varieties of chrysanthemums that were in season. Far from any cares, her mind was fixed completely on the moment and on the beauty surrounding her.

"Ma'am," she heard the maid's soft voice from behind her.

Still reclining with her eyes closed, trying not to lose the moment, she replied, "Yes, Abby, what is it?"

"There's a gentleman here who says he needs to speak with you."

"Did he say who he is?" Nancy asked a little impatiently.

"His name is O'Leary, ma'am. He says he's a lawyer from Dublin."

"Dublin? I don't know anyone from Dublin. At least not now, I don't. Did he say why he's here?"

"No ma'am, only that it's important that he speak with you."

Nancy sighed, then arose from her comfortable reclining position on the fainting couch and looked at the maid.

"Show him here," she said, gesturing towards the seating area on the terrace. "And have some tea brought out."

"Yes ma'am," the maid replied.

As she was instructed, Abby brought the lawyer out on the terrace and he immediately introduced himself as John Patrick O'Leary, who represented the estate of Mr. John Abraham Fisher.

"John Abraham Fisher?" Nancy exclaimed. "What does that sorry, piece-of-shit, excuse of a man want from me now?"

Mr. O'Leary, understanding the nature of the acrimony that existed between his client and Nancy for over twenty years, was sympathetic with her impetuous response and simply replied, "He wants nothing from you, Mrs. Braham." He cleared his throat. "You see, he's dead."

Nancy put both of her hands on her mouth and held them there. "He's dead?"

"Yes, madam," he said. "He died in June. I'm simply here to inform you of that fact and to let you know that you are now, officially his widow."

"You're telling me he's dead? Completely?"

"Yes madam," the lawyer laughed. "Quite dead, stone cold, rotting in the grave."

Nancy arose from her seat, her hands still cupped over her mouth. She turned and started to pace.

"I can't believe it," she exclaimed. "I can't bloody fucking believe it!"

Mr. O'Leary sat back in his chair and grinned, allowing Nancy her moment of elation and relief.

"I have a few documents for you to sign, Mrs. Braham. Unfortunately there was nothing left in his estate to offer you. He died with considerable debts."

"I want nothing of his," she said, bitterly. "What is it I have to sign?"

"Only a few documents stating that you release yourself from any claims to his estate. It's all right here, if you'd like to read it first."

"Of course," she said as she sat back down and began to read the papers.

"There is also a place that states that you may declare yourself officially wed to Mr. Braham by issuance of common law, of course, if you choose to do so."

She peered at him over the top of her round cobalt sunglasses. "And why should I desire to do that," she asked matter-of-factly.

"Well, I just assumed. Of course, it's not a requirement," he said, a bit taken aback by her response.

"I'd rather not," she said as she took the pen from his hand and dipped it into the ink.

"Of course, you and Mr. Braham are now free to have the union consecrated, which would take care of it as well," he continued.

Nancy looked up from signing the documents and replied, "Thank you Mr. O'Leary, for your concern over my legal marital status, but that is a decision that I would appreciate you leaving to Mr. Braham and me. As for now, I'm quite happy remaining officially a widow. If I change my mind, you will read about it in the tabloids, I'm quite certain." With that, Nancy signed the documents and thanked O'Leary for being the bearer of joyous tidings and sent him on his way back to Dublin.

When Braham returned home for supper, he was greeted with the tale.

"That's it?" Braham, said. "It's over? You're no longer married to him?"

"Well, of course I'm not. He's dead. I'm now his widow."

"Well, you won't have to remain Widow Fisher for long," he said as he picked up his fork and stabbed at a piece of roast beef on his plate.

"And whatever does that mean," she asked as she took a sip from her wine glass.

"It means, my love, that we are now free to wed."

Nancy lowered her head and thought for a moment before she spoke.

"I'm not quite ready to do that just yet," she said, softly.

"And why ever not," he asked, confused and hurt. "We've been together for over ten years now. We have a child together, a child who bears my name. We have a life, a home, and careers together."

"I know, John. I know this is difficult for you to understand. I'm not quite sure I understand it myself." She reached across the table and touched his arm. "This came as such a shock today, and at the same time a complete relief. I had no idea the strain I was living under for over twenty years, never knowing if he would return and try and lay claim on me, or my money and property."

Braham listened intently, trying to understand and be sympathetic to her feelings.

"The more popular and wealthier I became, the more fearful I grew."

"I had no idea you felt these things, Ann. Why didn't you tell me?"

"I didn't know I felt them this strongly until today when I realized that, for the first time in years, I was free. I am totally free now from any debts or obligations to that man and I don't wish to place myself in that position ever again."

"But Fisher didn't love you! He used you and beat you. How could you ever compare what we have between us to that? I love you, Ann," he said turning away with tears in his eyes, making it quite obvious how hurt he was. He drew in a deep breath, trying to remain composed, but his temper finally got the best of him.

"God damn it, Ann," he shouted as he got up from the table and threw his napkin on the floor in front of him. "I've been patient and understanding over this whole situation for ten years now! I've given in to your desire to retain your professional name and I've even given in to our maintaining completely separate financial accounts, but I only did so believing that once you were free from Fisher, it would be your desire to fully consecrate this union. Hell, everyone out there believes we're married. We call ourselves Mr. and Mrs. Braham for Christ's sake!"

He went down on his knee in front of her, taking her hands in his.

"I love you, Ann. For ten years I've been your loyal and faithful friend, partner, lover, and the father of your child. Now I want to marry you. Please, Ann, will you marry me?"

"Please, John," she said. "Please don't ask me this now. Will you give me some time—just a little time—to think on it?"

"What is there to think on? There's nothing left to think on!"

"Please, don't press me! I can't take this anymore," she shouted as she jumped out of her chair and ran from the room.

∞∞

That fall, a new piece by Mozart, who was largely unfamiliar to the English audiences, was introduced. Due in large part to the efforts of The Prince of Wales, Mozart's final serious opera, *La Clemenza di Tito* was to be performed at Drury Lane. Braham would sing the part of Sesto. When Nancy learned that it was on the schedule, she was assaulted with a series of mixed emotions ranging from tremendous excitement to overwhelming sadness and dread. As much as she tried to ignore these powerful feelings, she couldn't help herself. This was an opera that Mozart composed in the last year of his life, after he wrote his final letter to her in November of 1790. She had never seen it, nor had she ever heard any of the music from it.

"What is wrong with me," she asked herself. "I thought I buried these feelings for him in Vienna five years ago. I'm happy now. Why should this still be bothering me?"

When *Tito* was presented, Nancy, as usual, attended the opening night, for she was never known to miss anything in which Braham performed, even if she wasn't performing in it with him. As she listened to the opening measures of the overture, she heard him. It was unmistakably Mozart. A smile crept across her lips as she continued to listen. She closed her eyes. She could almost feel him.

In the very first act came a duet, *Ah, perdona al primo affetto*, in which the characters Servila and Annio confess their forbidden love.

Please excuse the emotions that I expressed that I shouldn't have.
They simply slipped out too naturally, for once upon a time that is

how I spoke to you. It was my lips fault, for that is the way they were used to speaking to you.

Nancy felt a tear run down her cheek, and she quickly wiped it away. Feeling a sudden chill, she pulled her wrap around her shoulders.

Pardon me, for disturbing your happiness, Wanze, but I had to express the feelings that I have so naturally expressed for you before. I saw you sitting there and I simply couldn't help myself.

She could barely force herself to sit through the rest. It was only through sheer determination and an intense desire to hear the music that she managed to make herself stay.

Only two performances of *Tito* were given, as the London audiences were not yet ready for the richness of Mozart's music. Their ears simply weren't attuned to it; they had never heard anything like it before. Nancy was both saddened and relieved that it was removed from the schedule. It wasn't the music that she couldn't tolerate, but the unsettling emotions that the music dredged up from deep inside of her.

"So, what did you think of it," Braham asked. Believing the London audiences needed the opportunity to try out their teeth on something a little more solid than the light Italian comedies and English frolics they were so used to, he was disappointed with *Tito*'s removal from the schedule.

"I loved it," Nancy said. "And you were wonderful, as usual."

"Is that all? You loved it? Seriously, Ann, you're generally more opinionated than that."

"I don't know what else you want from me," she said. Why did he always insist on pressing her?

"You hadn't heard this piece before, had you?"

"No," she answered, shaking her head. "He composed it several years after I left Vienna, just a few months before his death. The only other new piece I'd heard of his since I left were parts of *Don Giovanni.*"

"You sang some of those, yes?"

She nodded.

"So, did you like the piece?"

"Yes, very much. It reminded me of his *Idomeneo*, which I sang while I was in Vienna." In an attempt to end the conversation, she went to the shelf, pulled out a book out and opened it.

"Ann, what's wrong with you," he asked impatiently. "From the day I announced that I was going to sing in this piece you've been acting strangely."

"I don't know, John," she sighed. "Perhaps I'm simply tired. Or perhaps I'm just weary with everything having to be an issue with you. If I don't respond to something in just the way you think I should, there's something wrong, or you think I'm upset with you. You're too damned insecure!"

"That's because I never know where I stand with you anymore, Ann. You're back to keeping things—parts of yourself—from me like you did, before…"

"Before what?"

He paused for moment, then turned to her.

"Before we went to Vienna," he said quietly, still deep in thought. "Everything was different afterwards."

Nancy turned her attention back to the book, pretending to resume her reading.

He went to the window and looked out onto the barren, dark street below.

"That day you went out with Haydn. You said you visited the grave of an old friend. You were dressed in mourning. Everything changed after that."

Nancy went on reading, pretending she hadn't heard him.

"When I asked you whose grave you visited, you didn't answer."

She glanced in his direction, hoping that he wouldn't ask the next question.

"Whose grave did you visit that morning?"

Nancy slammed the book shut with a loud snap and said, "I'm sick of this, John. This is absolutely ridiculous!"

He turned to her and asked again, this time shouting. "Whose grave was it, Ann? I demand you tell me!"

"How dare you shout at me like that," she exclaimed as she threw the book to the floor and lunged toward him.

He grabbed her by the arms and held her there as she struggled to get free.

"God damn it Ann, it was him! You were in love with him, weren't you? And you're still in love with him!"

At that, she threw her head back and spat at him. Stunned by her reaction, he looked at her, his wounded pride ignited into a rage. Impulsively, he lifted his hand and slapped her across the cheek.

After she recovered from the shock, she glared at him and shouted, "I had one man rule me with his fists and I'll not have another one try! You'll rue the day you ever did that, John Braham!"

She turned and ran from the room, up the stairs to her bed chamber and slammed the door shut.

"I won't compete with a ghost, Ann!" he shouted at the door.

We want to be happy with love,
We live through love alone,
Love sweetens every torment,
Every creature offers itself to her.
It seasons our very lives,
It beckons us in the circle of nature.
Its higher purpose clearly indicates,
Nothing is more noble than wife and man,
Man and wife,
Reach the heights of Godliness.

Duet from *Die Zauberflöte*
By W. A. Mozart

Chapter Twenty

Margate, England, summer 1807

*A*fter the argument, a considerable distance stood between them for some time. However, after a few tense and uncomfortable weeks, the couple made up and decided to start afresh. Braham admitted that he had finally pressed Nancy too far, and he regretted the things he said and did. Knowing what she went through with John Fisher, he realized that after the regrettable mistake he made of striking her, a consecration of their union would be out of the question, so he never pressed the issue again.

A great deal of the summer of 1807 was spent on holiday in Margate, where Nancy, Braham, and five year-old Spencer spent lazy hours walking together on the beach and enjoying time away from the pressures of career and society. It was always a healing time for Nancy, who liked to reminisce over the first summer spent there, when she announced to Braham that she was going to have his child. It was among their happiest times together and she longed to recapture what they had somehow lost.

On a bright July morning, she decided to make the short trip to Ramsgate to visit an old friend whom she had not seen in a very long time. Braham wanted to spend some time alone with Spencer, so he opted out of the journey, agreeing that it would be fine for Nancy to go without him. As he put her on the coach, he gave her a sweet kiss on the cheek and told her he would see her in a few of days.

It was only a short journey from Margate to Ramsgate, through the small village of Broadstairs, so Nancy expected to arrive at her destination sometime in the late afternoon. As the coach made its way along the narrow coastal road, she watched out the window as the surf crashed upon the rough, rocky cliffs and visited with a woman passenger who was fascinated by Nancy's tales about hers and Braham's experiences on the stage.

Just outside the small coastal village of Broadstairs, one of the horses stumbled on a rock, causing him to falter. As he did, the coach began to weave, threatening to overturn. The driver struggled in vain to get control of it, but it crashed onto its side and slid halfway down a steep embankment, where it at last came to rest.

Inside, Nancy and the other passenger were tossed and thrown about and the driver, who had instinctively jumped from his seat, rolled down the hill, stopping only a few feet away from the coach.

Amazingly, the driver only suffered a few minor cuts and bruises, so he got up to check on the fate of his passengers. When he reached them, he heard moaning coming from inside the coach. Prying open a door he found one woman lying lifeless upon the other who lay crumpled into a ball in a bed of shattered wood and broken glass. Managing to pull the dead passenger out of the coach, he carried her body a small distance away and laid it down. Returning to the coach, he looked inside again.

"Ma'am," he called. "Are you all right?"

Nancy moaned and tried to move, but every inch of her body screamed in pain.

"I don't know if I'm all right, but I'm alive," she said as she tried to move so she could see the driver's face.

"Where are you hurt?"

"I'm not quite sure. I know I can't move my right arm."

"The village isn't far up the road," he said to her. "I'll go and get help. Will you be all right until I get back?"

"I think so. How long will it be?"

"I'd say only a couple of hours at most."

"All right," she said with a weak smile. "I'm sure I'll be here when you get back. Oh, the other passenger... Is she all right?"

The driver paused and looked around for a moment. "No ma'am. She's dead."

"Oh, dear....she seemed like a very nice lady."

"I need to go now, ma'am. Stay awake if you can."

"I'll try. Thank you."

As he predicted, it was only about two hours before he returned with another coach and three more men, one who was a doctor. Nancy was still lying at the bottom of the wreck, but she had managed to uncurl herself and find a more comfortable position, out of the sun.

Bearing two stretchers, the men carefully made their way down the steep, rocky hill to the site, two going to where the dead woman lay, and the driver, along with the doctor, hurrying to where Nancy lay.

"Ma'am," the driver called out. "Are you still with us?"

"I am," Nancy called back. "And I'm still awake!"

He peeked through the broken window into the coach and saw Nancy still lying there, but looking a bit more comfortable than when he'd left.

"I found a doctor visiting town. He offered to come."

"Oh, thank God," she said. "Thank you!"

"We're going to see if we can get you out of there. Can you stand, ma'am?"

"I'm not sure. I've been a little queasy, so I haven't tried."

The men agreed that the easiest way to get her out would to be to break the door off of the coach and pull her out. Once that was accomplished, it was easer for them to reach in and maneuver her so they could get in a position to support her as she tried to stand.

"Are you ready, now ma'am" the driver asked as each of the men grabbed underneath her arms to help lift her up.

"Keep your right arm close to your body, if you can," the doctor said.

"All right, I think I'm ready," Nancy replied.

"On three," the driver called out. "One…two…three!"

They managed to bring her to enough of a standing position that the doctor could lift her in his arms and carry her to the stretcher. They then carried her to a large rock that provided some shade.

"What is your name, madam," the doctor asked as he began to examine her.

"Mrs. John Braham… Ann."

"Signora Storace? Why, I know you! I've been to so many of yours and your husband's performances that I can't begin to count them all!"

Nancy smiled. "I do hope they were satisfactory."

"Oh, indeed. Far more than satisfactory—they were marvelous."

He examined her closely from head to foot and then said, "You've broken that arm, that's sure, but other than some nasty cuts and bruises here and there, you look well. You're a very fortunate woman. You could easily have been killed.

"Yes, I know," Nancy said, thinking of the passenger who didn't fare nearly as well. "God rest that poor woman's soul."

"Where is Mr. Braham?"

"He's in Margate, with our son."

"Well," the doctor said, "let's get you into town so that we can have you cleaned up and I can examine that arm more closely, shall we? We'll send word to your husband and he'll be here by the morning, I'm sure."

"You've been so kind, Doctor. Thank you for everything."

"'Tis an honor, signora. It's not every day I get called out on an emergency and find myself examining a celebrity of your caliber," he said with a cheerful grin.

Early the next morning, Braham arrived as the doctor had said. He found Nancy in a small inn where she was given a room to rest in bed and wait until he could arrive and take her home.

"Oh, my darling girl," Braham cried when saw her. "Look at you! Thank God you're all right!"

"I'm fine," Nancy said. "Just very sore and tired. I'm so glad you're here, John."

He picked up a small chair and sat it at the head of the bed, where he could be near her. As he leaned over to examine her more closely, he could see where she had cuts and bruises all over her face and arms.

"You didn't have any head injuries?" he said, concerned over her history.

"Apparently not. The doctor seems to think that my bonnet shielded me enough to prevent it. There was a lot of glass. That's why I have so many cuts. But they're not serious, either."

"Your poor arm didn't fare so well," he said as he examined the splint.

"Yes, well, the doctor said that would take a while. It's too swollen at this point for him to set it, so he said that we would have to find a doctor in Margate to do it."

"Yes, I spoke to the good doctor just before I came in. He seemed to be a very nice fellow. It was damned good of him to stay the night so that he could speak with me this morning.

Nancy laughed. "Yes, well, once he found out who his patient was, he was quite taken. He couldn't wait to meet you and go back and tell all his friends that he had treated the 'great Signora Storace' and had met her husband, the 'stupendous tenor, Mr. John Braham!' Those were his words."

"Yes, he did ask for my autograph," Braham said with a grin. "And he refused to charge me for his generous services. He said the opportunity to meet us in such a situation was payment enough."

After spending a couple of nights in Broadstairs, Nancy was able to return with Braham to their lodgings in Margate, where she spent several weeks recovering. She had once again escaped a brush with death, and that alone seemed to renew both of their desires to rekindle the relationship that they had started to neglect.

Upon their return to London, Nancy was immediately engaged in several productions not only in Drury Lane, but in the Haymarket was well. It was apparent from what the critics wrote that she was lacking the passion and conviction that she once had and that her age had started to get the better of her. Of one of her performances at the Haymarket, the critics wrote:

Storace has recovered from her accident. In the Haymarket Theatre her dancing days are over. It affords pleasure to the kitten to frisk and gambol but it becomes the well-fed cat to shun these pranks nor lose sight of the dignity of her age and bulk.

"Did you read this," Nancy asked as she pushed the paper over to Braham and began rubbing her temples.

"Another one of those damned headaches, darling?" he said as he took the paper from her.

"Read," she said, ignoring the question. "The bottom column."

Braham scanned the paper until he reached the critique, and began to read.

"Oh, dear," he remarked. "This is not good. What does he mean 'lose sight of the dignity of her age and bulk'," he asked indignantly.

"Oh, let's not kid ourselves, John. I'm old and fat, and everyone seems to know it but us."

"Well, you may be getting up there, but you certainly don't act your age. And I wouldn't call you fat."

Nancy laughed, and patted his arm. "You're so terribly sweet, darling, but that's what the critic is saying—that I need to start acting my age."

"But you're not fat!" he insisted.

"Well, yes, I am. But you're right, I've seen fatter. Good God, look at Elizabeth Billington these days. I could fit two of me inside of her! But it doesn't bother me, for I've always been criticized to some degree over my 'bulk'. I've always carried a few extra stones around the bosom and the hips. Some men appreciate it, others don't."

Out of the corner of his eye, Braham noticed that she was still rubbing her temples, so he rose to stood behind her chair and began to gently massage them for her.

"Well, I certainly appreciate it," he said with a frisky grin. "And your bosom certainly doesn't feel like stones—more like soft, silken pillows."

Nancy laughed at his ardent defense of her extra weight and thanked him for the compliment. "You do that so well, darling," she said as she relaxed beneath his tender touch, "I think I'll keep you around for a while. What say you?"

"I think that would be a grand idea," he said as he kissed the top of her head.

Several weeks later, Nancy announced that the 1807/08 season would be her last. She finished out the opera season with Michael Kelly in a production of her brother's opera, *No Song, No Supper,* and then several concerts with Braham and two other singers, Naldi and a new singer, in town Madame Catalini.

Her last night in the theater was on 30 May, 1808, where she sang in a gala concert of several pieces, including her brother's piece, *The Cabinet,* as well as a *Farewell Cantata* in which she was joined by her good friend Signore Naldi, and her adoring husband, John Braham. When it was finished, she walked hand-in-hand with Braham off the stage and into the wings, where they waited for a few seconds together.

"Are you ready, darling," he asked as he gave her hand a gentle squeeze and then a tender peck on the lips. "Take a deep breath and, when you get out there, remember how very much I love you."

As she walked back out onto the stage, the applause grew louder as the audience jumped to their feet. There was cheering and whistling, men and women shouting, "Brava!" and "We'll miss you Signora!" Flowers, ribbons, fans, handkerchiefs, confetti, were tossed upon the stage at her feet. For several minutes this went on and on until Nancy raised her hands and lowered them, indicating that she wished to speak. The audience finally grew silent and when she spoke, she merely repeated the last line of the cantata which she had only just finished singing.

"Farewell," she said, as her voice began to quiver. "And bless you all…forever."

The audience began to clap and cheer even louder as Nancy stood before them and wept. At that point she was so overcome that Braham, who watched her from the wings, ran out to support-her on his arm as he walked her off the stage.

In a final tribute to Nancy's brilliant career the critic, James Boaden wrote:

In the discharge of her public duty she was always highly exemplary; laughed at colds and nervous complaints, and had not a grain of affection about her.

How grave is my torment
In seeing you weep.
Ah, I wish in that moment
I could console your heart.

From the concert aria, "Quanto è grave il mio tormento"
By W. A. Mozart

The Celebrated
SIGNORA STORACE.

Chapter Twenty-One
London, June 1808

1 June 1789

Today I am recalling our days at Laxenburg and seeing you, my dearest love, in the gardens there—for that is where you belong, you know, in a beautiful garden. I close my eyes and remember that lovely day when we picnicked by the pond and as I slept in your lap you plaited a string of tiny white flowers that you made into a crown and placed on my head…

Forever and always I remain your true and faithful,
Wolfgango

"Take a home in the country, Ann," Soane said as he took a sip from his tea cup. "You're retired now and you've said to me over and over that it has always been your dream to own a large house with a pond and acres of garden."

It was a pleasant June afternoon as Nancy and Braham sat on their terrace with their good friend John Soane, who had stopped by to congratulate Nancy on her retirement.

"I know of a beautiful piece of property in Surrey. It's a small cottage on about four acres—lovely little spot. We could drive down there together tomorrow if you like."

Nancy looked over at Braham who grimaced. "What do you say, darling? How about it?"

"I'm just not sure I'm ready to move that far out of the city," Braham replied.

"Well, of course not," Soane answered. "You can keep this house for long stays in the city and keep the other as your permanent residence."

"Oh, please, darling. Let's at least drive out and take a look," Nancy pleaded.

Reluctantly, Braham agreed, so the next day Soane came with his carriage and drove them out to the property. As the carriage pulled up to the cottage, they saw that it needed work. It was in mild disrepair and was too small for their needs, but the bones were good and Soane believed that he could draw up plans that would be pleasing, as well as in keeping with what they were willing to spend. The house was nice enough, but it was the acreage that was most appealing.

Surrounding the cottage was approximately four acres of prime land wooded with fir, birch, and oak trees. There were several clearings that were perfect for the gardens that Nancy had always dreamed of, as well as a stream that emptied into a lovely, clear pond. Nancy was sold the moment she laid eyes on it.

"Oh please, darling," she pleaded. "Please, may I may have it? I'll never ask you for another thing in my life!"

Braham, who could never resist her when she begged, put his arms around her, squeezed her and said, "What am I to do with such a woman? You have me completely wrapped around your little finger. Of course, you may have it. You've worked hard for this, so who am I to say no?"

As soon as they returned to the city, they headed straight to the bank, where arrangements were made to draw out the money to purchase the property. Nancy and Braham agreed that since this had always been her dream, she would be the one to make the purchase and pay all the expenses towards renovations, and that only her name would be listed on the deed.

A few weeks later, after all the notes were transferred and all the deeds put into her name, Nancy visited Soane's office, ready to go over the renovation and landscaping plans that he had already begun. She was greeted by her nephew Brinsley, who had been taken on as Soane's apprentice.

"Good morning, Auntie Ann," Brinsley said, greeting her with a kiss on each cheek. "You're looking bright and cheerful this morning. I know you must be terribly excited."

"Indeed, Brinsley. I can't even tell you how happy I am! Everything is perfect—absolutely perfect," she exclaimed.

"Well, I think you'll be pleased with the ideas that Mr. Soane has drawn up. He's shown them to me and I've even had a little hand in them myself," he boasted.

"Well, then, I'm certain that they're perfect," she said, smiling.

"Let me announce you," he said, excusing himself. "I'll just be a moment."

What a handsome and clever young man Brinsley had turned out to be—so very much like his father. He even looked like him. Like his cousin Spencer, he had large, dark eyes, a swarthy complexion, and dark hair. They looked as if they were brothers; the Storace blood ran thick in both of them.

"Mr. Soane is ready for you to come in, now, Auntie," Brinsley said as he ushered her into the inner office. "I'll see you again after you're finished with him."

"Thank you, Brinsley," she said as he closed the door behind her.

"Clever young man, that nephew of yours," Soane said.

"Yes, he is, John. We're awfully proud of him."

"I'm sorry to say, however, that architecture isn't his cup of tea."

"Whatever do you mean," she asked as she took a chair in front of Soane's desk.

"Perhaps I'm speaking out of turn, but since you two seem to be so close, I'll tell you that I believe he has yours and your brother's musical talent. That's truly where his heart is."

"Oh, dear," Nancy said, "I had no idea that he was unhappy."

"Well, if I may be frank, I believe it was that new husband of Mary's that pushed him into it—completely discouraged him from the music profession and the stage altogether. As a reverend, he regards a life dedicated to the entertainments as vain and sinful."

"Mary has never mentioned anything to that effect. I had no idea," Nancy said, saddened by the news.

"Well, she wouldn't, would she? She's so very sweet and polite." He paused for several moments and then cleared his throat. "Anyway, on a happier note, I have your plans ready and I'm anxious for you to see them," he said with a ring of enthusiasm in his voice.

"Oh, good," Nancy exclaimed, happy to move on to a more pleasant subject. "I'm so excited, I've been acting like a giddy little girl!"

He directed her to a large, mahogany table, where the plans lay unrolled and spread flat, the corners anchored with heavy crystal paperweights.

"We'll start with the house," he said. "I've added another floor and several more rooms, plus expanded two of the rooms. The top floor, of course, will be for the servants, while the ground and first floors are reserved for two salons, one private and one public, a garden room, a dining room, a library and music room, a kitchen and, upstairs, six bedchambers.

"Twelve rooms altogether?"

"Yes, not including the top floor chambers and common area, reserved for the house staff, of course, or the front entry hall."

"Very nice," Nancy said. "Very nice, indeed. I like the size of the bedchambers. They're not too cramped, but not so large that they lack intimacy.

"I've added a large, arched portico to the exterior and eight-foot, palladium windows on the ground floor. The first and second floor windows are six-foot, and the top floor has dormers."

"Twelve-foot ceilings throughout," she asked.

"Yes," he said, nodding. "Now, are we ready to go over the landscaping?"

"Oh, yes," she exclaimed. "This is my favorite part!"

"Yes, I know how much you've dreamt of your gardens," he said with a warm smile. "I took extra care while drawing up these plans."

"Show me," she exclaimed.

"There is an exit from the garden room leading to the central garden, which will contain a large fountain and beds of roses. If you'll notice, there are five clearings that encircle the rose garden, with paths leading through the small wooded areas from the central rose garden into the various clearings."

"I love it already, John!"

"Yes, well, wait until you see what else I have come up with," he said with a smile. "Standing in the center of the middle clearing will be a scaled-down version of a pavilion you described from your years in Vienna."

"Yes, Diana's Temple, at Laxenburg."

"Well, it took me forever, it seems, but I was able to contact an architect in Vienna who found the original plans for that particular pavilion and he actually drew a scaled-down replica of it and sent the plans to me."

"Oh John, you're an absolute miracle worker! I had no idea when I asked if you could accomplish it, that you could! You just don't know what this means to me," she replied, nearly in tears.

"Well, the real miracle will be if I'm able to decipher the German."

"I still know a little," she said. "Perhaps I can help."

"I may call on you then," he said. "I have to admit that this is one of the most expensive aspects of the whole project. The plans alone were a costly venture, but I think you're going to be very pleased when you see it."

"I know I will. I trust you, John. You're the best in the profession!"

"Thank you for your confidence, Ann. I only hope that when it's all finished you'll be singing the same tune. I'm extremely glad that you're pleased."

"I am, and I can't wait," she exclaimed. "So how long will it all take?"

"I'm looking at about six months, at least to make the house livable. The gardens and landscaping will take a bit longer, but you can occupy the house well before that's all completed," he said. "You should be able to move in shortly after Christmas."

When Nancy returned home to Braham, she could barely contain her excitement over the plans for their new home in Surrey. The actual spot on which it stood was Herne Hill, so the name she chose for it was simply Herne Hill Cottage. Braham's enthusiasm was far more measured than Nancy's, but he feigned excitement for her sake, knowing how much it meant to her.

Late one night, as Braham started for the stairs to bed, a knock sounded at the door. Wondering who could possibly be calling at such a late hour, he waved the maid away and opened it to see Kennedy standing there, fumbling with the brim of his hat and looking quite agitated.

"May I come in?" Kennedy asked. "I'm sorry to call so late, but there's been an accident."

"An accident? Who? Where?"

"May I come in?"

"Yes, of course. Please do." He led Kennedy into the salon and called Abby to light some of the wall sconces, which had only just been put out. "Please, sit."

"I'm not sure how to tell you this," Kennedy said. "Has Ann already gone up?"

"Yes, but I can have Abby wake her."

"Perhaps that would be best. This news is regarding her nephew."

"Brinsley?" Braham asked, frightened of what was coming next. "What's wrong? Is he all right?"

"I should wait until Ann gets here."

"Abby!" Braham called. "Please wake Mrs. Braham and ask her to join us. Would you like some sherry, John?" he asked, going to the wine tray to pour himself a drink.

"No, thank you. I need to keep a clear head for the next several hours."

"What's all this," Nancy asked when she entered the room a few minutes later. "Is everything all right?"

"No, Ann, I'm afraid it's not," Kennedy replied.

"I think you'd better sit down, Ann," Braham said, taking her arm and leading her to the settee, where they sat down together.

"Brinsley came home very upset this afternoon from Soane's office," Kennedy began. "It seems that he was let go, something about his not having the desire it took to complete a successful apprenticeship in architecture. He was very hurt and angry, nearly to the point of tears."

"John, what's happened," Nancy asked, anxiously.

"It seems he went to a local tavern with some of his friends and got quite drunk." He struggled to control his tears, then continued. "There was an accident after they left the tavern. I don't know what happened, exactly, but Brinsley's horse got spooked by something. He was thrown and—I'm so sorry, Ann—he was killed almost instantly."

"Oh, God, no!" Nancy cried, breaking into sobs. Braham put his arm around her.

"I'm so sorry, Ann," he said. "I know how close you were to him."

"He reminded me so much of Stephen," she said, weeping. "Sometimes it was almost like having him back again."

"What about Mary?" Braham said. "How is she?"

"She's heartbroken. I've never seen her in such a state," he said as his own emotions finally overtook him. "We'll make arrangements tomorrow for the service, that is, if I can get poor Mary back to her senses by then. God knows she's suffering terribly."

"Is there something we can do to help," Braham asked.

"Perhaps there is. Mary is so fond of you, John. Perhaps you could drive out with Ann tomorrow and visit with her. She loves you both so, and she needs you."

"Yes, of course. Anything," Braham said.

"It's my fault," Kennedy said, shaking his head. "If only I hadn't pushed the boy as I did."

"Of course it's not your fault," Braham said. "You had nothing to do with the accident. The boy was upset, he went out and got drunk with his friends, and it happened. It could have been over anything."

"He was so much like his father; I feared him following in his footsteps."

Nancy lowered her head and said softly, "Yes, we know how you feel about a life dedicated to the entertainments, John."

"Well, I'm sorry for that now, Ann, and I humbly ask your forgiveness. I feel my judgment of you and your family has returned to me three-fold. Judge not lest ye be judged," he said as he stood to leave.

"We'll be out tomorrow to visit with Mary," Braham said as he gave Kennedy a pat on the back. "Tell her that we love her and please convey to her how very sorry we are."

"I will. Thank you."

The very next day they boarded their carriage and drove out to visit Mary. They arrived to find the front door draped in black crepe and on it hung a wreath of white lilies. Braham and Nancy were escorted into the main salon and found Mary dressed in mourning, going through a box of mementos, all things that belonged to Brinsley or that were associated with his childhood. It was evident that she had been crying, for she clutched her handkerchief tightly, and her eyes and nose were quite red and swollen.

"Look at this," she said to Nancy, as she held up a drawing that Brinsley made when he was a young child. "It's a sketch of his pony. Remember, Ann—the one that you and Stephen gave to him for Christmas a couple of years before Stephen passed away?"

"Of course I remember!" Nancy said with a smile as she leaned in closer to get a better look. "Oh my," she exclaimed, "he had his father's artistic talents as well as his musical ones. That's a very mature sketch for one so young."

"Indeed he did," Mary agreed. "I suppose that's why my husband believed so strongly that he would do well with architecture."

"We're so very sorry, Mary," Braham said, as he took a seat across from her. "We were shocked and devastated by the news that John brought to us last night."

"He feels so terribly about it all," Mary replied. "He blames himself. I've assured him that I harbor no ill feelings nor do I cast any blame upon him. He's a good man and he loved Brinsley as if he were his own son."

"I'm sure he did," Nancy said as she sat on the settee next to Mary. As she put her arm around Mary's shoulders, Mary collapsed, burying her face in Nancy's bosom and wept.

"I had no idea he was so unhappy," Mary said through her tears. "He never uttered a word about it. John and I both assumed that he was doing well."

"He was like his father in that, too," Nancy said. "Stephen kept his thoughts and emotions locked privately within himself as well. It's not your fault, Mary. You refuse to cast blame on John, so extend yourself the same courtesy. There was no way you could have known."

"But I'm his mother. We're supposed to know everything about our children, are we not?"

"I don't think that's possible, Mary," Nancy replied. "We're mothers, but we're mortals. We don't know everything, and we can't know what our children don't tell us."

For the next week, Brinsley Sheridan Storace laid in state as family, friends, and neighbors dropped by to pay their respects and condolences. Afterwards, he was given a small family funeral and committed to his final resting place in the church cemetery of his step-father's parish.

֍

Despite the tragic events that befell Nancy and her family, it still couldn't completely quell her excitement over her new home in the country. As the renovations progressed, she made arrangements for new furnishings, carpets, draperies, and decorations.

Again, no expense would be spared, and like with their home on Great Russell Street she said that she would bear the entire cost out of her own purse. The old furnishings, for the most part, remained at the town home, as Braham would retain it for his use whenever he had extended stays in London. Nancy also set about the business of hiring a new domestic staff for the home in the country as most of the old staff would remain behind at the old home in the city.

By Christmas of that year, the major renovations on the house were nearly finished. As Soane had anticipated, everything was on schedule, so after they spent the Christmas holidays in Bath, Nancy, Braham, six-year-old Spencer, Nancy's mother, Elizabeth and the new domestic staff made the move into Herne Hill Cottage the following January.

"I simply hate it that you're leaving us so soon," Nancy whined as she stood looking into Braham's armoire full of suits, deciding which ones would be the best for an upcoming trip to Dublin. "We've only just settled in, and off you go."

Braham chuckled. "You're a lady of leisure now. Some of us still have to work for a living. Besides, it's only for a few weeks, and then I'll be home again. You won't even miss me."

Nancy puffed up like a pouting child. "I will too miss you," she said as she grabbed his arms and placed them around her waist. "This will be first extended trip you've taken without me, ever."

He brushed his finger against her bottom lip, which was stuck out in a pretty pout. "For goodness sake, look at that lip of yours," he said as he kissed it. "Such a grown-up baby you are!"

"I'll hardly know what to do without you."

"You have plenty to occupy yourself. There are those two charity events coming up that you're planning, along with the landscaping plans with Soane. And then there's always your mother to keep out of trouble," he said with his characteristic ornery grin.

"Yes, well, Mother… She is a challenge, isn't she?" Nancy laughed. "I've been trying to figure out a way to get Spencer's boarding school to accept her, but they keep telling me she's too old. I tell them that may be so, but in terms of behavior, she's quite on a par with the average six year-old."

Braham laughed. "True, but seriously, darling, six weeks isn't that long, and then I'll be home."

"For a week," she sighed, frowning. "And then you're off again."

"Darling, this is how it's going to be from now on and we're going to have to get used to it," he said as he slid open a drawer filled with cravats and laid out several. "You'll adjust. And there's nothing that says you can't come on some of the trips with me, if you'd like."

"I know," she said, pouting again. "I just want you here with me, enjoying our beautiful new home. This isn't at all how I pictured our life together."

"You will adjust," he said, emphatically.

∞∞∞

Bratislava, 1809

"In nomine Patris, et Filii, et Spiritus Sancti. Amen," the priest said as he made the sign of the cross in front of the couple that knelt before him. "You are now husband and wife."

After nearly eighteen years since her husband's death in December of 1791, Constanze Weber Mozart married Georg Nikolaus von Nissen, a Danish diplomat who she had taken in as a tenant some years before in Vienna.

After Mozart's death, Constanze took on the formidable task of paying off her husband's debts. She accomplished this quite successfully by pulling off the deception that he had left her in abject poverty. By selling what possessions she had left and moving in with her mother, she saved a tremendous amount in day-to-day expenses, but it was by parading herself and her two young sons in old and thread-bare clothing, giving the impression that she was poorer than she really was, that she gained a widow's pension from the Emperor (due to the fact that Mozart died an employee of the court, though he hadn't yet taken on the duties).

Soon she began the task of compiling, publishing, and selling as many of her husband's compositions as she could (setting the price for many of them per written note), as well as organizing memorial concerts and other events. Many people saw her efforts as mercenary, and it wasn't long before she garnered a bad reputation among her fellow Viennese, especially when it was clear that she had accumulated quite a bit of wealth as a result and was soon able to send her two young sons off to Prague to be tutored privately.

In 1798 she and Nissen began to live together and they started the process of compiling documents, letters, and compositions all pertaining to Mozart, as it was their intent to write and publish the first biography about her late husband. A few months after they married, they moved to Copenhagen, Denmark where Nissen took the position of public censor.

Using his diplomatic connections, he began sending emissaries and representatives out all over Central and Western Europe in an effort to collect all the known letters, items, and documents pertaining to Mozart and bring them back for him and Constanze to compile and catalog for documentation.

"The first and obvious place to begin," Nissen said to Constanze who sat taking notes, "is Vienna, and then on to Prague. This process will take some time."

"I know," Constanze replied, as she wrote down the names of people who had connections with her deceased husband, and who might still have had letters or other memorabilia. "Wolfgang had friends everywhere. This could take years."

"Make sure you write them all down—even the ones we won't necessarily use in the book. Some of these people may no longer be living. I'll have to call upon investigators to find many of them, I'm sure."

"And if you find them, how will you get them to voluntarily hand over their items?"

"We'll coerce them well enough. Most will hand them over easily, if we offer enough in return. No doubt it will be an expensive venture, but well worth the price," he said, watching over his wife's shoulder as she wrote. "Just make certain you don't leave anyone out."

Sir John Soane

Chapter Twenty-Two
Herne Hill Cottage, Christmas 1810

"Oh, look! Mummy, look" Spencer exclaimed as he gazed out the salon window onto the circular drive. "Papa's carriage! He's here! He's here!" He ran out of the salon and through the entry to the front door.

"Spencer Harris Braham," Nancy called to him, "don't you dare run out there without your coat! You'll catch your death!"

It was too late, for by the time the words slipped off of her tongue, Spencer was out the door and halfway down the drive, running to meet Braham's carriage as it approached.

It was Christmas time and Braham was returning home for the holidays after another extended tour which included the towns of Bristol, Bath, Norwich, and Birmingham—a typical schedule for him. Over the past two years, Nancy had finally adjusted to the fact that life at Herne Hill Cottage wasn't going to be exactly how she'd pictured it, and that her husband, who was still at the height of his career, wasn't going to give it all up to enjoy the serene, pastoral life that she had always pictured for herself and her family. The disparity in their ages was more marked and defined than ever before, but it was something she had learned to live with, and accept.

"Papa! Papa!" Spencer called out over the rattle of the carriage wheels on the pea gravel drive. "You're home! You're home!"

When the carriage pulled to a full stop near the front entry, Braham burst out, leapt to the ground and ran, scooping his son into his arms and covering his cheeks with kisses.

"Oh, Papa, I've missed you so," Spencer exclaimed. "Mummy and I have been busy preparing a surprise for you, for Christmas!"

"Is that so?" Braham said, wide-eyed as he picked up Spencer and carried him on his hip to the front entry, where Nancy stood waiting.

"Well, I have some Christmas surprises for you and Mummy, too," he exclaimed.

"Oh, goodie! Can we see them now?"

"No, you cannot. You have to wait until Christmas!" he said as he playfully nibbled Spencer's red nose.

"Welcome home, darling," Nancy exclaimed as Braham walked up the steps to the front door. He put Spencer down and held out his arms to her for an embrace.

"It's good to be home," he said as he gave her a warm squeeze and a peck on the lips. "So how is my darling girl?"

"I'm well, my love, thank you," she said as he put his arm around her and walked inside with his family. "Emma has your room aired out and ready, and there's a fire lit. If you'd like, I can have her pour a hot bath so that you can relax, and freshen up a bit from your trip."

"Oh, thank you, Ann, that sounds quite blissful," he said as she helped him remove his great coat and handed it and his hat to the maid.

"Emma, please have the copper tub brought into Mr. Braham's chamber and prepared, immediately," Nancy ordered.

"Yes, madam," Emma replied with a curtsey.

Braham turned to Nancy again and, wrapping her in his arms, he gave her a deep kiss. "Mm… I've really missed that."

She giggled. "Oh, have you? Well, I shall have to see to it that you get more—after you've rested."

He raised an eyebrow, and grinned. "Tonight perhaps?"

"Oh I don't know," Nancy teased. "I thought you'd be so tired from your journey that perhaps you'd want to sleep in your own chamber tonight."

"But I was hoping that…well…"

"Oh, all right. If you insist," she said as she kissed him again. "I'll leave my door unlocked," she said with a coquettish grin. "You run on now. That bath should be ready for you in just a bit, and after you've had some time to unwind, we'll be ready for supper."

Braham gave her one more lingering kiss and then he climbed up the stairs to his room. "I'll see you after while," he said as he paused halfway up. "It is good to be home, darling. I've missed you very much."

Nancy smiled and blew him as kiss as he finished climbing the stairs.

That evening, after he took a few hours to rest, Braham enjoyed a fine supper with the entire family at the table and then he spent some time in the salon, sitting with Nancy and Elizabeth, as well as playing with Spencer.

After an hour or so, Spencer's nanny came to take him to bed. He gave everyone good-night kisses and then he was taken upstairs to give the adults some much-needed time alone, and allowing Braham time to catch up on the local reviews and tabloids.

Braham and Nancy sat and chatted for a while with Elizabeth, and then they shared with one another the latest town gossip and news from the war that raged with Napoleon. Braham kept glancing over at Nancy and grinning, giving her air kisses and playfully flirting whenever Elizabeth's attention was centered elsewhere.

Soon, Nancy gave a little yawn and said, "Oh, dear, I think I'm getting tired. Perhaps it's time for me to go up."

Braham looked up and she gave him a wink as she stood to leave.

"Good night, darling," he said. "I'll be following you very soon."

"I'm sure you will," she said as she bent over and gave him a kiss. "Good night, Mother. Rest well," she said as she gave her a kiss on the cheek."

"Good night, dear," Elizabeth said with a yawn. "I think I'll go on up as well."

Nancy took her mother's hand and helped her stand and then took her by the arm and led her to the salon door. She stopped to turn and wish Braham a good night, and then she climbed the stairs with Elizabeth to their bedchambers.

Closing her door, she put out all the candles but a few, which cast a soft, dim glow around the room. She let down her hair, undressed and put on one of her prettiest negligees and, climbing into bed, she tucked herself in neatly so that when he came through the door, she would look as pretty as a picture.

Not long after, she heard a quiet knock on her door.

"Come in," she said softly.

"Mm…there you are." He locked the door behind him then climbed into the bed, taking her into his arms. "I could hardly wait to get to this part of the evening."

"Me, too," she said as she slipped her arms around his neck and reclined into the pillows, pulling him gently down upon her. "I missed you so much, John."

"I missed you, too," he said as he brushed her cheeks with soft kisses. He ran his fingers through her hair, which, even despite Nancy's age of forty-five, was still as dark, long, and thick as it ever was.

"Oh, I almost forgot," he said as he stopped to retrieve a rectangular shaped box from his nightshirt pocket.

"Oh, no," Nancy moaned, "Do we have to, now?"

"You'll like this. I was gone on your birthday, so I brought you back a little something. I'm sorry it's so late, but it's from the heart."

Taking the box from him, she opened it to reveal an exquisite cloisonné hair comb in the design of a peacock, its long tail feathers dotted with semi-precious stones of different varieties and colors. Gasping, she took it out of the box and held it up.

"Oh, John. How lovely."

"I thought it would look pretty in your hair," he said, smiling proudly. He always seemed to pick just the right gifts for her. "Happy birthday, my love, even if it is two months late." He nuzzled close and nibbled on one of her ears.

"Thank you, darling. It's perfect," she said as she laid the comb aside and joined in the resuming of their amorous foreplay.

"Now, madam," he said as he brushed a loose strand of hair from her face. "Shall I proceed?"

"Mm… Yes," she said, slipping her arms through his and drawing him in close. "Please do."

The next morning, Nancy awakened to find her husband still asleep, snuggled up close to her, his arm draped contentedly just under her bosom. She gently laid his arm aside and kissed the top of his head.

He's so tired, she thought. I'll let him sleep.

Quietly, she dressed, then went downstairs, where the cook already had coffee ready.

"Mr. Braham is still asleep in my chamber," she said. "Please see that he's not disturbed. I want him to be able to sleep as late as he pleases."

"Yes, ma'am," Emma replied. "Would you like to take your breakfast with Mrs. Storace and little Spencer?"

"Yes, I think I shall. Thank you. There's no telling how long Mr. Braham will sleep, so I might as well," she said with a pleasant smile.

She sighed. This was the life of which she had always dreamed. She had her beautifully furnished and appointed home and gardens sitting on four acres of the most beautiful countryside in all of England. Her family was with her under one roof warm, safe, and well-fed. Her mother and child were content and her husband slept blissfully in her bed. Her life was good and she was grateful. She couldn't possibly want for more.

ဆပ္ဆ

"Only two weeks," she sighed as she stood facing her husband, tying his cravat. "You're gone from us for nearly two months and then you're only home two weeks before you're off again."

"I have to go, darling. You know that. We have a busy new season with two Mozart pieces that we've never seen before. And you know Mozart. He's so bloody difficult. I must start rehearsing those immediately."

The subject of Mozart had not been raised since the argument they'd had over the alleged affair between Nancy and the composer. They'd both regretted the altercation. Nancy dealt with it, reconciling the feelings that Braham's performance in Mozart's *Tito* had unearthed in her. She at last came to the conclusion that Mozart had been the love of her youth. She would never forget him, or the love they'd shared, but Braham was with her now, and she dedicated herself to loving him with all the passion and commitment that she had never been given the opportunity, due to their life circumstances, to give to Mozart. Mozart had been her first love; Braham her last.

She often thought it odd how a cocky, sometimes overbearing but insecure Jewish orphan had finally wormed his way into her heart, but when she recalled the moment that she realized she had fallen in love with him, it didn't really seem so odd at all. He was playful, charming, considerate, loyal, and absolutely delightful Of course, like all men, he had his faults. He was terribly vain and conceited, and he could sometimes say and do some of the most insensitive things. And, although he mostly paid his fair share of the expenses, he was a little too free with allowing Nancy to foot the bill for most things only to regard those things as joint property. But Nancy didn't care. He loved her and she adored him, and that was all that mattered.

"You know you can always come with me," Braham said. "We do own a home in town, you know."

"I know, but Spencer doesn't return to school for another three weeks. Besides, what would I do with Mother? She can't flit back and forth from town to country like we do, and I refuse to leave her out here alone for any length of time."

"These are the things you should have thought about." Braham said, shaking his head as if to say, I told you so.

"I know, I know. You've reminded me over and over that I should have thought of these things before I did this, but I still don't have any regrets," she said stubbornly. "We'll just do the best we can." She patted him on the chest and turned him around to face the mirror. "There. How does that look?"

"Perfect! How do you get it to look like that?"

"My fingers are as nimble as my tongue," she said as she put her arms around him and felt up his chest.

"Don't start that now," he pleaded, grabbing her hand and kissing her palm. "You'll have me so worked up that I'll never get out of here."

"That's the point," she said, winking.

In the following year, their lives became a whirlwind of Braham's performances and darting back and forth from town to country, as well as charity events, soirees, balls, and even a concert or two given with Nancy. She could still be persuaded, on occasion, to perform for charity concerts and other functions, as well as for private parties and soirees, and she still attended every one of Braham's in-town performances.

His summer appearances in Mozart's operas *Cosi fan tutte* and *The Magic Flute* were brilliant, and Nancy paid him the highest complement by telling him that she was quite sure Mozart would have been extremely pleased. Many times she spoke to Braham of Mozart and how he could so easily intimidate a singer if they failed to live up to his expectations. He was the harshest of critics, she told him, but he was also the best. Braham hung upon her every word and still heeding to her seasoned and well-worn advice. He had tremendous respect for her talents, instincts, and professional savvy, and he recognized that none of those things had diminished a whit since her retirement.

Everywhere they went, they still were the toast of the town, received in the most respected and honored households in London and Bath. They continued to holiday in the most fashionable places—Margate and Broadstairs—and Braham always insisted that his wife and partner of fifteen years be by his side. Nancy began to believe what Emma Hamilton had told her several years before when she said that Nancy lived a charmed life, for it seemed indeed, that she had it all.

Once the day seemed sweet to me,
Once love pleased me.
But now it is not so, no, no, no.
But it pleases me no more.

As long as I lived close to you,
My dear beloved,
When I saw you languish,
Full of love for me,
Sweet was that day love pleased me,
But it is no longer so.
But it pleases me no more.

The aria, "Dolce mi parve un di" from *Una Cosa Rara*
Originally composed for Nancy Storace
By Vincente Martìn y Soler

Margate, England

Chapter Twenty-Three
London, February 1812

"What an honor to meet you, Mr. Braham," Mrs. Wright said as she extended her hand, nervously peering over the top of her fan.

"And it is indeed a pleasure to meet you, Mrs. Wright," Braham replied politely as he gave her hand a polite kiss.

"I've been telling Mrs. Wright for some time that I simply must bring her backstage one day to meet you," Soane said. "She and her husband are both great admirers of yours and I thought it fitting that since I knew you in a personal capacity, I should extend to her this pleasure."

"Why, of course, John," Braham said with characteristic charm. "And I'm so pleased that you did."

Mrs. Sophie Wright of Teddington was the pretty wife of a ship's purser on the East India line. She and her husband were avid theater-goers and had been long-time admirers of both Braham and Nancy. Presently, Mr. Wright was at sea and not scheduled to return for several more months.

"And where is your lovely wife, tonight, Mr. Braham," Sophie asked. "It is my understanding that she never misses any of your performances."

"Unfortunately, you have met me on one of the rare nights when she isn't present. She's home with our young son, Spencer, who has a nasty cold. Nothing serious, mind you, but in times like these only his mummy will suffice, I'm afraid. "

"I have two children myself—twin girls—so I understand completely," Sophie said, as she gazed at him in awe with her large blue eyes.

When Nancy received word from Spencer's boarding school that he had taken sick, she immediately drove into town to bring him to the house on Great Russell Street, where she put him straight to bed and took charge of nursing him. The poor child was miserable with various complaints and his mother insisted on keeping a constant vigil. The entire staff was engaged in helping her nurse the child back to health, and the house reeked of the foul poultices, infusions, decoctions, and ointments that the cook had constantly simmering on the stove.

"I'll be god damned if this house doesn't smell like hell itself," Braham fumed when he walked through the door. "What the hell is that, Abby?" he asked, handing her his coat and hat.

"It's one of the poultices Mrs. Braham ordered for young Spencer," she said. "I think it's made with some type of fish oil, sir."

"Well, it smells like shit," he grumbled. "I don't know if I can stay in the same house with that. It might clog up my throat! Be a good girl and tell Mrs. Braham that I'm home."

"Yes, sir," she said.

Braham went into the front salon, where he poured himself a snifter of brandy and picked up the paper that he hadn't yet had the opportunity to read that day, and waited for Nancy. When, after fifteen minutes, she hadn't appeared, he grew a little concerned.

"Abby! Did you forget to let Mrs. Braham know that I was home?"

Abby ran to the door, drying her hands on a towel. "No, sir," she said. "I told her."

"Well, what did she say?"

"She said she was glad that you were home, but that she was too busy with Spencer to come down at that precise moment. She said she'll join you when he's finally asleep."

"Why didn't you tell me, then?"

"She sent me on another errand, sir, and I didn't have time."

"Very well," he said with noted agitation in his voice. He waited several more minutes, but finally, he gave up and went to bed.

Throughout the night there was constant noise—Spencer's cough followed by cries for his mother. The servants scurried about, retrieving ointments and bringing tea. Poor Spencer was having a miserable time of it and, as a result, so was the rest of the household.

Braham tossed and turned all night, putting pillows over his head to block out the noise and tying handkerchiefs soaked in rosewater under his nose to block the smell, trying desperately to sleep so that he would be fresh for the next day's rehearsals and performances. Finally, in complete exhaustion and frustration, he got up, grabbed a pillow and one of the blankets off his bed and dragged them downstairs to the salon, which was farthest from the noises. Grumbling as he shuffled his way through the doorway and into the darkened room, he stubbed his toe against a claw foot of a large, wingback chair. Frustrated beyond endurance, he threw down the pillow and blanket and fell back onto the settee, grabbing his injured foot and cursing.

"God damn, that fucking hurt! She's got this whole fucking household in a fucking uproar over a child's fucking cold!"

Finally, when the throbbing began to subside, he grabbed the pillow and blanket and lay down, settling himself on the settee.

The next day, Nancy was up and dressed at the usual hour. Spencer's fever had finally broken sometime in the early hours of the morning, and she and the servants were able to get some sleep. When she awoke, she went to his chamber to check on him.

"How is he this morning, Nanny Rose," Nancy asked as she placed her hand on his forehead.

"He's finally sleeping, ma'am," the nanny replied. "The fever's been gone for a few hours and the coughing isn't nearly as bad as it was. I think he's on the mend now."

"Were you able to get any rest?"

"Yes, ma'am, thank you. After he fell asleep, I sat right here and dozed off. And you ma'am?"

"Oh, I'm fine, thank you. I finally slept a little. I'm just relieved that he's better."

"That he is, ma'am. He can thank you for that."

Nancy smiled, leaning over to kiss her son's forehead.

"I'm going down to get some breakfast, Nanny Rose. Please call if you need me."

"Yes, ma'am, I will."

Nancy went downstairs to the dining room, where she found Braham sitting at the table, looking a bit disheveled and having his morning coffee.

"Good morning, darling," she said as she leaned over to give him a kiss.

"Hmph!" he grunted. "Morning."

"What a grumpy puss, you are. What's crawled under your rug this morning?"

"Couldn't get any damned sleep last night, that's what," he said, taking a sip of coffee.

"What kept you awake?"

Braham glared at her in astonishment.

"What kept me awake? Why, all that bloody noise everyone was making. Coughing, crying, the servants running back and forth, those God-awful smells from whatever fucking potions you and the cook had brewing. It was a god damned ruddy zoo!"

"I'm sorry, John, I had no idea—"

"And then, when I came in from the theater, you didn't even bother to come down to speak to me."

"I was taking care of our sick child," she said, defensively.

"He has a nanny for God's sake. You could have broken off for a moment to at least come down and say hello."

"He had a fever, John, and he was calling for me. I couldn't leave. For heaven's sake, you're acting like such a baby!"

"Well, this is my home now and I felt rather intruded upon, and discounted."

"Excuse me. Your home?" she said indignantly. "The last time I checked, darling, both of our names were on the deed. And if you do recall, I purchased virtually all of the furnishings with my own purse."

"Well, you're hardly here anymore now, are you? I pay the household staff now and you had them running and fetching for you so much, they barely had time to get their regular duties accomplished, much less meet my needs when I came in."

Nancy was astounded.

"I'm astonished at you. That was our son—*your* son—up there last night! The poor child was miserable with a fever and a terrible cough, and everyone was doing what they could to help him. Now you're sitting here this morning haggling with me over who owns this house and who pays for what, and God knows what else!"

Braham sat silently, eyes forward, sipping from his cup. When he refused to reply, Nancy got up from the table and went to the door, stopping only for a moment to look back at him.

"Sometimes, I just don't understand you, John."

ༀ

"How very good see you again, Mrs. Wright," Braham said with marked enthusiasm.

"And it is good to see you again, Mr. Braham," Sophie said with a pretty smile. "Your performance was brilliant last night, as usual. How is your son? If I recall, the last time we spoke, Mrs. Braham was home nursing him through a terrible cold. Is he better?"

"He's quite alright, thank-you. My wife, along with all of her miraculous potions had him right as rain in only a few days. He's back at school now, and she's back at her country house."

"Oh, so you're not living together," Sophie asked. "Pardon me if that's too personal a question."

"Oh, no. Nothing like that at all." He laughed nervously. "After she retired, she bought a small estate in Surrey—something she had always dreamt of—and we moved out there with her mother and our son a couple of years ago. We maintain our home here in London for whenever I have extended stays, or when I get the occasional break from my hectic schedule. But I manage to join her for a week or two at a time."

"Oh, dear," Sophie said. "That sounds very similar to the schedule Mr. Wright maintains."

"As soon as he's back in port, I should like to meet him."

"And I your wife," Sophie replied courteously.

"Well, then," Braham said, "we shall have to make it an occasion." He tipped his hat. "Until then, Mrs. Wright?"

"Until then, Mr. Braham."

It was only a few weeks later that Mr. Wright returned. Joining his wife at the theater, he asked to meet Braham, who promptly gave a favorable reply.

"Mr. Braham, this is my husband, Mr. Henry Wright," Sophie said. "He has only just returned home after six months at sea. When he learned that I had been introduced to you, he insisted that I bring him backstage so he could meet you as well."

"Mr. Wright," Braham said, extending his hand.

"It's an honor, Mr. Braham. A very great honor, indeed."

211

"The honor's mine, Mr. Wright. When I had the pleasure of meeting your lovely wife, I told her that I was quite anxious to meet you as well."

"Well, thank you, sir," he said. "And we're both quite anxious to meet your beautiful wife. We have a small place down in the Wells and, if it is at all possible, we would love to have the two of you down and visit for a few days."

"But of course," Braham exclaimed. "That would be quite lovely. Let me check my schedule and compare it with my wife's and then I'll get back with you on it."

"Good, then," Wright replied. "We look forward to it, sir."

It wasn't long before a letter arrived, inviting Braham, Nancy, and their son Spencer, as well as Elizabeth, to join the Wrights at their home in Tunbridge Wells over the Christmas holidays.

"All of us?" Nancy exclaimed.

"Well, yes. It is for the holidays and I'm quite sure they didn't want to take us away from our family. Right considerate of them, I think."

"Indeed, it is," Nancy said. "I'm just not sure Mother will be up to it."

"Why don't you ask Mary if she wouldn't mind having her over the holidays? She hasn't visited there in a while, and I'm quite sure both John and Mary would enjoy the company."

"That's not a bad idea. But what of Spencer? Do you think he would be too terribly bored by an extended visit like that, and over Christmas?"

"Oh, no! Quite the contrary, for the Wrights have twin girls who are around his age. He should have plenty of stimulating and, if I may say so, pretty company to keep him occupied," Braham said with a grin.

"Twin girls! Oh, dear. My head rattles at the thought of it," she said with a chuckle. "Poor Mrs. Wright."

"Poor Mr. Wright,' is more like it," Braham said, rolling his eyes. "I'm sure he looks forward to his times at sea."

෨෬

It was only a few weeks before Christmas when Nancy received an unusual invitation from her former colleague, Madama Maria Catalini, who had been scheduled to sing the role of Susanna in the upcoming

London production of Mozart's *Le Nozze di Figaro*. Knowing that the role was originally composed for Nancy by Mozart, Catalini desired to recognize Nancy at the London premiere. It was an honor bestowed on the Prima Buffa from a Prima Donna.

Braham was away on another one of his extended tours, and couldn't be with Nancy, so she chose Michael Kelly as her escort. Kelly premiered the double role of Don Basilio and Don Curzio along side Nancy, in Vienna. When the opening night of the premiere arrived, Kelly arrived in his carriage to pick her up, as she had come into London especially for the event.

"How ya feelin' about this performance tonight, darlin'?" he asked as she descended the stairs. He took her arm and gave her a kiss on the cheek.

"I'm not sure, Kelly," she confessed. Kelly was the only one, besides Haydn, who knew of the special relationship that she and Mozart shared. "I handled the other Mozart premieres admirably, I think, but this one's entirely different. I'm not extremely sure of myself. I'm just glad John's not here. He wouldn't understand."

"Well, I've full confidence in ya, me darlin' dove. Yer one of the finest actresses I've ever known. Ya kin keep it together in public. When ya get home ya can fall apart all ye need to. Jest know I love ya, Nancy, and I'll be sittin' there beside ya."

"Thank you. You don't know how much I needed to hear that," she said.

When they arrived at the theater, they found that Nancy's box had been draped with garlands of roses and various other varieties of flowers in honor of the occasion. She was so moved that tears welled in her eyes.

This isn't a good sign, she thought. I've got to do better than this.

When the conductor made his way to the harpsichord and lifted his arm to direct the opening notes of the overture, she took a deep breath and squeezed Kelly's hand.

"Here we go," she whispered.

As the conductor's hand dropped, the opening passage began—the bassoons doubling by the bass violins in rapid melismatic succession. Enter the winds in equally rapid fashion, but more legato. Followed by the entire orchestra at full fortissimo!

She felt a chill pass through her entire body and her stomach rose into her throat—the very same feeling she always got whenever she stood in the wings and heard the beginning of that overture. Next, the curtain would rise on Figaro and Susanna, as Figaro measures a place for their wedding bed, and Susanna tries on the wedding veil she made for herself.

It was difficult for her to understand why this opera was only just making its premiere in London, when she premiered it in Vienna in 1786—three years before the storming of the Bastille in Paris. It was 1812 and Napoleon was Emperor of France, and they had only just received word that he and his decimated troops were being driven out of Russia.

We Brits, she thought, shaking her head. If it doesn't happen on our own shores, we don't want to be bothered with it.

She made it through the first, second, and third acts with amazing ease. Even she was impressed by her fortitude. It helped, too, that Catalini, although an outstanding singer, couldn't act to save her life, something which this role especially demanded. Nancy was disappointed that her hometown audience wasn't able to see the role performed the way Mozart had intended it.

When they reached the fourth act, she began to grow a bit uncomfortable. The scene in which Susanna sings her love song to Figaro (who believes she's singing to the Count), in the garden was near. She shifted nervously in her seat.

Guinse alfin il momento! Che godro senz' affanno in braccio all' idol mio…

The first line of the recitative—Kelly took her by the hand. Take a deep breath, she thought. Just breathe…

Deh vieni non tardar, o gioia bella…

Mozart talked her out of the traditional diva's *bravura aria* for this scene in favor of this sweet little cavatina. Later, he'd confessed to her that his primary motivation for abandoning the formal rondo was because he wanted the tender cavatina to serve as their love song. Of course, no one knew this except them. He'd made it up to her later by composing a bravura *scena con rondo* with a piano duet part for him to play, as a gift to sing at her final concert in Vienna.

"I promise I'll make it up to you, Nancy," he'd pleaded. "A big aria simply isn't appropriate for this scene. It would completely break the mood we're trying to establish. It calls for something tender and from the heart. I'll compose something so sweet and so lovely that no one will ever forget that I composed it for you."

She understood, and agreed. Not just any prima donna would have.

The new aria was every bit as sweet and lovely as he'd promised it would be. Nancy knew from the first time she'd read through it that it was a tender message to her from his very heart.

Vieni, ben mio, tra queste piante ascose.
Vieni, veieni, ti vola fronte incoronar di rose."

"Come, my dearest, amid these sheltering trees. Come, come, I will crown your brow with roses."

She closed her eyes, listening intently, and in that moment she feared would stir painful memories and lonesome regrets, she was filled instead with a renewal of the tenderness and beauty of the love that they had shared. She felt him stirring within her, and for just a split second they were there, together again, under the moonlit sky of Laxenburg. No angst, no fear, not a tear shed—only a joyful reunion taking place between them right there in her garland-draped theater box, unbeknownst to anyone but her.

Diana's Temple, Laxenburg

Chapter Twenty-Four
Tunbridge Wells, Christmas 1812

"*A* happy Christmas to all," Wright exclaimed, "and many happy returns of the new year!"

Holding up their glasses, the company returned the toast. "Happy Christmas!"

Mr. Henry Wright and his wife Sophie, and their twin girls sat with Braham, Nancy, and Spencer. The large table was laden with traditional Christmas fare: a plump roast goose with chestnut stuffing and spiced apples, Brussels sprouts with roasted chestnuts, cranberry sauce, rich gravy, and of course, the crowning achievement, the Christmas pudding filled with dried fruit, nuts, raisins, and currants, flamed in brandy sauce.

After supper they moved to the parlor, where Nancy sat at the pianoforte and with Braham, entertained everyone with some favorite ditties and a few carols.

"Bravo, Mr. Braham! Bravo!" Sophie exclaimed after his first solo. She bounced in her chair as she applauded, her blonde side curls bouncing right along with her snow white bosom. "How lucky are we, of all people, to have the great Mr. John Braham to entertain us at Christmas?"

"And don't forget his lovely wife, the beautiful and talented Signora Storace," Wright politely reminded her.

After the entertainment the children went to another parlor to have refreshments and to play games while the adults gathered in front of the fireplace to open the small gifts they had for one another.

"This is for you, Ann," Braham said as he handed her a package wrapped in plain paper and tied with a bright red ribbon. "I bought it in Bath, thinking you might enjoy it."

Nancy opened the package to reveal a novel in three volumes entitled, *Sense and Sensibility*.

"It's published anonymously, but reliable gossip says it's by a spinster who lived a few years in Bath. Her name is Austen, Miss Jane Austen, I believe, the daughter of a clergyman. It's very possible that we've met her, in fact. I'm told that she and her family frequently attended many of the same gatherings as we. Anyway, I hear this novel is what all the fashionable ladies in Bath are reading these days."

"Thank you, John. What a thoughtful gift. I'm sure I'll enjoy reading it very much."

"I hear she has another novel coming out next year. If you enjoy this one, perhaps we'll get that book for you as well."

"Again, thank you so very much, John," she said as she gave him a kiss. "It's true that I have much more time for reading these days."

"I hear it's a very good book," Sophie said as she looked up from opening her gift from Henry. "I've been meaning to read it myself. Please tell me if you enjoy it."

"I shall," Nancy replied.

"So, what's it like to be a lady of leisure these days, Mrs. Braham," Wright asked as he sat back in his overstuffed chair.

Nancy smiled. "Quite different from the life I was used to. As one might imagine, it was a difficult adjustment at first."

"But you're still performing, are you not?" Sophie asked.

"Yes, some. For charity, mostly. And of course I do some singing for private parties, soirees, and such. But it's different than being in the theater every day. I miss the sights, the sounds… the smells. It was the life I was raised in, and I loved it."

"But your home in the country—you must love that," Sophie said.

"Oh, quite. It was my most cherished dream for almost as long as I can remember. The only thing I don't enjoy about it is that John isn't there with me as much as I'd like," she said as she took his hand and held it in hers.

"Long journeys away from home. The lot of both seamen and actors," Wright said. "Your wife sounds like mine, John. I suppose that we should be grateful they miss us!" He chuckled.

"Indeed," Braham replied with a grin.

"So, how much time do you actually spend away from home, Mr. Braham?" Sophie asked, diverting her gaze.

"It depends on the season, actually," he said. "Most of the time I'm in London, but then there's always the occasional tour. "I'm like your husband. I'm generally away more than I'm home."

"Then that means that Ann and I shall have more time to spend together," she said, looking over at Nancy. "Wouldn't that be nice?"

"Why, of course, Sophie. That would be very nice indeed," Nancy replied, politely.

As pleasant as it was, the Brahams spent only a few days in Tunbridge Wells, then returned to Herne Hill Cottage. Braham needed to be in London to begin rehearsals for the next season. As the coach lumbered along, Spencer slept, his head in his mother's lap.

"So, where exactly is it you said that you met the Wrights?" Nancy asked, breaking the long silence.

Lost in his thoughts, Braham gazed out the window of the coach, then absently replied, "I met them in London, backstage. They're friends of John Soane. He introduced Mrs. Wright to me first, actually, then, when her husband returned home from the sea a few weeks later, she brought him backstage to meet me. Why?"

"Well, they seem like very nice people, but they're not the sort we generally spend time with. They seemed genuinely interested in cultivating a friendship to that end."

"What do you mean by that," he asked, a bit defensive.

"Nothing insulting, but they're just not the type of people with whom we usually find much in common. Sophie seems sweet enough, but I find her rather muddleheaded."

"Really?" Braham replied. "I didn't notice that about her. I found her quite charming, and Mr. Wright a very warm and pleasant sort of fellow."

"I never said I didn't find her charming, but that seems to be about the only thing she has going for herself. That and the fact that she's quite pretty. If they're genuinely interested in developing a close friendship, I don't know what she and I would do together, or how we would manage to converse about anything but the weather and gossip. Oh, and I forgot, about how wonderful you are." Nancy rolled her eyes.

"Now, what exactly do you mean by that snide little remark?"

"Whenever she and I were alone together, all she seemed interested in talking about was you and your beautiful voice, your amazing talents, and how she just can't get enough of seeing you on stage. Every question she asked about our life together was about you. I think she has a crush," she said with a smirk.

"Hmph. I hadn't noticed," he said as he returned his stare out the window.

It was only a couple of days after they'd returned home that Braham was out the door again, on his way back to the city. Rehearsals were to begin soon and he wanted to report back early in order to study some parts that he wasn't familiar enough with at that point to commit to stage.

"So, how long will you be away this time?" she said as she tied his cravat. This had become such a routine for them, they could almost do it in their sleep.

"I'm not sure," he said as he watched her in the mirror. "Oh, look. You're not doing it right. You missed a tuck there."

"Well, if you can do it better, why have I been doing it for you all these years?" she fussed as he stepped up to the mirror to examine her work more closely.

"See here?" he said as he pointed to a spot. "That's not lying correctly." He untied the cravat, then turned to her to have her begin again.

"I think not," she replied, offended. "You've been watching me tie it for nearly twenty years. If I'm suddenly not doing it correctly, then you can tie it yourself from now on." She turned and left in a huff.

After several minutes Braham ventured downstairs, where he found Nancy in the salon, sitting in front of the fire reading the novel he had given to her for Christmas. In her hand she held a handkerchief, her eyes a bit puffy and swollen.

"I didn't mean to upset you," he said, calling from the bottom of the stairway into the salon, where she reclined on the settee, her reading glasses perched on the end of her red nose.

"It's all right," she said without looking up. "I'm fine."

"You're not fine. You're crying."

"I'll be all right, John," she repeated. "You'd best run along now. You'll be late."

Emma came in with his great coat. She helped him on with it and then handed him his hat. As he put it on his head, he turned towards the salon again and said, "I forgot to tell you that I took the liberty of inviting the Wrights to visit with us at our home in the city next Saturday. I didn't think you had anything on that weekend so I told them that you'd be there."

"Good," Nancy said again, not looking up. "I'll see you then, dear."

Braham stood silently, wanting to say something, anything to break through the wall of ice that they suddenly erected between them, but as he could think of nothing, he simply said, "All right then. I'll see you next weekend," and walked out the door.

಼ಣ೮ಚ

It had been a long, exhausting day getting Spencer packed and ready to return to school. All day, she and Emma had been going through Spencer's armoire, pulling out shirts, ties, breeches, and waistcoats to make sure they were clean and in order, and ready to be packed. His shoes had to be polished and inspected before they, too, could be laid out with the other things. As Nancy had never been the kind to shun work of any sort, it wasn't above her to labor right along with her servants in getting things accomplished—something her staff both loved and admired in her—so by the end of the day, she found herself quite weary, more than ready for bedtime when it finally came.

When Spencer was conceived, she knew that at the age of thirty-six, having a baby could be a challenge. It wasn't until after his birth, however, that it all began to catch up with her, and quite rapidly. The first thing she noticed was that it was extremely difficult to lose the weight she'd gained, despite the fact that she'd modified her eating habits and remained as physically active as she had ever been. She also began to notice little wrinkles and lines forming around her eyes and mouth, and that her eyesight had began to fail. She'd started wearing reading glasses when Spencer was still only a baby. Around the time that Spencer reached the age of ten, she began to recognize changes in her menstrual cycle—a slowing down and irregularity, accompanied by exhaustion, heat flashes, and mood swings that her mother always complained were associated with "The Change of Life".

As she climbed the stairs to her room, Nancy felt her knees creak a little, but she simply laughed it off.

I'm getting old, she thought absently.

At the top, she passed a mirror and, as she glanced into it, she suddenly noticed something that she hadn't seen before. She backed up and leaned in closer to get a better look.

221

"My hair," she exclaimed. "It's turning gray."

Quickly, she made her way down the hall to her bedchamber, where she sat at the vanity to look in the mirror there. Leaning forward, she examined her hair closely and saw several strands of gray around her widow's peak and her temples. She then removed the combs and pins, allowing it to fall loosely about her shoulders and down her back. Picking up her brush, she began to brush out her hair, to see if there were any more gray strands, but as soon as she pulled her brush away and examined it, she noticed that it was filled with hair. Frantically, she ran her fingers through the strands, checking for thin spots. Sure enough, there were places where it looked as if the hair had been worn off. She burst into tears.

In all the years she'd spent in the theater, her critics had always harassed her to some degree over her tendency to "plumpness", a criticism that she never took too seriously, realizing that men's taste regarding the size and shape of a woman varied to great degrees. Most men found her ample figure quite pleasing. It certainly never seemed to bother men like Mozart, Braham or even Napoleon, for that matter. It was only after Spencer was born and the weight accumulated to a point that even she admitted it was a problem, that she grew concerned about it. Even then, she realized it had much to do with her age and was one of the factors that led her to the decision to finally retire. However, if her weight, or the fact that she was olive-skinned and dark-eyed and didn't possess the ethereal beauty that was so much the fashion of the period were an issue with some critics, one opinion remained constant: they loved her thick, wavy, dark hair. Of all the youthful features Mother Nature could have robbed her of, this was the most devastating.

As she sat in front of her mirror sobbing, she became more and more determined that she would not give in to this injustice. There had to be a way she could at least cover the fact that the one physical trait for which she had always been just a little bit vain and prideful was being stolen from her in the cruelest of fashions. She wasn't going to give into this without a fight.

The next morning, Nancy and Spencer loaded into the carriage and were early on the road to London. Once they arrived at the house, Nancy saw to it that they were unloaded as quickly as possible. She ordered the servants to settle Spencer in without her for she had an appointment with her hair dresser and she was not to be disturbed by any one, for any reason.

"Do not despair, Madame! It is not the end of the world!" Pierre said in his typical flamboyant fashion. "I can fix this only too easily."

Pierre Girard was a miracle worker. He had been Nancy's hairdresser since 1802, after she and Braham had returned from their tour of the continent. Girard was a delightful, foppish little Frenchman who always made her laugh, and she had trusted no one else with her hair for over ten years. As the son of one of the wig makers to His Majesty King Louis XVI, he'd apprenticed with his father, quickly advancing to the rank of hairdresser to Queen Marie Antoinette. In 1793, just before the trial and execution of Marie, he escaped the Reign of Terror with his life, to London, where he was employed at one of the local theaters as a wig maker.

"But look at it, Pierre," Nancy said as she sat in front of the mirror holding out a section of hair. "It's a disaster, and it's only going to get worse, not better."

Pierre shrugged. "Then we cut it off," he said nonchalantly.

"We what?" Nancy exclaimed in terror.

"We cut it off," he repeated, "and we make for you a beautiful wig!"

"A wig?" Nancy said. The pictures that raced through her mind at that moment were horrifying. The only people she knew who still wore wigs were old, incontinent, bluestocking dowagers, and old men who still wore cut tail coats and laces, and who hadn't realized that the world had advanced into the nineteenth century over a decade earlier.

"You don't like only one? Then we make for you two or three— however many you wish!"

"No, no, that's not it," she protested. "I don't like the idea of even one wig or the idea of cutting off all of my beautiful hair."

Pierre pulled up a section of her thin, limp strands. "Pardon, Madame, but I would not call this beautiful. No wish to offend, but it has seen its best days."

"But wigs are so old-fashioned and ugly…"

"No, no, no! I make you a wig completely from human hair, matched to your precise color and texture and fitted to your own head so it is completely comfortable and fits so well that no one knows but vous et mois!"

"It can be worn and styled just like my own hair?"

"Oui. Any style you wish," he said with a smile.

"And no sores or blisters on my scalp?"

"No. We will not shave your head completely—only crop the hair short so the wig will have something to hold onto to keep it from slipping."

"And I can wear my bonnets and hats as I would with my own hair?"

"Precisely, Madame."

"Will it really make me look younger?"

"The Fountain of Youth," he said as he flipped his hands into the air.

"When will it be ready?"

"I take the measurements today and then I return to the shop and begin this afternoon. I first find a proper match for the hair. Once that is accomplished it should take only a month to complete."

Nancy thought for a moment, then stared at her worn out mop in the mirror. She took a deep breath. "Then let's do it."

With that, Pierre pulled a tape out of his waistcoat pocket and went to work. Nancy was impressed at how thorough he was, even measuring the distance between her eyes, and from the front of her ears around to the bridge of her nose.

When he was finished, he showed her some hairstyles that would effectively cover up the fact that she was thinning. He gave her a jar of pomade, colored with coal dust, to comb into the places where the gray was most obvious and to fill in the thin spots.

That evening when the Wrights arrived, Nancy's mood was cheerful and lighthearted. Together, she and Braham, Henry and Sophie, enjoyed a nice supper, which Nancy decided to prepare herself to show off the fact that she had other talents besides singing, dancing and acting. Afterward, they retired to the salon for a little entertainment provided by Braham and Nancy (upon the Wrights' insistence), followed by a rousing game of faro.

"Well, I must say, Mrs. Braham," Wright said laying a card onto the table, "I was quite impressed with that rib roast and Yorkshire pudding. You didn't tell me that the woman could cook, Braham. Very impressive." He gave his full belly a sound pat.

Nancy threw out her card and with it won the hand. Braham watched as she scooped her winnings from the table wearing a haughty grin, and said, "She also speaks five languages, can swear like a pirate, and plays chess with generals. And she's a damned good card player too."

Wright's eyes grew round. "Bloody hell! Where did that ace come from? You're right, Braham," he laughed. "Beware the woman who has too many tricks up her sleeve!"

Sophie looked at Nancy in astonishment and said nervously, "Oh, my, is there anything that you can't do, Ann?"

Nancy only smiled as Braham replied on her behalf. "I learned long ago, Mrs. Wright, that this is a woman of many talents and great tenacity, and it is just when you think that she has met her match, that she will pull one of those so-called tricks from her sleeve only to prove to you that she isn't defeated yet." He gave Nancy a warm smile and a kiss, and took her hand in his. "And I suppose that's why I love her and I've been with her all these many years."

"Bravo, Braham. Bravo," Wright said, applauding while Sophie simply sat in her chair wearing a disinterested grin.

Later that night, after the Wrights left and Braham and Nancy were heading up the stairs to their chambers, Braham stopped midway and took her by the hand and looked into her eyes.

"Ann, I meant all the things I said tonight. I don't know what's come between us lately, but I want you to know that I still love you. And I'm sorry for the things I said last week that hurt you. I can be such an arrogant and inconsiderate ass."

She cocked her head and peered into his warm, dark eyes. He always did have such expressive eyes. They gave away what he was truly thinking and feeling despite what he displayed.

"I love you too, John," she replied. "Thank you."

They turned and together they finished walking up the stairs, hand-in-hand.

At fifteen a woman
should know the ways of the world,
where the devil keeps his tail,
what's right and wrong.
She should know the wiles
that enslave lovers,
how to feign laughter or tears
and to make up good excuses.

At one and the same moment
she must listen to a hundred
but speak with her eyes to a thousand,
hold out hope to all,
be they handsome or plain,
know how to hide things
without getting flustered,
know how to tell lies
without ever blushing.
And like a queen on her lofty throne,
get her own way
with "I can" and "I want."

From the aria "Una donna a quindici anni" from *Cosi fan tutte*
By Wolfgang A. Mozart

Chapter Twenty-Five
Herne Hill Cottage, 27 October 1814

"Happy birthday, Ann," Wright exclaimed as he handed her a gift he'd brought for her forty-ninth birthday. "I do hope you like it. I found it last summer in a little shop near the harbor in Tokyo. I immediately thought of you."

She opened the neatly-wrapped package to reveal an exquisite red, lacquered Japanese card box which was adorned with pale pink hand-painted and mother-of-pearl inlaid cherry blossoms.

"Oh, Henry, how lovely. Thank you so very much!"

"Well, I do hope you like it and shall get some good use of it."

"Indeed, you know I will," she said, smiling. "Here, look, John," she said as she passed the box over for him to examine. "Isn't it lovely?"

"Yes, quite," Braham said. "Thank you ever so much, Henry. It's a lovely sheath for her lethal weapons."

"Oh, John, you're always so clever," Sophie said as everyone laughed at Braham's witty reference to Nancy's superior card-playing abilities.

"So, when do you go to sea again, Henry?" Braham asked as he leaned back into his overstuffed chair, lighting his pipe.

"Next month," Wright said as Sophie scooted closer to him on the settee and took his arm. "We've bought a house in London; we'll be moving Sophie and the girls in just before I set sail."

"Really?" Nancy said. "Have you tired of your lovely little place in the Wells?"

"Quite the contrary," Sophie replied. "It's just that I have family in London and Henry fears that I get too lonely while he's on his long voyages. He wishes for me to be closer to family and friends. He's quite thoughtful like that, you know," she said, wide-eyed.

"Yes, I'm sure he is," Nancy said with a smile. "So, that means we'll be seeing more of you?"

"Oh, most certainly, for now I'll be able to attend all those delightful soirees and parties that John gives in his lovely home!"

Nancy cleared her throat. "Yes, well, that is still *our* lovely home and *we* give all of those delightful soirees and parties together as a couple. John simply lives there alone when his work requires that he stay for long periods in the city."

"Well, anyway," Sophie said, unshaken, "whatever the situation is, I'm looking forward to being able to spend more time there."

Nancy looked up at Sophie, glaring. "I'm quite sure you are, Sophie."

Sophie's eyes darted to the two men, nervously shifting in her seat. When she picked up her tea cup, it rattled in her hand. Everyone diverted their eyes, for the tension in the room was so great that they were all at a loss as to how to cut through it.

Finally, Sophie recovered and commented in the cattiest fashion possible, "I've been noticing how gorgeous your hair looks lately, Ann. Tell me, what is your secret?"

There was a simultaneous drawing in and holding of breaths as Nancy rose and set her tea cup on the table beside her chair.

"Gentlemen, I think it's time for me to leave this party for quite suddenly I'm not feeling well at all. It's been lovely. Thank you again, Henry for the thoughtful gift."

As she left the room, the men glanced at each other and then at Sophie, who sat erect upon the settee, triumphantly sipping her tea.

After Braham made his apologies and saw their guests to the door, he ran up the stairs to Nancy's bedchamber and quietly knocked.

"Ann, may I come in, please?"

"No," he heard a pitiful voice from inside reply. "Just go away. I don't want to talk to you now."

"Ann, you're upset. Please, may I come in so that we may talk about it?"

"I'll be all right. There's nothing to talk about."

"You know I had nothing to do with this, don't you?"

There were several seconds of silence before Braham heard her unlock the door, allowing him entrance. She had removed her wig and was wearing her nightcap to cover her own cropped hair. Holding a damp handkerchief in one hand, she rubbed her temples with the other. Her eyes were red and swollen, and she had the hiccups.

Braham pointed to a chair. "Sit down, Ann," he said, gently.

She did as he requested and he walked behind her chair, removed her nightcap and began to massage her head.

"There, now, does that feel better?" he cooed softly.

"A little," she said between the hiccups.

As he massaged, he noticed through the thin hair the ugly, walnut-sized scar on her scalp from her operation many years hence. He leaned over and kissed it.

"Does that still hurt?" he asked.

"Sometimes. Scars stay forever. They never completely heal, you know."

৪০৪৪

It was an unseasonably warm and pleasing March afternoon. The sun streamed through the arched windows at Herne Hill Cottage as Nancy sat in her library going through a box of things that she'd somehow failed to unpack when they'd first moved in six years earlier.

As she rummaged through the box of mostly odds and ends—things that were simply thrown in because they didn't know where else to put them—she came upon Braham's old Hebrew prayer book. Opening it, she noticed that tucked inside were his winning ticket from the horse race they attended at the Prater in Vienna and the piece of paper upon which he had written the English translation of the Hebrew text he'd sung in the Synagogue in Prague—the very same day that she confessed that she had fallen in love with him, and on which Spencer had most likely been conceived.

As she adoringly fingered the articles, reveling in the memories of their new love, she came up with an idea. Braham's birthday was the following day. She would surprise him by driving into town to give him this sentimental memento of their young love.

"Emma," she called.

The maid came in from the hall, where she had been dusting some portraits. "Yes, ma'am," she said.

"Would you please tell Andrew that I would like to have the carriage ready first thing tomorrow morning? I've decided to make a trip into the city."

"Yes, ma'am," Emma said, perplexed. Nancy wasn't one to do things on impulse. "I hope everythin's all right, ma'am."

Emma had been one of the first servants hired for the new house. Nancy liked her from the first time she laid eyes on her. Only fifteen years old at the time, the dark-eyed, spirited girl reminded Nancy of herself when she was that age and she felt a special bond with her. Over the years it had only grown stronger.

"Oh, yes, everything's fine," Nancy said with a warm smile. "Nothing to worry over. It's just that I had quite forgotten that tomorrow is Mr. Braham's birthday and I have a special little gift to present to him that can't wait."

"Oh, good." Emma sighed in relief. "Ya had me worried there for a moment, ma'am."

"I'm sorry to have startled you, dear. Oh, Emma, you're just too sweet," she said as she gave her a warm hug. "Thank you."

"You're welcome ma'am. It's just, well, you and Mr. Braham and little Spencer are like family to me now and I'd be fit to be tied if anythin' were to happen to any of ya."

Early the next morning Nancy got up and dressed herself in the gown that Braham had only recently expressed was one of his favorites. She tied a pretty new pink ribbon into her hair—as pink was always his favorite color on her—and went downstairs to put on her coat and bonnet.

Andrew had the team hitched to the carriage and sitting in the front drive early, as Nancy had instructed. Soon, she was off to Great Russell Street, where she hoped to find Braham still lingering in bed. Her plan was to slip the prayer book, with the items inside, onto his breakfast tray and, as he opened it, to surprise him.

When she arrived, the house was quiet, as she had hoped it would be, so she slipped back into the kitchen where she found the cook preparing his breakfast, as she expected. When Nancy showed her the prayer book and told her the plan, the cook grinned from ear-to-ear.

"Oh, he'll love it, madam," she said. "What man wouldn't love to have his wife remind him how much she adores him in such a sentimental way?"

Nancy giggled and gave the cook a hug, thanking her, then proceeded to help in the final preparations of his breakfast by lovingly setting his tray with the best china and silverware, and a linen placemat and napkin that had come from a set that her mother gave them as an anniversary gift. As the cook handed the tray off to the maid, she gave Nancy a kiss on the cheek and said, "You're such a good wife. Mr. Braham's lucky to have such a fine lady by his side."

Nancy instructed Abby to take the tray into Mr. Braham's room and then wait by the door, leaving it cracked just enough for her to peek through and watch while he opened the gift. Once he opened it, she was to let Nancy know when to go in.

Quietly, they tip-toed up the stairs to the landing, where Abby told Nancy to wait. Nancy watched as Abby disappeared behind the corner and into Braham's bedchamber. Then, only a few moments later, she heard some scuffling, then Braham's surprised voice followed by two women's voices and the sound of two doors slamming. Abby ran back to the top of the stairs, where Nancy stood waiting for the signal, and shook her head vigorously.

"What's wrong, Abby? Is everything all right? Is Mr. Braham ill?" Nancy asked in a sudden panic.

Abby lowered her head and started to cry. "No ma'am, nothing like that."

"What is it then?" Nancy asked as she made her way onto the landing and past the maid.

"No, ma'am," Abby shouted. "Don't go in there!" She grabbed Nancy by the arm, but she shook loose and walked to Braham's door. When she tried to open the latch, she found it was locked.

"John!" she shouted as she pounded on the door. "John, are you in there? Is everything all right?"

When he didn't answer, she turned to Abby who stood in the hallway, crying.

"Abby, what's wrong? For God's sake what is going on here?"

With tears streaming down her face, Abby pointed to Nancy's bedchamber and said, "In there, ma'am."

Nancy quickly turned and opened the door to her own chamber and when it flew open, to her utter shock and dismay there was Sophie Wright, standing in the middle of the room wearing one of her negligees, weeping and trembling.

Nancy felt the roof of her mouth instantly go dry as hot, stinging tears began to pour from her eyes. Heat rose from the bottom of her feet all the way to the top of her head and her lower lip began to quiver. She felt that she was going to combust.

"What were... you, you... doing in my... my husband's room, dress... dressed in... my clothes? You fucking little whore!" she shrieked.

Sophie fell into a heap on the floor, sobbing as Nancy stood in the doorway and wept.

"How dare you do this to me, John Braham!" she screamed. "How fucking dare you!" She slammed the door, then turned and ran back down the hall to the landing and down the stairs to the front entry. As she ran out of the house, she slammed the door so hard, it shook a vase that sat upon a pedestal and sent it crashing to the floor.

She stopped on the front landing for only a moment to gather her composure and to try and decide what to do next, but before she could take another breath, she fainted.

O love, bring some relief
to my sorrow, to my sighs;
o give me back my loved one
or in mercy, let me die.

From the aria, "Porgi, amor" from *Le Nozze di Figaro*
By Wolfgang A. Mozart

Chapter Twenty-Six

London, 26 March, 1815

"Ann, Ann," Soane called as he gently pat her cheeks and ran some smelling salts under her nose. "Ann, wake-up now!"

Nancy opened her eyes to find herself lying on the settee in the middle of John Soane's salon. She startled a bit, not realizing at first where she was, but as soon as she recognized his face looking down over her, she burst into tears.

"Oh, John," she cried. "You know what's happened, then."

He gathered her up into his arms.

"Yes, I know, and I'm so very sorry."

"I don't know when my heart has ever been so broken," she cried. "How could he do this to me? After all these years, how could he betray me so?"

"I don't know, darling," Soane replied, trying to hold back his own tears. "I don't know." He held her there as she cried and cried, the tears soaking the shoulder of his coat. "It's all right, Ann," he said as he rocked her in his arms. "Go ahead and cry. Cry it all out."

Half an hour later, she finally fell into an exhausted sleep in his arms, so he laid her gently back down on the settee and got up to get his wife to help him move her to one of the guest rooms.

"She's too exhausted to make the trip home," he said. "She needs to stay here for a few days."

"The poor dear," Mrs. Soane said, shaking her head. "Only a cad could do such a horrid thing!"

"I worry about the scandal this will bring down upon her. I know Ann. She doesn't take this sort of thing well at all."

"I'll send word to Mrs. Storace that she's here, so she won't worry. I'll make something, anything, up."

"That's a good idea. She needs to recover from the shock first." He sighed as he went to the salon entry, but then stopped short. "You get her settled in her room. I'm going over there and have a talk with Braham."

"Are you sure you should do that, John? What if he's violent?"

"No, I know him. He's not the violent sort, plus he's a good friend. He'll speak with me. Perhaps I can talk some sense into the fool's head, before it's too late."

∞∞

"I'm so glad you came, John," Braham said as he ushered Soane into the salon. "Have a seat," he said nervously.

"Are you all right," Soane asked as he sat on the settee.

"I'm fine. Thank you for taking her in like you have," Braham said as he cleared his throat. "Under the circumstances it wasn't appropriate for her to remain here. I didn't know who else to send for."

"No, you did the right thing. I'm glad you felt you could call on me. We'll keep this as quiet as possible to prevent any scandal coming down on either of you and upon, well," he paused, clearing his throat, "upon Mrs. Wright."

"Thank you. I appreciate that," Braham said as he hung his head in shame. Finally, he looked up. "How is she?"

"She's not doing well. What else would you expect after she walked into what she did? It was careless of you, John, and terribly stupid. I understand a man's needs; I'm sure you have them. We all do. But did you have to do that in her home, in a place where she could walk into at any time for any reason? Have some discretion, man! And then the added humiliation of it being with a woman she knew and had been introduced into her company as a friend! Only a cad behaves like that, John!"

"I know," Braham said as he ran his hands through his hair. "I wish I could take it back."

"You can't be serious. You can't take something like that back. You should see her. She's devastated. The poor thing was passed out for nearly an hour and, after I got her awake, she cried for another half hour before languishing out of sheer exhaustion. What you've done is unforgivable. You've totally humiliated her."

"I don't know what to do for her now," Braham said.

"The first thing you do is to never set eyes upon that Wright woman again. Then you get down on your knees and beg your wife's forgiveness," Soane replied indignantly.

"I'm afraid it's not that simple."

"What do you mean,? Of course it is. There's no simpler answer, especially if you're to avoid a scandal."

"She's pregnant, John. It happened in November, right after her husband moved her to London and returned to sea."

"You can't be serious."

"I wish I weren't," he said as he got up and went to the fireplace. "The thing that complicates it even further is that there's no way Henry will ever believe the child is his. It can't be. He'd already been gone three weeks when we… well, you know."

"Pray the child's born early."

"Well, yes, that's our only hope, I suppose. I just don't know what to do. I still want to talk to Ann. Do you think she'll let me see her?"

"Not today, John. She's still in shock and quite beside herself. I fear for her health. Give it a few days and we'll see."

"Alright, then. But please tell her something for me, will you?"

"What's that?"

"Please tell her that I love her and that I don't want to lose her."

"Again, you can't be serious," Soane said, astounded by Braham's audacity.

"I'm totally serious. Tell her I love her and that I intend to come beg her forgiveness."

ഇരു

"Come now, Signora Storace," the Soanes' maid pleaded. "You haven't eaten a bite in two days. You're weak as a newborn kitten and if you don't eat something, Mr. Soane's going to have me head for it."

Nancy took a deep breath and looked at the spoonful of broth that the maid held in front of her. Finally, she opened.

"Fine, then," the maid said, as she put the spoon in Nancy's mouth. "That's a good girl."

"Well. I can't be wracked with guilt if Mr. Soane sent you to the gallows simply because I refused to eat, now can I?" Nancy said as she offered a sheepish grin. "Thank you, Mrs…"

"Ferguson," the maid replied. "Me name's Mrs. Margaret Ferguson. And you don't have to be introducin' yourself to me, 'cause I well know who you are," she said as she held up another spoonful of broth.

"Good morning, ladies," Soane said cheerfully as he peeked into the room. "How's our guest this morning?"

"Come in, John," Nancy said with a smile.

"I've finally gotten her to eat something, sir."

"I hear you threatened her with certain death if I didn't," Nancy said. "I think you've missed your calling. What a fine extortionist you'd make!"

"Well it's certainly good to see you smiling, again."

"Yes, indeed, sir. It most certainly is," Mrs. Ferguson agreed.

"Seriously, how are you feeling today, Ann?"

Nancy thought a moment before she replied. "I'm better—at least physically. The heart is a completely different matter, I'm afraid," she said as she started to tear up.

Mrs. Ferguson handed her a handkerchief and patted her arm. "I'll be goin' now and leave you two to have your talk. If you need anything, signora, don't hesitate to call."

"Thank you, Mrs. Ferguson," Soane said with a generous smile.

"Forgive me," Nancy said, wiping her eyes. "I fear I'm wearing my heart on my sleeve at present. I can't seem to help it."

"It's perfectly understandable, my dear." He pulled a chair up beside the bed and cleared his throat. "I've been to see him."

"Who," Nancy asked, stunned. "John? When?"

"The day you arrived. After you fell asleep I went over to talk to him."

"Why didn't you tell me?"

"I felt that you needed a few days."

Nancy's expression grew cold. "So what did he have to say for himself?"

"Well, Ann, he seemed quite remorseful."

"Hmph. As well he should be. Don't get me wrong. I understand you men. I know that I'm unable to give John what he needs in that capacity and I suspect that while he's been on tour and such, he's had plenty of little flings and affairs. I understand. But this was different. This was a betrayal of his loyalty, and in my own home, with someone I knew and regarded as a friend."

"Yes, you're right. And I said those exact words to him. He should be remorseful and, believe me, I do think he's paying for his sins with deep sorrow and regret." Soane had always been a quiet, soft-spoken, tender man. He had such a forgiving way about him that he easily led others into that same forgiveness. "He says he still loves you and he wants to come to you and beg your forgiveness."

"Do you believe him?"

Soane thought a moment and then he sighed. "Yes, I think I do. He seemed genuinely sorry for what he's done and he's extremely concerned about you and the state of your wellbeing. He was beside himself with worry."

"I just don't know if I'm ready to forgive him yet, John. I'm still so hurt," she said as the tears welled in her eyes again.

"And you have every right to the hurt you're feeling, so don't let me or anyone else talk you out of that. All I'm asking is that you give him a chance to speak so that there might be some chance for reconciliation."

He paused for a moment before he took her hand.

"You are my dear friends. I love you both very much and it is tearing me up to see you two hurting…and hurting each other, for that matter. I simply want to give you every opportunity to remember how very much you've loved one another. You have a child together. Nineteen years is a long time, Ann."

Nancy thought for a moment before she replied. "When does he want to come?"

"Tomorrow, if at all possible."

"I look terrible. I don't know if I even have the strength to get out of bed. I certainly don't want him seeing me like this," she said, her pride getting the best of her.

"I think he should see you like this. It will serve to show him the harm he's inflicted upon you by his actions."

She stared down at her hands. "Very well, then. Tomorrow it is."

"Thank you, Ann," Soane said as he got up from his chair. He leaned over and kissed her forehead. "You're quite a lady, you know. I must confess to you now that I've always borne a secret crush on you, and it's only out of my genuine heart-felt affections that I desire your greatest happiness and personal fulfillment."

"Thank you so much, John," she said as she took his hand, kissed it, then held it to her face. "I love you too. So very dearly."

The next morning, before Braham was scheduled to arrive, Nancy asked if she could at least have her wig so that she could maintain some dignity. Even if she was sitting in bed, it would help her to feel better about herself. Mrs. Ferguson agreed and even let the style down, working it into one long braid down the back. She then tied a night cap over it. She put Nancy in a pretty, white bed gown with eyelet lace at the sleeves and around the collar and sat her up against some fluffy white pillows, and gave her a book to lie in her lap.

"There, now, you look like a portrait sittin' there," she said.

"I don't look like a washed out old woman," Nancy asked, her confidence waning.

"Of course not. You look like the lovely, very dignified lady that you are."

"Thank you, Mrs. Ferguson. You've been such a dear."

"'Twas nothin'. Now, I want you to sit up there and show that man of yours the stuff you're made of."

Several moments after Mrs. Ferguson left the room, Nancy heard a soft, timid knock at her door. She took a deep breath, then she removed her reading glasses and laid them neatly on top of her open book.

"Come in," she answered, sweetly.

Braham entered the room, dressed in one of his best suits and wearing an expression of anxiety mixed with remorse. In his hand he carried an enormous bouquet of spring flowers—most of them bulb varieties, which were Nancy's favorite. As he handed her the flowers, he leaned over her and kissed her forehead and, as he did so, she felt a tear drip from one of his eyes onto her cheek.

"How are you feeling," he asked nervously as he looked around for a chair.

"I'm doing better, thank you," she replied formally. "The first two days were a little rough, but my strength is starting to return."

Finding the chair, he placed it directly by the head of the bed, where he could sit as close as possible.

"I've been worried sick."

"That's what I understand," she said, lowering her eyes to avoid direct eye contact.

"You look beautiful sitting there," he said with a soft smile.

"Thank you."

He reached over to take her hand, but she pulled it away.

"Ann..." He hesitated for a moment and looked around the room, gathering his courage. Bringing his gaze back, he settled it on her. "I've come to humbly beg your forgiveness. I know what I did was wrong and that I've hurt you deeply. I can't begin to express to you the remorse that I've experienced over the last several days, knowing that you've been lying here, languishing in such grief, humiliation, and despair—all hurtful emotions that I have inflicted upon you by my sins."

Nancy sat silently, refusing to look up.

"I don't know what to say to you. I'm sorry you've been in such pain."

"My pain is nothing compared to yours, I know that. All I'm asking is that you hear me, and give me the chance to make it up to you."

"What's done is done, John. The wound has been inflicted, and it's deep. You can't take this one back."

"I understand that," he said, lowering his eyes. "But is there a chance that the wound could heal with tender nursing, and over time?" His voice began to quiver. "Is there a chance we could begin again?"

"What are you asking of me?"

"Only that I be given a chance to prove that I still love you and that it is my greatest desire to live up to that promise that I gave to you so many years ago, to honor and cherish you till the day I die."

"I don't know if I can open myself back up, John. You can't even imagine the hurt and humiliation you've inflicted upon me," she said as tears began to pour down her cheeks.

"I know," he said as the tears fell from his own eyes. "I'll understand if you can't forgive me, Ann, but for the sake of all the years we've had together, all the wonderful times, and for the sake of our son, I'm begging you to try."

For several moments they sat, both weeping until, finally, Nancy looked into his eyes.

"All right, then," she said. "For the sake of all of those things, most especially our son, I'm willing to try."

Braham knelt down beside the bed and, taking her hand in both of his, he kissed her fingers, allowing his tears to flow down upon them.

"May I come again, tomorrow and sit with you," he asked.

"Yes," she nodded. "You may."

Sorrow has become my lot,
for I am torn from you.
Like the cankered rose,
like grass in winter moss,
my sad life withers away.

From the aria "Traurigkeit ward mir zum Lose"
from *Die Entführung aus dem Serail* by W. A. Mozart

Chapter Twenty-Seven

London, August 1815

*F*or several weeks throughout early spring, Braham continued to call on Nancy every day while she recuperated in the home of their friend, John Soane. As soon as she was well enough to travel, she returned to Herne Hill Cottage, where Braham's calls became less frequent, but remained every bit as devoted. His desire to make amends and do what he could to heal the broken relationship seemed heart-felt and genuine.

They agreed that because of the painful memories associated with the house in Great Russell Street, it would be best to sell it and move Braham into a smaller house at 6 Tavistock Square. Near the end of summer, after the contracts were signed and deeds turned over, they had all the household items and furnishings moved.

"It's much smaller," Braham said as he put his arms around his wife's shoulders. "But it will serve our purposes nicely, I think." He gave her a kiss on the cheek and went to his desk to begin unpacking and sorting his papers and correspondences.

"The furnishings look nice here," she said as she brushed her hand along one of the chairs. "I must admit I'll miss the old place, terribly. It was, after all, the first and only home we owned together."

Braham smiled, but said nothing as he continued unpacking his desk items.

"I suppose you won't make it back to Herne Hill for a while, will you," she asked.

"I seriously doubt it, darling. I have so much to do here what with settling into the new place and the end of the summer season. Then I have to get ready for the next touring season. You know how it is."

"I understand." She lowered her head. "I'm busy as well. I have to get Spencer off to school and then I have several annual charity events coming up that I haven't even begun to plan."

"Don't you have one of your little garden parties coming up as well?"

"It's not a *little* garden party," she said, perturbed by his condescending attitude. "But yes, I do. It happens to be a rather large event sponsored by the Prince Regent, benefiting a children's hospital."

"Whatever you call it," he said flippantly. "When is that?"

"Next month." She turned to the window, looked out onto the street and sighed. "Well, darling, I think it's time I be heading back home. I do have much to do and it's not getting done by my standing around here."

"Are you sure you have to leave so soon," he asked, barely looking up.

"Yes, I'm afraid so." She walked to give him a kiss. "Is there anything else you need me to do before I go?"

He looked around the room a little and then answered, "No, I don't believe so, darling. If anything comes up, I'll call on Abby to help me."

"All right, then. Send for me if you need anything," she said as she gave him a peck on the lips.

"I shall. Have a safe drive."

As soon as she returned home, Nancy was met with a whirlwind of activity. She barely had any time for herself, for reading, or any other leisure activities, due of all the private concerts, parties, and events that clogged her social calendar for the remainder of the year. It was a relief to be so busy, though. It kept her mind off of personal matters and the tension and difficulties that she knew still lurked under the surface between herself and Braham. If she didn't have to think about it, it made it easier to deny.

"I think that arrangement would look better over there," Nancy said as she pointed to a bouquet sitting on one of the tables in the garden room. "Move it there and let's see," she said to the servants, who helped her with the final preparations for the Prince Regent's event.

"Pardon me, ma'am," Emma said, coming into the room.

"Yes, Emma." Nancy picked up another arrangement and placed it on a nearby table. "No, no, no. Not there. Over on that side. I'm sorry, Emma. What is it you need, dear?"

"Mr. Soane is here to see you, ma'am."

"Mr. Soane? What's he doing all the way down here?"

"I don't know, ma'am. He just said that needs to speak with you."

"Well, it must be important for him to have driven so far," she said as she wiped her hands on her apron. "Here, help me off with this, will you?"

She turned so that Emma could untie the apron strings from around her waist and neck. "Show him into the salon, please."

"I already have, ma'am," Emma replied with a proud grin. "And I've already told the cook to put on the kettle."

"Good girl," Nancy said with a wink.

She followed the hall to the salon, where she found Soane standing by the fireplace, looking rather somber.

"Good afternoon, John," she said, coming through the doorway and extending her arms. "What a pleasant surprise."

He took her hands in his and gave her a warm smile. "You're looking lovely, as always," he said, as she gestured for him to sit.

"And what brings you all the way down here on this fine afternoon?" she asked as she sat beside him.

He hesitated a moment, then took in a deep breath.

"Oh, no…" Her expression fell. "That doesn't bode well."

"Ann, I have some bad news," he said softly.

Nancy braced herself to hear that a friend had fallen ill, or that there had been an accident.

"I don't know how to break this to you gently, Ann, so I'll come straight to the point, and tell you that John, well, he has left the country."

"Left the country? What do you mean? Where did he go?"

"He's gone to France."

"France? Whatever for?

"He's taken Mrs. Wright with him."

Nancy sat stunned, unable to reply.

"He's taken her and her two children, and the infant she bore him last month."

"Child? *His* child? But I thought… I mean we were… at least he told me that…" she said as tears stung her eyes.

How many more tears would she be required to shed over this man? How many more times would he break her heart before she gave in to the realization that he would only keep on breaking it? She looked down at the ring on her left hand—the wedding band he had given her just a few months before Spencer was born—and began to twist it around her finger.

"Please wear this, Mrs. Braham, in honor of the vow I have made to you to love, honor, and cherish you for the rest of your life."

She still recalled his words when he'd slipped it on her hand that day in Bath. One of the happiest days of her life.

No more, she thought, as she wiped the tears away. I'm through with tears now.

"I'm so sorry, Ann. I feel responsible for this."

"It's not your fault, John. Don't you dare blame yourself for his deplorable behavior."

"But I was the one who begged you to reconcile. I was convinced that his remorse was genuine, and now this…"

"You only did that out of your deep concern for our happiness, for my happiness, John. No," she said as she shook her head. "I won't allow you to shoulder the blame for this. This is his and his alone to bear."

"I must say you're taking this remarkably well, much better than I had expected."

"I'm through with being hurt by this man. I've had it. It's over. He has no integrity. I was told that years ago by someone who knew, and he has proven it to be true in so many instances. I chose to ignore it, thinking it was something the he would eventually learn, or that I could change in him."

"The thing that you must now brace yourself for are the tabloids. It will be all over them once word of this gets out."

"Yes, I know. Once the press gets a hold of this, it'll be in more papers than Wellington's victory over Napoleon at Waterloo," she said with a sheepish grin, trying to lighten the mood a bit.

Soane smiled, admiring her ability to cut through the gloom with her little bits of humor. It made things like this so much easier to bear.

Her expression suddenly turned more somber.

"Not only has he brought unspeakable pain with his betrayal, but now my son and I will have to endure the cruel scandal which he has brought down upon our heads."

"I know you loved him."

"I did," she said as she pulled his ring from off of her finger," but he has destroyed the love I had for him and left in its wake unspeakable contempt. I will not be his enemy, for that does not become me, but I am no longer his friend."

"What are you going to do now?" he asked as she lay the ring on the table beside her chair.

"I don't know," she replied, smiling. "I don't have time to think about it right now. I have a party to give tomorrow and I'm going to enjoy it. He won't steal that from me."

∞∞

"Storace," Constanze said to Nissen, who sat across from her at the table having his morning coffee. "Anna Selina Storace. She was a singer in Vienna for several years. She arrived about six months after Wolfgang and I were married—the Emperor's new Italian buffa."

"Oh, you mean the one for whom he created the role of Susanna?" he said as he picked up the list of names of people with whom Mozart corresponded by letter.

"Yes, that's the one," she replied, a knot rising in her throat. Even after all these years she still couldn't even mention the woman's name and not feel the same contempt and anger she felt then—when she learned that Mozart planned to abandon her and their son to go to London to be with Nancy.

"She went back to England early in 1787," Constanze continued. "Wolfgang wanted to go with her then, but Papa Mozart refused to take care of Karl while we traveled there together, and I refused to let him go alone. He attempted to get back to her again, about three years later during his last German tour, but I thwarted his efforts by sending my brother in law, Hofer, along with him as a travel companion. Wolfgang was in love with her."

"Seriously in love with her?"

Constanze lowered her eyes. "Yes," she confessed. "Quite seriously. Enough so that he was willing to close all his opportunities in Vienna to start a new life and career with her in London." She sighed. "Anyway, when his plans were thwarted and he was forced to return to Vienna, he was furious. We had a huge argument in which he confessed that over the course of several years he had written to her—'many letters', he said—but that he'd asked her to destroy them."

She arose from her seat at the table and went to the mantle.

"After that," she said, staring blankly at the wall, "he agreed to end all correspondence with her and to end the affair in order to save his reputation in Vienna. He was afraid the Freemasons would blackball him and make it difficult for him to get work. We never spoke her name again."

"You never told me any of this, Constanze," Nissen said, stunned by what she had just confessed. "Why?"

"I was ashamed—humiliated and ashamed. Hours before Wolfgang died I vowed that one day I would write his story and I'd wipe that woman's name out of existence, at least where her connections with him were concerned." She turned and faced her husband. "And that's what I intend to do," she said resolutely.

"It's imperative then, that we get those letters. If those should surface, they would ruin anything we write in the biography that is contrary. Do you know if she's still living?"

"The last I heard, she was. After she went back to England she grew rather famous there. I heard some gossip that she returned to Vienna for a visit several years ago with a companion—a young tenor. It was rumored that they were lovers."

"I'll have to use my connections then. We'll find her. We must find her and obtain those letters if they still exist, or all the years and hard work we've put into this endeavor will have been useless."

☞☜

The first news of Braham's infidelity broke out in the tabloids just after Christmas, in the form of a vulgar cartoon depicting Braham as a large-chinned, pointed-nosed Jew, crossing the English Channel with Sophie Wright on his back, along with her twin girls and an infant. On the other side of the Channel, Nancy was depicted lying on the ground, begging and crying, with their son standing by her side. It was entitled, "Mrs. Wright doing Wrong."

Rumors also flew of a lawsuit that had been filed by Henry Wright against Braham for Criminal Conversation, and that Wright had disowned his wife, as well as the children. He vowed that he would never set foot in

246

a theater again. Nancy, who had always been fond of Henry, who she had always believed to be an honest and honorable man, was almost as grieved for him, as she was for herself. But the cruelest, deepest cut of all came in the form of a commentary in a London paper which read:

From marriage to scandal is the most natural transition imaginable. Only think of Braham having at last run away from Storace and her wig. We are very sorry for it, since it may deprive us of Braham's sweet notes.

John Braham and Sophie Wright were in France for only a few months and, when they returned, he was once again performing for London audiences. In one performance, prompted by a few hisses and boos, he stood before his audience and gave them an obviously rehearsed speech in his own defense. The tabloids and papers quickly picked up on this, some taking his side and many others taking Nancy's, but in all of it, Nancy chose to remain as silent and hidden away from public scrutiny as possible.

She took several months to decide upon her course of action. She realized that in all of this it was against her best interests and her son's to remain completely silent, yet, not being given to vulgar public displays of temper or emotion, she wasn't going to rush into anything that she would regret later. It had to be calculated, well-planned, and above all, tasteful.

It was a bright and early morning in mid-March when Nancy showed up at Tavistock Square with a moving company and four wagons. Braham was away on tour, so she let herself and the workers into the house, and proceeded to enact her revenge. Following the same course of action that she threatened many years before in Paris (after Braham had decided to bring his whore under the roof that she provided with her own funds), she decided that she had given him ample time to pay his debts. It was now time for her to collect in full.

"I have an inventory of all of the items that are my property," she told the foreman as she presented him a list of everything in the house that she had bought—everything from dishes, silverware, linens, paintings, trinkets, and draperies to every single stick of furniture found in every room of the house. "I want it all crated and taken to the warehouse that I have reserved for storage."

"Yes, ma'am," the foreman said.

"How long should it take," she asked.

The foreman looked at the list, then around the most immediate vicinity of the house, and shrugged. "About three days, ma'am."

"That's good. This is where you may notify me once the work is complete." She handed him a slip of paper with John Soane's address written on it.

"Yes, ma'am," he said. "We'll get it done."

After three days had passed, Nancy received word that the job was finished and everything was at the warehouse, waiting for her to decide what to do with it all. Some of it she would bring back to Herne Hill and much more, she decided, would be auctioned, the proceeds donated anonymously to a charity benefitting widows and orphans.

The items she wanted to keep arrived, accompanied by John Soane, who had received word from Braham after he returned from his tour to discover what Nancy had done.

"So, what was his response," she asked with a devilish grin.

"Well, I wouldn't be standing there smiling if I were you, for I can tell you that his reaction wasn't at all a pleasant one."

"It can't have been all that bad," she said, trying to make light of what was probably Soane overreacting.

"It was very bad, indeed. You stripped him bare, Ann. You left him with little more than a carving knife and a desert fork! He wrote that to his 'latest breath' you would have his 'abhorrence' and 'contempt'. I wouldn't be at all surprised if there isn't a lawsuit to come out of it all," he said, shaking his head.

"I took what I was perfectly within my legal rights to take," she said indignantly. "I don't feel any obligation to Mr. Braham for having taken away what was *my own*, and I should be much obliged if you would have the goodness to write to him to that effect."

"I don't believe that my writing to him to any effect will deter him from what I am quite sure he's determined to do, Ann. Again, brace yourself, for I fear this is going to get rather ugly."

The vengeance of Hell boils in my heart!
Death and despair flame about me…

From the aria "Der Hölle Rache" from *Die Zauberflöte*
by W. A. Mozart

Chapter Twenty-Eight
London, June 1816

"Before I hand down my judgment in this case," the judge said, "I must first say that never in all my years on the bench have I presided over an enquiry in which there existed so much avarice and contempt between the two parties, who, for the better part of nearly twenty years existed as amicable and loving partners in business and domestic affairs, and by all rights could be considered bound in matrimony by issue of common law. It is a pitiful shame to see this union come to such an irreconcilable and odious end."

"Now, to my decision: Mr. Braham, you and Signora Storace have before you an itemized list of the property which you claim the signora stole from your home on twelve March, in the year of our Lord eighteen-hundred and sixteen. It has been determined by this enquiry, and is my judgment, that each item on that list indeed belonged to the Signora Storace, and that she was legally entitled to remove from them from the premises. It is also determined that, since you contributed to the general living expenses only minimally throughout the partnership, you are, in effect, still in her debt. Therefore, you are required to pay all of her legal expenses, as well as the cost of this enquiry."

"Signora Storace, I further find that your conduct in this situation is without fault and that you rightfully, and legally entered the premises at 6 Tavistock Square and removed only those things to which you had legal right to claim as your own. Therefore, you are forthwith exonerated of any and all charges of theft or misconduct."

"This is my final judgment. If you will each see the bailiff and sign the judgment, you will be free to go your separate ways."

৪১৩

It was over. After twenty years that she regarded as mostly happy and successful, Nancy found it incomprehensible that her partnership with Braham was over.

As she rode back to Herne Hill, she stared blankly out her carriage window. The judgment had been in her favor. She was triumphant. Why, then, did she feel as if she had lost everything? The carriage pulled onto the pea gravel drive in front of the house and 14 year-old Spencer came out to greet her.

"How did it turn out, Mum," he asked anxiously as he opened the door and helped her out.

"It went well," she replied. "I was exonerated of your father's charges against me and he was ordered to pay my legal expenses, as well as the court costs."

"And just what did he have to say for himself after that," Spencer asked, in a self-righteous manner.

Nancy stopped and took him by the shoulders, looking him squarely in the eyes.

"I well understand your anger towards your father. Believe me, Spencer, there is no one angrier or more hurt than I, but I will not tolerate you speaking of, or referring to him in such an arrogant and disrespectful tone as you just did. You will remember that he is still your father and that you bear his name. This will be my last word on the subject. It will not happen again in my presence."

"Yes, Mum. I'm sorry. I didn't mean to offend you."

"It's all right, son," she said, taking him in her arms. "This has been trying for us all, and I realize it is doubly trying for you to watch the parents, who you love dearly, going at it as your father and I have done. I don't envy your position in the least, but we must always remember to conduct ourselves in a manner that is measured with integrity and compassion so that we may remain above reproach."

"Yes, Mum, I'll remember." He paused for a moment, then gave her a kiss on the cheek. "Emma had a feeling you'd be returning soon," he said, changing the subject, "so she and the cook and I prepared tea and biscuits and took them out to your favorite spot in the garden under the pavilion, right in the middle of your roses. Shall I walk you there?"

"Of course," Nancy said as she took his arm and walked with him into the entry hall. "How very thoughtful of you all. Why don't you go to your grandmother and ask if she would like to join us?"

"All right. I'll be back straight away."

She went into the salon to wait for them when suddenly the desk in the corner caught her eye. It was an antique that had been hers since she was a girl, and had been one of the items she'd removed from the house on Tavistock Square. All at once her memory sparked and she went to it, pulled open one of the bottom drawers, and began rummaging through. As she felt towards the bottom she found a small wooden box adorned with hand carvings. It was locked, but if her memory served her well…

Yes! There's the key, she thought. Slipped right there between the pages of my diary where I put it. She put the key in the lock and opened the box to reveal the letters. How long has it been since I last read these, she wondered. She took them out, untied the cord and pulled the one from the top and opened it. It was dated April 1787, just shortly after she'd returned to London from Vienna. It was the first letter he'd ever written to her.

My dearest most precious Wanze…

"Mum," Spencer called. "Grandmamma is here and we're ready to go to the garden now."

"All right, darling, I'll be there in just a moment," she said as she slipped the letter into the hidden side pocket of her dress. She would get back to it a little later, but first, she needed this time with her family.

"There now," she said as she met Spencer and Elizabeth in the hall. "Shall we go?"

Spencer took her arm, leading both her and this grandmother to the garden room, where they made their exit outdoors and to the pavilion, where he and Emma had set up a lovely tea complete with little salmon and cucumber sandwiches and Nancy's favorite lemon-sugared biscuits.

"Oh, Spencer, this is very lovely," Nancy exclaimed.

"Indeed, it is, Spencer, thank you," Elizabeth agreed. "What a thoughtful young man you're growing up to be," she said as he helped her to a chair.

"Thank you, Grandmamma. Emma and I thought this would be something nice for Mum to come home to, after, well, after being in town on business all morning."

"And I trust that business went well," Elizabeth said to Nancy as she took her napkin from the table and laid it in her lap.

"As well as could be expected, I suppose, Mother," Nancy replied. "At least I retained my property and was exonerated of all charges, as well as released from the responsibility of any of the costs of the enquiry."

"Shall I pour?" Spencer offered.

"Yes, darling, thank you. Please do," Nancy said.

"And Mr. Braham? What was his response?"

Nancy glanced at Spencer, who hung onto every word.

"He agreed to the terms," she said, politely.

"Amicably?" Elizabeth pressed.

"No, Mother, I'm afraid it wasn't as amicable as I had wished it to be," Nancy took some biscuits from the plate as it was passed to her.

"What did he say? Did you speak with him afterwards?"

"We spoke a little," Nancy replied cautiously, wishing to shield Spencer from the worst of it. "I suppose he judges me by himself for, as he has proved to be my greatest enemy, he thinks I am to return the compliment. But let him say what he will, I shall never be his enemy."

"He's deluded himself into thinking that you are the wrong-doer in this situation," Elizabeth said. "A woman simply cannot have her rightful revenge without it coming back on her in some way."

"I suppose that's true," Nancy sighed. "I thought, by refusing to become ensnared again within the legal bonds of matrimony, that I could avoid all this, but apparently not. Not as long as men are in charge."

"Spencer, when you grow up and come of age, I think you should become a judge in the courts so that you can help to change some of this injustice," Elizabeth said, thoughtfully. "You've watched what your mother has endured so surely that would give you some insight into what we women are forced to suffer in these situations."

"It is indeed an injustice, Grandmamma, but I'm not sure I have a mind for the law," he said smiling. "I think you give me far more credit for that kind of intelligence than I deserve. I do know one thing," he said as he took his mother's hand. "I have learned from my father's example how not to treat a lady."

Elizabeth smiled. "Ann, I believe you've raised a fine, young gentleman. You should be proud."

"Indeed I am, Mother," Nancy replied as she gazed at her son. "I am very proud and very grateful."

After an hour or so spent in more pleasant conversation, Elizabeth excused herself, explaining that she wished to rest before supper. Spencer graciously offered to take her back to the house while Nancy remained a little longer, enjoying the fresh air and the fragrance of her roses. At last she was alone with the letter, which she'd kept hidden in her dress pocket. Eagerly, she took it out and began to read.

> *25 April 1787*
> *My dearest most precious Wanze,*
>
> *It is my greatest hope that this letter finds you well and settled once again in London. Just moments ago, I received a letter from your brother, who informed me of your safe arrival and gave me your address. I cannot tell you how overjoyed I was to hear from him, for it meant that I was that much closer to receiving word from you.*
>
> *I must confess to you now that, from the moment I saw you drive away (on that terribly cold and miserable day last February), I have longed for your return and am dreaming of that happy day when I shall greet you and hold you in my arms again. I only pray that day comes soon and that negotiations between His Majesty and you will be favorable for your return early next year.*
>
> *Oh, please do not forget me, my dearest love, for I languish here without you. Come back to me, and know that I remain always,*
>
> *Tuo Wolfgango*

She folded the letter, slipped it back into her pocket and smiled. "How I miss you, Wolfgango," she whispered.

As she stood under the pavilion—the one that Soane had designed after the one at Laxenburg—she gazed out over her beautiful rose garden. Taking in their fragrance, she closed her eyes, then felt the breeze as it gently caressed her lips and cheeks with soft kisses.

Oh, please do not forget me, my dearest love, for I languish here without you. Come back to me...

୧୦୯୫

"The post has arrived, ma'am," Emma said, handing Nancy a small stack of letters.

"Thank you. Would you please close the door when you leave?"

"Yes, ma'am."

Sorting through the stack, which seemed to consist mainly of RSVPs for her next upcoming charity event, Nancy came upon one addressed in a familiar hand.

"It's from Braham," she said, seating herself at her desk. "What does he have to say to me now?" She broke the seal and began to read.

"Oh, my God. The sodding little bastard! How dare he accuse me of such things?"

"Emma!" she called. "Emma, come quickly!"

"Yes, ma'am," the maid said as she opened the door, running into the room.

"What do you know of this?"

"Know of what, ma'am?"

"I have received a letter from Mr. Braham, who accuses me of conspiring with our servants to sabotage his upcoming trial over the charges which Mr. Wright has filed against him. He writes that you all have been gossiping with his servants, passing rumors that supposedly came from me and are libelous and intended to destroy his 'good name'."

"I know nothing of the sort, ma'am," Emma cried. "I wouldn't have part in such evil things. Me mum raised me better!"

"I know you wouldn't, Emma, but what about the others? Would they do such a thing?"

"I don't think so, ma'am. We love you. You're good to us. You make us feel like we're a part of the family. Mr. Braham, if I may say so, ain't like you. He treats servants like they was lower than him." She thought a moment. "I just had an idea pop into me head. Perhaps Mr. Braham's servants stayed loyal-like to you, ma'am."

Nancy considered this. "That's a brilliant observation, Emma. What a good girl you are," she said with a weary smile. "Oh, when is this all going to end?" She began to cry.

"Oh, ma'am," Emma went to her mistress and knelt down in front of her. "Please don't cry. The man ain't worth one drop of your precious tears."

"I'm just so tired. He's wearing me out."

"Don't let him do that to you, ma'am. You've got people who love you. We all love you. Chin up." She pulled out her handkerchief and dried Nancy's tears.

"I love you, too, Emma," Nancy said as she hugged her. "Thank you."

"Is there anything I can do for you now, ma'am? Would you like some tea?"

"Yes, that would be nice. Thank you."

"I'll have Cook put the kettle on straight away."

Nancy rose to go to the settee, but before she got there, she fainted to the floor.

"Ma'am!" Emma cried. "Somebody help me, Madam's fainted!"

Running into the salon, Spencer saw his mother and hurried to her.

"Mum! Mum!" he called as he knelt down and tried to rouse her. "Help me get her onto the settee. Mum, wake up now. Mum! Emma, tell Andrew to send for the doctor. Hurry!" He noticed a letter lying on the floor, and he picked it up. It was from his father.

...I am perfectly aware of your persecution and unnatural efforts to injure me—of your encouraging your servants to withhold and mutilate their evidence in favor of their Master. If you feel grateful in such conduct, I have nothing to say. I must bear it with fortitude. Go on then—fill up the Bitter Cup to the brim. Heap injuries upon me. Bury my few good qualities in Oblivion. I shall bear it without a murmur...[1]

When Emma returned from the stables, Spencer, who still held his father's letter in his hand, held it up.

"What's this, Emma? Did you know about this?"

"I ain't read it, but yes, I know what it is. Your mum was quite upset by the things Mr. Braham wrote in that letter."

"Well, that explains a lot, then, doesn't it? That man won't leave her alone. He's wearing my poor mother down."

---

[1] From a letter by John Braham.

"Andrew's on his way to fetch Dr. Hooper," Emma said.

"Good, then. Help me get her upstairs to her room."

❧❧

"She's suffering with dropsy," Dr. Hooper said to Elizabeth and Spencer who had been anxiously awaiting his diagnosis.

"Is that why she faints so often, Doctor," Elizabeth asked.

"Yes, Mrs. Storace. It's a condition that is aggravated by emotional or physical strain. It puts pressure on the heart, making it have to work too hard to keep up. It causes her to tire easily, to suffer bouts of dizziness and fatigue, and can cause swelling of the extremities."

"Is it serious?"

"Yes, it's quite serious. If the heart is taxed too heavily it can lead to heart failure, or stroke."

"What can be done?"

"Rest, Mrs. Storace. Rest and the elimination of all sources of stress and strain."

"How long before she can leave her bed," Spencer asked.

"That's entirely up to how she feels, but it is imperative that she be kept away from emotional and physical strain as much as possible. I would say a nice holiday in Brighton or Margate would do her a world of good about now."

"We understand, Doctor, thank you," Elizabeth said. "We'll see that your orders are followed."

Chapter Twenty-Nine

Brighton, September 1816

13 October, 1787
My precious Wanze,

Only imagine my grief when I opened your most recent letter explaining how the negotiations between you and His Majesty had fallen through! The only hope I had was for your eventual return. To what do I cling now? Perhaps the only hope is to come to England to compose for your theaters there. I pray that a commission will be forthcoming for the prospects in Vienna are quite dismal.

Oh, Nancy, I feel we are oceans apart now! How do we ever hope to cross them? Do I dare hold out hope that a commission will come and that I will be with you once again? Please write that you'll return to me. Come back to me, Wanze!

Forever,
Wolfgango

She folded the letter and placed it at the bottom of the stack. She was about half-way through reading all of them now. Sitting on the terrace overlooking the sea, she was struck by its vastness. The surf gently rolled in upon the beach, the waves calling to her.

Come back to me Wanze!

ॐ

"Good morning, ma'am." Emma entered Nancy's bedchamber carrying a silver tray upon which sat a carafe of coffee. "It's so good to have you home from holiday. We missed you!"

"Thank you, Emma. I missed you, too. I feel much better. Dr. Hooper was right, the rest did me a world of good."

"You look rested, ma'am. I can't tell you how worried we all was before you left."

"How is Spencer? Did he get himself back to school all right? I felt terrible about not being here to help you get him ready to leave. It's the first time I've not helped since he was very little."

"I know, ma'am, but he's a young man now and we managed just fine. You needed the rest more."

"Indeed, I did," Nancy agreed.

"I brought the last several days' papers up, just in case you wanted to catch up."

"Thank you. That was very thoughtful."

"You're welcome, ma'am. Again, it's right good to have you home!"

Nancy picked up the paper and began to read an announcement in the recent nuptials column.

"Emma," she said. "Did you know about this?"

"About what, ma'am?"

"It says right here, 'Mr. John Braham marries Miss Frances Bolton."

"Oh, yes, ma'am," Emma said with trepidation. "I didn't mention it because I thought perhaps you already knew."

"No, I didn't."

"He abandoned that Wright woman not too long after he lost the lawsuit that her husband had against him. Back in August, it was. The next thing I heard was that he was engaged to be married to a young girl—seventeen years is all—from a posh family in Manchester."

"How did he convince her family to allow her to convert?"

"He didn't, ma'am. Mr. Braham converted—at least that's what I heard. It was an Anglican ceremony, so he must have."

"My God," Nancy said, shaking her head. "The man has proven me correct. He has absolutely no shame whatsoever, and not a shred of integrity."

"I hope the news ain't too upsetting for you."

"Not in the least, Emma. The only thing that upsets me is my own stupidity at being taken-in by that cad for so long. Well, God bless him, is all I can say, and may he have a happy life. And God have mercy on the new Mrs. Braham!"

ಚಿ೦ಲ

30 September, 1789
My precious One,

How many times have I written that without you here with me, I am incomplete? I am a lost soul wandering in the darkness searching for my home. The night sky is filled with stars, yet my guiding star grows dim, for her light is so far away that I can barely see her now! Return, my Guiding Star! Do not leave me wandering in the night. Return to me, Wanze!

I love you forever,
Wolfgango

Sitting in her bed, Nancy felt a sudden chill as the wind blew in through her opened window. Getting up to close it, she was dazzled by the night sky and the millions of stars that cast their light upon the earth below. She stood for a moment, closing her eyes as the wind blew in the starlight and ran its fingers through her hair, gently kissing her brow.

Return, my Guiding Star! Do not leave me wandering in the night.
Return to me, Wanze!

ಚಿ೦ಲ

"We've located her, sir."

"Ah, you mean the Storace woman? Yes, very good then. Where did you find her?"

"She's still in England," the young investigator said as he took a chair in front of Nissen's desk and passed a detailed document across to him.

"It seems she retired a few years back and bought a small estate just outside of London."

"Then she's wealthy?"

"Oh yes, sir, quite. It's estimated that she's worth something over £30,000.

"That could present a little bit of a problem," Nissen said, stroking his chin as he read over the document.

"How so, sir?"

"If she has what I'm looking for, she might not be easily persuaded to give it up even for a good price. It means I shall have to offer more and perhaps back it up with a warrant to confiscate the items in question, should she still refuse."

"That's not so easily done," the investigator replied, "especially in England. They have much stricter laws than we do regarding the circumstances under which certain items may be forcibly confiscated. She seems quite the savvy woman; she might not give in easily to threats."

Nissen took a deep breath and continued to read. "Nevertheless, we've got to try. The items she my have in her possession are crucial." He paused before he spoke again. "Good then, thank you for your excellent work," he said as he stood and extended his hand for a shake. "I shall write to the Austrian embassy in London immediately and they'll take it from here."

⁖⁃⁃

Herne Hill Cottage, 19 July 1817

"Where the bloody hell did I put that?" Nancy said to herself as she looked frantically through the house. "I could have sworn I filed it in this drawer, along with my other important documents."

She'd been all over the house looking for the copy of the Last Will and Testament that she'd drawn up in 1797, after she and Braham had left Paris. At the time, she'd felt confident about their partnership, but all that had changed. She needed to change it.

Exhausted, she finally sat down at her desk, which was covered with stacks of papers, documents, and letters that she'd pulled from their places during her quest. She sighed and began to sort through the stacks, organizing them into two piles of which needed to be kept and re-filed, and which needed to be destroyed.

"Did you find what you were looking for, Mum?" Spencer said as he peeked into the salon.

"No, I haven't found it yet, and it's frustrating me to no end."

"Well, pace yourself, Mother," he reminded her. "Remember what the doctor said about stress."

"Yes, I know, but he doesn't realize how very important it is that I find this paper, does he?"

"Mother," Spencer chided.

"All right, all right, son. I'm listening," she said with a grin. "I'll be a good girl, I promise."

"All right, then," he said, sternly. "I'm going outside to the stables with Andrew for a bit to check on that new foal, but I'll have Emma keeping an eye on you, and she *always* reports back to me."

"Go on, then," she grumbled, waving him off. "Don't worry about me."

When he left, Nancy looked over the pile of papers and decided to move the ones that were to be burned onto the floor. As she picked up one of the stacks, she noticed that lying beside them were the letters that she had taken the better part of the entire year to read. She had finally come to his last letter.

Four years, she thought. Four years we wrote to one another of nothing but our undying devotion, and it all came down to this.

She picked it up and brought it to her nose to detect any of his scent that might still linger. She dreaded reading it, for she already knew what it said. Of all the letters that he had written to her, this was the one she had committed to her memory. Finally, she opened it:

My own Love, my Treasure, my Heart!

How I languish in the writing of this letter. Truly, there are no words to express the grief in my heart for what I must tell you, so I will come straight to the point and, as I have requested before, I make my most fervent plea that this be destroyed after you have read it.

It is with much sorrow and regret that I must inform you that I will not be accepting the commission that I know you, your brother, and Thomas Attwood have worked so assiduously to obtain on my behalf. I cannot express the gratitude I have for you all and for your diligence in this matter. However, there are circumstances beyond my control which compel me to decline, despite everything within me that shouts otherwise.

This brings me to another, even more painful matter: O Wanze, how can I bear to write the words? What cruel fate has brought us to this point? Again, I shall not tarry but shall come quickly to the point. This will be my last letter to you, my dearest love, not because my affections for you have diminished for, on the contrary, they have only grown deeper and more impassioned since last we saw one another, but because circumstances in my situation have developed to the place where, for the preservation of my reputation, my work, and my family, our affair must end. And although we will never see one another again in this life, my soul will always yearn for you. I vow to you my undying love for all eternity, whatever that is. I vow that whatever happens in this universe, I shall always find you and love you. You will never be alone. Whoever else may have my body, you will own my heart. Farewell, angela mia.

Forever,
Tuo Wolfgango

"Oh, Wolfgango," she said as tears began to stream down her cheeks. "Why, after all these years, is this still so painful?"

"Ma'am," Emma said, sticking her head in through the doorway, "Are you doing all right in there?"

Nancy took her handkerchief from out of her pocket and wiped her eyes. "I'm fine, Emma. Don't fuss!"

"I'm just following orders," Emma replied with a raised eyebrow. "Oh, goodness, there's someone at the door. Who could that be?"

"I certainly wasn't expecting anyone to call today," Nancy said as she hurriedly wiped the last of the tears from her cheeks.

Emma turned toward the entry and went to the front door and opened it. Two gentlemen dressed in formal black suits, both rather young looking and carrying large leather portfolios stood on the step. They looked like lawyers, or government officials.

"Good morning, gentleman," Emma said. "What can I do for you?"

"Good morning, Fruelein," one of the men said. "If you please, we are here to speak with Signora Storace."

What a strange accent, Emma thought. He sounds German.

"Come in, please, and I'll let her know you're here."

Emma went into the salon, where Nancy sat at her desk reading a letter.

"Well, who is it?" she asked.

"It's two men, ma'am. Two German men. They say they want to speak with you."

"German? How do you know they're German?"

"They sound German to me, ma'am."

"Did they say what they want?"

"No, ma'am. Only that they must speak with you."

Nancy sighed. "Go ahead and show them in," she said impatiently. "Oh, and Emma, have Cook—"

"Yes, I know. Have Cook put the kettle on."

"You're a good girl," Nancy said with a smile.

Emma left, and returned to the entry, where the men waited.

"You may go in now," she said as she showed them into the salon.

"There are two gentlemen callers," Emma said to the cook when she went into the kitchen. "Better set some extra cups and saucers. Oh, and some extra biscuits, too."

When she went back into the salon, Emma quietly set the tray down on the table in front of Nancy and the two men.

"Thank you," Nancy said. "That will be all for now."

"Yes, ma'am." She left the salon and quietly shut the door, but, her curiosity getting the better of her, she stood outside, placing her ear against it to hear what was being said inside.

"So, gentlemen. What may I do for you?" Nancy asked as she began to pour the tea.

"We were sent by an important gentleman who has employed us to inquire about the letters from Vienna." Her eyes narrowed. Who was this gentleman, and how did he know about her letters?

Clearing his throat, the younger of the two men quickly added, "Our employer is writing a biography and he would like to have these letters to add to his research."

"Well, gentlemen, I am not about to hand personal letters over to someone whose name I don't even know, if I indeed have what you think I have."

"I can assure you that he is willing to pay you generously for them."

"And what if they're not for sale?"

"We are more than prepared to negotiate a sum with you, Madame."

"And I am prepared to tell you to convey to him that, if I had these letters, they would not be for sale."

"We understand that no amount of money could replace the sentimental value that they must hold for you."

"Nevertheless, you can see I have no need to sell my personal belongings."

"In that case, we regret to inform you we have a warrant pending to confiscate them should you refuse our employer's generosity."

"Excuse me, gentlemen, but I believe this conversation has reached its conclusion. Emma! Show these gentlemen out."

Emma opened the door and saw Nancy standing in front of the two seated men, pointing toward the door. Emma gestured, saying, "This way, gentlemen."

"Good day, sirs," Nancy stated firmly.

"You're making a grave mistake. We know that you have the letters, and we will use whatever means necessary to obtain them. Take care, Madame Storace. You do not know with whom you are dealing."

"And you do not know with whom *you* are dealing, gentlemen," she said, her anger rising. She was a woman who didn't like to be controlled, not after all she had survived in her life. "I have politely asked you to leave. I don't believe I could have made my feelings on the matter more clear."

"This is not a stage play, Madame. I suggest you abandon the dramatics and discuss this with us in a civil manner."

"Dramatics? You've not begun to see the full range of my dramatic talent!" She slipped her hands through each man's arm and pulled them to the front door.

"The nerve!" the older man huffed. "You may live in a fine house, and you put on some very fine airs, Madame, but we know that you were little more than his slut!"

Nancy opened the door and, shoving them onto the doorstep, she shouted, "You can take that bloody warrant and tell your employer to shove it up his sodding bum! And if you two bloody bastards ever set foot anywhere near my house again, I'll send for the constable!" She slammed the door in their faces, falling back against it and catching her breath, her blood pulsing wildly in her temples. "Emma! Get my smelling salts. I think I'm about to faint," she said as she slid down to the floor.

Emma, who had learned to keep some smelling salts with her at all times for just such situations, pulled a vial out of her pocket and bent down, waving it under Nancy's nose.

"Ma'am!" she said as she patted Nancy's cheeks. "Don't faint, ma'am! You're all right. They're gone now."

"Emma? Are you there?"

"I'm here, ma'am. Everything's fine."

"What happened?"

"You gave them two men the bloody shove off, that's what happened!" Emma said, laughing.

Laughing with her, Nancy said, "I did, didn't I? Oh, dear. What an ordeal!"

"I don't think I ever even heard you yell at Mr. Braham like that!"

"I don't think I did, either. Please help me back into the salon."

"Yes, ma'am. You sure you're up to standing now?"

"I think so. I just need a bit of support, that's all."

Emma helped Nancy up and took her arm, then led her back into the salon, where she helped her into a reclining position on the settee. She propped her feet up on some pillows and told her to lie still while she went to get Spencer.

"Oh, don't bother him. I'll be fine."

"No, ma'am, I think it's best that I fetch him. He's the man of the house now, and he needs to know when things like this happen."

"Of course, you're right, Emma. You're such a good girl."

"Thank you, ma'am."

When she got to the stables, she found Spencer with Andrew, the two of them kneeling down to examine the foal that had been born only the night before.

"Yes, Emma. What is it?"

"There's been an incident at the house involving your mother."

"What kind of an incident? My father hasn't been harassing her again, has he?"

"No, nothing like that. Two strange men—foreign men—came to the door demanding some letters they claimed someone from Vienna wrote to her. They threatened her if she didn't hand them over."

"What type of threats?"

"They threatened to get a warrant!"

"What did she do?"

"She got bleedin' angry is what she did. She got so angry that when they wouldn't leave, she railed at them. Then she grabbed them by the coat sleeves and dragged them into the entry and shoved them out the door!"

"Oh, my God, Emma! Is she all right?" I should go and check on her," Spencer said.

"That's what I thought too, Mr. Spencer. That's why I came out here to fetch you."

When Spencer rushed into the salon, he found Nancy sitting at her desk going through papers again.

"Mum, are you all right? Emma said that you were threatened by two foreign men."

"Emma exaggerates. It's nothing as serious as that. Buggering bastards were blowing hot air, that's all. I handled it."

"She said you nearly fainted!"

"Well, yes, I did. The bleedin' sods got me worked up and I lost my temper."

"I want you to settle down," he fussed.

"Why is everyone so worried about me today? I'm just fine, but everyone insists on carrying me around on a pillow!"

"We love you, Mother, and we're just concerned," he said as he went to her and kissed her cheek. "Now, stop being such a grump and tell me what it is you're doing. You should be resting"

"I'm just sorting through some old letters and papers, trying to decide which ones I need to keep and which ones I should burn."

"Do you need help?"

"Yes, dear," she replied. "That would be awfully nice of you."

"What do you need me to do?"

"Well, if you could get the fire going, it would be extremely helpful."

"All right, then," he said.

After doing what she'd asked, Spencer turned to her. "Would you like me to start tossing some of this in now?"

"Yes, but would you first mind opening up the windows? It's a bit stuffy in here. One doesn't usually light a fire in July." She chuckled.

As he went about opening each of the casements, Nancy picked up the different piles of papers and laid them within Spencer's easy reach, but when she came to the stack of letters, she hesitated.

Do I really want to destroy these? she asked herself. They're still all I have left of him.

She thought about the two men. How did they know about these? Who was their employer, and why did he want them so badly that he was willing to pay them to threaten her for them?

Yes, she thought. I have to burn them. The sentiments expressed in them are too passionate, too personal. No one was meant to read these letters but me. I can't take any risks.

As Spencer began tossing the papers onto the fire, she picked up the stack of letters, which she had tied into a neat bundle, and then she kissed it.

"It's time," she whispered. "I'm ready now." She handed them to Spencer.

"Are you sure you want to burn these? They look as if they're special to you."

"They are very special, but as they were for my eyes only, it's time for them to go now. I don't need them anymore," she said with a smile.

"All right, then." He took the bundle of letters from her and tossed it in the fire.

You burn now, and soon, my loves,
no trace of you will remain:
but oh, the man who wrote you
may long burn within me still.

From the Lied *Als Luise die Briefe* by W.A. Mozart

Chapter Thirty

Herne Hill Cottage
19 July, 1817

"I'm being bloody serious, Kelly. It was the damnedest thing I ever saw! There, standing before me were two German men. They actually threatened me with a warrant if I didn't hand over some letters they assumed I have."

"Did they say who's supposed to have written these letters?"

"No, but I think it's Mozart. Who else could it be? Vienna? The real question though, is how did they know I had letters from him?"

"Perhaps he told his wife that he'd carried on a correspondence with you, or she assumed—"

"Constanze?" She laughed. "Even if she did know, why would she want them? I seriously doubt there would be anything in them that she'd wish to read."

"I heard that she remarried several years ago, some Danish fellow who's a diplomat of some sort."

"Still, what would she want with my letters? It's strange. Very strange indeed. Well, then, on to pleasanter subjects. I'm so glad you were able to drive out for supper, Kelly. It's been a while and I've missed you!"

"It has been a while hasn't it, me dove? I've been keepin' meself busy enough with still managin' the theater, and now me own pub! Old Sheridan, God rest his soul, left the place in a mess, but I'm gettin' it back on its feet."

"I'm so sorry my mother isn't feeling up to joining us tonight. She's getting older, and she retires early most nights now. Spencer's at a party with some friends. In fact, I think there's a young lady who's caught his eye and is supposed to be there."

"I'll bet me last farthing the lad's grown ta be a handsome one."

"Indeed, he has. He's fifteen years old now and is a handsome devil like his father, although nothing like him in character or personality. He's quite a darling boy."

"I'm sure he is," Kelly said with a smile. "He certainly has a darlin' of a mother. Why, I'll never forget the night the lad was born and I turned to that husband of yers and reminded him of what a darlin' woman he had." He noticed Nancy's color had suddenly paled. "Nancy me dove, are you alright?"

"I don't know. Suddenly, I'm not feeling well at...all..."

"Nancy! Wake up, Nancy! Someone come quick! She's fainted!"

ೠೞ

"She's had a stroke," Dr. Hooper said, closing his black leather bag.

"How serious?" Elizabeth asked.

"It's serious, but I think she can recover, given the proper amount of rest and time."

"How will it affect her abilities," asked Kelly.

"Well, there seems to be some paralysis, mostly concentrated on the left side. She's having difficulty with her speech and, of course, movement of the limbs, but again, given rest and time, I think she has the ability to recover most everything she's lost."

"May we go in and see her now?"

"No, Mrs. Storace. Not tonight. I've given her some laudanum. She needs rest. Miss Walthen will sit with her through the night. I've given her all the instructions and she seems quite capable."

ೠೞ

"How is she this morning, Emma?" Spencer asked, anxiously.

"She's better. At least she rested well last night."

"I could just kick myself for not being here when it happened. I knew I shouldn't have left after the kind of day she'd had."

"It's not your fault, Mr. Spencer. There's nothin' you could've done."

"May I see her?"

"Doctor says it's fine. Just don't stay too long and don't try to talk to her too much. She don't speak so well. And remember to sit on her right side 'cause she don't have much use of the left."

"All right. Thank you, Emma."

Spencer went quietly in the chamber and placed a chair near the head of Nancy's bed. She appeared to be sleeping, but when he leaned over her, she opened her eyes.

"Mother," he whispered.

"Ma... da...dahling... buh...boy..." she said, struggling.

"I'm so sorry, Mummy," Spencer said as he began to weep.

"No...no..." she said, shaking her head slowly. "Not cry..." She raised her good hand to stroke his cheek. "Beh...better... soo...soon."

"Don't try to speak, Mummy. Doctor Hooper says you need rest more than anything right now."

"Rest..." She smiled. "Love... you..."

Spencer's chin began to quiver. "I love you, too, Mummy. So very much."

&OCB

16 August, 1817

"John! How good to see you," Nancy said as she extended her hand to her good friend John Soane.

"Miss Walthen told me that I'd find you out here under the pavilion. She says you spend a great deal of time here these days."

"It's my very favorite spot in the garden, thanks to you and your brilliant piece of arc...arc...arch-i-tec-ture. Sorry," she said, embarrassed. "I'm still struggling a bit with some words."

"But it looks and sounds as if you're doing so much better!"

"I am. At least I can speak for the most part, without sounding like an imbe...imbe-cile." She laughed. "And I'm using my left hand much better. I still have to walk with this bloody cane, though."

"If I know you, Ann, you'll be rid of that thing and dancing the night away in no time."

"I don't know about that. I fear my dancing days are over now. I'll be happy when I can simply walk on my own."

"I hear from Dibdin that you're still planning to attend their charity event next week. That's amazing, Ann. You're quite a woman."

"You know me. I've cheated death so many times, I can't even count them anymore. I'll be there, even if I do have to use this bloody cane."

∞

18 August, 1817

"But I don't understand, Doctor," Elizabeth said, distressed. "She was doing so much better. Everyone remarked about how quickly she was recovering. What happened?"

"I'm afraid her defenses are still weak, Mrs. Storace. She's contracted a type of unknown fever that I can't put my finger on. I fear we may be approaching the end. I'm so sorry, Mrs. Storace. I wish I could give you more hope."

"You've been of tremendous help, Dr. Hooper. I thank you."

"Your daughter's a lovely woman, Mrs. Storace. I can't tell you how many times she has delighted my wife and me with her work. And getting to know her as her personal physician has been a singular honor. She's a remarkable woman."

∞

20 August, 1817

"She had a bad night, Mr. Spencer," Emma said. "You may see her, but she's very weak."

"I understand, Emma. Thank you."

He went to her bedside and as soon as she sensed that someone was there, she opened her eyes.

"There's my handsome son," she said with a weak smile.

"Hello, Mummy…"

He took her hand and knelt beside the bed. "Emma said you didn't have good night. I'm so sorry."

"Oh, don't bother about it, Spencer. It's all right. It's to be expected." She choked a little and swallowed hard.

"Can I get you some water?"

"Thank you. My throat's just a little dry."

"Here," he said as he put his arm around her and helped her lean forward so the liquid wouldn't drip down her chin. She took a small sip, then leaned back.

"Thank you, darling. That helps."

Unable to hide his emotions any longer, Spencer finally broke into tears, burying his face in his mother's lap. "Oh, Mummy, please don't die. Don't leave me here all alone!"

Nancy placed her hand on his head and ran her fingers through his dark curls. "I'm not leaving you alone, son. You have your Grandmamma and, of course, your father. They both love you dearly," she said, trying to comfort him.

"My father doesn't love me," he said, bitterly. "If he loved me he wouldn't have done this to you. It's all his fault! It's his fault you're dying!"

"He did nothing to cause this. My body is worn out. Your father has his faults, there's no denying that, but I can assure you that he loves you. He loves you with all his heart."

"But I don't want you to die."

"I don't want to die, either, Spencer. But we all do. Death comes to everyone sooner or later, but I have a secret."

"What's that?" he said, wiping his eyes with his sleeve.

"Love doesn't die. It won't die. When my body has finished its work and nothing else remains, my love for you will still be here. I won't leave you, my darling son. I promise you."

"I love you so much, Mummy…"

"And I love you, Spencer, with all my heart."

Sir John Soane, London
My dear Sir,

Valuing your friendship and great kindness to my daughter, as well as her family, I would not let you leave town without knowing how she is—I'm sorry to say she has had a very bad night. She has a fever, but from what cause we don't know. It must reduce her more than really now I begin to lose my courage, as I fear there's but little hope. We must submit to God's will what a stroke to us all, particularly her dear Boy.

Dr. Hooper was here yesterday, he thought her more animated but no abatement I her complaint they seem to think there's much danger.

I wish you a pleasant journey. I shall hope to be favour'd with another recall on your return – she expressed great pleasure of your kindness in calling her and was much obliged for your great goodness in your offer.

I am, dear sir,
Your much obliged and grateful servant,

E. Storace
Herne Hill

You'll excuse my blunders, but I hardly know what I write.[2]

ഇൽൽ

24 August, 1817

"I'm afraid, Mrs. Storace, there is simply no hope. Sometime during the night your daughter suffered yet another stroke," Dr. Hooper said.

"When will it be, then," Elizabeth asked in tears.

"I can't say exactly, but sometime today—this afternoon, perhaps. Her pulse is very weak and her breathing is labored."

"Shall I fetch the lad so that he can sit with his mother in her last hours," Kelly asked.

"I'm sorry Mr. Kelly, but Spencer refuses to come into his mother's room now. The poor boy is utterly inconsolable."

---

[2] Letter by Elizabeth Storace.

As the clock ticked away the hours from early morning until early afternoon, Elizabeth and Kelly sat together in Nancy's chamber, keeping watch. Several times, Emma came in to offer them tea and to urge them to eat a little if they could, offering to bring a tray to the room so that they wouldn't have to leave Nancy's side.

Shortly after one o'clock in the afternoon, Kelly moved his chair by the head of the bed to be closer to the friend and colleague he had met at the harbor in Italy, in 1780, when she was only a girl and he a lad. He told her that he would never forget her and how she and her brother had been the dearest friends he'd ever known. Then he kissed her forehead and said farewell to his friend with his tears.

It was one-thirty in the afternoon when, suddenly, he noticed a breeze that wafted through the open window, making gentle ripples in the lace curtains as it passed.

"Wake up, Wanze. It's time to go now."

"Wolfgango, is that you?"

"Indeed it is! I told you I would come. I promised you. Don't you remember?"

"Yes, I remember." She rose from her bed and took him by the hand.

"Come, my love," he said. "I'm taking you home with me."

I vow to you my undying love for all eternity, whatever that is. I vow that whatever happens in this universe, I shall always find you and love you. You will never be alone. Whoever else may have my body, you will own my heart...

The End

Afterword & Acknowledgments

The greatest challenge a writer faces when creating an historical fiction piece based on the lives of real people is the balancing of the actual historical facts with good story-telling. Often the cold, hard facts fail to meet the criteria that make for a good story with the rises, peaks, and falls in the proper places. That was not the case with the life of Anna "Nancy" Storace, for her life was so packed with famous people and events that I had to choose which notable historical events and figures to highlight and which ones to give slight mention to or no mention at all. To say Nancy Storace led an interesting and exciting life is a vast understatement, and it has been both an honor and a sheer pleasure to devote the better part of thirteen years in getting to know this amazing, fascinating and courageous woman. I have to admit that now that I'm finished with the telling of her story, I'm really going to miss her.

After becoming familiar with this incredible character through both academic and personal research, it is baffling to me that only one biography has been written about her. It's by a British lay music enthusiast and researcher, Mr. Geoffrey Brace, and it is here I will thank Mr. Brace for his exhaustive research and for compiling and organizing the facts and events of her life into one, concise work. Brace's book, *Anna...Susanna: Anna Storace, Mozart's first Suanna: her life, times and family* (Published by Thames Publishing 1991), has been invaluable to me and has served to provide the factual "skeleton" upon which I have structured both *So Faithful A Heart* novels.

My greatest disappointment in Brace's work, however, is in some of the incorrect data and the deliberate omission of the event towards the end of Nancy's life which appeared to be a major catalyst in the progression towards her final illness and death. In an apparent effort to press his own admitted agenda of separating Storace from the belief held by some of the most noted Mozart historians (most notably Alfred Einstein), that there at least existed an emotional affair between Mozart and Nancy (Brace himself even admits that both of Mozart's first biographers, Joseph Lange and Georg Nissen claimed that Mozart was in love with Nancy), Brace failed to make even casual mention of the maid's testimony at Storace's death inquest regarding the visit from the two "German" men and their demands that Nancy hand over the "letters from Vienna".

There is abundant documentation of the fact that Nissen, using his diplomatic connections, spent nearly a decade sending emissaries out all over Central and Western Europe, searching for and purchasing, as well as confiscating letters, documents, musical scores and memorabilia that were connected with Mozart. It was his desire to collect virtually everything that had anything to do with his wife's deceased husband and either use them as documentation for the biography he and Constanze were writing together or to destroy evidence that would contradict the cleaned-up image of Mozart that they sought to present. Nissen admitted in the foreword of the biography (which wasn't published until 1828, years after Nissen's death in Salzburg, Austria), that it was his intention to present a view of the composer and his life without "harming the fame and esteem of the name-human."

> *There is a need for a lot of selection to extract something attractive and characteristic in the letters, which can be offered to the public, without harming the fame and the esteem of the name-human. ... One desires not to, one must not show one's hero publicly in the way in which he portrayed himself in evenings of familiarity. By all truth, one can harm his fame, his esteem, and the impression of his works...*

–Extracted from the foreword of *A Biography of Mozart*, by Georg Nikolaus von Nissen

It seems very clear why Brace chose to leave out the aforementioned facts when discussing the end of Nancy's life, considering his stated purpose to suppress the idea that anything but a warm professional and personal relationship existed between her and Mozart. However, his choice to do so was a disservice to his readers, leaving them with an incomplete and inaccurate picture of his subject and her life, as well as her death. In this unfortunate choice, he proved himself to be little better than Nissen.

I also found other facts in Brace's biography of Nancy that were skewed to apparently manipulate the reader to his view, as well as some other statements that were simply based in poor research, the two most glaring regarding Nancy's close friendship with Lady Emma Hamilton. The first is where he stated that Nancy most likely attended Admiral Horatio Nelson's funeral and sat with Emma. It is a well-established fact that Lady Hamilton was forbidden to attend the funeral of Lord Nelson, so it is more likely that Nancy either didn't attend at all or, if she did, sat near her common-law husband, John Braham, who sang at the funeral. The other was at the end of the book where he states that Emma Hamilton attended Nancy's funeral on 2 September, 1817 which would have been impossible as Hamilton died in exile in Calais, France on 15 January, 1815. These two glaring errors, along with Brace's apparent need to skew and omit important details and facts made it difficult to trust anything in the book that wasn't backed-up with hard documentation.

Brace was also very free about casting value judgments on the relationships between Nancy and various important people in her life such as her brother, Stephen, her son, Spencer, and her common-law husband of twenty years, John Braham, labeling them as bordering on an "unhealthy closeness" and using terms such as "pathetic devotion" in regards to her commitment to Braham. I'd personally like to know how Brace found himself so in the midst of these relationships that he could make such judgment calls, and how, after he had gleaned so many facts about Nancy Storace that screamed otherwise, he could ever say that this woman was "pathetic" about anything. The truth is that there wasn't a pathetic bone in the woman's body; Brace's own research proves it. He had the facts (well, most of them anyway), but his insights into the facts were pitifully lacking.

History has long taken a hard, and I will add unfair view of strong, independent, successful women like Anna Storace. One of the most unfair views that seem to run common among historians familiar with Storace's life and career is the idea that she was involved in a "string" of unsuccessful love affairs. In Nancy's nearly fifty-two years she was only involved in three, what can be documented and proven, "love affairs", (aside from her disastrous marriage to John Fisher, which I don't in any way count as a love affair). The three were with, Francesco Benucci who was Mozart's original Figaro, the Spanish composer Martìn y Soler, and the English tenor, John Braham (I don't include Mozart because no affair between them has been documented other than through hearsay and circumstantial evidence, although I believe there is plenty of both to establish the probability of an affair and that it was one of the two most significant in her life). How anyone could judge these affairs as unsuccessful is beyond me. Were they unsuccessful simply because they ended? I'd like to know what the criteria were in making this judgment.

The obviously most significant documented love affair was with John Braham. It lasted twenty years, produced a child (who grew up to be an educated and respected member of British society), brought in a tremendous amount of material wealth to both parties, and in Braham, produced one of the greatest singers Great Britain has ever known. If that isn't success, I don't know what is! The relationship ended badly, but its tragic ending in no way diminishes its duration and accomplishments. Again, how does one define success in a love relationship—simply by one that ends only in "till death do us part"? I've known many a marriage that lasted fifty years or more that didn't produce half the amount of success created in the twenty years that Nancy Storace spent with John Braham.

I'd also like to fill my readers in on some of the factual details concerning the fates of both Braham and the couple's son, Spencer. According to Brace, after Braham's marriage to seventeen-year-old Frances Bolton, he went on to have six children and to die in 1856 a "pillar of Victorian society." He was regarded as the finest tenor England had ever known, and also according to Brace, continued with his rather disingenuous and cynical attitude towards his profession as a musician by playing up to whatever audience for which he happened to be singing at any given time. Lack of integrity continued to follow him through the rest of his life and in all aspects of his life, including his relationship with his son, Spencer.

William Spencer Harris Braham was fifteen years old (not fourteen, as Brace miscalculates in his book), at the time of his mother's death. Spencer was never reconciled with her death; going on to blame his father for the decline in Nancy's health that led to her demise—something for which his father never forgave him. Apparently Nancy never did find the copy of the Will she searched for, and perhaps destroyed it by accident, along with the "letters from Vienna" on the day to which her maid, Miss Walthen ("Emma" is a name I gave her after my inability to find her actual first name), testified at Nancy's death inquest. Because Nancy's Will was never changed, the bulk of her massive estate was not passed on to Spencer as she intended, and the £2000 designated to Braham in the older Will, did go to him. However, Braham in this case did do the right thing and gave it back to his son in the amount of £150 annually. Spencer struggled in school for several years after his mother's death, but eventually did go on to obtain both a B.A. and M.A. from Oxford. With the help of his father, he obtained a post in the clergy and married in 1851, changing his surname to Meadows (the name of his wife's family), to rid himself of any connection to his father. It was quite obvious that the animosity between them lingered on until Braham's death. Spencer, too, had six children and when he died in 1883, he held the post of rural dean of Chigwell, Essex.

Finally, I would like to express my thanks to the people who have worked with me, inspired and encouraged me, and lent their help and expertise:

First, I would like to thank my daughter, Lauren Weaver, for lending her knowledge of the French language as well as helpful information and an excellent timeline outlining the periods of the French Revolution and Napoleonic Wars.

Special thanks go to Dr. D. Allen Scott for writing the Foreword to this book. There are certain people who come into your life and you know from the moment you meet them that they're there for a special reason. Allen is one of those people to me. I can honestly say that without Dr. Scott's encouragement and inspiration, neither of my *So Faithful A Heart* novels would have been written.

As always, I appreciate the unending love, support, expert advice, listening ear, patience, and professional assistance of my life partner, SK Waller. There is no greater joy than sharing one's life and work with one's best friend.

Last but not least, my heartfelt thanks go to the lovely, talented, warm, spirited, and courageous woman whose life and career inspired these novels, Anna "Nancy" Storace. I only hope I did your story justice, Signora. Thank you for a life well-lived and for choosing me to be your messenger. Brava, Prima Buffa!

K. Lynette Erwin
Autumn, 2011

Made in the USA
Lexington, KY
31 October 2014